LYCEUM

WOLVES

IMMORTALS OF NEW ORLEANS

BY
KYM GROSSO

DISCLAIMER

The characters, locations and events portrayed in this book are a work of fiction or are used fictitiously. Any similarity to real persons, living or dead, is coincidental and not intended by the author.

NOTICE

This is an adult erotic paranormal romance book with love scenes and mature situations. It is only intended for adult readers over the age of 18.

For the love of my life, Keith.

You inspire me to write romance that speaks to true love,
and of course, sexy love scenes that steam up the pages. No
one could ask for a more supportive husband.

I am so lucky to be your wife and partner.

Acknowledgments

I am very thankful to everyone who helped me create this book:

~My husband, for encouraging me to write, editing my articles and supporting me in everything I do.

~My children, for being so patient with me, while I spend time working on the book. You are the best kids ever!

~Julie Roberts, editor, who spent hours reading, editing and proofreading Tristan's Lyceum Wolves. I really could not have done this without you!

~Carrie Spencer, CheekyCovers, who helped me to create Tristan's sexy cover.

~My beta readers, Stephanie, Liz, Nadine, Katrina, Elizabeth and Sharon, for volunteering to beta read the novel and provide me with valuable feedback.

~My street team, for helping spread the word about the Immortals of New Orleans series

~⚜ *Chapter One* ⚜~

Tristan smoothed the sleeves of his tux and straightened his tie. His platinum locks had turned a darker shade of blonde after the accident. Yearning for the warmth of the sun, there'd be plenty of time to run wolf later. Right now, he had other plans; tearing the city apart brick by brick in order to find the asshole who'd torched his club.

A mixture of anger and excitement simmered like a raging fire underneath the cool exterior of his Alpha façade. Not only had he survived the building's collapse, he'd orchestrated the unthinkable, a new club opening within a week. Tonight, he'd publicly demonstrate his steel resolve to the hundreds of patrons eagerly anticipating the grand opening. His team of warriors, trusted comrades, would seek retaliation for the destruction of his property and attack on his sister, Katrina. Whoever had sought to attack his family was in for a day of reckoning, as he was already strategizing in preparation for the battle.

The heavy pounding of a techno beat reverberated throughout his private office, reminding him that he needed to go upstairs to greet his guests. The new club was on the penthouse level, fifty stories into the troposphere. Customers, subjected to heavy security on the ground level, took express elevators that emerged to a spectacular indoor twenty foot, cascading waterfall which flowed into a limestone-encompassed Koi pond. Stunning crystal chandeliers and spectacular black marble floors presented an understated sense of elegance.

The main club, encased in floor to ceiling glass, gave way to a breathtaking, three hundred and sixty degree, panoramic view of Philadelphia. A large spiral mahogany staircase led to a magnificent rooftop deck, which opened to the warm September breeze. Landscaping adorned with tiny white lights, presented patrons with a romantic ambiance in contrast to the pounding club scene below.

Private luxury rooms, located below the main floor, allowed vampires and supernaturals alike, the privacy they sought for feeding and sexual escapades. State of the art video feeds fed into a central security station. Every corner and crevice of the club, including bathrooms, was meticulously monitored for suspicious activity by a team of experts.

Tristan hadn't had to rebuild the club; his real estate investments were both lucrative and substantial, but the club was popular with supernaturals and humans alike. While wolves and witches were welcome, it was the vampires who enjoyed the greatest benefit; easily finding willing donors to satiate their thirst without relying on bottled blood. Humans, on the other hand, often sought to indulge in an orgasmic feeding experience or simply enjoyed walking on the wild side, delighting in the paranormal conversation and sexual ambiance. It was a synergistic relationship, one that he intended to continue to cultivate.

A new beginning, Tristan thought, as he curled his hand around the cold brass doorknob. This was his city, his territory. Outsiders were already painfully aware of his presence, as he'd placed a moratorium on any new wolves from entering his territory. If found trespassing, they'd be killed without a blink of an eye. There were times when Tristan overtly exerted his dominance, reminding all those around him exactly why he was Lyceum Wolves' Alpha. And so it began. Letting his power flow out toward his wolves, alerting them to his presence, he advanced toward the partygoers. After a brief appearance at the opening gala, he'd meet with his advisors, then retribution would commence.

As the private elevator door opened, Tristan smiled confidently at his guests. Urbane and handsome, he nonchalantly strode into the room, commanding the attention of every male and female. He waved to Logan, his beta, who was chatting up a sultry redhead at the bar. Spotting Marcel, his brother, the New Orleans' Alpha, he crossed the dance floor. Tristan embraced his older brother in a sturdy hug, enough to hurt most men.

"Hey, why didn't you come up to the office?" Tristan questioned.

"What can I say, Bro? There are some mighty fine women down here who required my undivided attention. Nice job with the new club by the way." Marcel looked casually around the club. Calvin, his beta, sat at the bar, carefully observing the interaction.

"Always the ladies' man," Tristan joked. "Sorry, but tonight is all about business. When I finish my speech, we're meeting in the conference room. Logan and the others are aware of the schedule." He patted his brother on the back.

"Sounds good. See you in a few. Good luck," Marcel added, knowing his younger brother fully enjoyed the attention of speaking in front of a crowd.

Tristan smiled back at his brother as he made his way through the crowd toward the stage. The sea of patrons on the dance floor parted as he made his way toward the microphone, uber-aware the good looking Alpha was in close proximity to their gyrating bodies. Women strained to catch a glimpse of the sexy Alpha, demurely curtsying while showing off their cleavage. Males bowed their heads in respect, clearing a wide breadth for the lethal wolf.

The striking Alpha was the picture of exemplary health and strength; not a scratch or scrape gave a hint that a building had collapsed on him less than a week ago. As he strode through the crowd, he silently acknowledged pack members. His dominant aura permeated the room. The band stopped playing. All talking ceased. Suave and cocksure, he grabbed a glass of champagne off a tray held by a passing waiter, and walked up onto the stage, commanding the attention of the entire room.

"Welcome to Noir, mes amis!" Tristan cheerfully announced to his guests as he took the microphone. "I am pleased to have all of you here tonight to celebrate the grand opening of Philadelphia's premier nightclub." A cool smile broke across his face as he raised a hand to quell the surge of applause. "Yes, yes, I know. It is quite impressive. I'd like to thank Logan for assisting me in this spectacular accomplishment. Please be sure to check out the magnificent views of the skyline from our rooftop bar."

He raised his glass to the crowd in celebration. "Once again, thank you for coming tonight. Vive les loups Lyceum!"

A loud cheer erupted as Tristan exited the spotlight, determined to meet with his pack leaders. While he felt a splinter of satisfaction with the expedient and successful opening, revenge consumed his thoughts. He'd let his patrons celebrate, while he strategized his plan of action. Shaking hands as he made his way through the crowd, Tristan eyed Logan and nodded. The band started up again, firing off a sultry rock song. Undulating bodies filled the dance floor, writhing and grinding to the music.

This is why he was Alpha. The blazing fire had barely made a dent in his daily existence. He had easily rebuilt in the face of the fools who'd attacked his territory. The cool vibe of his new club exemplified just as much about him as it did about what was coming; a day of reckoning. Whoever had decided to torch his property had knowingly declared war on his pack. It was time to get to business, find the enemy and obliterate the threat. No one attacked Lyceum Wolves and survived.

Tristan approached the private entrance behind the bar, and pressed his hand into the biometric security pad. Greeted with a ping and a green light, he typed the code and the door slid open. He marched down the mahogany-lined hallway. Logan and Marcel brought up the rear, making sure that no one followed as the door closed. As he turned the corner, a svelte blonde, well-dressed in a camel-colored suede suit, leaned against the wall admiring her long manicured nails. Mira.

"Ah, ma chère. You look beautiful this evening." Tristan slowed his approach, admiring her long legs. Mira Conners, alpha female of the pack, attracted every wolf on the East Coast. She and Tristan had made love on more than one occasion, but they couldn't seem to make it work as a couple. They were more than 'friends with benefits' but less than lovers. Mira was the first female to teach him that sex didn't equate with love. But his relationship with her also taught him about friendship and respect. A century of being together had a way of weeding out those you could trust from those you couldn't.

Tristan caged her legs and set his hands upon her hips. "Nice leather."

"Nice tux." She smiled, fully appreciating how delicious he looked dressed up for this evening's event.

"Listen Mira, we got work to do. I can't afford to get distracted, and you have a way of doing that to me," he whispered into her hair.

Without looking, he yelled over his shoulder. "Marcel. Logan. We'll meet you in two minutes. Make sure everyone's here."

Marcel and Logan looked at each other, before stealing a glance at Mira, avoiding Tristan's gaze. She'd been part of the pack since they were kids, and had been the strongest female they'd ever known. Both her physical and intellectual acumen set her far above other female pack members. Like Marcel and Tristan, she was destined to be Alpha.

Abandoned at birth, Mira had been raised by the Lyceum Wolves' Alpha. Both the Lyceum Wolves' Alpha and Tristan's father had been the best of friends, so they'd decidedly forged a strong alliance with their children. From a young age, she'd summered in New Orleans, running with her boys: Marcel, Tristan and Logan. Tristan's parents, the Louisiana Alpha and his mate, had welcomed the addition of the little female wolf to their home and pack. Tristan's mother had always wanted a daughter, so in a way, Mira had filled those shoes, at least for a few months each year.

Summer after summer, they ran the bayou and raised hell. As Marcel grew older, he had become focused on learning the role of the Alpha, determined to take over for his father. In his absence, Tristan, Mira and Logan had strengthened their friendship, spending their days fishing in the swamp and warm summer nights making love in the fields. There had been a time when the three wolves had been inseparable lovers. In retrospect, Mira honestly wasn't sure who she'd loved first, Tristan or Logan, but in the end, neither man had become her mate.

After attending graduate school, Tristan had come to Mira's side after her father died. Determined to protect her, he'd fought to be the Alpha of Lyceum Wolves. In his newfound position of authority, Tristan had taken her under his wing, ensuring she continued her college education. Once she'd graduated from Wharton Business School, she'd smoothly slid into Tristan's life as his executive assistant. She was the perfect fit for his real estate holdings corporation. Sharp dressed and tongued, she wielded great power in the boardroom and the pack house. Mira was in a league of her own among the females of the pack. And while she'd occasionally made love to both Tristan and Logan, they all knew it would not result in a mating pair for the pack. Still, she fit nicely into Tristan's life as his confidant and friend.

Tristan liked to play the field but Mira could still make him hard with just a look. As she laid her fingers on his cheek, he let out a small sigh. She bowed her head, her eyes not meeting his. "Alpha, your new club is amazing. Sorry

I'm late. Good news is that I wrapped up the Rapkus deal but got stuck in rush hour traffic."

Tristan placed a finger under her chin, catching her gaze. "Great work, Mira. I'm glad you made it to this meeting. I know you usually work the business end of things, but I need you on hand to ensure the security of all ongoing deals. Something tells me this attack wasn't the last, and I'm about to go on the offensive."

Mira reached her hand up to cup Tristan's hand and rubbed her cheek into his fingers, seeking his touch. He responded by holding her hips still, bringing her body flush against his. His warm breath teased her throat; she moaned as he licked her flesh.

"Please," she begged.

Tristan laughed, knowing full well they didn't have time to make love. "No time, ma chère. But look what you do to me," he teased, groaning as he pulled away from her. Painfully aroused, his manhood pressed against his zipper. Damn, it had been a long time since he'd been with a woman.

"Later tonight, perhaps? Or do you have a date this evening?" he asked with a lopsided grin, knowing damn well that he had several wolves vying for her attention. She could have whoever she wanted any day of the week. Yet they both knew it didn't matter. She was his first, no matter what plans she'd made.

"Maybe," she hedged with a small teasing smile. "But I could reschedule for my Alpha. Seriously, Tristan, you know that you and Logan have ruined me for any other wolf. I mean, really? How will I ever find a mate who'll satisfy me the way you do?"

"Ah, come now, Mir. You know that when you meet your mate, no one will compare. That's just the way it is. Sadly, you'll forget us like yesterday's news...no matter what mad skills I have in bed." He shot her a seductive grin, like a spider drawing her into his web.

While Tristan was truly an incredible lover and she was a desirable female, they both knew that once she found her mate, she'd leave him in the wind. When a wolf found his mate and initiated the final bond, no sexual rival existed. Sure, a wolf could consensually decide with his mate to play with another during the full moon activities, but the wolf pair would make decisions as one party. All decisions would be in the best interest of both wolves. And their love would bond them only to each other.

But until they each found mates, they were all happily single and available. While the threesome didn't make love regularly, their strong friendship could easily turn into hot sex on the right night, waxing and waning like the moon. Given the kinky things they'd done to each other, Tristan knew it would be difficult for her to find another male who'd match the intensity of their trio.

Tristan held her gaze and reached for her again, sliding his fingers along the curve of her jaw, down the side of her neck until the back of his hand brushed over the swell of her breasts.

"But until you find your mate, you'll just have to compare them all to me...Someday, though, I'll have to give you up for good. You'll leave Logan and me to go have a house full of pups. We'll be hopelessly heartbroken." He feigned sadness.

"And what about you, Tris? Sydney's married now; it's time to get serious about finding your mate. The elders believe it is your time," she countered with raised eyebrows.

Narrowing his eyes on Mira, he released her and raked his fingers through his shaggy blonde hair. "Please don't start. I'm single for a reason and you know it. Besides *I* run Lyceum Wolves, not the elders. I appreciate their input, but we do not need a breeding pair to run things," he grumbled, irritated that she'd brought up the topic of his mating, which was so not happening any time soon.

"Okay, okay. God, I'm sorry I even brought it up." She smoothed her hair and stood a bit straighter, but still lowered her eyes in submission, sensing his agitation.

"I'm serious, Mir. I really do hope you find a mate soon, but I'm good. In fact, I'm perfect...single...the way I like it. Really," he emphasized with a grunt as if that would convince her to give up the subject. Granted, he knew she'd been waiting over a hundred years to find a mate. But that didn't mean he wanted any part of being tied down to one woman. *No thank you.*

"Come on, let's go. The boys should be ready for us."

Tristan had bristled at her questioning, knowing full well that he was not ready to settle down. Sure, he had asked Sydney Willows to move in with him over a month ago, but he did so knowing that they were not mates. Sydney had been his steady 'friend with benefits' for over a year. But now that she was married to his friend, Kade, he had no excuse not to play the field. Besides Mira and Sydney, Tristan didn't date nearly as much as was rumored. When he was younger, he'd sowed his oats as much as the next wolf, but he'd refined his tastes in recent years and was quite happy with his selective but dynamic sex life.

As they walked toward the door, he deliberately said nothing, letting the cooling sound of silence speak volumes. They entered the soundproofed meeting room without speaking another word. He'd had top of line conference facilities installed in the new club, including LCD projectors and wall to wall plasma screens. An oval cherry table with tan leather seating for twenty took center stage.

Tristan strode to the head of the table, where Marcel and Logan were already seated to his left and right. Three distinguished pack members, who Tristan held in high regard, also sat in attendance. Willow Marrow, the oldest living elder, had seen a lifetime of pack wars. When Tristan had fought to win Alpha, she'd been grateful, because he ensured her safety and status. Her brothers, also elders, Gavin and Shayne, flanked their sister.

Gavin's son Declan sat to his right, and was considered a senior wolf, strong and competent. Tristan could sense Declan had been itching to challenge him, yet he'd always been loyal to the pack. There was a good chance Tristan would need to call upon Declan in the coming weeks, and he wanted him on board with his strategy. As a leader, sometimes it was better to coax an opponent into becoming a friend, rather than cause fractures within the pack.

Tristan silently nodded at Mira to shut the door; she entered the security code to lock down the room and then gracefully sat down next to Logan and looked to the Alpha to begin. Tristan closed his eyes slowly and blew out a cleansing breath, aware that his power rolled off him, commanding the attention of his pack. His eyes flew open; the others felt his tension and waited anxiously for him to begin.

"Okay, people, listen up. As you all are aware, someone decided to wage war with Lyceum Wolves by attacking my club last week. Now that Noir is up and running and we've had a chance to investigate, it's time to go on the offensive. However, before we talk about how this is going to go down, let's review what we know so everyone's on the same page."

Heads nodded toward Tristan in acknowledgment but no one spoke; they all knew better than to interrupt the Alpha. While Tristan presented a cool and charismatic appearance, he was also reserved and lethal, like a Samurai sword waiting to be drawn from its sheath. Picking up the remote, he confidently circled the table. Punching a button, the large plasma screen flicked to life. Through the grainy video of a room in flames, a small, cloaked figure dashed across the room toward the aquarium behind the bar.

"Most of the video was damaged in the fire, but we were able to get this footage. Notice the one person we've got here. We're not sure, but we think it's a human woman. I smelled the blood before the collapse, and the one thing I could tell is that she's not a shifter or vampire. I couldn't tell at the time why all the blood was concentrated behind the bar, but as you can see here in this clip, she breaks the glass to get to Eve."

Eve was a large yellow boa constrictor, who'd been a centerpiece behind the bar. Tristan had raised her as a baby and had built an incredibly elaborate terrarium for her, including lights and trees. Yet, when he'd gone into the fiery building to save her, the snake was missing.

"There's only a few seconds left on this clip, and as you can see, she appears to cut her arm. She wraps it in a bar towel and proceeds to grab Eve. I find it damn interesting that someone would go through the effort to torch the place, and then take the time to save an animal, a snake at that. But this is what we've got. The only prints I saw when I went in were bloodied footprints, presumably hers, since they were small. There was no evidence of anyone else in the place, but then again, it was burning pretty good. I could barely breathe in there let alone detect the scent of a wolf or vamp. Magic is also still on the table as a possibility."

Tristan flicked the screen off, walked back around and sat down. He felt a silent vibration on the table, picked up his cell phone and read the message: *'D. on premises. Waiting for you in Luvox Suite'*. Tristan impatiently tapped his fingers on the table on learning that the vampire was present in the building.

Looking over to Marcel, he directed him to speak to his wolves. "Marcel is going to update you on the stray wolves that attacked Kat. Not sure how they tie into this situation yet, but I know they are a piece of the puzzle. Marcel?"

Marcel nodded and scanned the faces at the table. He was not their Alpha, but commanded the respect of Tristan's pack. "The day of the fire, Kat's car was attacked and her driver, Paul, a young member of our pack, was killed. Kat managed to draw two wolves into an area where we could trap them but both of them committed suicide before capture. I'll tell you that I've never seen anything like it. Cyanide tablets. That tells me they were fiercely loyal and didn't want to risk our interrogations. Unfortunately, the bodies had no identifiable markings. We did find the car; it'd been stolen. New York plates. And that's all we've got."

Marcel pinched the bridge of his nose and blew out a deep breath. He continued, "Now I've talked to Chandler by phone. He continues to deny any involvement. As much as I want to believe the guy, we can't be sure. I mean, he didn't give up wanting Kat for his mate until both Tris and I confronted him. So he's not one to take no for an answer. He may be pissed and looking for retribution. He could have sent those wolves to kidnap Kat and force a mating. Now, on the other hand, if it isn't him, it could be that there's someone trying to stage a coup within his pack. You can be damn sure that if he's clean, he's pickin' apart his pack lookin' for traitors."

Jax Chandler was the New York Alpha. Dangerous and cunning, he'd spent the last couple of months trying to convince Tristan's sister to mate with him.

Tristan stood again, interrupting his brother. "So for now, Kat is safely tucked away in New Orleans. Marcel's leaving tonight to keep a close eye on her and his pack. As for Lyceum, we are locking down. This new building has several empty apartments with state-of-the-art security. All pack members are welcomed and encouraged to stay here when in the city, or remain at the pack house up state. To date, no one's claimed responsibility for the fire, but that doesn't mean this is over. Logan?"

Logan, calm and stoic, raised his gaze to meet his Alpha's. He was Tristan's best friend and confidant. As beta wolf, he took second in command, and often shared responsibilities with his Alpha in both work and play. Logan had idolized Tristan when growing up, knowing his power first hand. Until recently, he'd helped run Eden, but now he vowed to stay close to Tristan, guarding him with his life. Over the past century, Logan had become accustomed to the visions that plagued his sleep; good or bad, he usually only shared them with Tristan. Today, he'd been asked for the first time to talk with a group.

Tristan strode over to Logan and put his hand upon his shoulder, giving him assurance of his protection. He wouldn't push Logan too far, realizing that he preferred to keep his visions private. But this time, Tristan needed him to tell the others what he'd seen.

"I've seen a dead wolf. A male. I felt he was ours. He definitely wasn't one of the wolves down in New Orleans. My visions," he looked up to Tristan, then back to the others. "My visions, they aren't always clear. But this, what happened to the club, what happened to Kat, it's only the beginning. All members of the pack need to be on alert for out-of-territory wolves. In the past, we've been relatively lax about wolves entering and leaving our territory. No more. Tristan's put out an advisory to all other Alphas. Anyone who comes into our territory as a non-pack member must seek the Alpha's permission or else there will be consequences."

Consequences. Mira and the others knew what that meant. Death. Tristan wouldn't hesitate to kill another wolf after the recent attacks. Nor would Marcel.

"In addition, there is no traveling outside our territory until after this issue is resolved," Logan explained; his serious expression cast a dark cloud over the room. No one was used to Logan speaking about his visions, and they now knew death was coming for one of their own.

"That means all wolves need to be brought up to date on this mandate. Willow, you're in charge of pack communications, so as soon as the meeting's over, get on it," Tristan ordered. "The visions. It's possible things can change, but our wolves are indulged, used to freedoms. It has not always been peaceful, and unfortunately, such is the way of territorial disputes. I expect everyone here to read and digest the security dossiers that Logan's put together in front of you. Any questions, see Logan."

Tristan looked over to Mira. "Mira, from here on out all deals through my corporation will need to be approved by Logan. In addition, I expect you to run in-depth background checks on all prospective clients, whether we're buying or selling properties."

She nodded in agreement. "Yes, Alpha."

"As for me, I'm setting up a face to face with Chandler to be held off territory in a neutral location. This meeting will be held within the next few days. Even though the location is neutral, that doesn't mean there won't be a confrontation. If I sense he is responsible, I will take action. You must all be prepared," Tristan pointed out with a calm demeanor. He heard Mira let out a barely audible gasp. They all knew it could mean his death if he didn't win.

Without encouraging their fear, he continued speaking. "Also, Léopold Devereoux is here in Noir, tonight. For those of you who don't know him, he's my friend Kade's maker. I'm not sure what he's got, but Kade said he's bringing me intel on the arsonist. So I expect I'll have more info within the next thirty minutes."

Tristan raised an eyebrow, surveying his wolves, and then looked down to check the time on his cell. "Any questions? Now's the time to ask them."

Declan was the first to speak up, yet again trying to assert his dominance over the other wolves. "Why are we bringing a vamp into pack matters? Wolf battles need to be fought by wolves."

Tristan smiled coolly at Declan, eyeing him until he lowered his gaze. "Ah, jeune loup. *'There is at least one thing worse than fighting with allies – And that is to fight without them'"*.

A flummoxed Declan stared back at him. "What?"

"Churchill," Tristan quickly responded. "You will learn with experience that allies are allies, no matter the species. Wars are won based on both strength and information. It is foolish to cut off areas that bring you either. Any other brilliant questions?" He was losing his patience, knowing that Devereoux was on the premises. There was no time to waste. Whatever information the vampire had, it was important enough that he was visiting the club.

Léopold Devereoux was not only ancient and powerful, well over a thousand years old, but he was quite elusive. Tristan had been surprised when Kade called him to let him to know to expect a visit. He was even more surprised that Léopold was coming to see him and not Kade. Whatever the vampire had to say must be damn important for him to travel to Philadelphia, and Tristan wasn't waiting a minute more to hear it.

With no other questions, Tristan stood. Mira hurriedly entered the security code, unlocking the door.

"Well, then. Carry on with your orders. Anything out of the ordinary, contact Logan or me immediately. Meeting adjourned. Be safe, my Lyceum Wolves." With those words, Tristan strode out of the conference room with Logan close behind. Mira watched as her men walked away, knowing danger awaited them all.

Tristan knocked once. A response, "Come in", registered, before he proceeded to open the suite door. Entering, he heard the faint sound of a zipper being zipped as a man adjusted his pants, dressing in front of a long mirror. The debonair vampire turned to face Tristan, a smile on his face, quite comfortable with the intrusion. Léopold Devereoux, Kade's maker, looked as if he was in his late twenties, with short dark hair spiked into a shark's fin. Lethal and quick-witted, he casually and smoothly proceeded to button his tailored shirt. Admiring a naked blonde and brunette, who both slept contently on the bed adjacent to the long leather sofa, he licked over his fangs in delight. A moan escaped one of the women as she turned to spoon the other and found the warm breast she sought.

"Lovely, aren't they?" Léopold asked nonchalantly with a slight French accent. "Your club Noir... c'est magnifique. Exquisite blood and even better sex."

"Monsieur Devereoux?" Tristan questioned, confirming his assumption that the man before him was indeed Kade's maker.

"Oui."

"Monsieur Livingston?"

"Oui."

"Please call me Léopold," he insisted, checking his appearance once more.

"I'm pleased you've had a chance to enjoy Noir's amenities but we need to speak privately." Tristan eyed the nude women, smiling at Léopold. As much as he enjoyed viewing the opposite sex without clothing, business came first.

"Ah oui." Léopold snapped his fingers loudly and the women on the bed began to stir. "Up now, my lovelies. Time to go. Next time in Philadelphia and all that good stuff. Now off you go." He handed each of them a white fluffy spa robe, complementary from Noir. Each woman grabbed their clothing and shoes off the floor, sheepishly giggling as they left the room.

Tristan proceeded to sit in an overstuffed leather chaise, and propped his feet up on the ottoman. He gestured for Léopold to join him.

"Let me say that I am appreciative of any assistance you can provide with regards to finding the arsonists."

"Nasty business, no? Kade informed me of your troubles, cowardly, indeed. Not that I mind revenge or war, when justified," Léopold commented flatly.

"I can assure you that I do plan on revenge. And when I do, I'll look straight into their soul when their life leaves this earth."

Léopold let out a hearty laugh. "A man of my own heart. No wonder you and Kade are friends. Well then, I'd say you'll enjoy this little tidbit of information I have for you."

"I imagine I will." Tristan grinned, tasting the justice he was readying to mete out.

"Let's get to it then. You know Alexandra? My fille. My daughter. She runs our Philadelphia operations."

Tristan silently nodded with an utterly emotionless expression. Did he know Alexandra? Who didn't? She ran her vampire operations with a silk-covered, well-manicured, iron fist. Animalistic came to mind when he thought of how she lusted after anything with a cock, and provided little mercy for her enemies. Tristan considered her neither friend nor foe but generally avoided contact.

While it was true that he allowed her and her vampires to patronize his club, he'd had to refuse her sexual advances on more than one occasion and didn't relish the thought of having to interact with the black-hearted mistress.

Alexandra was interested in one thing and one thing only; Alpha blood. Alpha blood equated to power. As far as Tristan was concerned, it'd be a cold day in hell before he ever fucked her, let alone let her drink from him. He silently prayed that whatever Léopold said next didn't involve quid quo pro.

As well as Tristan tried to hide his disdain for Alexandra, Léopold began to chuckle to himself. "Alpha, you need not conceal your feelings about her. I am not fond of the little witch, myself. But for now, she leads. And it just so happens that she's found a toy which you'd like very much."

Tristan raised an eyebrow. "A toy, you say?"

"Oui, a toy. If you know my fille; she sees most things or people as either food or toys. In some cases, they are one and the same."

"So let's say she does indeed have what I'd like to call a 'person of interest'. Why hasn't she come to me herself? Why send you?"

"Well, first of all, she very much likes her toy at the moment. And secondly, she'd want something in exchange for her troubles. However, when I heard you were looking for this 'person of interest', and I found out about her toy, I decided to force her to hand it over to you. You see, unlike Alexandra, I am very fond of Kade, and unlike most parents, I do play favorites. Sometimes she needs to be spanked a little to stay in line, no?" Léopold stated plainly as he fastened his cufflinks.

"Monsieur, I do appreciate your, shall we call it, intervention."

"You can go do a pick up tonight. She's expecting you. I can't promise your 'person of interest' won't be unharmed. I can, however, say that said person will be alive."

"You sure about that?" Tristan didn't mean to question the vampire but he knew Alexandra was nothing short of ruthless.

"Trust is a delicate thing, Alpha. You don't know me well, so I shall let this pass. But know that my children do not cross me. For if they do, well, let's just say that the immortal are not truly immortal. Death can come to us all given the right circumstance," Léopold responded indifferently as he stood and put on his suit jacket.

Tristan knew his words to be true. Stake or remove a vampire's heart or decapitate them, and a vampire would indeed die. Werewolves were nearly immortal and could suffer great injury, yet they could be killed by evisceration or broken neck. On that somber thought, Tristan stood up and faced the ancient vampire eye to eye.

"I want you to know that Lyceum Wolves is appreciative of your willingness to help. It will not be forgotten. If I can be of assistance to you in the future, do not hesitate to call on me." He extended his hand.

"Alpha, you've been there for Kade many a time, no? I am only returning a favor. And I must say that after visiting your club, I see why it is so important to our upper echelon vampires. Willing donors for blood and pleasure combined with a decadent atmosphere is quite the attraction in the City of Brotherly Love. C'est une excellente." Léopold reached for Tristan and returned his offer with a solid handshake. As Tristan opened the door, Léopold briefly raised his hand in a salute, before gathering his things to leave.

Logan gave Tristan a small grin. He'd stood watch outside, overhearing the entire conversation. "He's quite the vamp, huh?" Logan commented. "Hard to believe Alexandra's his daughter, although I will say they're both as deadly as a rattlesnake in a pit."

"That is true, my friend." Tristan put a hand on Logan's shoulder, not fancying a visit to Alexandra. Nevertheless, he couldn't contain his excitement over the possibility that the arsonist could be in his custody within the hour.

-๏๛ *Chapter Two* ๛๏-

K alli slowly opened her eyes, entrenched in a hazy nightmare. Kidnapped and bled out, she could barely move her limbs, let alone try to sit up in bed. Two days ago, she'd left the hospital only to be attacked from behind by vampires. They'd knocked her out and brought her here, wherever here was. At first they'd chained her to the bed, but now her own body's weakness shackled her. For two nights, she'd been visited by a diabolical bloodsucking mistress. The demon sucked her blood only to spit it out; something about poison, she remembered her screeching.

Kalli wasn't naïve to supernaturals, far from it. She knew how evil they all were, and this nasty detour only proved her point. But Kalli was a survivor. She'd survived her so-called family; she'd survive this too. The effects of her pills were starting to wear off, as she could feel the beast within calling, begging to fight. She supposed she needed the extra strength it could bring her, but her brain refused to allow the animal to surface. She was human now, at least on the outside.

Looking around the opulent room, she craned her neck, struggling to identify where they'd brought her. If she didn't know any better she'd have thought she was in a luxurious hotel. But the thousand-thread-count Egyptian cotton sheets could not mask her hideous isolation; her deafening screams while tortured beyond reason. Still no one came to her rescue. Someone would have surely heard as she strained against the blood red talons that held her down while razor sharp fangs pierced her skin.

She spied a bottle of water and saltines on the nightstand. Had they been feeding her? Keeping her as some kind of blood bag? She didn't remember eating, but she couldn't deny she needed water. With great effort and a moan, she reached for the bottle and opened it. She felt almost human as the cool liquid slid down her sore throat. *Almost human.* That was the key, she thought to herself. For now, she thanked God that she was human enough to fool them. Repulsed by her blood, they hadn't discovered her secret. She could sense the bitch's confusion as her medicated blood hit her tongue. Damn straight, it didn't taste good. Yet the greedy bloodsucker kept going, probably to make her weak on purpose. She might have succeeded in draining her, but Kalli was a fighter.

Letting the beast take control was seemingly her only option for escape. She hadn't seen or heard anyone in the hallway. She reasoned from the short car ride, that she was still in the city. If she could just get out of this house, people wouldn't be far; refuge was within her grasp. But her medicine suppressed the beast. She wanted it that way. Being human was far underrated, yet in this situation she could not deny that being supernatural would give her the strength to at least walk, find help, and hide.

Seeing no other choice, Kalli closed her eyes and breathed deeply, searching for the one within who could save her from the torment that would surely seek her out again. Determined to find deliverance from the incubus, she let the power of the beast fill her veins.

Tristan pulled his SUV up to Alexandra's four-story, Victorian brownstone. While she preferred her ostentatious mansion in the suburbs, he knew for certain she'd be waiting for him in the city. Alexandra's narcissistic tendencies would drive her to make an appearance at the exclusive opening of his club. Anyone who was anyone was there tonight; she considered herself *the* one. It probably was killing her to have to wait for him to retrieve 'the toy', as Léopold called it.

Tristan conceded that she had her place in the supernatural world. Vampires needed a leader, and she kept hers on a tight leash, preventing them from wreaking havoc in the city or his club. For the past fifty years of her rule, vampire on human crime had been minimal. If someone was killed, it was with her knowledge and approval. Tristan respected her leadership toward shifters; she generally respected their existence. She never questioned Tristan's punishments on her own vampires if they got out of hand at his club, and they'd been able to amicably work out any disagreements.

But the one thing Alexandra coveted the most, she could not have; Tristan's blood. He'd refused her his vein many a time. The denial only fueled her desire, convinced she could seduce him given the right circumstances. But he knew that no matter how beautiful or alluring she was, he'd never give in to her wishes. She only wanted his blood to increase her power, and as far as he was concerned, she already had too much, paired with little restraint.

Tristan looked over to Logan who'd been deep in thought on the ride over to Alexandra's. Since the attack,

Logan had had more visions and Tristan was certain that he wasn't sharing all he'd seen. He didn't press him, understanding that it was both a gift and burden to sense the future.

"Hey, man. You ready to do this?" Tristan asked, shutting off the car.

"Yeah, sorry. Just thinking," Logan grumbled.

"You okay, Logan? I know seeing that death wasn't easy. I'm not sure what's going on here, but it's not my first time to the rodeo. Things will be okay," Tristan assured Logan, hoping he would snap out of it.

Logan knew that whatever was in that house, more like whoever was in that house, would change things forever between him and Tristan. He couldn't get a feel for whether that change would be good or bad, blanketing him with uncertainty. But now was not the time to tell Tristan what he'd seen. Not only would the Alpha be pissed, he'd fight fate every step of the way. It had the potential to throw Tristan off his equilibrium during this time of battle; he couldn't risk divulging his speculation without being sure. Logan had decided, with heavy heart, to cautiously watch and wait before telling him.

Blowing out a breath and unbuckling his seatbelt, he placed a hand on his Alpha's shoulder. "I'm okay. Now let's do this thing. Not sure about you but I'm ready for a little action, myself."

"Okay, here's the game plan. We're in and out. You know Alexandra. She's goin' to want to keep me there, going all Playboy bunny slash Martha Stewart on me. Sex or food, she knows what I like." Tristan grinned; she knew him well enough to know his favorite things. "A man has his weaknesses."

Logan shook his head disapprovingly.

"Hey, at the end of the day, I'm a man. Who doesn't like a little cookie with their milk? Seriously though, we're in and out. No cups of tea. No bonbons. We get the package and get out. This is too serious to waste time."

"I'm with you."

"One more thing. The package may be damaged. Léopold promised it'd be alive, but knowing Alexandra and the fact that he referred to it as her toy, well, let's just say we may have to carry it out."

"As long as we can do an interrogation at some point, it'll be okay," Logan commented.

"Okay, you ready? Let's do it," Tristan ordered, getting out of the car.

Logan followed him up the cobblestone walkway. The extravagant brownstone had been fully restored and probably looked better than it had during the eighteen hundreds. Gas lights illuminated the heavy wooden, intricately carved door. Tristan knocked hard on the stained oak, knowing full well she was aware of his arrival. Survival instincts would alert her to the powerhouse standing outside her home; she'd be waiting for him.

A well-toned young man dressed in a turquoise harlequin vest and black tights opened the door and greeted them with a blithe smile. "The mistress awaits," he announced, ushering them into a spacious, octagonal foyer. Stained glass windows and dark mahogany moldings set against cream textured wallpaper with red swirls created an antiqued illusion for guests. Dark hardwood floors accentuated the expensive oriental area rugs.

Tristan and Logan watched the odd-looking man walk into a larger parlor where he lounged on a long, velvet sofa.

He closed his eyes, ignoring them. Through an archway, they saw Alexandra gracefully navigate her way around a baby grand piano. Dressed in a red satin corset that pushed up her already firm breasts, she smiled coldly, baring her perfectly white teeth. A tight, black leather pencil skirt hugged every inch of her bottom, leaving little room to walk in a typical stride. Her jet black hair had been swept into an intricate updo that drew attention to her creamy pale skin. She looked every bit the enchanting, but dangerous sanguisuge. And while her beautiful looks most certainly drew men like bees to honey, Tristan knew all too well that her sting was deadly.

"Tristan, darling," she crooned, extending her arms for a hug. "Come now, I won't bite."

"Ah chère, but you do," he teased.

Tristan grabbed her bony hand in his and quickly blew air kisses to each of her cheeks. It was more a gesture of peace as opposed to genuine happiness to see her. He knew she'd appreciate the thought.

"And Logan, so glad you could join us as well," she smirked, feigning geniality, never taking her gaze off of Tristan. Her irritation with Tristan's second was hardly a secret, since she wanted to be alone with the Alpha. Logan would only serve as a barrier in her quest for blood.

Logan ignored her comment, scanning the room for others. He didn't give a shit if she was happy or not. There was no way in hell that he'd let his Alpha walk into that hornet's nest alone.

"Please, Tristan, come have a drink. Cognac perhaps? And I'd be remiss not to mention how sexy you look in that tuxedo. Sorry I missed your opening. As you know I'd been planning to be there right on time, but…"

28

"Stop. Alexandra. You know why I'm here, and I don't have time for nonsense. Give it to me now," Tristan commanded, not moving from the foyer.

Alexandra ran her palms up and down the lapels of his jacket. "You mean my mouse?" she purred. "Léopold really is no fun. I was having such a good time playing with her."

"Her?" Tristan raised an eyebrow.

"Please, don't pretend you didn't know. Surely Léopold must have told you."

"No, and frankly I don't care whether it's a man or woman. Whoever torched my club knowingly started a pack war. That being said, I'm interested in how you procured her. How do you know she was there?"

Alexandra admired her long nails, preparing to boast about her extraordinary hunting skills. "My strong Alpha, you do know just how important your little club is to me and my vampires. While you may not appreciate my interest in your venture, you know that I've always wanted you."

Tristan rolled his eyes. "Yes, tell me something I don't know."

"My vampires. They do treasure being able to go to the club for a bite to eat and to seek carnal pleasure. They watch. They protect what they value."

"You have surveillance on my club?" Tristan could hardly believe she'd go so far as to stalk him, but at this point, he just wanted answers.

"Please, darling, don't make it sound so crass. They weren't spying on you," she countered defensively. "They were merely making their rounds, making sure our ranks were behaving. They are my eyes and ears. As their leader, I'm acutely aware of their activities. One must keep vampires in line."

"Yeah right," Logan grunted under his breath. He didn't trust a single word that came out of those finely painted lips.

"Did you have to bring him?" Alexandra asked Tristan, quite annoyed that Logan was allowed to speak in her presence.

Tristan shot him a pleading look as if to ask him to curb his anger. He knew Logan didn't do diplomacy, whereas the Alpha was trying to get as much information as possible about what had happened. The last thing he needed was war with the vampires, as he might need their help with whoever had attacked the pack.

"Please go on," Tristan encouraged.

Alexandra huffed, smoothing her hair. "The day of the fire they were merely doing rounds of the city. All they saw was her leaving with that dreadful snake of yours in tow. Honestly, I don't know why you even kept that vile reptile." She rolled her black eyes in disgust. "But I digress. Long story short, we tailed her then snapped her up a few days later in a parking garage."

"What else did your workers see that night? Did they actually see her set the fire? Was she with anyone?"

"No, they did not see her set the fire, nor did they see anyone else. Please, Tristan. As if I would lie to you." She batted her heavily mascaraed eyelashes at him. "Now that I've already told you what they knew, can we please go into the parlor and sit like civilized people? I'd love to hear all the details about your new club," she pleaded, and turned to walk away.

"What do you mean by 'knew'? I want to talk to the vampires who saw her that day and the ones who captured her," he demanded. "They might be able to tell me something you overlooked."

She stopped in her tracks, slowly turning around with a cold sneer plastered across her face. "I'm afraid that's not possible, as they are no longer with us. The vampires who saw her and took her were one and the same. Unfortunately for them, they did not understand the meaning of 'do not touch' and tried to play with my new toy." *Vampire justice was swift and merciless.*

"Okay then. Since we are about to do a transport, I need to know if the woman's supernatural," Tristan inquired. He stoically waited for answers that did not come, while Logan began to pace.

"From what I can tell, she is not of a supernatural origin, now please, let's just go sit down and..."

"Alexandra, I don't have all day. If you have no further information, then we've got to get going. Where is she? Oh and she'd better be alive," Tristan snapped. He was growing impatient.

"Mouse? Don't worry, I didn't *kill* her," she scoffed. "I merely *played* with my toy. But if you are in such a hurry, I'll ask James to bring her down to you. Honestly, I'll be glad to be rid of the nasty little thing. I'll tell you this, my dear Alpha, the twit may not be supernatural, but I'm not convinced she's entirely human, either. Never in all my years has a human tasted so foul."

Kalli heard voices. Her beast had risen for mere seconds only to cower inward. Even though her medicine was starting to wear off, it wasn't enough to allow a transformation. After opening herself to what lay within, she'd hoped she'd have more energy. She was grateful that she could at least walk, which was more than she could have managed earlier. Slowly, she turned the door handle, sensing there were no guards. As she peeked around the corner, she spied the staircase.

She hesitated and looked down at her bare feet. What the hell had they done with her shoes? And even though they'd left her in her jeans, they'd torn her sleeveless turtleneck, exposing her bra. Out of modesty, she tried gathering the material together, softly gliding her fingers over the welts on her neck in the process. It was September, so she wouldn't freeze. Kalli made a split second decision; she needed to leave. It was either flee or die. A coward she wasn't.

She quietly padded down the long hallway, cringing at every little creak her feet made on the old hardwood floor. A shiver ran down her spine when she heard the demon female voice she'd come to know the past few days. Startled at the sound of a man's voice raised in anger, she jumped. Had she brought more vampires here? Were they here for her? She had to get out quickly. She'd die if she lost any more blood.

As she intrepidly descended the stairs, she found they led into a kitchen. Kalli caught sight of a backdoor only twenty feet away; freedom was so close she could taste it. A few steps more and she could reach the handle. She didn't see or hear anyone and darted for the door.

Pain seared through her body as a pair of large hands wrapped around the loose tendrils of her hair, yanking her backward toward the floor. Choked in fear, she gasped for air as vomit rose in her throat. A gut-wrenching scream tore from her lungs as the man dragged her flailing body along the stained wooden planks. Although fraught with confusion and despair, she took note of his perplexing attire; a clown? No, it was another monster, a vampire. His fangs bared, he silently continued to pull her toward the voices. Thrashing about, she grabbed onto his hands, trying to free herself from his iron grip. A flash of the vampire who'd bitten her and two strange men crossed her vision. *Saviors?*

"Please! Help me! They're going to kill me!" she cried out, begging for rescue. Tears streamed down her cheeks as she tried kicking her abductor in an attempt to escape the bloodthirsty, fanged savages who'd been holding her hostage.

Breaking his silence, the harlequin man stopped and straddled her. "Silence! The mistress wants her mouse quiet!" She recoiled as he raised the back of his hand to hit her.

As Tristan heard the screams, he caught a glimpse of the evil smile blooming across Alexandra's face. Growling, he rushed the vampire who sat atop the young woman, shoving him so hard that he flew across the room and smashed into a wall. Tristan cradled the woman's head in his lap, while Logan blocked Alexandra.

Tristan looked down at the battered woman, who looked emaciated and bloodied. Dark raven curls covered her face. Gently, he pushed the strands of hair aside. She whimpered and cringed in fear, balling herself into a fetal position. At first sight, Tristan found it hard to believe that such a vulnerable creature could be involved with starting a pack war.

"Logan, coat!" Tristan barked. He would have given her his own but he refused to let go of the woman for fear that she'd run. Obediently, Logan removed his tuxedo jacket and placed it over her quivering body, never taking his eyes off of Alexandra.

Even though one of his best friends was a vampire, Tristan was irate as he saw the puncture marks all over her skin. *Animals.* She might be a suspect in the fire, but he didn't condone torture. He scooped her small body up in his arms, and stood.

Without another word to Alexandra, Logan opened the door for Tristan, protectively shielding him. He slammed the door as they left, pissed at the vampire. Rage rolled off his Alpha, nearly making him tremble. If it hadn't been for the abused woman lying on the floor needing aid, he was fairly sure Tristan would have killed Alexandra. And he would have gladly helped.

-⊛· *Chapter Three* ·⊛-

"That went well," Logan quipped from the driver's seat. He'd settled Tristan and the stranger into the back seat; she was tightly curled on her side, lying in his lap. Her eyes were still closed and she was breathing in soft, rapid pants.

"What a clusterfuck," Tristan responded. "I swear to God, I'd like to kill that bitch. Look at what she's done to this girl."

"Tris, hate to point out the obvious. But number one, Alexandra has been and will always be a bloodsucking monstrosity. And number two, the girl, as you put it, could have been involved with starting the fire. She could be involved with the wolves who killed Paul. So if it makes you feel any better, that woman back there may not be all that innocent."

"Goddamn Alexandra. It's not her place to do this," he snarled angrily, waving his hand over Kalli. "This...this is torture. And it will never, ever be condoned by me or anyone in my pack, understood?"

Logan solemnly considered his words, knowing that this woman was about to change everything, regardless of her culpability in any crime.

"Just playing devil's advocate. You know I'd like nothing more than to take that vamp's head. And I'd smile doing it," Logan affirmed. "So…how's the girl? She doesn't look too good."

"Still breathing at least, but she's going to need to be cleaned up." Mentally and physically, Tristan thought to himself. His wolf stirred, intrigued by the human nestled in his lap. He absentmindedly stroked a finger across her scratched forehead. She was beautiful, even with the bruise that was starting to form above her left eye. *How did she get mixed up in this nastiness?*

Kalli first became aware that she was no longer in the house when she felt the movement of the car beneath her. The scent of two different males roused her wolf. *God, she needed her pills; she was losing control.* She thought she must be dreaming. She could feel the dominant male calling to her. He'd come for her wolf, and she wouldn't be denied. Kalli clutched his jacket, pulling it up to her face, breathing in pure maleness. She needed more. Seeking comfort, she turned her nose into the soft material couched underneath her head, snuggling against the warmth. *Where am I?*

Tristan shifted uncomfortably in his seat as the female turned towards him, settling her head well into his crotch. He took a deep breath, praying Logan wouldn't look back and see what was happening. Not that he usually minded a woman with her lips on his zipper, but this was all wrong. Regardless of what he knew should not happen, his cock, apparently having a mind of its own, jerked in response to the pressure. There was no denying the warm sensation of her breath on his groin; her nose pressed against him. He tried to back into the seat, slightly moving her to relieve the pressure. Of all the things he'd expected on the car ride back to his condo, this wasn't one of them.

A gentle push on her shoulders roused her senses. Forcing her eyes to open, her vision came into focus, and she was shocked to see a belt buckle. *What the hell?* As she turned her head, golden eyes locked on hers. He was the most gorgeous man she'd ever seen, but it was the sheer amount of energy that took her breath away. *Authority. Domination. Alpha.* Even though it had been years since she'd been around an Alpha wolf, there was no denying the infinite potency emitting from this man. Her wolf sang for it, while her mind panicked.

Kalli started to shake uncontrollably as her wolf fought to emerge. *Oh God, this cannot be happening. I need my medicine.*

"Please," she begged, gasping for air.

"Calm down, now. You're safe," he assured her. She'd thankfully moved away from his zipper, but now was starting to climb up toward his face.

Kalli writhed in his lap, trying to fight the change. She found herself clawing at his shirt, placing her forehead against his chest. Her wolf wanted at this strange man, and she couldn't let that happen.

"Please. I need...I need my pills. The hospital. I'm sick," she lied. But Kalli considered changing a worse fate than being ill. She was content living her life as a human in hiding. She couldn't risk having others finding out she was still alive.

"The hospital? Sorry, ma chère. We'll tend to you when we arrive at the club." If they took her to the hospital, it was likely she'd try to escape. She was a bit scraped up and very much needed food. He'd have his healers tend to her once they got home.

"No, you don't understand. The University Veterinary Hospital. Garage, third floor. My pills are in the car," she cried, digging her fingernails into his chest.

Tristan remembered Alexandra saying something about how she tasted "foul". Perhaps it was whatever medication she'd been taking. Was she really sick? He needed her alive if he was going to get information out of her. Erring on the side of caution, he decided a quick detour couldn't hurt. Perhaps they could get her identification or other information from her car.

"Logan, drive over to UVH. We can check out the car while we're there. It'll only take a minute," Tristan called over to him. She stopped rubbing herself against his chest, and dropped back into his lap again. *Here we go again.*

"Got it, boss. What kind of car are we looking for?" he asked.

"Black. Black convertible. BMW," she replied, her voice starting to calm. Out of exhaustion she laid back onto Tristan. Thank God he'd agreed to take her to the car. She'd get her pills and regain control. Again she pulled the black fabric to her body, pressing it over her mouth in an effort to hide her face. Tired, hungry and weak, she knew there was no way she'd escape an Alpha wolf. But if she took her antidote, she'd get well and bide her time until she could escape him. Kalli wasn't sure why he'd saved her or what he wanted, but there was something about him. He wasn't hurting her; it appeared that he needed her for some reason. For what, she had no idea.

As Logan pulled into the garage, he glanced back at the girl who was still wrapped round his Alpha. Seeing her face, he knew for certain she was the one from his dreams. *Poor Tristan.* He silently groaned, knowing Tristan would have his hide once he found out the truth about the girl, and worse, found out that he'd seen it. But he wasn't sure how it all fit together with the fire or the death of the driver in New Orleans. Sure, the girl looked innocent, but he knew better than to trust a woman based on looks.

Logan navigated up to the third level, slowing as he approached what he assumed to be the car. All four tires had been slashed, presumably in an attempt to prevent her from getting away during her abduction.

"This it?" Logan asked, knowing it was more of a confirmation of what he already knew.

Kalli reached forward with both arms until she found the door. Slowly she rose, sliding up until her fingertips reached the lip of the car window. She moaned, unable to go any further.

"Hold on there. Let me help you." Tristan carefully slid his hands underneath her torso; one hand supported her just above her waist and another under the swell of her breasts.

She peered over the window's horizon to see her little convertible. Breathing a sigh of relief, a rush of hope washed over her. The silly car had been the one extravagance she'd allowed herself after she left. The hospital, where it was parked, was her home; it was everything to her. But would she ever get her life back now that an Alpha had her in his grip?

"My pills are in the center console," she cried, as a single tear rolled down her cheek. "Let me down. I won't run." She let her body go limp and fell onto her back, staring blindly up at the leather ceiling.

Tristan heard a resigned acceptance in her voice. It was better this way. Guilty or not, she had stepped into his world, and one simply didn't walk away after becoming a person of interest in a territorial war. He looked down into her sky blue eyes, realizing she'd disconnected from him. She needed time before he'd be able to get all the answers he needed.

Logan got out of the car, fully prepared to break open a window. Looking to get lucky, he tried the car handle but both doors were locked. Circling the car, he noticed a pair of shoes thrown against the concrete wall. He squatted to inspect them, and guessed that they belonged to their girl. As he stood, he noticed metal glinting underneath the front rear tire. A silver keychain, shaped as a dove. He picked it up and looked at the writing, 'Libre Volonté'. *Free will? From what or whom was she fleeing?* Clicking the key, the car locks clicked open.

"Look at that," he commented, smiling over at Tristan who was watching him. "I'm good."

Tristan rolled down the window. "Yes you are. Now move your ass, Logan. There's something not right with this girl. Did you find her pills?"

Logan held up a brown tube and shook it. "Got it." He rummaged through the car a few minutes more, before he got out and shut the door.

"Took you long enough," Tristan commented as Logan handed him the bottle of pills. "Water?" he asked, hoping for the impossible.

"Sorry, man. I've got nothin'. Can't she just chew it?"

"Guess that's how it's going to have to be. Come on, ma chère. We've got your pills." Tristan opened the unmarked bottle, and he wondered what kind of medication it was. Even though he wasn't human and didn't use their pharmacies, he knew for certain that most pharmaceuticals were labeled. It seemed strange, but she obviously needed the pills.

"Please, just one," she whispered, her eyes locking on his.

Tristan took out a white chalky tablet and placed it on her tongue. She closed her eyes in relief while her lips sealed around his finger. The sweet bitterness burned her throat. *Thank you, God.* Her wolf whined in grief as she was pushed to the back of Kalli's psyche, jailed yet again.

A small sigh escaped as he pulled his wet digit out of her mouth. Goddammit. The woman was scratched and sick, possibly his enemy, and he was thinking of a damn blow job. Shit, he needed to get back to the condo, and fuck something, even if it was his own hand. The pressure of helping Kade, then the fire, his sister; it was getting to be too much. Something had to give.

"What's happening, Tris?" Logan asked, wondering if it had worked.

Tristan didn't want to tell him what was happening, because what he was feeling was inappropriate, to say the least. "She's falling asleep. Whatever was in those pills seemed to calm her. Let's get back to the condo. Call Julie. Tell her to meet us up in my condo. She can heal and watch over this woman. Then call Mira and have her meet us at your place."

Thirty minutes later they pulled up in front of Livingston One. The brand new skyscraper, home to Noir, offices and several luxury condominiums set aside for pack members only, gleamed with reflective black glass. Tristan had already owned the property prior to the fire; call it serendipity, but construction had just finished. With Noir taking the top five floors of the building, Tristan's penthouse rested safely underneath it, with Logan's under his.

As the car pulled up to the entrance, Logan handed the keys to the valet. "Hey Ryan, take care of my girl, here." He patted his car.

"Will do, sir," Ryan, a young wolf, assured him.

"Tristan's in the back. Hold it a second while I get Toby," Logan instructed. He whistled over to Toby, who jogged over, giving him a smile.

Both Toby and Ryan had been adopted into the pack by Tristan after they'd been abandoned as teens. He'd been putting them through college, and both kids worked for him, valeting cars.

"Toby, hold the door for me. Tristan's in the back with a guest," Logan said casually, wondering what else he should call her. Guest hardly seemed appropriate, but prisoner didn't suit the situation either. He shrugged; either way she was going upstairs. They'd have her name soon enough.

"Yes sir," Toby obediently responded.

Toby opened the car door, and held it wide open, and Logan leaned in to help Tristan. But Tristan held up his hand, gesturing for him to step back. *It's starting already*, Logan thought to himself.

"I've got her," Tristan told him as he effortlessly exited the car cradling Kalli against his chest as if he were holding a baby. "Thanks. Hey, how's school going? Keeping your grades up?" he asked in a parental tone.

"School's going well. My chem class is tough but I'm studying hard," Toby beamed.

"Good to hear. Just make sure you keep your mind on your grades and keep the distractions to a minimum. I've heard you two are turning into quite the ladies' men," Tristan teased, looking over at Ryan through the glass, who'd been playing with the radio, but glanced up in time to catch what his Alpha'd been telling Toby. He smiled and gave Tristan a thumbs-up through the glass.

Tristan nodded toward and smiled at him, acknowledging his response.

"Yes sir," Toby laughed, shutting the car door. He and Ryan had had a great summer, parking cars and meeting the sexy women who frequented the club. They weren't hurting for dates.

"Ready to go, Alpha?" Logan asked, rescuing Tristan from further conversation. "I'll run interference."

Tristan looked down at the tranquil woman who slept in his arms. "Yes, let's go."

They took the private elevator up to Tristan's penthouse, avoiding prying eyes. As the doors opened, Tristan immediately started toward the guest room.

"Did you get ahold of Julie?" he asked Logan, without looking at him.

"Yeah, she's on her way up. I'll wait for her here and let her in," Logan told him, knowing she'd have to be let in. Even though the private elevator opened directly into the foyer, only he and Tristan had the code to take it. All other guests arrived separately.

Julie was a nurse practitioner and all-round pack healer. While wolves healed fairly quickly on their own, given a full shift, it wasn't always possible to engage in a transformation. Younger wolves didn't transform until after puberty, and often got into scraps. Julie was also a midwife and attended most, if not all births, depending on what the mother wanted. She practiced both traditional and alternative medicine, catering to supernaturals. On occasion, she'd treat a witch or vampire, if it was a friend, but they generally didn't need aid.

Tristan nudged the guest room door open with an elbow, careful not to hit Kalli's head. She'd need to be cleaned up and fed before they settled her under the covers, so he decided to lay her atop of the comforter. Gently placing her down, he slid his hands out from underneath her warm body.

He sat on the edge of the queen-sized bed and sighed, watching her chest rise and fall under Logan's tux. His wolf had been gnawing at him the entire car ride home; he begged to smell her, nuzzle her, lick her. And shit if Tristan didn't want the same thing. He couldn't understand why he was having these feelings toward a mortal woman he'd just met, one who could be involved in the fire. Still, staring down at her sweet face, he wanted to touch her.

Julie and Logan watched as the Alpha ran his fingers through the woman's hair. *Shit, here we go*, Logan thought. He coughed, drawing Tristan out of his trance.

"Hi, Alpha. Sorry to interrupt," Julie apologized. She walked over and looked at the girl in his bed, shaking her head. "Now, I know you missed me, big guy, but there are easier ways to get me in your bedroom." She winked at him, trying to lighten up the atmosphere.

"Ah, Jules, thanks for coming," Tristan greeted her, reaching over to squeeze her arm, welcoming her to his home. "This, here, is a very important person of interest." He looked down at Kalli, and continued. "She's been roughed up and fed on by vampires. But I need her well enough to question. You should know that we think she's sick."

"Did she tell you that? What happened?"

"No, but during the car ride, she started freaking out, screaming for her pills. We managed to get them out of her car and gave her one. Alexandra claimed there was a strange taste to her blood. I don't know."

"So she's been with Alexandra? How long?" Julie asked in a professional manner, yet she was well aware that the girl had probably been tortured by the bloodsucker.

"Yeah. About two days."

"Can I see the pills you gave her?"

Tristan reached into his inside jacket pocket, pulled out the small bottle and dropped it into her hand. "Here, this is it. Logan grabbed her purse. I'll see if he found anything else."

Julie pushed down and screwed open the safety cap, and shook a few tablets into her hand. "Hmmm. Bottle's not marked and neither are these pills. Could be some kind of generic."

"Not sure, but she seemed damn anxious to take one. Almost like she was having some kind of a panic attack. As soon as she took it, she calmed right down. She's been sleeping for a good thirty minutes now. But I really need to talk to her."

"Okay, well why don't you go take a break and I'll get her cleaned up. Try to feed her something. Here, let me get my bag," She walked back into the hallway, where she'd left her medical kit. Picking it up, she caught Logan's eyes. She smiled and mouthed: "It will be all right." She could tell he was worried about Tristan.

"Okay you two, leave me be. I've got some work to do," she ordered.

Tristan stood, rubbing his hand over his face. Before he walked away, he turned again to Julie. "One more thing. She might be a runner. I'm going to have Simeon stand guard at the elevators. Unless she can sprout wings and fly out from forty stories, she won't get far. But we don't know if she's dangerous, so be cautious, okay. Text me when you think she's ready to talk. I'm gonna go downstairs for a while to Logan's."

"No problem. Will do, Alpha." Julie knew Simeon wouldn't let the girl out of the condo. He was one of the strongest wolves she knew. If anything happened, she'd call on him right away.

"Thanks."

"Thanks, Jules," Logan added.

Clapping a hand on Tristan's shoulder, he walked down the hallway toward the elevators, relieved to get away from the girl for a while. Logan sensed Tristan's frustration about not getting immediate answers, but even more overwhelming was his Alpha's attraction to a stranger they'd just met. Unable to stop fate, he'd be damned if he didn't fight tooth and nail to protect Tristan from being hurt. Despite his visions, he still wasn't sure whether her nature was good or bad. Regardless, he was certain that the woman they'd just saved was about to rock Tristan's world.

⊰⊱ Chapter Four ⊰⊱

Tristan fell back onto the soft leather sofa and sighed. "Well, that was fucking fun."

"Yeah, I hear ya. I was two seconds away from staking that vamp bitch tonight. Seriously Tristan, I don't have your diplomacy skills," Logan quipped. He went over to the bar and poured them each a sizable glass of whiskey.

"I know. If she didn't keep the vampires in this city on such a tight leash, she'd be dead. And I'd be the first one lined up to kill her," he declared flatly. And after tonight he meant it. *How did someone torture a human like that and feel nothing?* He just could not relate. It was as if the vamp was completely devoid of compassion. The only feelings she had were about her own needs.

"Not only is she narcissistic, she's a true sadist. Not that I haven't seen it before with other vamps, but damn, she's nasty." Logan fell alongside his friend, shaking his head and handing Tristan a tumbler.

Tristan took a large draw of the amber liquid, savoring the flavor as it danced over his tongue. "Thanks, brother. I swear I feel like I'm ready to punch something. I need to shift. Run. Something. I love the city, but it would be nice to just go wolf right now."

"I hear ya." Logan needed to run too, blow off steam.

"Have you got the purse?" Tristan asked. He needed to know more about the mysterious woman lying upstairs in his bed.

"Yeah, it's over by the door. Not much in it. Standard girl stuff. There was identification. Name's Kalli Williams. Twenty-nine years old. City address. Nothing really out of the ordinary for a human."

"Any more strange pills?"

"Nope, nothin'. Listen, I know you're frustrated, but the girl will wake up soon and we'll get answers." Logan wasn't really sure that what he was saying was true, but he was always the optimist.

"Will we? I gotta tell ya that I'm not convinced that girl laying upstairs in my bed has anything to do with the fire. What do we really know? She's guilty of taking a freakin' snake? And while I'd like to know where the hell she took Eve, not even the vamps saw anyone go into Eden. I'm telling you, Logan, something else is about to happen. I know you saw it in your vision, but I can feel it and it's not good. The meeting with Jax can't come soon enough. I've got to know if he's in on this." Tristan raked his fingers through his hair.

"Well, friend, nothin's happening for at least a couple of hours so we might as well just chill...maybe with Mira," Logan suggested, slyly raising an eyebrow at Tristan.

A grin broke across Tristan's face, knowing exactly what Logan was thinking, and it didn't exactly involve relaxing. But after sporting a hard on for the last half hour in the car, he couldn't deny that he needed to get laid as much as Logan did.

Soft knocking at the door got their attention. "Come in, Mir," Logan yelled, unwilling to get up to answer the door.

Mira walked in with a clipboard in her hands, tapping it with a pen. Tristan and Logan watched as she slammed the door and started pacing, immersed in thought.

Without looking up, she began speaking. "Hi guys, just wanted to bring you an update. Talked to Willow, and about fifty percent of the pack will be moved in with her by the end of the weekend. Most of the others are going up to the mountains. You may need to talk to Zed and Nile; both want to stay in the city at their own places. I don't know what's up. They told Willow it was work related, but I'd bet you it has to do with a woman. Probably human." She rolled her eyes and kept talking. "Um, let's see. What else did I need to tell you? Oh yeah, I ran through the list of all potential clients. Most are screened and clear. I have one or two that still need clearance."

She stopped in her tracks and looked over to the men, who were staring at her with wide grins on their faces, enjoying an adult beverage. "What? Am I boring you? Or is it that you've started without me?" she joked. She'd freed her long blonde hair from the confines of its clip.

"More like stopping," Logan responded.

"Thanks for the update. I'm glad to see you have it under control," Tristan replied, complimenting her work. She was nothing if not a type A person who could teach a course on responsibility. Her driven personality was quite congruent with her Alpha status within the pack.

"Want a drink?" Logan asked, toasting his glass up in the air.

"No thanks, I'm good."

"Yes you are," Tristan teased. He patted the cushion in between Logan and him. "Come, Mir. Sit with us. Relax a bit. It's been a long night."

Mira took off her suit jacket and kicked off her pumps. Obediently, she listened, and squeezed herself between the two strong men.

"Now, you don't think you're going to get away with sitting like that, do you? Come here." Tristan set his glass down on the coffee table, and then reached to swing her around so that the back of her head rested in his lap. Logan pulled her legs up onto him and began to rub her.

"I love it when you don't wear stockings," Logan remarked.

Tristan smoothed her hair out of her face and rubbed her head with one of his hands, resting the other below her breasts.

"Oh my God, okay, I think I died and went to heaven. What did I do to deserve this?" Mira moaned.

Tristan wanted release and Mira could give it to him. His wolf had been clawing at him; there was something about that human woman upstairs. Rarely did Tristan feel confused about his emotions. One of the benefits of being Alpha was the serenity of knowing what to do in almost every situation. He was a born leader: decisive, authoritative. Having the ability to quickly assess the state of affairs and determine the correct course of action, he didn't vacillate. He and his wolf were always in sync.

Yet ever since he'd taken Kalli into his arms, his wolf wanted what he shouldn't have. Not that Tristan's cock disagreed, but his head told him otherwise. You couldn't trust a woman based on looks alone. He didn't even know her. Perhaps Sydney marrying had affected him more than he thought. Or maybe it was that he simply hadn't had a break since the battle he'd helped Kade fight. He'd been dealing with Jax Chandler's relentless pursuit of his sister. Then the fire and club rebuild.

As he stroked Mira's hair, he reasoned that sometimes things just didn't make sense. What he did have was a red-blooded female in his arms, and his beta, both of whom would ease any tension he'd been feeling over the past month. Instead of worrying about the suspect, he needed to ease his own sexual needs.

"Logan, isn't Mir looking lovely today?" Tristan massaged her shoulders. She closed her eyes and moaned.

"Yes she is, Tris. You know, it's been a long time since we played. The three of us...together. I've missed this," Logan said as his fingers glided along the inside of her calves. He watched Mira's lips fall open as he teased up toward her thigh. Her hips began to wiggle slightly, calling him toward her center.

Tristan looked over to Logan and met his eyes. "I've missed it too. Now look at how beautiful she is, Logan. I bet she's nice and wet for you. Yeah, that's it," he encouraged as Logan pushed a hand under her skirt, still only barely touching her thighs. "Mir, tell him what you want."

"Please, Logan. Touch me," she whispered, reaching for Tristan's chest.

Tristan found the side opening to her skirt and unzipped it. Then Logan tugged the skirt off until all that remained were her panties. Tristan began to unbutton each pearl of her blouse. Before long, her breasts were bared save only her bronze-colored silk bra. He rubbed his hands all over her chest and tummy, teasing her without touching her breasts directly.

Mira sucked a breath as the cool air hit her skin. She stared into Tristan's eyes, intent on making love to both of her men.

Logan gradually slid his forefinger into the flimsy material, only enough to tease her.

"Logan. Tristan, please," she begged.

Tristan's cock hardened as she pleaded. Burying himself into her sweet heat could take the edge off of his day. God, she was so responsive, even after all these years. No, she wasn't his mate. But she was loyal, sexy and available. What else did he need? His wolf roared in protest, and Tristan pushed him aside. The rational thing to do would be to make love to this ready and willing woman in his lap. He'd done it many times before, so why was the wolf upset? Ignoring his beast within, he extended a claw, and cut her bra free, exposing her creamy flesh. Her nipples peaked in response and she gasped at the act.

"Touch me," she demanded.

Tristan, happy to oblige, grazed his fingertips over a nipple.

"More," she cried.

"Logan, I think our little she-wolf is getting impatient. Shall we help her?"

"Ah yes," Logan groaned as he slipped his fingers down into her slick folds. "She's so warm and wet. Aw baby." He withdrew his hand for a second, only to tear the panties off her body.

She moaned in protest. "Don't worry, we'll take care of you, Mir," Tristan assured her, cupping her warm breast in his hand. Shit, Logan was turning him on by the way he touched her. Sometimes Tristan wondered if he could ever give up having threesomes with his beta. Sharing sexual experiences with his best friend completed everything he needed. He and Logan never had sex alone with each other nor were they in love, but he loved him and wanted to share everything with him.

Logan circled her nub slowly with his forefinger. She pushed her hips upward seeking more pressure, but he wouldn't give it to her yet. No, he wanted to draw it out, make the tension and pleasure last.

Mira reached for Tristan's belt, frantically trying to free him. She desperately wanted him in her mouth, seeking out his steely length through the fabric of his trousers.

"Fuck," he hissed at her intrusion and cuffed her right wrist.

She moaned again in protest.

"Not yet, ma chère. Don't move, just feel. Concentrate on what Logan's doing to you."

"I need more," Logan grunted as he moved onto his knees, putting her legs over his shoulders. "I can't wait to taste you."

She reached for her breast and squeezed it, but Tristan took that hand as well and pulled her arms over her head, gripping her wrists firmly.

"No, no, no," he scolded. "No touching yourself, either. Hmm, we might have to spank her lovely little ass tonight. She's not listening." Tristan knew just the thought of it would push her over the edge; she loved being smacked on the bottom while he made love to her from behind.

"Stop teasing me. I can't take it. Oh my God!" she screamed, as Logan trailed the tip of his tongue between her inner lips.

Tristan reached down with his other hand and pushed her apart, allowing Logan better access. Mira raised her hips upward, seeking relief. The pressure of her orgasm was built. She was almost ready to come, but she needed just a little more.

"She tastes so good," Logan groaned as he pressed his fingers deep inside her. Mira began to shake; she was falling over. Logan's lips took her sweet pearl, sucking gently as he pumped into her. She screamed in pleasure as she flew apart into orgasm.

Aroused and ready, the spell broke for Tristan as his cell phone buzzed in his pocket. Releasing Mira's wrists, he immediately reached for his phone to read the text, *'She's awake'*. Tristan's thoughts slammed back to the woman upstairs in his bed.

"Sorry guys, party's over...well, at least for me. But please keep having fun, okay?" Tristan kissed Mira's head as she smiled up at him, sated for the moment. He gently moved away, straightened his clothes and walked toward the door.

"You need me?" Logan prayed he didn't.

"No, I've got this. I'll call ya later."

Logan scooped Mira up into his arms as if she weighed nothing. "Okay then...I guess your loss is my gain," he declared, smiling as he carried Mira away to his bedroom. He knew better than to ask twice.

"Bye, Tris!" Mira waved giggling as she disappeared into the hallway.

Tristan's mind raced; he couldn't wait to interrogate the suspect. There was something about the whole situation that didn't make sense. And Kalli was the key to getting the answer.

⟶⟨ Chapter Five ⟩⟵

W arm water pulsed around her body as the fragrant smell of lilacs danced in her mind. She felt warm and safe. Then images of Alexandra flashed. Blood. Vampires. An Alpha. Screaming, her eyes flew open, scanning her surroundings. Panic coursed throughout every cell in her body in a flight or fight response.

"Hey, you're safe. You're okay," a comforting female voice advised her. She looked over to see a young woman with long brown hair kneeling at her side by the tub. A tub? Her heart raced, realizing she was stark naked in a bath full of steaming bubbles and jets pulsating around her bruised flesh.

The woman regarded the tub as if she knew what Kalli was thinking. "It's just a warm bath to get you cleaned up, hun. Nothing happened. I'm a nurse. Really, see?" She leaned over and pulled a stethoscope out of her black bag.

Kalli said nothing as she surveyed her surroundings. She was in a large whirlpool Jacuzzi; warm heat lamps shone overhead. The bathroom felt dark and rich with its umber painted walls and fawn-stained crown molding. The flicker of a single candle danced across the black speckled granite countertop of a chestnut vanity. Although she could think of worse places to find one's self, waking up in strange places was really getting old.

She struggled to find her voice, aware that her throat was raw from screaming. "Where am I?"

"You are at the home of Mr. Tristan Livingston, Alpha of Lyceum Wolves," Julie answered cheerfully. "You're safe, but a bit scratched up from your run-in with that dreadful vampire. Don't worry, though. Your vitals are good. We just need to get you some rest and something to eat. You should be good in a few days."

"A few days? I really need to get home and..." her voice trailed off as Julie held up a hand, silencing her.

"Hun, I know you've had a rough time of it and all, and I'm not going to judge, but the Alpha wants to talk to you." She went about her business, readying up a warm towel. Throwing it over her shoulder, she bent down and slid her hand behind Kalli's back and under her arm.

"Come on now, I want to see if you can stand. Lean on me, and I'll wrap this towel around you. That's it."

Kalli let her weight fall back on the strange woman as she tried to stand. The Alpha wanted to talk to her? Oh God. She knew she shouldn't have gone in to get that snake. He was going to ask about the fire and what she'd seen. She didn't want to be involved. She could not let *them* find out she was alive.

Finding her legs, she pushed upright until she was standing. She sighed as the warmth of the towel engulfed her.

"That's it. Look at you, standing all on your own. God, Alexandra's such a viper. I can't believe she did this to you. Can you step out of the tub? Just hold onto me as you move, okay?"

"Alexandra?" Kalli did as instructed as if in a daze. She let Julie dry her, trying to focus on staying stable on her feet.

Weakness was not something she was used to feeling and she disliked having to rely on someone to help her, but at this point, she had no choice.

"Yeah, you know, the bloodsucker who drained you?"

"I…I didn't get her name. I shouldn't have gone out to the parking garage alone. I should have…" Kalli's soft voice trailed off as a small tear ran down her cheek. She should have known that someone would have seen her at the club. Embarrassment washed over her, knowing that she had let this happen. But there was another emotion that racked her mind. Anger? Yes, she was mad all right. But most of all, at the moment, she felt violated. Was there no place on this earth she could be safe from the violence?

"Hey there, I know what you're thinking. Just stop it right now. The vamps. They can even get to us wolves, you know. A human woman is just no match for them. There's nothing you did to cause this to happen to you," Julie told her. A somber expression flashed across her face.

If you only knew, Kalli thought silently.

"Now, come on, let's get you dressed and in bed."

"I don't have anything to wear," Kalli began to say and stopped when she saw Julie hold up a large man's t-shirt with a black wolf insignia on it that read: 'Harley-Davidson'.

"This will do. Wait 'til the Alpha finds out I was digging around in his skivvies," she joked. "Ah, the thrill of it all."

Kalli had a hard time trying not to smile back at the lovely nurse. She gratefully allowed Julie to pull the shirt over her head. It was better than being dirty and infinitely better than being covered in her own blood and body odor.

"Now, for the pièce de résistance." Julie held up a black pair of man's boxer briefs. "You'll probably swim in these, but I found a new package in his room, and well, it's better than no undies. I'll leave it up to you."

"Thanks, I'll, um. I'll take them. They'll be okay until they stretch out." Then they'd probably fall right off of her, but there was no way in hell she planned on staying in a wolf's den with no underwear. She had to figure out a way to escape the hell she'd gotten herself into. Glancing over to the door, she considered making a break for it. Dizziness racked her brain as she started to wobble.

Julie grabbed onto Kalli's arms as she wavered, almost falling onto the floor. She eased her into a sitting position and rubbed her back. "Okay, I'd say that's enough exercise for today. Just take a second and breathe. That's it. You're sitting well. Better now?" Kalli nodded as Julie ran a towel over Kalli's long raven hair. After patting it dry, she dropped the towel on the floor, pulled out a comb and began to tease out the knots.

"Oh and hun, don't even think about leavin' this room right now. Yes, I saw you eyeing the door," she said, continuing her work.

Busted, Kalli groaned inwardly. Who was she kidding? She was barely well enough to stand, let alone walk.

Julie finished up and set the comb on the nightstand. "I probably failed to mention that you are on the forty-fifth floor of a city skyscraper, so there's just one exit out of here and my friend, Simeon, is keeping watch on that one. Besides, I'm telling you that you're safe, okay? Nothin' is gonna happen to you up here. I promise. And besides, you're in no condition to leave, anyway."

A skyscraper? Shit. There was no way she was getting out of here. Kalli liked a nice view of the city as much as the next person, but was terrified of heights. Resigned to the fact that she'd have to face the Alpha, she let Julie tuck her into the feather-soft bed.

"Let's see, so, soup is next on the agenda. I sent for some plain broth and crackers. It should be here about now. So is there anything else I can get you?"

"No, thanks for helping me," Kalli managed, wringing her hands nervously.

"No worries. You just rest, and I'll be right back."

Kalli let her head fall on the pillow and stared up at the intricate light fixture, which was made out of tiny royal blue, glass butterflies. The pretty winged creatures exquisitely complemented the shades of brown and tan of her warm and inviting gilded cage. She breathed deeply and blew out a breath, relaxing into the bed. Unable to deny how serene amenities helped to calm her nerves, she curled into her comforter, willing herself to heal. Closing her eyes, her thoughts drifted to the Alpha who'd rescued her.

In her mind's eye, she remembered how the handsome stranger had saved her from the vampire dressed in the ridiculous harlequin vest. A tall, muscular man with dark blonde hair, he looked like a sexy James Bond in the tuxedo. Struggling to picture his face, his piercing amber eyes came into focus. Like yellow-orange supernovas, they'd been striking and memorable. Did his eyes change when he went wolf? What color was his fur? His power rolled off him like a tidal wave in the car. Authoritative and deadly, an Alpha who took what he wanted.

Kalli thought back to her days in the pack she'd escaped; her stomach tightened. She'd been hybrid. Her mother, a human, had died when Kalli was only fourteen, leaving her to survive on her own within the brutal pack. Three years later, her father, a mean son-of-a-bitch, had fought to be Alpha and lost. The reigning Alpha had sent for her soon after, attacked her and explained how she'd be servicing his men for the rest of her life. Tired of the never ending violence, she'd made a decision to leave.

She knew that even though she was considered lower than omega because of her human genes, they'd never let her leave their ranks. They'd use her up and spit her out. Death was the only way out of the pack, an option she'd have willingly chosen, if necessary. So one late summer's afternoon, she'd taken her father's fishing boat out into the Atlantic off the coast of South Carolina, and jumped off into the cold dark water. Of course, her body was never found, but the small vessel was recovered two days later. The weather had forecast a small squall, so no one had questioned her disappearance; just another soul lost to the sea. With nothing but a backpack and some cash she'd saved over the years, she took off to New York City.

Upon arrival, she'd picked up a waitressing job and saved her money. It was easier than she'd thought it would be to find someone to change her name. With a few Benjamins, Kalli Anastas became Kalli Williams. Afterward, she'd continued working to put herself through college. By her sophomore year, however, she could no longer prevent the wolf from emerging. As a teen she'd starved herself, preventing the shift. But once on her own, she'd gained weight, and shifting into wolf became inevitable. For weeks she'd suffered nightmares, always with the animal scratching to come out and have its due. She'd remembered the tales the other pack girls had told, describing the symptoms of their first time. That was how she looked at it; an illness to be cured. Kalli knew it would come on the full moon, and there was nothing she could do to stop it.

Scared and alone, she'd managed to get out of the city and into the mountains in preparation. She'd rented an isolated cabin in the Catskills, and waited. The excruciating pain of the shift took her by surprise even though she'd known it was coming. After running and killing throughout the night, she'd woken up naked, curled into a hole of a rotted-out tree. Covered in blood and dirt, she'd cried hysterically, believing she was cursed for life. For years she'd repeated the ghastly process, month after month, until she became a doctor and discovered 'the cure'.

After graduation, she'd earned an assistantship, which paid for her grad school. The residency opportunity in Philadelphia had led to a permanent position at UVH. She was able to practice, utilizing state of the art medicine, while continuing to blend into society. And it was there she'd found salvation from the beast.

In reality, her drug didn't cure her of her wolf. But it kept her at bay, caged and unable to shift. Relentlessly, Kalli had worked; she'd rarely eaten or slept, determined to develop a drug to stop the transformation. On the twenty-second trial, it had worked; Canis Lupis Inhibitor (CLI) kept her from shifting, even on a full moon. Side effects, aside from preventing shifting, included chills and aches, but they only occurred if she missed a daily dose. Enhanced hearing and smell were slightly suppressed but not entirely gone. The discovery allowed Kalli to go months without shifting, and she reveled in finally being human. Best of all, no wolf or vampire could detect her wolf, as far as she could tell, anyway. Of course a simple blood test would reveal her true nature, but other than that, she appeared wholly human.

After she began taking CLI, she kept refining the drug, seeking other useful purposes for it. She experimented, theorizing the drug could help aggressive animals in the canis genus to reduce anxiety. Since they were not supernatural, she envisioned a one dose treatment that would positively affect their emotions. She hadn't come too far with that side of her research, but initial projections looked promising. Still, she kept all of her work under lock and key in an effort to hide her identity.

Truth be told, Kalli avoided purposeful contact with supernaturals. She'd only done one full-fledged test of the formula to see if she could or could not be detected as wolf. By all accounts, the exercise had been a success, yet that one experiment had proved to be her most critical mistake. Last month, she and a co-worker had gone to Eden. Well aware that it was run by a wolf and frequented by vampires, her curiosity had got the better of her.

Kalli had danced all night, hoping her pheromones would attract a vampire or wolf. Yet every man who approached was human. She'd even approached female wolves and vampires, engaging them in casual conversation, and not one had identified her as wolf. Rather, she was called out as a human by more than one supernatural. She'd left the club in triumph, celebrating the success of her drug.

But in her efforts to do research, she'd also noticed the fifteen foot yellow boa slithering around behind the bar. A spectacular and healthy specimen; it was like having a private viewing at a reptile exhibit at the zoo. While she didn't specialize in reptiles, she held an appreciation for a species that had survived through the ages.

The vivarium, extraordinarily large, with its heated rocks, trees and flowing water, was an excellent example of how a large snake could be kept safely in captivity. Personally, she did not advocate anyone owning or raising a wild animal, but boa constrictors were routinely sold these days in pet stores. It was refreshing to see how a pet owner would go to such great lengths to care for it, as opposed to what many careless owners did when the snake got too large; releasing it into the wild to fend for itself where it could procreate or die. Florida had a serious issue with the large serpents these days.

So that fateful day, she'd known that she had to save the snake. It had been her lunch break, and she'd been out taking a walk, clearing her head. As she rounded the corner, she smelled smoke and watched as two wolves ran out of the building. They were in human form, but she could tell that they'd been about to shift, noticing the claws extending on their hands. She'd ducked into an alley, waiting for them to pass. Wondering where the fire department was, she'd waited. But then when no one came, she ran into the club on instinct, to make sure everyone was out of the building. Noticing no one, she smashed the glass enclosure and pulled out the slithering animal. Unfortunately in the process, she'd cut her hand. But she'd still managed to carry the poor animal out of the building. As the fire engines raced toward the inferno, she'd made a rash decision to take the snake back to UVH to have it evaluated.

When she'd later pondered over the fact that the snake belonged to a supernatural, she'd decided to have a nurse call Eden and leave a message for the manager. But before she'd had a chance to issue the order, she'd been attacked in the parking lot. She wasn't supposed to have been working that day; having been called in for an emergency consult, she'd rushed into the hospital with only her ID and keys, locking her purse in her car.

After she'd finished, she'd returned to her car. Instantly, her skin had pricked in awareness as she saw two strange men approach her. Trying to run had proved futile, as they'd snatched her up with preternatural speed. Vehemently protesting, she'd kneed the first of her attackers in the groin. And even though he'd released her, the other vamp had quickly grabbed her by the shoulders, slamming her head against the concrete. By the time she'd woken with a splitting headache, Alexandra was at her neck.

As the history of what had happened to her racked her brain, she felt sick. Opening her eyes, unable to rest, she wished she was like one of the butterflies so beautifully reproduced in the lamp above, able to fly away from her troubles. At least she was clean, in a warm bed and about to be fed, she reasoned. She'd been upgraded from the house of horrors and was no longer a blood bag.

Closing her eyes, she flipped onto her side, hoping this new position would help her find the rest she desperately needed. As her body started to drift toward dreams, she heard the rustling of fabric. Frightened, she sealed her eyelids tight, feigning sleep.

"Hello, Kalli," a deep sexy voice said, startling her. Her heart began beating quickly. She didn't want to answer him. *Please go away*, she silently prayed.

Tristan had talked to Julie in the kitchen as she was preparing soup. She'd sternly warned him not to upset Kalli, updating him on her condition. She was afraid the little bird would try to fly, and was confident that if she tried, Kalli would fall flat on her face.

But Tristan was anxious to see the intriguing woman who had found herself in Alexandra's nest. He needed to see her face, smell her skin, touch her. Rolling his eyes, he cursed himself. His wolf had to be influencing his thinking. Struggling not to go to her, he took off his jacket, unbuttoned his sleeves and fell back into a large velvet lounge chair that sat diagonal to the bed. Her enticing hair sprawled over the white bed linens, begging to be touched. When he listened to her heartbeat, he knew she was awake.

"Kalli," he repeated, louder this time. "I know you're awake. Come on, now, ma chère. Let's have a chat, shall we?" His voice had a barely detectible southern Cajun accent to it.

Kalli gritted her teeth. She hated that wolves had such good hearing. Her heartbeat gave her away. Running her hand through her untamed locks, she pushed the unruly hair aside and turned over in bed. She pushed up so that she was laying more at a forty-five degree angle, not quite sitting, but clearly aware of his command. Averting her gaze, she played with her hands, hoping they could do this quickly. Determined to get the upper hand of the situation, she struggled to raise her eyes and direct the conversation.

"Dr. Williams. My name is Dr. Williams," she corrected, trying to separate herself from the wolf ranking that she knew all too well made her opinions less than important. She was human now, she reminded herself. She purposefully shielded herself in her title, embracing the professional decorum that always managed to seal off unwanted feelings.

"What?" Tristan asked, surprised at her pretentious tone. *Was she for real?*

"I said my name is Dr. Williams." She nervously forced herself to sit a little taller, but her breath caught as she made eye contact with the charismatic Alpha. He was ruggedly handsome, with those striking amber eyes she remembered. Except now, she felt as if he was seeing straight through to her soul. His slicked-back dark blonde hair framed his tanned face; a sexy five o'clock shadow broke the surface of his skin. A sensuous smile revealed perfectly white teeth. Why was he smiling? *Better to bite you with my dear.*

Her stomach dropped in anticipation. What was happening to her? Involuntarily, her nipples strained against the fabric of the shirt as her body recognized the incredibly virile male addressing her. Her wolf howled, begging to run to and jump on him. She took a deep cleansing breath, trying to force her body to relax. This could not be happening. *I am human now.*

Tristan laughed. So this was how she was going to play it. He could sense her arousal and damn if it didn't make him want to actually enjoy this little interrogation. Her heart was beating like a hummingbird, yet she played it cool. He licked his lips, and raised an eyebrow, shooting her a wolfish grin.

"Okay, Doc. Personally I think we'd both be a little more comfortable if we'd go informal, but by all means, suit yourself. I'm Tristan Livingston, Alpha of Lyceum Wolves. Welcome to my home."

Chapter Six

Kalli immediately lowered her head, gazing downward. "Thank you, Alpha," she said softly, taken aback by his commanding presence. Within seconds of doing so, she became conscious that she'd reverted to pack protocol. Confused by her own behavior, she quickly looked up, adjusting her posture. How could this have happened? She'd been away from wolves for nearly seven years, yet the man before her sent her reeling. His smooth voice registered deep within her as if she'd known him long ago. But he wasn't the Alpha from her childhood.

His manner was cool and dignified with a hint of humor that could be seen in his smile that reached his eyes. Instead of physically attacking her, he'd sent a healer to her side. He'd rescued her from the vampire, and ensured she was clean, warm and fed. Yet she knew deep down not to be fooled by his kind exterior. A dominant wolf lurked inside him; remarkable good looks and a compelling personality were only one side of the man before her.

She glanced down, noticing the gooseflesh on her arms. What was he doing to her? Bunching the silky sheet, she pulled it up over her pebbled breasts and held it under her chin.

"I, um, I really appreciate you saving me from the vampires. I didn't think I'd survive," she stammered, struggling to sound coherent.

Tristan considered her initial response, 'Thank you, Alpha'. It wasn't so much what she said but how she said it. Her submissive positioning came so naturally that he would have sworn she was wolf. Knowing that she was human was a paradox, given the gesture. The only explanation could be that she'd spent a lot of time with wolves. And then just as quickly, as if a light switch had been clicked, she easily transposed back into an underlying confident tone of voice.

He could detect her internal struggle as to how to appropriately interact with him. Watching her defensively bring the cotton material to her chest told him she knew she was teetering on the edge of arousal, fighting to gain control of her own body. While he was very much used to young adult wolves displaying erratic behavior in the presence of their Alpha, going from servile to aggressive, he could not reconcile why she, a human, would display a conflicting demeanor.

Her paled olive skin tone had not regained its healthy color as yet, but her beautiful blue eyes were bright with excitement as she studied him. She smelled of clean soap and lilacs, which pleased his wolf. Shiny raven curls spilled down over the sheets, teasing her elbows. The sight of her drove Tristan to imagine how he'd like to run his fingers through her hair, bury his face into it, wrap his fist around the tendrils while he slammed into her from behind. His breath caught, and he quickly looked away, averting his gaze while attempting to hide his feral thoughts. *What was he thinking?* He was here to get information about the fire, not to figure out how he could get into her pants. But the more time he spent near her, the more he wanted her.

He needed to get control, and fast. Taking a deep breath, he attempted to get the conversation moving in the right direction. "Well, I too, am quite happy that you are alive. Alexandra can be quite deadly." He ground his teeth just thinking of what she'd done to Kalli. "But we were lucky. Jules said you'll recover quickly."

"Yes, thank you again for your kindness," she replied formally.

"Would you like to tell me why you think the vampires took you?" He was toying with her a bit, but he found people were more likely to talk when the discussion wasn't centered on the real topic.

"Well, I really don't know. You see, I'm a veterinarian at UVH. I got called in for an emergency consult. When I got back to the car, there were two men…waiting for me. I don't know why. I tried to fight, got in a few hits, but I couldn't get away," she explained through the tears that ran down her cheeks. Determined to stuff every horrible thing that had ever happened to her deep inside where she could compartmentalize the hurt, she swore she would not cry about this. Wiping the eyes with the back of her hands, she raised her gaze to Tristan's. *Please let me go home. I can't do this.* Silently she willed it to be, but knew it wouldn't happen.

"You're a vet?" Tristan asked, intrigued by her profession. Initially when she'd said she was a doctor, he thought she healed humans.

"Yes, I work in the ER."

"Interesting. So you wouldn't happen to treat reptiles at UVH?"

Her eyes widened. "Reptiles? Um, well, yes, I am more of a generalist, but I do treat reptiles now and then." Her heart began to race. The boa. *Please don't let it be his…please don't let it be his…please don't let it be his.*

He smiled, pinning her with his mesmerizing eyes. He could hear her pulse rate increase, smell her fear. Leaning forward, he placed his forearms on his knees and tilted his head.

"So you wouldn't happen to treat snakes on a regular basis, then? You know, like a fifteen foot yellow boa constrictor, for example?"

Like a dam bursting, she couldn't hold it in any longer, and the words began to spill forth. She wasn't sure whether to beg for forgiveness or simply tell her story. And before she knew it, she'd done both.

"Please Alpha; you must know that I was going to have my nurse call the owners of that club. I swear to you. I am *so* sorry. At first I wasn't sure who to call, and then I decided to have her call Eden and leave a message. But then I forgot. I've been so busy. And then I got kidnapped, but you know that part. And oh, I guess I should have started with this first, but yes, I do treat snakes, and she's very healthy despite the smoke inhalation. A beautiful specimen, really. I promise that I will have her returned to you as soon as possible."

Shaking his head, he held up the palm of his hand to silence her. Resisting the urge to go to her and hold her in his arms, he opted to pace over to the end of her bed. Grabbing the end of the sleigh bed as tight as a vise with his two hands, a serious look washed over his face.

"Look, Dr. Williams, I am not sure why you took the snake but I need to know everything, and I mean everything, about the day of the fire. Did you set the fire?"

Oh my God. He thought she set the fire. She cringed. If she told him about the wolves she had seen that day, he might ask her to identify them. If she identified them, it might somehow get back to her pack that she was alive. Or worse, they'd come after her and kill her. What a damn fine mess. She should have just kept walking that warm September day, but it wasn't in her nature to stand by and do nothing. She was a doctor. A healer. And a fighter; she was no coward. She didn't think twice about running into a burning building to make sure others made it to safety.

"Kalli," Tristan said firmly, shaking her from her thoughts. He let go of the bed and circled around, stalking her like the wolf that he was.

"I was there the day of the fire," she began quietly. Determined to keep her dignity, she stiffened, and stared at him. "There was smoke. Two men exited the building. No one was there. No sirens. Nothing. I had to go in, because I knew that animal was in there. I mean, I did call in before I entered, you know. But no one answered. And then I saw the snake. What was I supposed to do? Let it die? I couldn't. So I ran in behind the bar and broke the glass, cutting myself in the process. But I managed to get her. I got the snake and left."

He sensed honesty in her words and mannerisms but had to know the extent of her involvement. "Did you set the fire?"

"God no," she gasped. "How could you think I'd do that?" It dawned on her that he didn't know her, not to mention that she'd admitted taking the snake.

He moved closer and sat on the edge of the bed, mere inches from her feet. "Tell me about the men. Can you describe them? Were they human?" His voice was like steel, every bit the cold tone she remembered from her pack days.

"Yes, but..."

"Yes, you can describe them, or yes they were human?" He interrupted.

She swallowed her fear, refusing to be intimidated by a wolf again. "Yes, I can describe them. But no, they were not human. They were wolf," she said in the most even voice she could muster.

"Describe them," he ordered.

"Oh God, please don't make me do this. It was just a fire. A building. No one was hurt. If I tell you, I know what will happen. You might find the wolves and begin some kind of a territory war, but I'll end up dead. You and I both know they will find me," she countered. Kalli inwardly shuddered, realizing how frankly she'd just told the Alpha to basically fuck off; also she'd revealed to him yet again her inner knowledge of pack society.

"Look, Dr. Williams, as a courtesy, I will overlook your insolence given that you are not wolf, but let me be perfectly clear. You will describe the men you saw. And pack business is none of your concern. Now tell me why you think these men were wolf," he demanded.

"Fine, Alpha," she drawled out the word, hoping he'd feel the anger in her words. "First off, I told you that I am a vet, which means I also understand human physiology. So unless a new trait for humans is to sprout claws, they were wolves." She refused to tell him that even though she didn't know their names, she recognized the two men as pack members from her old pack. But even if she couldn't name names, Tristan would know that she was in danger.

"Secondly, if they were vampires, they'd be moving more like a flash rather than running." She could feel emotion bubbling up like a fountain she couldn't control. As grateful as she was to him for rescuing her, she was also scared of him questioning her like he was.

Tristan could see she was on the edge of bolting out the door, before she even knew what she was thinking. He decided to press on; he had to get answers.

"Did you know the men?"

"No, I did not know them," she lied. She pulled her legs up to her chest and put her arms around them protectively. What if she was wrong about this Alpha? What if he was prone to violence like all the others she'd known? She needed to escape.

"Are you sure you didn't know them? Did you speak with them? Did you see them set the fire? Did they see you leave?" Tristan relentlessly fired questions at her, testing her honesty. Everything she'd said rang true, but it felt like there was something she wasn't telling him.

"I told you that I didn't know them. And no, I didn't speak with them or see them set the fire. I told you, I saw them leave and then I saw smoke. There was no one else around. I don't know anything else!" she yelled, her eyes darting to the exit. What was that last question he'd asked her? *Did the wolves see her leave?* The realization that the wolves could have identified her felt like a punch to her gut. She'd worked so hard to build her life as a human. A life that she treasured.

"Oh my God, I've got to get out of here. I've got to get back to my life. My job. Please let me go," she begged, as she threw her legs out of the bed onto the floor. After being held captive by Alexandra, she couldn't take any more of his inquest. Her stomach rolled at the thought of being forced back into her old pack. She refused to let that happen. In a foolish attempt to run, nausea and vertigo overcame her; she was pulled toward the floor as if she had an anchor around her waist.

Tristan cursed, realizing that he'd gone too far. His desire for the truth had pushed Kalli into hysterics. *Goddammit.* He should have assured her of his protection. After surviving being a human pincushion over the past forty-eight hours, no human would have been this strong. He could tell she'd been thinking of running, but couldn't believe she'd actually tried. Not only was she sick, she should have known there'd be no way she'd be faster than him. What sane person ran from an Alpha wolf? *What was she thinking?* She was thinking he was a total dick, and she was right, he thought to himself.

As she fell, he effortlessly caught her before she hit the carpet. Holding her in his arms, he backed onto the bed and sat, just staring at her. *Who are you, Kalli Williams?* There was something about her fiery spirit that called to him; something he couldn't quite identify. Her sweet warm body fit so nicely into his arms, and he suspected that cuddling her in his bed would feel nothing short of heavenly. He shouldn't be thinking about her this way given her condition, but damn, his wolf didn't care. It was so wrong. Brushing back the hair from her forehead, he watched as her soft pink, very kissable lips parted.

"Tristan," she whispered.

He stiffened, hearing his name on her lips like a lover's breathy call. "Kalli, you're okay, I've got you," he assured her.

"Doctor," she replied softly with a small smile on her lips.

He laughed. Fainting and unable to stand, she was joking with him.

"My fault," she croaked with a weak voice. "I shouldn't have tried to stand. What was I thinking?"

"You were thinking that I was giving you the Spanish Inquisition, and like any good prisoner, you tried to run. Granted, I've never seen someone in your condition try to outrun me, but you get points for trying," he added, hoping to make her smile.

"I'm scared," Kalli admitted. Her head had finally stopped spinning.

"Please don't fret, chèr t'bébé. No one can get to you here. It's safe." He sighed, pissed that he had purposely pushed her to the edge. "I'm sorry for all the questions, but I have to know what happened. It's not just the fire. I can't go into it all right now, but please know, that I had to ask. And I'll need your help finding them. But right now, you need rest. Come, get in bed. Please stay, I promise not to hurt you."

She wriggled away from him as he stood to place her gently back in the bed. In the process her shirt rode upward, scrunching up near her breasts. Her taut stomach exposed to the cool air, she glanced down to see her bare skin and caught Tristan's eyes as they roamed slowly down to her underwear. He raised an eyebrow at the discovery and smiled coyly.

"What? Julie said they belonged to you but were new. Would you rather have me wear no panties at all?" she quipped, tugging the shirt down. Flirting with the Alpha? She was playing with fire.

"Now that you ask, the thought did occur to me," he replied, not missing a beat. "Clothes are highly overrated, you know. But I might not get much work done if I knew you were sleeping nude in my guest room, not to mention that we've only just met. But don't you worry, we'll have plenty of time to get better acquainted tomorrow," he promised.

Kalli smiled, and closed her eyes, pretending he had not just said what she thought she'd heard. *Naked? With Tristan? Together.* She breathed in a deep breath and released it, trying to tamp down her arousal. Within minutes, a wall of exhaustion crashed into her, ushering her into a much-needed sleep. Her last thoughts were that she'd worry about her feelings for the sexy wolf tomorrow. Right now, she had to heal.

Tristan felt all the blood in his body rush to his cock at her mention of wearing nothing. And seeing her sweet body in his shirt and underwear...Jesus, was she trying to kill him right there? He would have to make sure Julie got her proper clothes to wear.

He pulled up the covers to her neck, willing his erection to subside. If he couldn't see what was under the fluffy mound of covers, he reasoned, he could get it together. Damn, he was losing it. Maybe he should send her down to stay with Logan? Staying in his condo, she would most certainly cloud his judgment when he needed to be at the top of his game. He was confident that his beta would guard her with his life and make sure no one got to her. But he knew his beta as well as he knew himself, and couldn't stomach the idea of Kalli naked in Logan's bed, at least not without him.

Tristan reached for her hand and slowly rubbed circles into the small of her palm. There was something about her that seemed extraordinarily supernatural. Bringing her satiny wrist up to his nose, he inhaled her delightfully feminine scent, detecting only human blood. He wasn't sure what to make of it, but as long as she was in his home and bed, he planned to fully explore the attraction.

Julie poked her head around the corner in time to see Tristan making his way down the long hallway. She quickly got back to work, annoyed that he'd gone so far with his investigation. Their voices had carried well into the kitchen during the heat of their argument. She'd been tempted to intervene, but knew better than to interfere with Alpha business.

Padding into the room, Tristan eyed Julie standing next to the stove, pouring the broth into Tupperware containers.

"She sleeping?" Julie asked, already aware of the answer. He'd been down in her room for well over an hour, sitting in total silence, watching Kalli sleep, and she found it curious that he was taking such an interest in the injured human woman.

"You didn't bring the soup," he commented.

"You were busy," she curtly replied.

"What gives, Jules? Just say it."

"I guess it shouldn't surprise me that you don't take direction well, Alpha. Although I guess you're more used to giving directions than taking them," she huffed. "I could hear the ruckus all the way in here. No disrespect intended, but I did say not to upset her, didn't I?"

"Yeah well, it's not easy being king," he remarked with a smart-assed inflection, grabbing a bowl of soup. He sat down at the counter and began eating while she finished working.

"Sorry, I don't mean to be so hard on you. I know you've gotta do what you've gotta do. It's just that seeing her like that....all those scrapes and bruises and bite marks. My God, she was a mess. I suppose I'm going a little mother hen on you. I'm not used to having to deal with such violence. You are good to us, here."

"No worries. We worked it out. She's a tough one, you know. Believe me; she'll be right as rain, soon. My spidey sense tells me so," he joked.

"All right then, I'm going to leave you some crackers and ginger ale to put next to her bed in case she wakes up in the middle of the night starving. I was able to get a little bit of the electrolyte fluid into her before she woke up all the way. I have to say that it's unusual for a human not to be dehydrated. I guess she must have been really, really healthy before this happened to her. It's almost as if...well, never mind."

Tristan stopped eating and stared over at Julie, who looked deep in thought. "What is it?"

"Oh, I'm just being crazy. I was just going to say that it's almost as if she had the constitution of a wolf. Silly, huh?"

"Yeah, silly." Tristan bit into a cracker, considering her assessment. Silly? Or right on target? He felt it too. Something about that woman wasn't exactly human, but then again, she wasn't at all supernatural.

Julie gathered up her purse and gave Tristan a quick hug and kiss on the cheek. "Okay, hun, well, call me if you need anything. I'll stop by tomorrow to check on our girl. Maybe bring up some clothes for her, too. Get some rest, okay? Love ya!" she chirped as she entered the elevator and the doors slid shut.

Tristan reveled in the quietness surrounding him. He needed to think about his next steps, his strategy. He planned to bring in a sketch artist, so they could put a face to the arsonists. The meeting with Jax Chandler was in another two days, and he needed to get his shit together before it all went down. Throwing his bowl in the sink, he went to take a hot shower. He needed to think, without his libido interfering. It was as if he'd just been given a few more pieces of a jigsaw puzzle for which he didn't have the picture. But he was cunning, and that's what he did best, work with the impossible to make the possible happen. He was Alpha.

Chapter Seven

Crimson droplets splashed her face. She tried smearing them off with her hand but they kept coming down harder until she was drenched in the sticky sanguine spray. She felt heavy, her clothes sodden with blood. Then she heard it; the voice. Whipping her head toward the ear-piercing scream, she winced, covering her ears. Then she saw it; the vampire, the fangs.

In a flash of a dream, she was shackled by iron cuffs to a wooden cross, teeth snapping in the distance. She squeezed her eyes shut, willing it to go away. But the creature wanted all of her: her flesh, her blood, her mind. Metal cut into her wet wrists; she was almost loose. A little more and they'd fly open. Escape was imminent. Her eyes snapped open; she only caught a glimpse of the razor sharp fangs before they sliced into her neck, tearing the tender skin to shreds.

Kalli screamed bloody murder, jolting upright in bed, throwing the covers aside. Sweat misted over her entire body. Clammy, she shivered from the cool air conditioning that stung her skin. She surveyed her surroundings; the quiet hum of a noise cancellation fan rested on her nightstand. Used to the urban sounds of the city, she reached over and flipped off the switch. Noticing the food and drink that had been set out next to it, she grabbed a few crackers and some ginger ale, sighing in relief at how good it felt to put sustenance back into her body.

After using the bathroom, she sat back in bed, still so very tired from the blood loss. She hoped by morning she'd feel stronger, be able to leave. Uncomfortable, she yanked at the collar of her t-shirt, finding it dampened. She couldn't sleep in the wet shirt, so she pulled it up over her head and turned to hang it on the corner of the headboard. Reacting to the cold, her nipples hardened instantly and goosebumps broke out all over her skin. As she twisted back around to grab the blanket, she saw the shiny eyes of a wolf standing in her doorway.

Deep in sleep, Tristan had heard the bloodcurdling scream emanate from down the hallway. *Kalli.* Immediately he shifted to wolf, readying for a fight. As he raced toward her room, he sensed that no one else was in his home. He poked his head into her room, careful not to scare her, and saw her consuming the snacks he'd left her. Thank God she was all right. She must have been dreaming.

He quickly fell back into the shadows, and stole off to check the rest of his condo. It would have been nearly impossible for someone to have gotten into his home without him knowing. Guards blocked the only elevators up to his home twenty-four by seven, and once inside, one needed a security code to ascend and then a separate code to open the door into the home. Both the private and public elevators had different combinations. The stairwell was the only other way in, and he'd installed a double set of steel security doors, again with sequencing codes and biometric security scans. He couldn't be too careful, sensing a war was upon them.

One more check of Kalli, and he swore he'd go back to bed. His brain and body needed rest, so he'd be one hundred percent in the coming days. Coming up to the guest room, he padded slowly and quietly, trying not to alarm her. She hadn't seen his wolf yet. Being that she was human and a veterinarian, she might not take too kindly to seeing a wild animal on the loose.

Within minutes, he returned to her and came upon the most fascinating and spectacular sight he'd ever seen in all his long life. *Kalli.* In the dim light, he observed intently as she grasped the hem of her shirt, exposing her creamy white breasts to the midnight light of the moon. Her perfect peaks protested the brisk temperature in response. As she moved to hang up her shirt, her hair swept over the tightened, pink areolae, hiding then revealing them, teasing him as he watched.

He knew he should leave, but was undeniably captivated by her beauty and the mere sight of her skin. She reached for the blanket, and froze. He was tempted to leave but instead he found himself slowly stalking her bed, as he had earlier in the evening as a man. Surprisingly, she sat still, letting him view her bare and defenseless.

Kalli knew it was him. *Tristan.* My God, he was magnificent. Lush black fur with the same amber eyes that had enthralled her earlier, he was the most stunning wolf she'd ever seen. She glanced down at her skin, well aware of her nudity, and realized that she wanted him to see her. Her wolf wanted it too, but unfortunately, she was well caged and could only admire how strong and dominant he truly was from afar.

Slowly she reached for the covers, and laid her head back on the pillow, never losing eye contact with her wolf.

"Tristan," she whispered and curled onto her side facing him. "Come lie next to me. I'm not afraid. You can stay how you are. Please come sleep and protect me," she asked in a soft voice. There was no denying that she wanted the man, but tonight in the darkness, she felt safe with the wolf.

Tristan's heart jumped at her words. Even if she were unsure of wanting him as her Alpha, she wanted his protection and accepted his wolf. He found it extraordinary that she was capable of knowing it was him and that she spoke to him, cognizant that he understood her as if he was man. He went to her, curling into her side.

Kalli laid motionless, wrapped in soft fabric, oddly relieved he'd come to her. Within minutes, she could feel his warmth radiating through the covers. She relaxed, certain he would not shift. The last time she had slept next to a wolf, she'd been a young girl, nuzzling with her friends as the adults ran without them. But as an adult, she'd feared both the males and females, well aware of the brutality they could inflict. But at the moment, she felt a sense of tranquility and closeness that she'd never experienced as a woman.

No words were spoken. And while she knew he'd seen her naked, there was nothing sexual about the experience. It was a demonstration of trust. He revealed himself to her, and she revealed herself to him. It may have appeared as a physical exchange to an outsider, but she recognized the importance of the interaction; a significant milestone that created a bond between them. With deliberation, she reached over and placed her hand upon him, silently thanking him for saving her.

Tristan eased into her touch, trying to ignore the message his wolf was sending him. But he couldn't deny that he hadn't felt such intimacy with a woman for as long as he could remember.

❧ Chapter Eight ❧

L ight streaked through the window, waking Kalli. Although it had only been a day since she'd been rescued, she already felt better. She knew it was her lupine genes which supported the advanced healing. The pills stifled the shift and lessoned other traits, but they could not completely change her underlying cellular structure. If someone tested her blood, it would present positive for wolf.

Stirring in bed, she became acutely aware of heat emanating under her hand. Slowly opening her eyes, she quietly gasped, recognizing the feel of skin. Warm, tanned, manly skin. Skin that belonged to one very naked, very muscular, Tristan Livingston. Without moving, she allowed herself the indulgence of taking in an eyeful of the powerful Alpha while he lightly snored. Riveted, she couldn't take her eyes off his face; he was incredibly handsome. A straight nose, masculine jawline with smooth lips. She imagined he was very skilled with those lovely lips and shivered thinking about the things he could do to her with them.

Given that he was perfectly nude, lying atop her bed, she thanked goodness her own body was underneath the covers. She wasn't sure whether to be happy or upset that he'd fallen asleep on his stomach, but she couldn't help appreciating the hard contours of his body, from his well-corded back to his firmly sculptured ass to his strong thighs and calves. Dear Lord, the man was sheer perfection. Michelangelo's David paled in comparison.

She'd somehow fallen asleep with her hand on his shoulder and now let her fingers voluntarily wander down the length of his back. Curious, she couldn't resist, indulging in the experience of touching such an amazing male. Gently, she pushed into a sitting position as she continued to slide her hand over the cheek of his bottom and onto his thigh. Squeezing her legs together, she forced herself to concentrate as her arousal peaked. No internal conflict plagued her as the impulse to touch him took over her thoughts. Neither wolf nor human, she simply was a female who very much wanted the desirable male in her bed.

Tristan flinched slightly, awakened by the touch of her hand on his back and the sweet smell of her excitement. Shifting back after she'd fallen deep into REM sleep, he had to force himself to calm down. He could have sworn he'd been hard all night. This morning, he feigned sleep, knowing that if he opened his eyes, she'd go tearing off his bed like a scared alley cat. But when she skimmed over his butt with her fingers, he swore his steel shaft threatened to catapult him off the bed.

The subtle flinch alerted her that he could be waking up, and she didn't want to be in bed with him when it happened. So she snatched his shirt off the bed. Now dry, she slid it over her head and slipped into the bathroom to freshen up. After brushing her teeth and hair, she tugged again at the too large underwear that clearly had stretched out and no longer wished to stay on her hips. Losing the battle, she let them fall to the floor and decided to go without, resigning herself to a pantyless morning. Because his extra-large shirt fell down over her thighs, she felt relatively covered. Ready to face her Alpha, she cracked open the door.

She wasn't sure where Tristan had gone when she exited the bathroom, but she was hungry and wasn't waiting for him. Within a few minutes, she quickly found the kitchen and the ever-important coffee machine. She turned it on, popped in the coffee pod and started opening cabinets looking for mugs. Setting two cups on the counter, she opened the door to the refrigerator and pulled out creamer then continued looking through the clutter for the eggs. She felt ravenous, and needed protein. "Come on, where are you, little eggies? Tristan has to have eggs. Everyone has eggs," she mumbled, talking to herself.

"Tristan does," he told her with a grin, surprised to find Kalli rummaging around in search of food. Despite taking a cold shower, he was instantly hard again at the sight of her lovely bare ass which peeked at him from underneath his shirt. He wanted nothing more in that moment than to take her from behind and slide deep into her warm heat. The temptation was great, but he restrained his desires.

Kalli jumped at his voice, quickly turning around. "Hi, um, I was just going to make us something to eat," she said nervously.

"By all means," he agreed confidently, walking by her wearing only a towel around his hips. His erection tented the fabric, and he made no attempt to conceal it.

It was nearly impossible to ignore both the charisma and raw sexuality Tristan exuded. Slowly, Kalli's eyes roamed up and down his lean torso, astonished at the audaciousness he exhibited while wearing practically nothing. His hair, dampened from the shower, fell shaggy over his eyes. Hardened abs rippled down toward his low slung towel. Struggling for the words that never came, she couldn't help her natural reaction, which was to look him over one last time. Embarrassed, she just knew that he knew that she'd just looked at his groin area, which appeared to be growing. *Oh God.* She rubbed her hand over her eyes and smiled to herself. *What was it about this man? Get it together, Kalli. Say something.*

"Um, okay then, so the eggs." She opened the refrigerator, careful to hold on to the shirt so it didn't ride up again.

"Like what you see?" he asked seductively as he set a coffee mug next to her hand, proceeding to wait for the next cup to fill.

"What did you just say?" Shocked, she grabbed the egg carton and quickly stood up, banging her head. She turned around holding the package in one hand, rubbing the sore spot on her head with the other.

He set his eyes on hers, taking the eggs and putting them on the ledge. She backed into the counter as he caged her, pushing her body flush against his. "I said...Do. You. Like. What. You. See?" he whispered into her ear, accentuating every word.

She sucked a breath as a million pithy responses filled her head. But the hard bulge pressed against her body and her dangerously hard nipples made it impossible for her to speak coherently.

"Um." God, she felt like a complete idiot. Eight years of college and all she had was 'um'?

"I'll take that as a yes," he replied playfully, kissing her ear softly. He reached over to grab his coffee cup, which made him press against her even harder.

She sucked a breath at the welcome intrusion. There was a part of her that thought he might kiss her. Immobilized against his hard torso, he had her exactly where he wanted her, or rather, where she wanted to be.

Instead of kissing her, however, he wrapped his fingers around the clay handle and walked away with a broad smile across his face, without saying another word. He proceeded to sit down at the island, and switched on his i-Pad, checking his email as he pretended to ignore her. When Kalli turned around again to make the eggs, he let his eyes drift to her soft supple cheeks that strained to stay covered by his shirt. The hem teased higher as she bent over slightly to turn on the stove. Damn, this woman was killing him.

Tristan could not remember the last time he'd slept naked with a woman. Sure he'd fucked many, but not truly just slept with one. He'd stayed wolf as long as he could, treasuring her trust, teaching her that he wouldn't hurt her. But now that she was healing and walking around his home like she belonged here, he felt the pressure in his chest along with the ache between his legs.

They'd forged a bond last night, and he didn't want to rush forward and scare her off. At the same time, he knew she was withholding information. Something small, perhaps, but it was there. Bringing his full attention back to his tablet, he tapped out a quick email to Logan asking him to run a full security clearance on one "Kalli Williams". He wasn't a fool. The woman may have been a brilliant vet, but he found it coincidental that she just happened to be at the fire.

She could have gone any direction that day when she decided to take her break, but she'd passed his club. Why not just call right away after she'd rescued the snake? And then there was her hesitation to tell him about the wolves and what they looked like. He understood that she was in serious danger, but she had to have known the minute she saw them that they could find her based on scent alone. She said she didn't know them personally but her eyes held a terrifying trepidation, a foreboding of sorts, as if she knew exactly what they were capable of doing to her.

And then there was the odd way about her mannerisms, which suggested she'd spent time around a pack. He could tell that she was aware of protocol from the way she'd bowed her head submissively to him when she'd first caught a glance of him in the bedroom. Sure, she'd snapped out of the spell, dragging her eyes to his, but it had been forced. It was as if she was trying to hide the fact that she'd been around an Alpha in the past. Her 'tell' gave her away. She'd acted on instinct when she'd averted her gaze. But the confident posture she'd then adopted had been rehearsed. Like an actor playing the role of a prizefighter, it might have been believable to most audiences, but not to a champion. Others might not notice, but he knew. It was the little things that always gave people away, no matter how much they believed the lie.

Kalli breathed deeply while making the omelets, never turning around, afraid that he'd see right through her soul. Read her mind. She didn't want to lie to him, but she'd just met the man. The intimacy they had shared the previous night spoke volumes to the type of man he was but she wasn't ready to trust him with her secret. He'd never understand what it was like being a hybrid in pack, not even omega; she'd been the lowest of the low.

He was a beautiful, strong Alpha, who'd most likely been like that since birth. How could he possibly fathom the terrifying childhood she'd experienced? He might be able to empathize, but he was neither hybrid nor female, both of which were insubstantial, undesirable and often, irrelevant within pack life. Alpha females were utilized to mate and breed, but even that life wouldn't have been hers. She wasn't Alpha; she wasn't even full wolf; she was seen as nothing more than a tainted half-breed.

As such, the Alpha would have sent her to work for the pack in whatever capacity the others deemed necessary. Come the full moon, when the wolves were most sexually active, they had planned on pimping her out like a prostitute to any lower ranking males who hadn't earned the right to breed. And if by chance she'd become pregnant, it was made clear they'd abort the child, by force if necessary. No one wanted her to propagate the human genes within the pack. From puberty, the Alpha had made sure she learned pack protocol. He had no intention of letting her leave, but wanted her groomed for her new 'role' when she turned of age. Her life had already been a living hell growing up, and she refused to accept the brutal, misogynistic future he'd planned. Running was the only way, and she could trust no one but herself.

Yet Tristan seemed so different than the others she'd known. There was no mistaking his dominant spirit, but he'd saved her, asking for nothing in return but information about that night. She needed time to think, time to assess whether or not she could implicitly trust him with not just her secret, but her life.

"Hey, here you go. Hope you like lots of cheese," she said, placing a plate in front of him.

He raised his eyes from his work. "Thanks. It's been a long time since I've had someone make me breakfast." He started eating, only to be stunned by her next comment.

"I find that hard to believe. You're Alpha. Bet you have lots of women lined up to serve you." The words were out of her mouth before she could take them back. *Oh my God. What the hell did I just say?*

"What makes you say that? Have you spent a lot of time around an Alpha before? Do you have personal knowledge about how Alphas behave and who cooks their meals?" he countered, wanting to know exactly where she'd learned about packs.

She nearly choked on her eggs.

"Sorry, I shouldn't have said that. I'm just so nervous. You know, open mouth, insert foot." Glossing over her faux pas, unwilling to answer him, she forcefully swallowed her food and pressed onto her next agenda item. "So, Tristan, I really need to get back to work today," she stated flatly, changing the subject. She knew he was too keen not to notice, but she wasn't about to start discussing her knowledge of wolves.

"Yeah, about that. No." Nice try, he thought to himself. She may not want to talk about how she knew what she did, but damn if he was letting her out of his sight. "Great eggs by the way."

Did he just tell me no? "But I have to go. I've been missing for days. How am I supposed to explain this to my boss? I have patients; they need me."

"Again, that would be a no. You will not be returning to work until my pack business is resolved. I have a sketch artist coming over this morning. You can work with him, and we'll see what we get."

Frustrated, Kalli accidentally slammed her coffee mug on the counter a little too forcefully, spilling coffee. "Did you hear what I said? I have patients. A job. I don't want to get fired."

"Oh I heard you, but you need to remember who you are talking to, Doctor." He used her professional title hoping it would alert her that he meant nothing but business when it came to the topic of her returning to work. He stood, towering over her petite frame.

"But I need…" she stammered, immediately feeling small in his shadow. She was tempted to cower in his presence, but stiffened her spine and raised her chin at him. Thankfully, he moved around her to put his plate in the sink.

"But nothing. You're in danger. You're not returning until this is over. End of story. After we've done the sketches, we'll take you over to the hospital, so you can wrap up whatever you need for your 'leave of absence'. You can talk to your boss and explain that you need a medical leave due to the attack in the garage. I'll make a call over to Tony at PPD, and report it for you, if the hospital hasn't reported you missing already. If they give you any trouble, I'll put in a call to the president of UVH. I donate enough money to that place that they can go without you for a few weeks."

Kalli stood in awe that he had already worked it all out in his mind. She knew he was right. Where would she go? Her apartment? The vampires had easily found her at her work; it would be even easier to attack her at home. If the wolves decided to come for her, there would be nothing she could do to stop them. She reached up to her neck, feeling the freshly healed scars, and shivered. What if the spawn of the devil, Alexandra, came for her again? She conceded that she needed Tristan's help. And as much as she didn't want to admit it, he needed hers as well.

"You're right. I'll stay," she acquiesced. Going over to the sink, she began washing dishes in defeat. She tried to think of what she was going to tell her boss.

"Did I just hear you say I was right?" He laughed in triumph. She really had no choice. It almost was comical that she actually thought she did. He'd overlook her insolence, considering she wasn't in his pack. But in truth, he simply didn't want to argue with her. With the ladies, he'd much rather be a lover than a fighter.

"Yes I did. And I'm quite sure that you hear it all the time." He was Alpha. Deciding not to give him any more ammunition, she tried another request. "But I need to go by my apartment and get some things. Are you sure it's okay that I stay here with you? I could go to a hotel if you…"

"No," he interrupted coming up against her from behind. "You'll stay with me…in my home…in my bed. I am not letting you go, Dr. Williams." His firm tone left no room for misunderstanding. Standing close enough to her, he could feel the warmth of her skin. He wanted to rip off his towel, bend her over the sink, and slam his cock into her sweet pussy until she screamed his name over and over. But he wouldn't even consider talking her into it. No, when they made love, she would willingly submit to him, begging him for release. He wasn't sure why it was so important to him that she behave like pack; she was human, after all. Maybe it was his wolf warning him, but he just couldn't have her any other way. Until then, he'd tease and seduce her every second she was with him.

She wasn't sure if it was his commanding tone that set her on edge. Or perhaps it was the knowledge that his bare arousal lay directly underneath the towel around his waist, but Kalli's entire body hummed in excitement when he grazed the back of her shirt with his strong body. There was no imagining the sexual tension; it threatened to set the room ablaze. Tristan was incredibly magnetic, and she felt like a box of paperclips that was about to explode; she'd be stuck to him all over. She'd spent so many years hiding her true identity, never getting close to anyone. The men at work had asked her on dates, but she'd conveniently thrown up her "professional morals" speech. She couldn't let anyone into her bed, let alone her heart. But Tristan was larger than life in every way. Overnight, she'd become unraveled, and it was all because of him.

The alluring Alpha threatened to break down her carefully, hermetically sealed, stronger than steel emotional walls. The heat was just too much. And like any metal, given a high enough temperature, it would melt. She tried to concentrate. How was she going to collect herself? Needing to cool down, she looked for an escape. Setting the last clean dish in the rack, she turned off the water and slipped away past him.

Even as she squeezed by him, she knew it was because he'd let her go. She was practically shaking with arousal by the time she reached the corner to the hallway. She swore silently at the dampness between her legs. Tristan eyed her from the kitchen with a sly grin on his face. He knew. There was nothing she would get past him, except for maybe the secret that lay in her pill bottle.

"Ma lapin, I thought you were done running last night. You faced the wolf. Welcomed him." He stalked toward her then stopped and placed his hand on the end of the island.

Kalli's eyes caught his. Looking relaxed and confident, he was deliciously cool, like an ice cream cone on a warm summer day. Ready to be licked all over. She parted her lips, unconsciously moistening them in response. She knew that if he hadn't smelled her wet arousal that he'd surely seen her nipples, which pressed through the thin fabric of his shirt.

"Last night." She stopped midsentence as the memory flashed. Bared to him physically, emotionally. Welcoming him into her bed. He'd proved that he was trustworthy, revealing himself to her. Maybe it was time she gave him more of herself, as much as she was capable of, anyway. It might not be enough for him, but it was all she had.

He slowly moved toward her, sensing her internal struggle; the scent of her flooding his olfactory system, the sound of her quickening heartbeat assaulting his ears. But his little rabbit wasn't afraid; she was sexually excited, wanting him, even if she couldn't yet act on her feelings.

"Tristan," she began as he came nearer. "Last night, I needed you. I guess I didn't really know how much," she confessed. "Your wolf was…he was…you were magnificent, so beautiful. But you need to know that I've never…I've never done anything like that before. It was so intimate. I'm…I'm trying to make this work. You saved me," she whispered, hoping he could understand what she was trying to tell him. Intimacy had always seemed formidable for Kalli, if not unattainable….until last night. She shook her head in disappointment over her lack of articulation.

Her admission floored him. He'd felt it too, but he didn't understand how hard it was for her to talk about how she felt until now. Granted, he barely knew her, but he wanted to know her. He wanted to know every single thing about her, inside and out.

It was all too much, her arousal, her words. He couldn't hold back. In two strides, he had her backed against the wall. The wolf had the rabbit cornered yet again, except this time, she wasn't running. This time, she looked up at him with sad dreamy eyes. Her mouth parted slightly and he struck.

Raking his fingers into her hair, he pulled her mouth to his, sucking, tasting. Kalli felt relieved when he made the first move, kissing her, allowing her to finally act on her passion. As he pushed his tongue into her mouth, she teased hers into his, reveling in the power of his kiss. She moaned, but refused to release him as her hands wrapped around his neck.

Tristan was drowning in her sweet mouth. Needing more, he reached under her knee, grinding his body into hers. His towel came undone, and his flesh met hers.

Kalli felt his rock-hard cock press against her bare belly as his towel fell and her shirt bunched up around her breasts. Lost in his embrace, her lips broke free of his for a mere second, enough time for her to moan his name: "Tristan."

"Kalli," he groaned in response, finding her mouth yet again. He planned to thoroughly kiss her until she knew what he wanted from her; everything.

She slid a hand down his strong chest, fingering each ab and then reached down to cup his firm ass. At her touch, he shoved her harder against the wall, letting his own hands wander until he found her soft breast. He pinched a pointed nipple, making her cry out in pleasure, and then bent his knees so that the tip of his shaft ran up and over her mound. As much as he'd like to fuck her up against the wall, and he was about a minute from doing so, he wanted her in his bed with her neck bared to him in submission. The first time he took her, it had to be. She needed to give all of herself to him, no secrets.

A ding from his private elevator alerted him that Logan was about to come into his home. He tore himself away from her lips, peppering her neck with small kisses. "Kalli," he panted, trying to get her attention.

She was lost in ecstasy when she heard him call her name. Breathlessly, she dropped her leg as he released it from the crook of his arm. She instinctively pulled down the rim of the shirt which had been pushed clear up to her neck. She sighed, "Tristan."

They each had an arm wrapped around each other, reluctant to let go. Gazing into each other's eyes, registering the fireworks between them, a voice jarred them out of their erotic trance.

"Doesn't take you long, Alpha," Logan remarked. He wasn't trying to be disrespectful, but was naturally skeptical about Dr. Williams. He'd seen her in his dreams, but still, he was unsure of her intentions.

Tristan growled. "Enough, Logan. Living room, now. Leave us," he ordered over his shoulder, shielding Kalli from his beta's view and never taking his eyes off hers. "The sketch artist will be here soon, as will Julie with some clothes. Why don't you go relax in your room?"

Snapping out of it, Kalli realized what had almost just happened. It terrified her; making love to the Alpha, he'd tear her apart. But like a moth to a flame, she couldn't resist.

"Yeah, okay," was all she managed to say, slipping from his arms. She scurried down the hallway toward her room, needing to collect herself.

"Oh, and Kalli," he called.

She stopped dead in her tracks but didn't turn around. "Yes."

"This isn't over, not by a long shot. We'll finish this later. I promise."

Kalli didn't respond, choosing to flee to the safety of her room. What was she going to say anyway? She had practically thrown herself at him in the hallway. And she knew as Alpha, he could have whatever he wanted, at least that is how it worked in the pack. But she wasn't pack.

❦ *Chapter Nine* ❦

Tristan adjourned to his room and got dressed before talking to Logan, who was sitting on the couch reading the news on his tablet.

"Hey," he greeted him as he went into his kitchen to get another cup of joe. The open layout of his condo was such that the kitchen, living room and family rooms were essentially one large, shared space. "Coffee?"

"No thanks," Logan replied, not looking up.

"So, did you get my email? Give me the rundown."

"Yeah, I'm running her clearances right now. Should have some info by this afternoon. Tony's sending someone over to do the sketches within the hour. Meeting with Chandler is set up; two days from now. Neutral territory. Jersey. It's all been arranged. And don't forget the mayor's charity ball is tomorrow night."

"Anything else?" Tristan walked over and stared out the sliding glass doors.

Logan set his tablet down on the coffee table and looked up. "Uh, yeah. Are we going to talk about what I just walked in on?"

"What's to talk about?"

"Really? Okay, maybe the fact that we don't know her story yet. Or that you just met her yesterday. Come on, Tris; tell me that you didn't sleep with her." Logan had to ask, considering the strong scent of arousal that had hit him when the elevator doors opened.

"Seriously, bro?" Tristan shrugged. "Okay, let's go there. I questioned her, and yes, she's concealing something. But I can also sense that she's not dangerous nor did she set the fire. And no, I didn't sleep with her. Well, technically, I did sleep with her, but if you are asking if we had sex, then no." He wouldn't lie to Logan, but Tristan knew it was just a matter of time before he'd make love to her. And he planned on doing it all night long.

"Good to be the Alpha, huh?" Logan joked.

"Yeah, something like that. What about it?"

"So let me get this straight. You, my friend, just slept with her last night as in lying in a bed, eyes closed, no hanky panky?"

"It wasn't planned. Kind of just happened. I went wolf," he admitted.

Logan raised an eyebrow at Tristan. "Okay."

"She had a nightmare. She needed me. Come on, stop looking at me like that," he replied with a small smile. He held his hands up in protest. "Look, I'm nothing if not a gentleman."

"Yeah, okay, but do me a favor. Don't jump in any deeper until we find out what's going on with her. I know she's important to you, but…" his voice trailed off. He was tempted to tell Tristan about the visions, but they were unclear. If he told him that he'd seen her, there was no telling how he'd react.

"I got this. She's fine, really. And speaking of Kalli, we need to take her to the hospital today to tie up loose ends. I don't want her out of my sight. She saw two wolves leave the club on the day of the fire. They could have seen her go in or have seen her leave with the snake. And I still can't trust Alexandra to keep her fangs away from her. She was out of control yesterday. I'm sending a text to Kade so he can get a message to Devereoux. He needs to put the smack down on her, so she doesn't decide to try to snatch Kalli again. The look on her face yesterday when we walked out…she's one mean bitch."

"You can say that again." Logan shook his head. "I think that we should keep her out of Noir, too. I know she'll be pissed but she crossed the line."

"Agreed. But let's put that one back on Devereoux. He made her, and he needs to deal with his own. I can't have her going off when I'm in the middle of a territory war."

"So, is there anything else that I need to know about Kalli?" Logan asked, just as she walked into the room wearing Tristan's robe.

Tristan sucked a breath seeing her freshly showered, and hardened at the thought that she was completely naked underneath the black cotton terrycloth. He jumped to his feet, taking her hand, pulling her to his side. "Aw, chére. Sorry about the clothes. Listen, Julie will be up in a minute with something for you to wear. I promise."

Kalli felt shy, barely dressed. She awkwardly tried to stand behind Tristan in an effort not to look at Logan. Another wolf. Fear swept through her.

Tristan immediately noticed Kalli's apprehension and tried to reassure her. "Kalli, it's okay. This is Logan, my beta. Do you remember him from yesterday?"

Her wide eyes met Logan's, and she quickly averted her gaze. "I do remember seeing two men," she responded fearfully.

Concerned she was displaying the submissive behavior of a wolf and that he'd recognize her as something other than human, she forced herself to meet his eyes and extended her hand. "Hi, my name is Dr. Williams, but please call me Kalli. I can't thank you enough for coming to my rescue yesterday." There, she'd done it. Inwardly she congratulated herself for acting so completely normal....human.

Logan shook her hand, watching her curiously. It was as if she'd switched from submissive to dominant within seconds. He looked over to Tristan, shooting him a knowing look and then back to Kalli. *What the hell was that?* He'd ask him later what was going on with her. Tristan had to have noticed it. Subtle, but the Alpha missed nothing.

"Hey, no problem. Just sorry you had the unfortunate experience of meeting Alexandra. I'd call her evil but that would be an understatement," he told her.

"I will give her this; the mistress of Satan is true to her nature. Not that all vampires are bad people, but they definitely skate the line of morality. Alexandra is a predator and doesn't care who knows it. I have a feeling, though, that will get her staked. She's gotten worse over the past ten years," Tristan commented.

"Without a doubt," Logan agreed.

True to her nature. Kalli considered how she'd avoided her nature. Self-preservation had a tendency to drive one to do desperate things.

"Kalli is a veterinarian," Tristan explained. "Which explains why she was at UVH. She rescued Eve."

"Well, that's a good thing. I'm not a huge fan of snakes, but the old gal has grown on me. Where is she?" Logan asked.

"She's at the hospital. I have her in the observation area now. Such a beautiful snake, very calm, likes being held. She's thriving." Her eyes lit up as she talked about her patient. Anyone could see how passionate she was about her work. "If you want to send someone to get her, I'll sign the release papers when I go in today. I know I'm going to have to take a leave until this mess is figured out, but there were a few severely dehydrated puppies that someone had left abandoned in a dumpster. I want to see how they're doing. They might be ready to go to the shelter by now. I really don't know how people can just abandon animals, abuse them. People can be cruel," she remarked, thinking how humans could be every bit as evil as Alexandra. "I know my patients will be fine with the staff but I have to know how they're doing...peace of mind and all. I know you're not supposed to get attached, but sometimes, I just can't help it."

"That reminds me." Logan walked over to the elevator and picked something up off the floor. "Here's your purse. We got it out of your car. I'm afraid someone cut your tires. We'll call in a tow for you and get it fixed up, don't worry. Tristan here, tells me you'll be spending time with us for a while, so sounds like you won't need it."

"Thanks, and um, thanks for my pills," she coughed, remembering her desperation in the car. Rifling through her purse, she looked up. "You didn't happen to find my work ID by any chance?" The sequence of events was blurry, but then she recalled taking her ID and keys with her and leaving everything else in the car.

Before Logan had a chance to speak, she answered her own question. "It must have fallen off when they took me. I left my stuff in the car. Just took my keys."

"Hey, I know you've been through a lot, but I want you to know that we appreciate your help," Logan offered.

"Well, to be honest, I'm still in considerable danger. Those wolves I saw could be after me...if they weren't before, they will be once I do these sketches. And there's the vampire; I know she didn't give me up out of the goodness of her cold dark heart. Not happy about it, but I've got to lay low for a bit...if I want to live that is. And I do kind of like living. Pretty fond of it, actually," she joked half-heartedly.

"Alive works for me, too. Seriously, though, we'll keep you safe here. It'll be all right," Logan encouraged with a small smile.

Even though she'd initially been afraid of Logan, she soon found it was easy to talk to him. It didn't hurt that he was good-looking either. Like Tristan, he was at least six four, well-built and charming, she thought to herself. His dark brown hair fell past his shoulders, but even with long hair, he somehow looked quite the all American guy.

Logan studied the fine doctor, cognizant of her easygoing personality. He could see why Tristan found her attractive, with her innocent face and baby blue eyes. And that hair; the black curls were beginning to dry in shiny spirals, cascading over her shoulders. She seemed so vulnerable but at the same time, she exhibited strong tendencies. It was just yesterday she'd been passed out in the car, bitten and bloody. And today, although still bruised, she was conversing with them both as if she'd been around supernaturals her whole life.

Tristan watched his beta cautiously from across the room, as if he could hear Logan's thoughts. Was he flirting with her? His wolf growled; *mine*. Oh hell no, Tristan thought. He was not claiming this woman as his own. He hadn't even had sex with her. One night of sleeping with her, and his wolf was ready to take her? A human? Why did the wolf want her so? It was insane, yet the human side of him felt a sharp pain deep in his stomach as he watched Kalli flash Logan a smile. *What was that?* As Logan reached to put a comforting hand on her shoulder, Tristan heard himself growl.

Both Logan and Kalli stilled at the menacing warning. They both knew what it meant without hearing a single word spoken. Logan stared over at Tristan, surprised at the territorial admonition.

Tristan raked his hand through his hair, realizing what he'd just done. Like a common dog protecting his bone, he'd just snarled at them. *Fuck.* He couldn't believe that he was even capable of such an intense reaction. Yet there was no denying the confusing emotions swirling inside his chest. Relieved to hear the elevator ringing, he silently strode over and punched in the security code.

Julie's eyes darted from the Alpha to his beta and back again. She wasn't sure what she'd just walked in on, but the tension seemed thick. Regardless, she had a job to do.

"Good morning, peeps!" she chirped, walking in with a large tote bag. "Kalli! You're up. Oh my, I didn't expect you to be walking around today. Are you sure you're all right? Did these he-men drag you out here for another interrogation? Um, I mean questioning," she corrected, shooting both Tristan and Logan a questioning look.

"No, they're fine. Um, I'm fine, thanks," Kalli responded, purposefully moving away from Logan.

"Well, let's get down into your room. I want to check your vitals. Brought you clothes too, which I'm quite sure you'll appreciate. You're already at a disadvantage around these two. And being naked won't help you. Maybe them, but definitely not you," she said with a wink to Tristan. Looping her arm around Kalli's, she led her down the hallway.

"What. The. Fuck?" Logan snapped, once the girls were out of earshot. He'd heard Tristan growl a million times, but rarely was it directed at him and never over a woman. Spending his life protecting the guy kind of earned him that privilege, to talk to him the way he just had. Logan was the only person in the world that when push came to shove, Tristan would allow to call him to the carpet.

"It's nothing," Tristan protested.

"Denial must be a great place to be, Tris. Seriously? Over her?" he pressed.

"All right. I'm sorry I, uh…growled. Let it go. End of discussion," Tristan replied, aware that he'd momentarily lost control.

"Yeah, okay," Logan agreed looking down at his phone, reading a text. "Hey, the artist is here. Mira's bringing him up."

Logan needed that clearance report on Kalli stat. He prayed it came back clear. She was alluring, no doubt, both physically and intellectually. But his sole purpose was to defend his Alpha and pack; something said he couldn't trust her. Not yet. He planned to stick close to her until he had something on her, and even closer to Tristan. Clearly irritated with his territorial nature over Kalli, Tristan had shut down. Logan backed off, knowing he needed space to get it together.

The Alpha was being sucked into the vortex of the mystery woman, and he suspected he knew the cause. Logan wished he could spare him from it; but like all things in life, it was the natural cycle of things. Fate was a coldhearted bitch. It didn't make sense to him how the Goddess would bring a human to mate his Alpha. Perhaps she wasn't the one. His visions weren't clear, but being around Kalli, seeing her face, her mannerisms, he felt more and more certain she'd been the one in his dreams.

⊸⊛ *Chapter Ten* ⊛⊷

Tristan took a deep breath, centering himself. He had to remain in control; so many people depended on him. He couldn't wait to get the sketches done. Not only would he share them with Marcel and Chandler, he planned to send the drawings over to Tony. They might help on his end. Tony Bianchi, Sydney's former partner, still worked homicide in the city police department. Since the fire had been ruled as arson, Tony wasn't working the case, but he was the only one Tristan trusted on the force.

P-CAP, the Paranormal City Alternative Police, was aware of the fire, but since no supernaturals were murdered, they wouldn't take the case. Tristan didn't want them involved anyway; given that Alexandra had vamps entrenched in their organization. The previous month, when a serial killer had been stalking young women, Kade had assigned himself to P-CAP in an effort to expedite the case. At the end of the day, pack business would be handled from within; he would mete out justice, not leave it up to the police.

But Tony could put out a city-wide bulletin on the suspects, or perhaps get a name on them prior to his meeting with Chandler. It was a long shot that Jax would even know the wolves who'd set the fire. And even if he did know them, Tristan wasn't certain that he'd cooperate. Working all angles was prudent given the lack of information.

Logan tapped in the code, allowing the ever-polished-looking Mira to saunter into the room. She wore a smart pink plaid dress suit with black pumps, her hair pulled neatly into a French twist. He smiled to himself, thinking how she could go from looking like a business barracuda one minute to a purring kitten the next. And had she ever purred for him last night.

A disheveled man, carrying messenger bags, followed her, stumbling into Logan.

"Logan. Tristan. This is Mr. Mathers. He will be doing the sketch. And before you ask, yes, I checked his badge," she stated, walking over to Tristan first, giving him a quick peck on the cheek.

"Please, sit," Tristan requested, gesturing to a guest chair in the living room. "Do you need anything to work?"

"Ah, no. Just the witness. I'm going to do the sketches. Afterward, I can send them to whoever you wish," he explained. Pulling out an oversized tablet and stylus, he situated his equipment. "It may be easier for me to work at the dining room table. Do you mind?"

"No, not at all. Mir, can you get him set up? I'm gonna go get Kalli," Tristan told her.

Kalli exited the bathroom, dressed in hip-hugging jeans and a tight yellow cotton short-sleeved t-shirt. Brushing her hair aside, she gratefully accepted a pair of beige ballet flats from Julie and slipped them onto her feet.

"Thanks again. I promise to get this stuff back to you once I get my clothes from my apartment. It feels good to finally have some clothes on again. I almost feel normal," she declared, smiling.

"No problem. I have to say that I'm pretty amazed at how quickly you're healing. You sure you're not feeling any more dizziness?" Julie asked, intrigued by how quickly she had recovered from her blood loss.

"I'd be lying if I said I wasn't a little tired, but no dizziness. I must have a strong heart," she suggested, knowing it was her wolf genes that helped her heal so quickly.

"Well before ya go, do you want to talk about these?" Julie held up the tiny bottle that held her pills.

"Um, well, they're just something I take to help keep me on an even keel. Helps control muscle spasms. It's kind of experimental; something I've been working on," she lied somewhat.

She hated deceiving Julie; the woman had been so nice to her. She'd always heard that if you had to lie that you should do it by sprinkling the fib into a story that was mostly truth. *Muscle spasms?* Well, technically that is what happened when she shifted. And being undetectable as wolf definitely was good for her mental state. As long as no one knew her true identity, she had been able to relax. Her old pack couldn't find her.

Kalli slipped the container into her purse, and rummaged around for her makeup. Finding a small tube, she pulled it out and slid the light pink gloss over her lips. As she dropped it back into her bag, she noticed Tristan by the door, watching her with the same heat he'd shown when they kissed. She smiled over at him, hoping that she'd be able to trust him soon with her secret. She felt guilty not telling him everything. He deserved to know the truth, but should she put her life into his hands?

"Can I take a break?" Kalli asked, after the first sketch was finished.

"Well, I really suggest we keep going. I need to get back to the station," Mr. Mathers replied, clearly annoyed that she wanted to stop working.

"Well, okay then, but it might be more productive if I just take a small break to refresh myself," she persisted.

Her face began to flush as she approved the first drawing. It brought back the reality of her situation. She was not going home or back to work. No, she'd decided to stay with strange wolves, when she had spent the past ten years trying to stay away from them.

Looking at the drawing of the wolf over and over again was enough to send her into a full-blown panic attack. Seeing his face reminded her that she'd been living on borrowed time. If they found her, they'd drag her kicking and screaming back to South Carolina. And if they decided not to kill her on sight, she'd be subjected to monthly rapes by the men who weren't worthy of breeding. *Oh God. I can't go back.* At the thought, her chest tightened; it felt as if she had an elephant sitting on top of her, making it difficult to breathe. *Air, I need air.* Her throat began to constrict. She put her head into the palms of her hands.

Tristan was talking to Logan and Mira about the latest acquisition when he heard Kalli gasping. Alarmed, he ran to her, pulling her into his arms.

"What did you do to her?" he yelled at the artist, who was tapping away on his tablet.

"Me? Well, nothing. I mean, she wanted a break, but it works better if we just keep going while the details are fresh," he explained nervously.

"Idiot," Tristan mumbled under his breath. He stroked Kalli's face with his hands, in an effort to get her to breathe normally again. "Time for a break. Come on, baby, it's okay. Breathe. That's it. Just feel me."

Tristan led her over to the sofa and lifted her onto his lap. He sent calming waves to her, hoping that his powers could be felt by a human. She cuddled into his warmth, trying to concentrate on his words. Hearing his breaths and strong heartbeat, she focused on matching her own to his as if they were one.

Logan and Mira both gaped, taken aback by the scene, as Tristan took the human to his breast. He acted so protective of her, as if he was mated. Yet he didn't know it. They both felt slightly voyeuristic but couldn't help but be drawn to the sight before them. Mira was more than astonished, she was irritated. *How could this happen? She was human.*

"I'm okay," Kalli reassured Tristan, lifting her head up and pressing a palm to his chest. "Oh my God. I'm so embarrassed. Really it was just a tiny panic attack. I'm fine."

"Don't be embarrassed. You've been through a lot in the past seventy-two hours. You're overcoming blood loss. He was a jerk. You asked, and he didn't listen. No worries, chére." Tristan felt as if his heart had been ripped out of his chest seeing Kalli so stressed over these pictures. He fully understood what they represented, but her face was as pale as if she'd seen a ghost.

Realizing that everyone was staring at them, Kalli attempted to get away from Tristan. She couldn't afford to show weakness in front of his wolves; they'd eat her alive.

"Hey, where're you going? You sure you're okay?" he asked, refusing to let her up. He held her tight, not caring what anyone thought.

"Thanks, I'm fine. You're right. It must be the blood loss. I think I'm okay now. I'll use the bathroom and be right back," she told him, hoping he'd let it go.

"Okay." Tristan released her, watching as she tore down the hallway. It may have been panic, but he could sense the sheer terror coursing through her body. She was afraid of something. Perhaps the wolves she'd been sketching scared her. But he got the distinct feeling she was not telling him the truth. It was just a matter of time before he found out what the hell was going on with her. Giving Logan a look, he gestured for him to come over to the sofa.

Logan complied. "What's up, boss?"

"How's the clearance going? Anything yet?' he asked impatiently.

"Not really. All we got so far is criminal records, which didn't tell us much. No arrests. Not even so much as a parking ticket. Pays her bills on time. Been on staff at UVH for two years. Still diggin'. Should have more information this afternoon."

"I want to know as soon as you hear from our guy. And I mean as soon as you hear it. No delays," he directed. "She's hiding something, and I damn well want to know what it is."

Mira overheard their conversation from across the room and came over to see what was happening. Tristan's intimate display with the human woman troubled her on a visceral level. What the hell did he see in her? Mira wasn't usually a jealous woman. He'd fucked lots of women over the years. He'd even been serious, holding long-standing booty calls with detective Sydney Willows. He'd even asked her to move in with him, but she had the good sense to turn him down.

But this woman had insinuated herself into his life in less than twenty-four hours. The only way that could ever happen would be if he met his mate. Mate? No fucking way. No Alpha had ever mated with a human. Besides, she would have known if he'd found a mate. Logan would know. The entire damn pack would know. They'd all feel it. And knowing Tristan, he'd be broadcasting it over a satellite. There was something about this human woman that was all wrong, and she was determined to find out what it was. In the meantime, she planned to make her life a living hell, even if Tristan had decided she was staying with him.

"Hey, what's up?" she asked innocently.

"Nothin'. Just talkin' to Logan about running a security clearance on Dr. Williams," he explained.

"Doctor, huh? Looks like she's the one who needs to take a pill if you ask me. And while we're all sharing, why the hell were you chasing her all over?"

Logan rolled his eyes, hoping Mira would know when to stop.

"I don't know what you're talking about," Tristan grinned, trying to get her to lay off the subject. "I'm just givin' her a little sweet Alpha love medicine. You should know all about that, Mir."

A chuckle came from Logan. The man had mad lines. He could talk the pants off a nun.

"Yeah, well, you'd better watch yourself, Tris. She's human. Not to mention that you barely know her," she warned.

"Thanks for your concern, chére, but I assure you that your Alpha can take care of himself."

"But you can't seriously be thinking of letting her stay here," she interjected, raising her voice.

"Already done. She's staying with me, in my home and will not stay with anyone else," he remarked, looking at Logan, remembering the incident earlier in the day.

"But…"

He interrupted her before she could get another word in. She was overstepping her boundaries. Pinning her with his eyes, he forced her to drop her gaze in submission. "Drop it, Mira. Seriously, not another word. She's in my care. She's mine."

He understood the implications of claiming her, the instant the word 'mine' left his lips. Looking at Logan and Mira's faces he knew they interpreted it as much more than the context in which it was meant. As Alpha, all wolves were his. They were all his responsibility. Just because she was human, well, it shouldn't make a difference. She needed his protection, and he needed her, for information only, of course. Sure, she was incredibly alluring and gave him an aching erection just about every time he talked to her, but it was just attraction, pure and simple. He'd have to be dead not to want to have sex with her.

As Mira and Logan gave each other quizzical looks, he narrowed his eyes on them. "What?"

"Nothing," they both said at the same time.

Finishing up the description of the second wolf, Kalli waited for the artist to work his magic. She sat patiently, anticipating that he'd ask for her to confirm the sketch. The tall blonde had been shooting daggers at her ever since she'd returned from her room. Kalli stole glances over at Tristan and Logan working on the other side of the room and noticed the woman never left Tristan's side.

Her business attire and laptop suggested she worked for Tristan in a formal capacity, but her intimate gestures toward both men indicated more than a professional relationship. *Friends?* No, her occasional touch to Tristan's face implied more. *Lovers?* For some reason the thought of him having other lovers gave her a slight twinge in her stomach. She silently admonished herself for the feeling. She'd only known him for a day. So what if she was lusting after him like a bitch in heat? He wasn't hers.

The phenomenon of physical attraction was undeniably compelling given the right chemistry between the right people. It could hardly be controlled. And then there was the very hard to ignore fact that Tristan was an Alpha who appeared to have made an art form of seduction, with the ability to turn on and off his intoxicating charm with the blink of an eye. Any woman who even looked his way would be hopelessly lost. She didn't stand a chance.

She damn well knew that he probably had a stable of women, supernatural and human, ready and willing to warm his bed. What kind of idiot would get involved with an Alpha when she, herself, was pretending to be human and was on the run from her own pack? *A fool.*

But she could not deny that she wanted him sexually, and not in a nice hand-holding, missionary position kind of way. Visions of her gripping the headboard while he slammed into her hard, fisting her long hair in his hands was more in order. And she, screaming as the pleasure bordering on pain sent her plummeting into orgasm…oh yes, that was how she wanted him. Fast and hard. Biting and scratching. Animalistic.

Regardless, she couldn't let these temporary lust-driven feelings cloud her judgment. She didn't do jealousy. Perhaps what did bother her, though, was that this woman who didn't even know her did not like her. Kalli didn't understand why but then again, it didn't really matter. And if she was reading things correctly, there was the possibility she'd also have to spend time with her over the next few days.

Not that she wasn't used to dealing with cantankerous and even cruel pet owners from time to time; she'd become an expert at pulling down her professional aura, speaking to them in a dominant but calm voice. Articulately eviscerating pet owners who were abusive was an unfortunate reality of life in the city. She wasn't the type to take shit from anyone when it came to protecting her animals. She reasoned that she could take care of the uptight blonde; it might not be pretty, but she wasn't here to do pretty. She needed to stay alive and help Tristan find the wolves who'd killed that man in Louisiana and set his club ablaze.

Once this ordeal was over, she planned to go back to her life's mission of healing animals and teaching others how to help them. She'd return to hiding as a wolf in human clothing. Maybe finally date a human who didn't mind a brainiac who worked long hours and was covered in pet hair when she got home. A hot kiss, one that brought her to her knees, with a spectacularly gorgeous Alpha wasn't going to change that very real outcome. She glanced over at him again, hoping he wouldn't see her looking yet again. *God, he is delicious. I could lick him up....*

"How does this look?" the artist asked, jarring her from her carnal thoughts.

"Um, yeah, that uh, that looks good," she stammered. "We done?"

"Yeah, just saving them and then I'll email them over to Tristan, Logan and Tony," he murmured, continuing to work.

"Okay, thanks." Tired from working, Kalli stood, unconsciously stretching her arms over her head like a cat who'd just awoken from a long nap.

Tristan stopped talking, noticing she was finished. His dick snapped to attention as she began stretching in front of everyone, her hard nipples pressing through her t-shirt. Was she aroused? Cold? He needed her close, thanking the Goddess that the artist wasn't watching her. He'd have a heart attack at the delectable sight.

A low growl emanated from him as he strode across the room and wrapped his hands around her waist. He didn't want anyone else seeing the lovely sight he'd just witnessed. Oh, he wanted to see her nipples hard, all right, but he didn't need other males seeing them, especially in his own home. Before he knew it, he hugged her, running his hands down her back where they rested right above her rear. Taking in a long draw of her scent, he moaned, and then released her, realizing they had an audience. He caught a glimpse of Logan's wide grin. Mira's mouth was drawn in a tight disapproving line.

"All done?" he asked Kalli and looked down to the artist who was putting away his tablet.

"Yeah," she said, surprised he'd just hugged her out of the blue. She wasn't sure what to make of it, but it felt so good to be in his arms.

"Mr. Livingston, I've sent the files to your email address. Tony should have them by now. Pleasure working for you."

"Thanks, I appreciate your work. And remember, you are to keep this in confidence. That means you are to tell no one, got it? Not even your mama," he ordered.

Apprehensively, the artist shook Tristan's hand. "Yes sir."

"Logan, please see Mr. Mathers out, would ya?"

The artist hurried over to the elevator, looking like he couldn't wait to leave. Sympathetic, Kalli understood what it was like to be intimidated by supernaturals. Even if the poor man didn't spend a lot of time with them, he'd be aware of the danger. They exuded a natural intimidating aura, and most humans had the good sense to be wary. An elk didn't need to know to be afraid of a pack of wolves skulking toward him. He instinctively knew to run.

"Come on over here. I want you to meet someone before we leave for the hospital," Tristan insisted, dragging her by the hand over to meet ice woman.

"Mira, I'd like you to meet…"

"Dr. Kalli Williams," Kalli interrupted, donning her professional mannerism. She extended her hand to her as she would a patient, looking her directly in the eyes. "Since you are friends with Tristan, please call me Kalli."

Mira shook the human's hand, astonished that she was so bold. Any wolf would have recognized her as an Alpha female and lowered their eyes. *Humans.* They grated on her last nerve. "Charmed I'm sure," she uttered briskly, darting her eyes to Tristan's.

Kalli quickly removed her hand. She didn't have time for pissing contests. And if there was going to be one, her opponent was going to drown trying.

"Yes. Okay, well, nice to meet you, Mira," she replied, not knowing what else to say to her. She wasn't sure what came over her but before she knew it she'd turned her back on Mira. Closing the distance, she pressed her body to Tristan, not quite touching, her breasts mere inches from him. Resting a hand possessively on his waist, the other touched a palm to his chest. The electrically charged tension hung in the air between them.

"I have to go freshen up. Then can we swing by the hospital? I've got to get in there before they fire me."

"Sounds good. I'm going to review the sketches real quick with Logan to see if anything about them seems remotely familiar. We'll get them out to the rest of the pack so they can be on the lookout, too. You go ahead. Take your time," he suggested, not moving an inch.

"Thanks." Kalli took a deep breath, removing her hands from him, but letting her breast brush him slightly as she turned.

Before Mira had a chance to say another word, Kalli spoke. "Nice to meet you." With confidence, she flipped her hair aside and walked away to go get ready.

"Humans," Mira sniffed. "God, Tristan, it's probably a good thing she's not wolf. I might have to take her down a peg or two."

Logan came up from behind her, wrapping his hands around Mira's waist, snuggling into her shoulder. "Mir, what's wrong, baby? Didn't we have fun last night? I've never seen you so prickly. Tris, our girl got up on the wrong side of the bed. You see what happens when you leave us in the middle of our play?"

Tristan tried to focus on Mira's reaction to Kalli, but was having a hard time, given the ache he felt below. The mere touch of Kalli drove him mad. He needed to take her soon, get her out of his system so he could think straight.

"What?" he asked, not having listened to the question. Ignoring it, he looked back to Logan and Mira. "Listen, Mir, I don't know what's gotten into you but you need to be nice to Kalli. She's already skittish around wolves."

"I was perfectly nice," she protested, gathering her up her things. "If you'd stop drooling for five seconds, you might notice that she was the one who was disrespectful."

"Seriously? Because she didn't avert her eyes? She's human. You need to get used to it. And she also holds a position of authority. In case you didn't hear it right the first time, she's a doctor. I get the feeling that she doesn't mince words. Despite what happened to her, she's no shrinking violet. She's tough. It's in her nature," he told her.

Humiliated, Mira rolled her eyes. "Human nature. Don't forget that, Tris," she countered, cupping his face briefly. She turned, giving Logan a brief kiss on the cheek, before entering the elevator.

Tristan considered what had just transpired. Consciously or not, Kalli had physically blocked Mira from touching him, possessively rubbing her hands all over his torso, thereby asserting her role in his life. And she happened to put on the display in front of his beta, who also took notice. Mira's feathers had been justifiably ruffled. He understood why, but it didn't change what had just happened. However vulnerable Kalli had appeared yesterday, there was no mistaking the lurking dominance within her.

❧ *Chapter Eleven* ❧

Kalli sat across from Dr. Marcus Cramer, who wasn't at all happy with her request for leave.

"Dr. Williams," he began. "We really can't have our doctors taking leave willy nilly. I understand you had an incident in the garage a few days ago, but you look fine to me."

"Dr. Cramer," she addressed him using his professional name, thinking that two could play that game. "You don't seem to understand. I really don't have a choice. I'm requesting a personal leave, effective immediately, which under my contract, I am entitled to do. And while I really do want your approval, I will escalate if necessary."

She didn't want to burn any bridges but she also wasn't about to let the jerk push her around. She reasoned he was trying to strong-arm her, because he knew that it was just a matter of time before she was completely in charge of her own department. She supposed he felt she needed to pay her dues before moving upward within the administration. But then again, the man just seemed to be a generally disagreeable person, regardless of who he spoke to, staff and patients alike.

"I feel that as a courtesy you should tell me why you are taking the leave. Is it medical? Are you pregnant?" he challenged, raising his voice.

"What?" she nearly shouted back at him, incredulous that he'd even ask such a personal question. "That is none of your damn business. I need to take a personal leave. I am under no contractual obligation to explain the reasons."

Tristan had heard quite enough. Kalli's boss did not just ask her if she was pregnant. *What the hell? Was that even legal?* Even though he hadn't wanted to leave her side, she'd insisted that he and Logan wait for her in the hallway while she explained the circumstances of her absence to her supervisor. Of course that didn't stop him from listening to the entire conversation, given his enhanced senses.

Logan raised his eyebrows at his Alpha and took a deep breath, realizing that the shit was about to hit the fan. Truthfully, Kalli's administrator seemed like a total dickhead and was about to get what was coming to him. He smiled, thinking to himself that this was going to be fun to watch.

Tristan launched out of his seat and stomped across the waiting room. To the dismay of a very concerned receptionist, Tristan opened the door to her boss's office like a wild tornado. Dr. Cramer literally jumped in his seat at the sound of his door hitting the wall. As it bounced back, he looked up to see a large, very irritated male glaring down at him.

"What are you doing in here? Who are you? Get out of here right now, before I call security," he demanded.

Tristan growled, hands fisted at his side. He restrained the beast within, which was ready to rip out the good doctor's throat.

Kalli shot to her feet, ready to pull him away. "Tristan, it's all right."

He shot her a look, warning her. "Sit, Kalli."

She found herself complying without argument. Nervously watching him, she tried to stifle the seed of excitement growing in her belly. His dominance called to her inner wolf.

"Dr. Cramer, allow me to introduce myself." Tristan leaned forward, putting his palms onto the desk.

"I'm calling security right now," the doctor tried interrupting.

Tristan grabbed the receiver from his hand and forcefully ripped the phone out of its outlet. Flecks of dry wall splattered all over the floor.

"So glad to have your attention. As I was saying, my name is Tristan Livingston." He deliberately emphasized his last name.

"Livingston? As in the Livingston Equine Rehabilitation Center?" The doctor's face paled. Mouth agape, he sat silently stunned.

"Yes, that Livingston. Now this is what's about to happen. You're going to apologize to Dr. Williams for your atrocious behavior. And if I ever hear you speak like that to her ever again, you'll be looking for more than a new job. Are we clear?"

"Yes, yes sir. I'm terribly sorry, sir. Mr. Livingston, please know that we very much appreciate your donations and contribution to our fine institution. We wouldn't be able to function without donors such as you."

Tristan rounded the desk in two seconds, grabbing the man by the scruff of his collar, lifting him out of the chair. "Apology. Now."

"Yes, yes, I'm so sorry Dr. Williams. Don't worry about a thing. Dr. Kepler can take over your caseload, and everything will be in order when you return." He actually looked like he was about to cry.

Kalli's eyes widened at the display of her Alpha's protection. *Her Alpha.* Her wolf wanted to roll over and bare her throat.

"Glad that's settled. Thanks so much for your understanding, Dr. Cramer. We'll be leaving now," Tristan snapped at him, taking Kalli's hand and gently helping her to her feet.

As they walked down the hallway, Kalli said nothing. She wasn't so much upset about what Tristan had done as she was about her reaction to it. To say she was aroused was an understatement. She swore silently as she felt the dampness in her panties.

"Tristan, I have to grab a few things from my office. Right here." She pointed to an open area, with several cubicles. "Um, I'm in here...over in the corner. Oh hi, Lindsey." She waved to a young woman whose cube was directly across from her office door.

"Hi, Dr. Kalli. Where ya been?" Lindsay, a pretty young graduate student shuffled papers behind her desk. Her long blond hair, streaked with bright red highlights, fell into her face.

Kalli had befriended Lindsey when she'd started interning over a year ago. She taught her how to help with research projects, and also the basics of day to day animal care. Kalli admired Lindsey's determination and strong work ethic. Her compassionate attitude toward the animals had her convinced Lindsey would make a fine veterinarian someday.

"Hey, just wanted you to know that I'm going to be on leave for a few weeks. If you need something, call my cell.

Also, expect a call today or tomorrow for a pickup on the yellow boa. I signed the release."

"Okay, Doc. Is there anything I can do while you're gone? I can work on compiling the statistical data for you on MAO36, but I'd need access. Is your laptop here?" she asked cheerfully.

"No, all research will go on hold until I get back. I don't want anyone messing with my data. You know how it is," Kalli called through the opening of her door. She was shoving a few files into a bag, looking through her stuff to see if there was anything she really needed to take with her. She was hoping to be back in the office within a couple of weeks, but she wasn't entirely sure when things would be back to normal. Looking over at Tristan and Logan who both seemed to be studying her overflowing bookshelf, she was pretty sure things would never be the same for her again.

"I scent wolves. Stay back," Logan directed, as he pushed open the door to Kalli's apartment. Kalli had insisted on getting a few things to wear, since she was going to stay at Tristan's. But as soon as they entered the building, the smell was so strong that even Kalli had recognized its deathly scent: wolf.

"Hey Tris, maybe you ought to take Kalli back down to the car," he suggested, eyeing the disheveled mess they'd made.

"No," she cried, pushing past Tristan. "Goddamn fucking wolves." She could not believe they'd torn her apartment apart.

"Don't hold back, Kal," Tristan joked, slightly amused at her temper. Good, she needed to get mad, pissed even. This fight wasn't going to be easy.

"Why the hell did they have to do this? I mean, if they wanted me, they could have just opened the door, had a looksee and left. Why tear everything up?" she huffed.

The sofa was torn apart, knifed. Her bookshelf had been dumped. All the kitchen cabinets had been opened; the dishes and canned goods were strewn all over the counters and floors. She sighed, looking around at the mess. Sitting on a kitchen table chair, she put her head in her hands, while Tristan and Logan poked around in the bedroom and guest room.

She couldn't believe her world was coming unhinged. Why had they made this mess? It was as if they'd been looking for something. Something important. In a split second, Kalli's heart began to race in panic as the reason for the mess became altogether apparent. *No way. No one knew. They couldn't know.* All her research had been secret. She'd told no one. No one even ever saw her take the pills. Sure, in the beginning stages of her research, she'd taken her laptop to work. She printed only a few things off, but always on her private printer and always making sure there were no copies, shredding any remaining trash.

Since the actual development of CLI, she'd stopped carrying her laptop completely. After memorizing the composition and deleting all the data off her computer, she'd stored all the information on a flash drive which she kept hidden. But if someone knew....if they knew of CLI's existence or even suspected it was possible to devise a like drug, it'd be disastrous. It wasn't as if she hadn't gone through the scenarios during its creation: its possible use by the unscrupulous as a punishment by preventing a wolf from shifting, or worse, deriving the compound into a weapon. In the wrong hands, wolves everywhere would be vulnerable.

But she couldn't be sure that's what had happened. At this point, she had to assume that the wolves most definitely had seen her leaving the fire, and knew where she worked and lived. They could have just been on a power trip, trashing her apartment to scare her. There was only one way to find out if they knew. The only other supply of pills besides what she had left at Tristan's was her emergency supply, which she also hid. And she had to look for it now without alerting Tristan and Logan.

She jumped, startling as Tristan laid his hand on her shoulder. "Kalli, the bedrooms are a mess. I'm really sorry. Do you want Logan and I to help you get a bag together?" he asked softly. No matter how tough she was, this intrusion was bound to shake her.

Standing up, she pulled away from him. The impending lie felt like a lump in her throat. If the pills or thumb drive were missing, then she had to come clean. There was just no other choice.

"Can I just have a minute alone in my room?" she asked.

"You sure?"

"Yeah. I can do this. I have to do this."

"Hey Logan," Tristan called.

"Yeah, what's up?" Logan answered, walking back into the kitchen.

"She's going back to get her things. Alone."

"I just need some privacy. A minute to think." She gave them both a small smile, which didn't reach her eyes.

"Hey Doc. I'm real sorry about this. Assholes," Logan remarked, taking in the mess all over the kitchen. Cracked eggshells and dried yolk stuck like glue to every surface.

"Yeah, I won't lie. It feels like such a violation. Strangers going through my house, tearing it up. Really, really sucks. But you know, this stuff," she gestured to her torn books, cracked pieces of china and knickknacks. "It's all just…well, it's all just stuff. As opposed to animals or people, it can all be replaced."

Logan set a comforting hand on her shoulder. At the same time, he shot Tristan a nod, careful not to overstep his boundaries. Logan loved his Alpha. He knew things were changing. He'd dreamed of Tristan's mate. But unlike his Alpha, he'd had time to mentally prepare. However, he never imagined the sense of protectiveness he'd feel toward her. Confusion swept over him as he tried to resolve why. Considering she was human, not pack, it didn't make sense to him that he felt so compelled to shield her from danger, hurt. He'd first noticed it at the hospital. While he always enjoyed watching his boss dominate, hearing Tristan attack her nasty boss had given him unusual delight. He'd known that if his Alpha hadn't intervened, he would have been the one to do it.

Tristan studied him, tamping down his unreasonable possessiveness regarding Kalli. It continued to aggravate him that he cared at all. He kept coming back to the fact that he'd just met her. On top of that, it wasn't as if he didn't ever share women with Logan, so why was this any different? Logan was more than just a friend, given how many times they'd been intimate. They never were intimate with each other sexually during their trysts, but they did touch each other, share a caress; perhaps even direct each other's play with the lucky woman. Whether it was Logan's girlfriend or Tristan's, it was always understood that neither man was with their mate. Therefore, jealousy never reared its ugly head. There were no limits.

But with Kalli, he'd felt the need to possess her, mind and body. And if he ever shared, he knew it would be on his terms only. No one would touch her without his permission, and she'd only be touched the way he commanded. It could be no other way. Tristan grew irritated as his territorial feelings grew stronger every hour he was around her. It felt uncomfortable to think about a woman in this manner, yet it seemed as natural as being born.

As Kalli caught a glimpse of Tristan observing her interaction, she pulled away from Logan's touch. She was appreciative that he cared, but guilt ate her. She had to tell them about her formula. Dreading it, she'd have to confess sooner rather than later if the flash drive or pills were missing.

"Guess I'd better get my stuff," she commented as she resigned herself to her task. Looking terribly defeated, she walked out of the kitchen. When Kalli reached her room, she locked the door. She knew that either wolf could easily break it down if they really wanted to, but they didn't seem the type who'd go bursting in on a lady in a locked bedroom.

She ran into the master bathroom, trying to avoid the shards of glass scattered all over the room. They'd smashed the mirrored closet doors as well as the sink mirror. Opening up the vanity drawers, she searched for the small pill boxes where she kept the spares. One by one, she came up empty. Her stomach lurched at the thought. *They'd stolen the CLI.*

Thinking she might vomit, she bent over at the sink and took deep breaths, willing the bile back into her stomach.

She prayed silently that they hadn't taken the thumb drive. Without the data, they probably wouldn't be able to replicate it. Even if they analyzed the chemical composition, its creation was a complicated process. And said process and all the underlying details were on that drive.

Opening the bottom of the vanity, she looked for her cosmetic bag, the one she used to hold her makeup. Cleaning supplies had been spilled inside the cabinet and the boxes of tissues had puffed up, smelling like pine and bleach. What she didn't find was the drive. Bending her knees, she squatted, scanning the entire floor. Behind the toilet, her little pink bag peeked at her. She leaned over and scooped it up; even though it was open, most of the contents were still in it. Eyeshadow. Eyeliner. Foundation. Blush. Lipstick.

"Thank God," she breathed. Her pink lipstick was still there. Gently screwing off the top, it popped open, revealing its secret compartment. The drive was safely nestled inside. She'd bought the little diversion safe on an online spy shop. Given a choice of soda cans, shaving cream and books, she'd decided on the lipstick. It was small enough that she could easily transport it, but easily concealed, especially among a collection of lipstick tubes.

Pressing it into her pocket, she exited the bathroom and went to her closet to pack a bag. After collecting some casual clothes, underwear and shoes, she unlocked the door. Luckily, she had a small bag she kept for traveling which was already stocked with toothbrush, baby powder, razor and other convenience items. With a sigh, she took once last glance at the mess that used to be her room and shut the door.

They rode in silence on the way back to Tristan's condo. Tristan and Logan had both heard the lock click as she went to retrieve her things. Why did she feel the need to lock a door unless she was doing something in secret? Something she didn't want them to know about? She hadn't changed her clothes and was barely gone for ten minutes. What was she hiding? A nagging pull at Tristan's gut reminded him that she hadn't been entirely truthful. The feeling of distrust was confirmed when she refused to look him in the eyes after they left the building. It also didn't help that he could not stop wondering about the way the wolves had torn apart her place. Sure, they could have done it out of spite, but more likely they'd been searching for something. And if that was true, then Kalli was involved up to her eyeballs in trouble.

As the elevator ascended, Tristan decided he needed a break from her. He was angry she wasn't telling him everything. If he stayed with her, he was either going to force her to tell him what the hell was going on or take her up against the wall again. While both were feasible options, neither seemed like the right thing to do. He needed space. Time to think and get his head together. Tristan really didn't want to leave her alone with another man, but even he had his limits.

When they got to his floor, he addressed Logan, ignoring Kalli completely. "I need you to stay here with Kalli for a few hours, okay? I'm goin' up to my office to do some work and then may go for a ride or hit the gym. If you need me, text me."

"No problem. Take your time," Logan replied, sensing the tension. His Alpha looked like he was about to snap. And Kalli was running a close second.

Kalli said nothing as the elevator doors closed. She dropped her bag at the door, walked into the living room and fell back into an overstuffed lounge chair that faced the long wall of ceiling to floor windows. Throwing her head back, she put her hands over her eyes and blew out a big breath. She needed to tell them about CLI.

"Hey Doc. What's going on? Wanna talk about it? I'm a good listener," Logan offered, sitting on the sofa perpendicular from her.

Removing her hands, she stared out the windows. "I've gotta talk to Tristan about what happened today."

"What happened with your boss or what happened to your apartment?"

"They were looking for something," she stated flatly.

"Yeah, I assumed as much. Pretty sure Tristan already suspects that too."

"They took something." She bent over, placing her forearms on her knees and pinching the bridge of her nose with her fingers.

"You wanna tell me what it was?" he asked, biting his upper lip. He wished she'd just spill it.

"Yes. No. Okay, yes, but I have to tell Tristan first." She sighed in frustration. "Tell me, Logan, did you ever have to tell somebody something? Something that was a really big secret? But by telling the secret, you'd be putting your own life at risk?"

He silently regarded her, well aware her life was already on the line. She was a smart woman and had to know how much danger she was in; she had agreed to stay with Tristan after all. What the hell did she know that would put her in even more danger? Whatever it was, he could tell it wasn't going to be good.

"Here's the thing, Kalli. In Lyceum Wolves, we're pack. Lies don't fly too well here. And yes, I've kept things to myself on occasion." He didn't want to mention his visions to her yet. "But I can't say it put my life in danger. If my life were in danger, my pack would be behind me, so I wouldn't keep the secret."

"How well do you know Tristan?"

"Like a brother. Hell, I know him as well as I know myself."

"So what's he really like?"

"He's badass," he boasted smiling. "Has more confidence than I've ever seen in a wolf, but it's well deserved. He's extraordinarily powerful, both physically and mentally. Fierce in battle and loyal as the day is long. And here's something you'd do well to remember; at the end of the day, he's fair. I'd even go as far as to say that he's caring."

"You love him, don't you?" she blurted out.

"Well now, aren't you the inquisitive one? Come on, Doc. Of course I love him. I'm his second. We're best friends and do almost everything together. It's our way," he revealed thoughtfully.

"Wolves?" she questioned.

"Yeah. I mean, sure, there're fights within the pack every now and then, but we live to support each other. It's how it's meant to be. The communal love and devotion, it's in our nature and whatnot. Kind of hard to explain to someone who's human, but I'm sure you feel it a little. Right?" He wanted to tell her she was Tristan's mate, but it wasn't his place. They needed to find their way to each other via their own journey.

"Yeah, but what about the brutality? You know, the forced breedings and matings? The fights for dominance? That's not so loving," she remarked directly, remembering her life in South Carolina.

"Hold on there, Doc. That's old school shit and I can assure you that it doesn't happen around here. Now, it could be part of the reason we're about to have a territory war, who knows? I can tell you that Tristan and Marcel don't schlep out our females like prostitutes. They make their own decisions about mating when they're damn ready. As for the violence, put a group of human men together and you'll see what happens isn't too much different than around here. But I'll guarantee you won't see any 'brutality' as you so delicately put it." Logan narrowed his eyes on Kalli. Where the hell was she coming up with these things? Sure, brutality was common long ago, but things had changed, in most packs anyway.

"I'm sorry, Logan. I didn't mean to insult you or the pack. I...I just have a different experience is all. I spent some time around wolves before...not here...it wasn't pleasant," she admitted.

"No offense taken. Doc, I like you. I'd like for you to stick around a little and not just because you have to. Can I give you a bit of advice?"

She rolled her eyes and smiled. "Yeah, sure. Why not? I sure as hell could use some."

"Whatever is going on with you, we'll deal with it, okay? But you've got to tell Tristan. Like soon. I'm gonna be honest with you. Your life is already in danger. So whatever little nugget you've got stowed up your sleeve, it's not going to put you more at risk. But by not showing all the cards, you could very well be putting others in danger. I know you're not pack, but you should consider joining our team so to speak," he said with a grin. "And hey, it's a pretty good team. The only requirement for membership is honesty. Other than that there's all kinds of great benefits; not only do you get the protection of a tough Alpha wolf, you get his beta. It's a twofer. Also, there are lots of great friends here, runs in the wilderness, although you might need a horse for that," he joked.

Kalli laughed softly. "I'll talk to him tonight."

He cocked his head to the side, as if not quite believing her.

"I swear," she promised, standing. "Okay, I think I'm going to go take a long hot shower and try to relax before he gets back. Thanks. I really appreciate the talk."

As he watched her walk down the hallway, Logan found himself wanting Kalli to be Tristan's mate. She was intelligent, beautiful and full of life. The more time he spent with her the more it confirmed his visions. But he worried about her reasons for lying, sensing something very, very bad had happened to her. If he had to guess, he'd say she'd been abused. Something drove her fear of wolves, yet she exhibited a knowledge of wolves that could only be learned by spending a lot of time with a pack. The subtle way she lowered her gaze around Tristan told him she'd been with an Alpha.

But up until just now, she wouldn't readily admit she'd been around a pack. Why? Was she afraid of the 'brutality' she'd referred to in their conversation? Had a wolf done something horrible to her or her family? Now that he thought of it, she hadn't mentioned her family. Her entire being was wrapped up in her work. None of it made sense. But he prayed she'd come clean soon. She was wrapped tight. And Tristan. Shit. He'd been coming unglued since the minute he'd met her. Things were getting out of hand. The pack, including Kalli, needed to be strong if they were going to prevail.

A text came across the screen of his phone, slamming him back into reality. As he read the words, he shook his head. Knowing that Tristan was receiving the information at the same time, he took a deep breath and blew it out. Things were about to get real serious but quickly, and Kalli had better get ready to provide his Alpha with the truth as soon as he got home.

Tristan slammed down the weights. The text from Logan's investigator was the last damn straw. No past on a Dr. Kalli Williams since college. Everyone who was a real person had a past; good or bad, exciting or boring, rough or easy, it existed. On the contrary, people who didn't leave a paper trail of their past, were hiding something, possibly using another person's identity. They were liars. He'd like to pretend it wasn't a significant finding, but he just couldn't.

There was no doubt that the beautiful woman he knew, the one who'd gone to school for eight years in New York, who'd been working at UVH, was Dr. Williams. But before that, there was nothing. No birth certificate. No driver's license. Not a high school diploma. And then poof, one day Kalli Williams is a freshman at NYU. It was if she materialized out of the freakin' air.

Goddammit. Kalli was driving him crazy. He wanted to scream at her. Make her tell him the truth. At the same time, he wanted to fuck her senseless. The situation was maddening. What the hell was she lying about and why the hell wouldn't she tell him? Her apartment was totally trashed, and she was as cool as a cucumber. 'Things can be replaced' his ass. Who says that anyway? She'd had to leave her job. Her shit was destroyed. You'd need a fucking jackhammer to get the eggshells off the cabinets. Hell, the entire apartment would need to be gutted.

And what was her reaction? She calmly went to her bedroom and packed a bag. Seriously? Oh, and she'd locked the door while doing it. The million dollar question was why and what was she doing in there? When she'd returned, she'd refused to look him in the eye. Like a cat on a hot tin roof, she'd scampered out of the building. During the torturous car ride home, she'd said nothing, pensively staring out the window.

He was so damn mad that he could have thrown the hundred pound barbell through the window. Instead, he grabbed his towel, wiped it across his face and headed toward the locker-room. Fuck. He needed to get laid. Blow off some steam. He knew Mira would be down for anything he asked for sexually; she'd do whatever he wanted. If not Mira, others were willing and ready to service him. With a text, there was nothing he couldn't have. A one on one. Threesomes. The women were plenty. Wolves, humans and even vamps, as longs as they didn't bite, there'd been a time when he'd have been up for it. The women were available and willing twenty-four seven. And he was an equal opportunity lover…used to be, anyway.

Therein lay the rub; he wasn't that person anymore. For the past couple of years, he'd quietly made love to Sydney on the side; sometimes indulging with Logan and Mira. Was it a release? Yes. But was it fulfilling? Was his wolf at peace? Unequivocally no. But what was he supposed to do? Go in search of a mate? So not happening. He was happy with the freedom of knowing he could do what he wanted, when he wanted, and wasn't about to give that up. He wouldn't submit to a forced pairing, something that was done in the old days. It'd never feel natural. He'd be trapped like a zoo animal, never again allowed to run in the wild.

But meeting the good Doc had flipped his world upside down, and he wasn't sure it was in a good way. Within twenty-four hours, he'd gone from cool and confident to hot and horny, unable to think straight. He wanted to strip her, flip her and fuck her and not necessarily in that order. But then there was that damn thing that was stopping him, his conscience. How could he make love with her, knowing she was lying to him? He was pretty sure that she wasn't even *Kalli Williams*. Not that he needed to know the name of every woman he'd been with but when he had the Doc, he was going to make love to her hard and long. And he'd be damned if he'd do it not being able to call her by her real name when he sank deep inside her.

That settled it. There was no other option; he had to find out what she'd been keeping secret. No matter what it took, he needed to find out, deal with it and then get it together, so he could concentrate on finding the asshole who'd burnt down the club. And at this point, it wasn't just about the club. One of Marcel's wolves was dead, and they had no idea if it was even related. Kat was in hiding. There were too many loose ends. Unanswered questions and lies in the air.

Stomping into the bathroom, he flipped on a spigot. Tristan tried to shake off the feeling of foreboding that blanketed him as the hot spray of the shower danced on his skin. He planned to go back to his apartment and interrogate Kalli. He didn't want to hurt her but the responsibility of the pack settled on his shoulders. The truth was coming, and he'd see it realized.

⋘ *Chapter Twelve* ⋙

As Tristan strode through the elevator, ready to tear into her, demanding an explanation, he stopped short. *Candlelight? Garlic? Tomatoes? Shit. What did she do? And where the hell was Logan?* The anger he'd spent the last three hours building was melted away within seconds as it dawned on him that she'd cooked him dinner. No one, aside from his mother, had cooked him dinner. Sure, many a woman had tried, but he'd always managed to avoid the experience, knowing full well what it represented: commitment, love, marriage. His jaw fell open as he walked toward the heavenly scent. *No way.* He rubbed his hand across his face in disbelief.

Shock would be the best word Tristan could use to describe the surreal situation he'd walked into. Fully anticipating questioning her until she spilled the truth, he found his mind going haywire, like he'd stuck his finger in an electrical socket. Logically, he knew he should tell her they needed to talk now, force the argument to happen. But the food…the wine…and where did all the candles come from? He owned candles? And what was she dressed in? Boy shorts and a camisole, covered with an apron? What kind of woman cooked in underwear? He smiled, shaking his head at the sheer absurdity of the situation.

Kalli was bent over his stove languidly stirring a boiling pot. And yet again, the globes of her creamy ass beamed at him as the back of her apron rode up her back. The length of him immediately reacted at the sight of her. Of all the things he'd expected tonight, this was the very last thing he'd envisioned.

"Kalli?" He muttered, at a loss for words. "Where's Logan?"

"Hi there. He left just a minute ago; said he knew you were in the building," she explained, continuing to stir the pasta.

Tristan growled softly to himself, irritated that Logan had left her alone. He'd talk to him later.

"So, I hope you don't mind but I thought I'd cook us dinner tonight. Kind of like a thank you for saving my ass from Alexandra. Nothing fancy."

"Yeah, okay," he responded, walking toward her as if he was caught in a magnetic ray.

Kalli stopped stirring for a minute to look at Tristan. She'd been thinking all afternoon about how to tell him everything about her past, the formula and most importantly, the *stolen* CLI. She was terrified of the kind of violence she'd grown up with, never knowing when her old Alpha would strike. Even if Tristan managed to control his anger, she considered the possibility that she'd lose his protection, that he would toss her out to the wolves...literally.

As her gaze fell upon him, she instinctually lowered her eyes, letting them roam down his chest to his feet and up again. She sighed and briefly closed her eyes, as her belly pooled with desire. Tristan looked incredibly sexy in his tight white t-shirt and loose jeans. She looked to his feet, which were clad in black military boots. In his left hand he carried a black motorcycle helmet, and she wondered what kind of bike he rode. Rolling her eyes in an effort to gain her own composure, she reasoned she didn't care what kind of bike he had. She'd ride him, um, ride with him, any day of the week. She could feel her panties dampen at the thought. Clenching her thighs together, she prayed he wouldn't know how wet she was from just looking at him. *Get it together, Kalli.* He's going to know that instead of this wonderful dinner, you'd rather eat him right here, right now, she thought embarrassedly. He's Alpha. He'll know.

Kalli decided changing the subject was in order and looked back to the stove. She struggled to get her composure. "So yeah, I was going a little stir crazy being cooped up in here. Um, I mean not that your home isn't beautiful. It's really nice, warm and open feeling. I've never actually been to a penthouse before....you know, the kind where the elevator door just opens up into the apartment," she rambled.

She knew things were about to come to a head and figured that maybe if she tried opening up a little about herself, just crack that steel door on her past, just a tiny bit, maybe he'd soften.

"I actually like to cook, but I'm all by myself, so I don't ever really get to it. My mom," her voice became softer at the memory, "she was Greek. She was a wonderful cook. Made all kinds of great stuff. She was really amazing. I wish I'd paid attention."

"Where is she? Your mom?" Tristan asked, treading carefully, realizing that this was an in to his line of questioning.

"She's dead. She died when I was only fourteen. It was really hard losing her. Dad's gone too. Died when I was seventeen. I've got no family, well, blood related anyway."

She stopped stirring the pasta and turned to grab the romaine lettuce that'd been drying on a paper towel. "I really work a lot. And I co-run a no-kill shelter, so whenever I get the time, I'm there. I consider the animals my family. I need them as much as they need me. I'd really love to have my own pets someday, but I spend too many crazy hours away from my apartment. And my apartment isn't that great for animals anyway. It's small, doesn't have a yard, you know. Well, I guess I could do a cat, but it's not fair to the animal if I'm not there."

"Do you like horses?" Tristan sidled up to her, watching her chop the lettuce and toss it into a bowl. He wanted to discuss her parents, but he could tell she'd been on the verge of tears when she'd mentioned her mother dying. He figured if she started talking about her life, she'd continue to share with him what happened.

"Oh yeah, I love them. Of course, I never had any growing up, but I did do an equine rotation. By the way, I didn't say anything at the time, but I'm really impressed that you funded the rehab center. It's a terrific facility; helps so many horses. We should go there sometime and tour it. It's funny, I know all about it, but because it's so far outside the city, I just never get there." Kalli stopped talking after suggesting plans for the future…a future with Tristan in it.

Tristan smiled, catching her slip. Before there was any kind of a future for them, he needed facts. He could tell she was trying, but he needed more. He needed honesty.

"Yeah, sure, we could go to the center. We could ride, too, if you want. Hit the trails," he suggested.

"Really? We can ride? Oh my gosh, that would be so great. I did get to do it a few times when I was in school, but never for long, and I wasn't with a friend," she exclaimed excitedly.

Tristan smiled broadly this time, gazing into her wide eyes. She was like a child who'd been told she could go to an amusement park. It was almost as if she'd missed out on a lot in life and was getting an opportunity to live, experience. His heart squeezed at the tragic thought.

"Sure thing," he replied, picking up the salad she'd created. He walked over to the table and set it down.

"Um, so, I also thought we could talk after dinner. I, uh, I have some things I need to tell you. But let's eat first, okay?" she croaked. She was not looking forward to the conversation.

"Yeah, sounds great," Tristan struggled to reply, deciding that it could wait thirty minutes so they could eat dinner. He could see that she was getting ready to tell him, and he preferred for her to submit on her own and tell him without a quarrel. But if it was the last thing he did today, he would have verity from her within the hour.

Somehow, they'd made it through dinner without choking or ripping each other's clothes off. Both of which seemed possible considering the incendiary tension that threatened to combust the room. After everything was cleaned up, the time of reckoning had arrived. There were no more dishes to wash or food to put away. It was just Tristan and Kalli and the truth waiting to be told.

Tristan walked over to the sliding glass doors, sensing her hesitation. She'd cleaned the countertop and stove from top to bottom, procrastinating in order to avoid the inevitable. He was done waiting. As he was about to call her over, she nervously played with her hair then untied the apron, revealing a hot pink cami and black boy shorts. All the blood rushed to his cock, responding to the sight of the second skin material. Jesus, she was killing him. He prayed their talk would go quickly so he could peel her out of her barely-there excuse for clothing.

He pointed his finger at her and then crooked it, indicating it was time. He knew it. She knew it. He could hear her heartbeat quicken as she closed the space between them. Her breath hitched as she met Tristan's eyes. His finger beckoned her to join him. Her legs were moving before she thought she'd said yes. By the time she was within a few feet, he slid open the door.

"Come, Kalli. Let's talk," he instructed. He held out his hand gesturing for her to go outside.

"I…I can't go out there," she stuttered. "I'm not even dressed. Well not really." She was petrified of heights. The entire time she'd stayed with him she'd avoided the windows as much as possible. The view was lovely but her stomach dropped as soon as she got within a foot of the glass.

"Yes you will, Kalli. Truth. Now. Why don't you want to go?"

A test?

She looked down to her feet and then met his eyes yet again. She crossed her arms protectively across her chest. "Okay, fine. I hate heights. Satisfied? Let's just stay in here…please," she begged.

"No, Kalli. We're going outside. It's a beautiful night. Very few people get to see the city like this, alone on a Penthouse balcony. Call it my gift to you."

"Gift? I don't understand how…"

"As long as you live in my home, my building, I am your Alpha. You accepted this when you accepted my protection. The wolves, I protect them too. Guide them when necessary. From the youngest pup to the eldest grandwolf, I have their best interests in mind in everything I do. This is your gift. Teaching you to trust your Alpha. Now come to me, Kalli," he demanded with a smooth sexy voice.

It seemed as if there was nothing she'd consider denying him as she reached for his hand.

"That's it, chére. Come with me," he encouraged as he led her outside. He chuckled as she looped her arm within his, clutching him tightly.

She tried concentrating on her breathing in an effort to calm the fear that threatened to take over her sense of reason. As her bare feet touched the warm terracotta tiles, she closed her eyes.

"See how nice it is? There's nothing better than a warm September night." He looked down at Kalli to see that her eyes were completely shut tight.

"Cheating are we?" he laughed. "Okay, brave girl. Close your eyes all you want, for now. But I've got something I want to show you, and you will open your eyes," he stated confidently.

As he led her over to the wrought iron fence, he smiled. "All right, come on, turn around for me."

Extricating his arm from her deathly grip, he gently took her by the waist and slowly turned her toward the skyline. He peeked at her and saw she still wasn't looking. She was a stubborn little thing, he thought to himself. What fun it was going to be breaking her of that habit. He planned on teaching her a lesson she'd not soon forget.

Placing his hands on her shoulders, he rubbed them gently. A small moan escaped her lips. "That's it baby, relax. I want you to enjoy my gift." With a final caress, he let his hands roam down her bare arms, never losing contact with her skin. When he reached her hands, he pulled them over to the fence and placed her palms on the cool iron bars. He proceeded to wrap each of her fingers around the metal until she fully grasped it.

Sliding his hands around her waist, he pressed his body against her until the hard bulge of his erection was nestled into the crease of her bottom. She released a small gasp at his delightful intrusion.

"Okay, Kalli. It's time. You can do this. Your Alpha is with you. And you're safe. I won't let anything happen to you. You must trust me. Ready? One, two, three. Open your eyes. Now," he demanded.

By the time her eyes flew open, she was so aroused she'd forgotten where she even was. With Tristan holding her waist, and her hands clasped to the bars, she let her fear go and gasped at the incredible sight. The city vista danced with lights to an orchestra of urban music. It was magnificent, like nothing she'd never experienced.

"Tristan, oh my God. It's beautiful. Thank you," she breathed, aware that she truly had been given a gift, one that she'd never have experienced if it weren't for Tristan and the trust she put in him.

"What do you see Kalli?" he asked.

"Lights, buildings, shadows…" she wasn't sure of what he meant.

"Yes, all that is true. But let me tell you what I see. I see my city, my wolves. I see my responsibility. And whether my wolves are up the mountains or in the city, they know they can trust me to lead them and protect them. And you Kalli, you can trust me too."

"Yes, I know," she moaned again. She trusted him. But part of her was done talking; she simply wanted this man. "I have to tell you. Tristan...my apartment. They took something. Something really important."

"What, chére? What did they take?"

"Pills. My medicine. But I'm afraid... I need...I need..." She took one of her hands off the iron and reached behind her to touch his thigh.

Something in Tristan snapped. He knew he should keep up with her confession, but the feel of her warm hand on his thigh, mere inches from his hard arousal, flared his desire. His fingers slid under her stretchy cotton cami, until his hands were full with her soft breasts. He gently pinched her nipples, enjoying the feel of her tender, excited flesh.

Kalli released a loud breath at Tristan's touch. The sweet sting sent a rush of desire to her core. Needing more, she wriggled backward, relishing the feel of his cock on her ass.

"Yes, please," she begged.

"Ma chérie, what do you need? Tell me," he whispered into her ear. As the word, 'chérie' left his lips, he briefly took note of what he'd called her. It was a term he'd reserved only for a girlfriend. Intellectually, he knew that she wasn't, but his body disagreed.

"Please. Please touch me. I want you."

She was begging for him to take her. At her admission, Tristan groaned. He swore his dick was going to tear through his zipper as it pulsed in exhilaration. He promised himself he wouldn't make love to her without knowing everything, but that didn't mean he couldn't get a small taste. While sprinkling small kisses behind her ear, he slipped his hand into her panties. Stroking his forefinger into her slick folds, he ground into her from behind. Damn, he felt as if was going to come in his pants like a teenager.

"Fuck Kalli, you are so wet for me," he grunted. He slowly brushed her clit back and forth, loving the feel of her smooth skin.

"Tristan, yes," she cried. The touch on her bundle of nerves sent chills through her body; she could feel the precipice of her orgasm within reach. She didn't want to come so quickly but she could no longer control her own body. He was powerful and sexual and Alpha. And she wanted all of him.

He was teasing her, circling her nub then backing off. Reaching down further, he finally plunged two long fingers into her hot sheath, thumbing her clit. "Ah, that's it, baby. Take my hand. You are so damn tight."

She was panting hard. The city lights flashed in the sky, horns beeped. As soon as he penetrated her, Kalli's body exploded as the wave of a release crashed over her. She shook in orgasm, while he supported her body with his arm, clutched her waist.

"Tristan, yes!" She screamed, unable and unwilling to restrain her emotion.

"Ma chérie, you're so beautiful when you come," he crooned as he spun her around to face him.

Without giving her a chance to recover, Tristan quickly kissed her. It was a hard, forceful kiss that let Kalli know that he was her Alpha. She responded in kind by hugging her arms around his neck and jumped to wrap her legs around his waist, while he supported her butt. Their lips sucked and bit, tongues dancing with each other. Kalli had officially lost control. Her wolf cried, begging to be released. This man was hers; she'd give up anything to be with him, even being human.

"Tristan." A male voice called from inside.

"Ignore it," Tristan growled as Kalli bared her neck to him. His wolf howled at the submission. He gently bit at her throat, alternately licking and kissing it.

"Tristan!" Logan yelled again. He stopped still, watching Tristan and Kalli on the balcony. *Was she submitting to him?* He wished he didn't have to interrupt the intimate and very erotic sight of his Alpha at her neck, but he had no choice.

"Tristan," he repeated softly as he approached them. He knew Tristan was far gone and his wolf would consider attacking him, given the interference.

"Go away, Logan. Not now," Tristan ordered without turning around.

"Tristan, it's Toby and Ryan. Something's happened. We've got to go now."

⤳❀ *Chapter Thirteen* ❀⤶

Tristan had hauled ass on his bike, knowing city traffic could be a bitch by car. In the rush, he'd forgotten his helmet, but took off anyway. He asked Logan to drive Kalli, so they'd be there shortly. But he couldn't wait; nothing mattered, but the kids. He barreled into the Intensive Care Unit, seeking out a nurse.

"Ryan Pendleton. Toby Smith. Where are they?" Tristan more demanded than asked.

A young nurse peered up at him, while still typing into the computer. "I'll be with you in one second," she replied. After a few more key strokes, she looked up at him expectantly. "And you are?"

"Their father," Tristan bit out angrily. Toby and Ryan should not be in the hospital. Wolves rarely ended up in a human hospital, given their extraordinary healing powers. Generally, most injuries could be healed with a shift. And in other cases, they paid witches who could help with healing spells.

The nurse eyed him over and came around the desk. "Come with me, please," she instructed. "Their mother is already here."

Tristan assumed she meant Julie, who he'd been advised was already at the hospital. As they walked down the hallway, he caught sight of Detective Tony Bianchi, talking with doctors and nurses. *What was he doing here?*

The nurse pointed on the left. "Here we are."

"Ma'am, what's his condition?" Tristan asked quietly. He could see through the long rectangular window, Ryan appeared unconscious.

"The doctor has explained his condition to your wife, um, their mother," she corrected. "He came in with multiple gunshots. One in the leg. Another to his shoulder. The hits weren't in vital areas, but he lost a considerable amount of blood. So we're keeping an eye on him here for a while before transferring him down to Med-Surg."

"And Toby?"

"Sir, I'm terribly sorry," she said looking to her watch. "I'll send the doctor down to speak with you as soon as she's done with the detective. You go on in now....only two people at a time, okay? The doctor will be right with you, I promise."

A surge of grief hit Tristan upon hearing her words. He'd been around long enough to know that the nurse was avoiding telling him that Toby was dead. As he pushed his power outward in search of the boy, there was nothing. His jaw tightened in anger. He wanted to force the nurse to tell him more, but through the glass, he could see Julie crying. She needed him. And so did Ryan. Goddammit, why hadn't the boys just shifted?

Julie looked up through puffy eyes, tears still evident on her face. She rushed into his arms. "Alpha, thank God you're here. The boys. Ryan, he's better. But Toby. Oh God, Toby," she cried. "They killed him. He's dead."

Hearing the actual words of Toby's death felt like someone had shot him; his gut burned in grief. It wasn't possible. How could he be dead? Both boys were like sons to him. He and Logan had unofficially adopted them when they were just pups, late teenagers really. They'd lost their parents in a territorial fight, and Tristan found them wandering the city streets. He took them into his pack, gave them shelter and food, sent them to school. The other mothers in the pack helped raised them. Pack was like that. It was everyone's responsibility to help raise pups. A parent was never left short of support.

Tristan held Julie, hysterically crying in his arms. He stared at Ryan, praying to the Goddess that it wasn't true. It didn't make sense. Gunshots could seriously damage a wolf, but a shift would surely heal most wounds. It could take several shifts before they were truly back to normal functioning, but most wolves survived.

Filled with rage and sorrow, Tristan stoically shoved his emotions away. He'd deal with it later. Right now, his pack needed their Alpha. The calm in the storm, he'd guide them out of the pain.

"Julie, what happened to Toby? Have you talked with Ryan?" he inquired.

Wiping her tears, Julie sat down again next to Ryan and held his hand. "Toby was shot, multiple times. But I think they may have used a knife," she cried; her voice wavered. "The doctor wouldn't let me see him. Whatever it was, it was awful."

Tristan moved to the other side of the bed, sat in a chair and took Ryan's hand. He stopped and sniffed Ryan's wrist.

"Did you smell it?" he questioned her with a firm voice.

"I know, Alpha. He smells…he smells…"

"Human." Tristan finished her words as she nodded in confirmation. "What the hell happened? We both know he's wolf."

"He took something," Julie replied. "Before you ask, I don't know what it was. He was awake for like a minute and said they'd been at a college party all afternoon. He and Toby took something…a drug."

"This doesn't make any sense. I know my boys; they don't take drugs."

"I know. But what else could it be? Something had to do this to him."

Tristan shook his head in confusion. None of it seemed real. Sensing Logan, he worried they would make it down to the room, given the rules. But then again, a little rule breaking was the least of their problems. Before he had a chance to ask Julie to go get Logan, both Logan and Kalli came into the room.

"Sorry we're late. Traffic was a killer as usual. Had to sneak in here 'cause they said only two people were allowed, so I arranged for a distraction. What is going on with…" Logan's words ended abruptly as he noticed it too. He rushed toward the bed and sniffed. "What's wrong with Ryan? What did they give him? He smells…" Perplexed, Logan ran a hand over Ryan's forehead in concern.

"Human. I know. We smell it too. Julie said he may have taken something," Tristan added.

"Where's Toby?"

"He didn't make it. He's gone."

Logan stumbled toward a chair in shock. "No, no, no."

Julie ran over to Logan and hugged him as they both wept openly.

Anxiety seized Kalli as she came to terms with what must have happened. There was no way in hell someone went from wolf to human without intervention; without CLI. Someone had taken her pills, and that same someone had given them to Tristan's wolves. Someone took the CLI, and used it as a weapon just like she'd imagined in her worst nightmares. Her heart sank in guilt and anger. Like it or not, she had to confess.

"CLI. Canis Lupine Inhibitor," Kalli whispered. "It's why he smells human."

Stunned, Tristan turned to Kalli. *Did she just say she knew why Ryan scented human?* How did she know this? Missing pills. On the balcony. She'd said that they took something from her apartment. His vision tunneled onto her, and for a few seconds, he felt as if he was seeing things through a kaleidoscope. Kalli was involved in Toby's murder?

Before he realized what was happening, he'd sprung out of his seat, growling. Logan jumped in between them, holding up his hands. "Calm down, Tris. Just let her explain," he pleaded.

"You knew about this?" Tristan accused Logan.

"No, I don't know anything. But we need her help. She might be able to help him or at the very least, tell us what the hell is going on."

"By all fucking means, Dr. Williams, which probably isn't even your real name, explain away. I mean, one of our young wolves is dead. And Ryan, here, is apparently human. For once, I'd like the damn truth," Tristan yelled at her.

Both Julie and Logan cringed slightly upon hearing his voice raised. Tristan was consistently calm, even during the most tense discussions or negotiations. But Toby's death had sent him completely off the edge; he was boiling over in anger.

Kalli, unable to deal with the situation on a personal level, reverted back into her professional persona. The only way she could deal with violence or death was to compartmentalize the information, otherwise she'd simply break down in tears, especially knowing it was her formula that had caused this. She straightened her spine, readying to face the Alpha.

"I tried to tell you earlier, Tristan. You know I did. But we...we ended up, you know what happened," Kalli insisted. "Can I look at Ryan? I mean, I need to see him to be sure."

Tristan nodded furiously and gestured for her to move toward the bed. He was pissed at her, and he was pissed at himself for fooling around on the damn balcony. He should have pressed for all of the truth but instead, he was weak. He darted his eyes to Kalli, watching her grab a stethoscope off the wall. She inserted the ear tips and began pulling open Ryan's hospital gown.

"I'm sorry Tristan. So sorry I didn't tell you everything but I was scared. And now," She looked down to Ryan. "Well, you wanted the truth? Here it is...the sad horrible truth. I told you that my parents died, but what I didn't tell you was that I was pack. That's right. My son of a bitch father was wolf, and my mother was human. And I was a lowly hybrid. Cross that. I was a lowly hybrid, who managed to survive abuse day after day. I was the hybrid that the great, almighty Alpha planned to utilize as concubine for the wolves who weren't allowed to breed. I hated that pack and everyone in it. So I ran far and wide. Changed my identity. But it wasn't enough. I needed to be human. Nothing else would do. They'd find me. Excuse me a minute."

Kalli stopped to listen to Ryan's heart. Then she picked up his wrist to listen to his pulse. Tristan and Logan stared at her in disbelief as she continued her confession. "I've been working on the formula ever since I was in grad school, but it wasn't until two years ago that I perfected it. No more shifting during full moons, waking up alone naked in the woods. No more fear of being discovered and dragged back to that hellhole. For once in my life, I could just live quietly with my work and my animals."

Kalli pushed the hair out of her face, and walked over to the other side of the bed. Her voice started to waver as tears brimmed her eyes. "And if I hadn't gone for a walk that day, saved your damn snake, I'd still be living that way. But that wasn't in the cards. The wolves I saw, they're from my old pack; I recognized the faces. As for the pills, someone, I don't know who, knows about my research. It's what they were looking for. They took my spare pills, and it's without a doubt what is running through this boy. But after looking at him, it appears that they didn't give him a full dose. Maybe they slipped it in his drink and he didn't drink it all?"

Kalli pulled the ophthalmoscope off the wall, lifted Ryan's eyelids and examined him. "I'd say, from my experience of taking CLI, he should be able to shift in another two to four hours. It's wearing off already. Whoever gave this to them knew what it was supposed to do. They probably were testing it, wanted to see if he could shift when injured, because that is exactly what this drug does, prevents shifting." Kalli sighed, looking to the exit.

She'd had enough: enough lies, enough violence, enough of pack. But at least it was out in the open; they all knew. And even though she was terrified the wolves from her old pack would find her, the worst thing was how Tristan was looking at her; she couldn't bear it. She feared that he'd never forgive her. Even though she hadn't intentionally set out to hurt him or anyone in his pack, her creation had killed that boy. Sure, it kept her hidden from others who'd see her dead, but now someone out there was using it to kill wolves.

Feeling as if she was going to be sick, she made toward the door. She had to go. She didn't belong here with Tristan or his wolves. After everything she'd told him, she wouldn't be surprised if he loathed her.

Tristan balled his fists at his sides, reeling from her confession. She was a fucking wolf and hadn't told him. He wanted to hate her, yet his wolf wouldn't allow it. But his human side was enraged. He watched in astonishment as she tried to leave the room, without even discussing it. *So not happening, Doctor.*

"And where the hell do you think you're going, Kalli? Is that even your real name?" he sneered.

"I told you that I had to change my identity. I had no choice. They'd find me. But just so you know, Kalli is my real name. Williams isn't, but I'm still the same person inside. And for all intents and purposes, Dr. Williams is who I am," she countered, stifling a sob.

"It's one thing to lie to me, but don't lie to yourself. You aren't human, no matter how much you want it or how many of these pills you take," he spat at her. "I can't talk to you right now. Fine, you want to go; then just go. Get out of my sight. I can't even look at you. Logan, take her to your condo. Move her things."

"I'll just go to a hotel…"

"The hell you will. Listen to me, Doctor, like it or not, I may need you to find the sons of bitches who did this…the fire…Toby's murder," he choked out, trying not to scream. "You're not safe. If anything, you're in even more danger.

They know where you live; where you work…I will not lose you." Tristan shook with passion, well aware that he still wanted her badly. Conflicted, he needed space. As much as he hated the idea of her staying with another man, he knew he could trust Logan with his life.

As she realized that Tristan no longer wanted her, Kalli's heart felt like it was breaking into a million pieces. Filled with shame and disappointment, she deserved it, she thought. But, still, how could he send her off to live with another wolf? Logically, she shouldn't have been surprised given how she was raised, and the way the males treated the females. It was just that with Tristan, he seemed so progressive, kind…loving, even. Feeling downcast, she silently accepted that she'd have to move. Why bother arguing? He needed her to help him find the killers. She needed his protection. So she had to stay with Logan. Who else would she stay with anyway?

Raking her fingers through her long hair, she looked at Logan. "I've gotta get out of here. I'll be in the waiting room. Come get me when you're ready." Casting Tristan a sorrowful look, she walked out of the room, fairly certain that he and Logan wouldn't try to stop her. It would cause a scene and she was pretty sure they didn't want that.

Tristan considered going after her, but the doctor entered the room at the same time. Concerned that they already had too many people in the room, he looked to Julie to leave. With a nod, she understood, and left.

The doctor looked to be about forty years old with short, thick curly hair, wearing a traditional white coat with her name embroidered on it. Regarding the two males, she extended a hand to Tristan. "Hello, I'm Dr. Shay. The nurse said she'd filled you in on Ryan's injuries. He's a lucky kid," she commented, looking down at her patient. "Almost bled out, but we got to him before he hit hypovolemic shock, so he's going to make it. Both shots were fairly clean, in and out, but apparently he sat in the alley for quite a bit before someone found him. So we're going to keep him here for a few more hours just as a precaution, then he'll be transferred down to the fourth floor. Once he's released, he'll have to come back for follow-up to have the stitches removed. My biggest concern right now is the risk of wound infection. Even though we cleaned it out, bacterial infections still occur. Do you have any questions?"

"Yes, it is my understanding that anything we discuss needs to be kept in confidence, is this correct?" Tristan asked, already knowing the answer.

"Yes, that's right," she replied.

"I'm going to tell you something, and I don't want you to repeat it, not even to the nurse. Nor do I want it entered into his record," Tristan explained. "I'm not sure how much experience you have with supernaturals, but I'm Tristan Livingston, Alpha of Lyceum Wolves. And this boy, he's mine."

The doctor flushed at the revelation. "Why yes, of course I'm aware that there's others. Those who aren't human. But sir....well, there's no way he's wolf. I just operated on him, so I think I'd know if he weren't human. No, this can't be," she protested.

"Well, Doc. Sometimes things aren't always as they appear." He shot a look at Logan who knew he meant Kalli. "And when that happens, it truly is a bitter pill to swallow. Let's just say that I've come into knowledge that Ryan, here, was exposed to something very dangerous that thwarted both his shifting and his natural healing abilities.

Both of which would have prevented him from visiting your fine establishment. We think he's going to shift in a few hours, and we'd like to stay with him until he does. Afterwards, we're going to walk out the front door."

"Well, I don't know. But I guess if he shifts, then I can't really oppose his release, but I'll need to examine him first," she insisted.

"Thank you for your cooperation. But there's one more thing. That dangerous thing Ryan was exposed to...I need you to keep a tight lid on it until we find out who gave it to him. Tony...Detective Bianchi. We're going to have to meet with him too. He'll back up what I'm telling you. We're looking at a murder."

The doctor nodded solemnly. "Yes, I just spoke with the detective, but as I told him, I didn't see the other boy. He was found dead on the scene. The paramedics said he'd been shot and stabbed quite badly. I'm very sorry for your loss."

"Thank you," Tristan said quietly. The meeting with Jax Chandler couldn't come soon enough. When he found the wolves Kalli had helped to sketch, they'd die a slow death at his hand.

The doctor exited the room, leaving Tristan and Logan. No words could describe the loss of Toby. All that was left to do was to wait until Ryan shifted so they could find out what had happened. How did he even get the drug? He knew Ryan and Toby partied hard, but nothing that most college students didn't do. They never took drugs; he'd scent in a minute if they'd tried. No, someone gave this to them without them knowing, perhaps as Kalli had suggested in a drink or maybe even food.

The vigil was broken as Ryan stirred in his bed. Slowly opening his eyes, he licked his dry lips.

Logan rushed to hold his hand, while Tristan stood on the other side of the bed. He rubbed his hand over Ryan's matted hair, and leaned in to talk to him.

"Take it easy, Ryan. You're safe. We're all here with you," Tristan comforted him.

Tears filled Ryan's eyes. "Toby...he didn't make it," he whispered, weeping silently. "We couldn't shift."

"We know, Ry, we know. Trust me, we'll grieve. And we'll avenge his death. I promise you. But right now, I need to know what happened. Who drugged you?"

"We were at a party. Nothing big. A girl. Lindsey. She asked us if we wanted to take something. You know us, we said no. I swear it," Ryan asserted. His eyes locked on Tristan's. "We stayed for another beer, and left to go home. We walked. We always walk. Two men. Wolves. They had a gun and backed us into an alley. We knew we could've taken them, Tristan. But then we couldn't shift. We tried to run, but our wolves wouldn't come. I hid in a dumpster after I got hit, but Toby..." his voice trailed off as he looked away and closed his eyes.

"You listen to me, Ryan. This wasn't your fault. Someone drugged you. There's no way you could have known. You need to rest now. Kalli said you'd be able to shift in a few hours. Afterward, we'll get out of here. See...Julie's here. Logan's here. We're all here for you. And when we get home, you know you'll be pawing off the pack mothers; they're never going to let you out of their sight. We'll make it through this."

Lindsay? Wasn't that the name of the girl from Kalli's office? He planned asking Tony to send someone over to

UVH to find her. Tristan stood and turned toward the door in an attempt to hide the pain that threatened to rip him in half. Listening to Ryan recount what had happened through guilt-tinged tears killed him. It shouldn't be this way for them. They were only kids, yet someone deliberately went after his pups. Killed Toby. One thing was certain, blood was about to rain down in his city and it would be Lyceum Wolves who shed it this time. There'd be nothing sweet about this revenge, but it would happen.

"Logan, keep an eye on Ryan. I've gotta find Tony," Tristan grunted. He needed to tell him everything he knew about what had happened. There was no way in hell he'd let P-CAP take over the investigation. For all they knew, a human had been shot and killed. But on the off chance they decided to become involved, he'd call Léopold and seek his assistance. As much as he despised Alexandra, he knew he could count on her as an ally.

As he rounded the corner, he caught sight of Tony engaged in an intimate conversation with Kalli. *What the hell?* She nodded her head in agreement to whatever he'd just said to her. Her baby blue eyes, rimmed in red from crying, were focused on the detective.

Without a doubt, Detective Tony Bianchi, Sydney's former homicide partner, was one of the best cops in the city. Tenacious but good natured, the good-looking Italian detective never left a clue unturned. But Tristan could tell by the looks of him, that tonight he'd seen Toby's body. His dark, olive-skinned face appeared to be drawn and his cropped raven hair was no longer carefully coiffed. Like a bloodhound knowing where to find his bone buried deep in the yard, Tony was busy digging for his next lead.

Tristan ground his teeth as Tony put a comforting hand on Kalli's shoulder. She began to cry once again, and he could see that she was hurting too. Tristan wanted to be the man holding her, telling her everything would be all right. Deep down, he also knew that part of the reason she was coming unglued was because of him. Instead of mauling her on the balcony like a sex-starved maniac, he should have let her finish telling him the truth. He'd told her she could trust him, but the minute she'd confessed, he'd laid into her and ordered her to stay with another man. He felt like an asshole, but he could only deal with so many things at once. Coughing loudly, Tristan cautiously approached them.

Kalli scowled at Tristan before turning her back. She couldn't look at him without hysterically crying, and she hated being *that* woman. The woman who was so weak, she'd put all her trust and feelings into a man and now couldn't control her own emotion. She hated being a woman who a man would use sexually and then toss to one of his friends. She hated that she was the woman who'd created the drug that had eventually got Toby killed. Kalli refused to let him see how badly she hurt inside. If he didn't want her, she had to at least salvage what was left of her dignity.

"Kalli," Tristan offered, unsure of what to say to her. He wasn't ready to apologize but at the same time, he needed her. He needed her comfort as much as she needed his.

"I'm getting coffee," she snapped, unable to take another tongue-lashing. She'd spent the last hour telling the detective everything she knew about her past, the people who she worked with, every detail about CLI and how it worked and the names of every wolf she could recall. She didn't know the full names of the wolves she'd helped the artist sketch. She guessed the one was Sato and the other

Morris, but wasn't sure. She could, however, remember the name of her old Alpha, Gerald. She'd even told him about everything that had happened to her including the fire, the kidnapping, and her rescue. She'd described in detail what she'd been doing at Tristan's, which involved a brief mention of what had happened on the balcony. Of course she left out the play by play, but she wanted to make sure he understood how she lamented her decision to trust Tristan enough.

Oddly, the detective empathized with her decision, given her past history of abuse. He said he'd too often seen battered women and children and could understand the deep-seeded fear that had been planted in her psyche long ago. Simply telling her to share information that could expose her to her abusers again was not enough to get her to open up about her past. She found it ironic that the one person who seemed to understand her plight was human.

Seeing Tristan as he rounded the corner, she fought back her first instinct which was to run into his arms. Despite his angry words, she didn't want to give up on their budding relationship, which definitely was well rooted into the 'it's complicated' category. At the same time, her healthy sense of self-preservation overrode the need to pursue a man who clearly didn't want her, no matter how incredible he was.

Tony nodded at Tristan. The pain rolled off him like an overflowing river. Even though Tony wasn't wolf, he swore he could feel it. He'd known Tristan for a long time, having been introduced to him by Sydney. Tony regarded him with admiration, as a leader who cared about his wolves and what happened in his city.

"Sorry for your loss, Alpha."

"Thanks Tony. You talk to Kalli?" Tristan inquired, already knowing he had. He just wasn't sure of the extent of their conversation.

"Yeah, she filled me in on everything. It's amazing given all the trauma she's been through," Tony remarked.

"Yeah, I guess she mentioned that Alexandra took her."

"Yeah, she mentioned that, but when I say trauma, I guess I'm referring to the abuse she suffered growing up. She's terrified, but she comes off so composed."

"Detached?" Tristan countered.

"In a sense. If you'd been beat down, told you were going to be tortured for the rest of your natural life, you'd build some walls too. We're talking about survival. Anyway, from her childhood to Ryan's examination, I feel confident that she's told me everything. You, uh, might want to go easy on her." Tony gave Tristan a concerned look.

Tristan inwardly cringed. Just how much had she told him? About what happened between them on the balcony? How he'd yelled at her? How he'd sent her to stay at Logan's?

"Anyway, it's a good thing she's still under your protection. She's sure gonna need it. I understand she was staying with you but now she's staying with Logan?" Tony questioned him, reading between the lines.

Yes, it appeared that she had, indeed, told him everything. Damn.

"Yeah, she's stayin' with Logan tonight." He tried to sound indifferent, but the words tasted like poison as he spoke them aloud. "My entire pack has moved into the new building except for a few wolves. Some have moved to the mountains."

"All right then. Well, I've got some names of males from her old pack. I'll run them tonight. A bulletin was issued of the sketches you sent me. The priority will be upped now that we're looking at murder. Anything else you want to tell me?" He gave him a small smile. "You know, while bearing in mind that I'm an officer of the law."

"Ryan mentioned that he was at a party with a girl named, Lindsay. Could be a coincidence, but Kalli's got an assistant by the same name. She works over at UVH, and she's a college student. Can you check her out?"

"Sure, I mean, we don't know how they even knew she had the CLI. Best guess is that someone at the hospital found out about her research. It's possible the wolves went there looking for Kalli and somehow got mixed up with this, Lindsay. If Lindsay knew about the drug's existence, she could have spilled."

"Yeah, I don't know. It's a long shot but I agree, someone at the hospital must have found out about her research. According to Kalli, she doesn't have much of a social life outside of the hospital and her shelter."

"Anything else?"

"Tomorrow night is the mayor's ball. The following evening we have a summit with Jax Chandler, the New York Alpha. Hoping that it'll be a fruitful meeting. Other than that, there's nothing more I can tell you…officer of the law and all that."

A silent understanding settled between the two men. Tristan was lethal when crossed, as were most supernaturals. Whatever their brand of justice, Tony didn't want to know the details. It wasn't his place to judge their ways; his purpose was to find a murderer. And if Tristan just happened to find the guy before he did, well, then that was all the better in his book.

"Listen, man, we'll do our best to find these sons of bitches. I've made Toby's autopsy a priority. The coroner will start tomorrow morning. I'll be honest, I'm not sure what else she'll find, but the killers may have left a trace. Unofficially, exsanguination from gunshot and stab wounds is listed as COD," Tony speculated.

"I'd like to get his body as soon as possible. Can you text me when he's done? We'll be taking him home. The burial needs to occur as soon as possible," Tristan told him quietly. Home referenced to their mountain compound. While it wasn't often they were forced to bury one of their own, Lyceum Wolves adhered to their own funeral rituals.

"Sure. It'll probably be a couple of days before they'll release the body. Again, I'm real sorry about your wolf. I understand he was in college." Tony extended a hand to Tristan in condolence.

Tristan nodded sadly, shaking his hand. He didn't want to reveal the explosive rage that begged for deliverance. Its time would come, though. Vengeance was coming, and he planned to ride it hard, until every last wolf involved in Toby's death was nothing more than fur and bones.

~⊛ *Chapter Fourteen* ⊛~

After finally getting Ryan settled in Julie's condo, it was nearly three in the morning. Even though shifting had healed Ryan's wounds, it did little to help the emotional scars that cut deep. Instead of having Ryan return to the small apartment he'd set up for the boys, Julie and he agreed that he should stay with her. Despite the fact that she had two younger sisters, it seemed the extra female attention would go a long way toward aiding his recovery.

Tristan had slept in until eleven in the morning; tossing and turning as he tried to resolve his feelings for Kalli and the fact he'd sent her away to spend the night at Logan's. As he sat at the dining room table, drinking coffee and doing work, he couldn't help but notice the emptiness around him. Within a day of her being in his home, he'd grown unusually accustomed to having her around. He smiled, thinking that it didn't hurt that she had a penchant for walking around in her underwear.

Of course, now that he knew her true nature, it didn't surprise him as much. It wasn't as if wolves were exactly known for their modesty. Even if that medicine suppressed her shifting, it couldn't erase the telltale signs that she was wolf. It also now made perfect sense why his wolf wanted her so badly. It was as if he'd been looking at an image, thinking he saw only a woman. But if one looked closer, the wolf was revealed, exposing the optical illusion. Aware of the mirage, he could now see both the woman and the wolf; never again would he be fooled by the trick of the eye.

He tried focusing on his email, noticing that Mira had sent him three different dossiers on potential real estate acquisitions. Tristan considered getting Logan's input before moving forward with the deals. In reality, he knew he could've made the decision himself, but part of him was just looking for an excuse to see Kalli. Unable to resist, he picked up his cell and tapped Logan's number.

"Logan here."

Tristan could barely hear him through the static-filled connection. What did he say? And did he just hear dogs barking? What the hell?

"It's me. Can you hear me?" he asked, sounding like a television commercial.

"Send you a text," was the last thing he heard before the call dropped.

His cell buzzed, alerting him to the text from Logan. 'At animal shelter with Kalli. Bad cell service.'

Where the hell were they? An animal shelter? Goddammit. Did no one listen? He'd specifically instructed everyone to stay home except for essential activities. And Logan was with Kalli at a shelter? Shit. They'd been alone less than twelve hours and already they'd started doing things together? It rubbed him raw thinking about Kalli, sleeping in Logan's bed. He wondered if Logan went to her like he had that first night. Had she bared her beautiful breasts to him? Thoughts of his beta and Kalli nearly drove him mad.

He tapped out an angry response: 'Where r u? Address?'

Tristan had to see her, unsure what he'd say. He was still angry about her lying. But he felt horrible not being around her. The conundrum was killing him. Facing it head on was the only option. Grabbing his helmet, he took off out of his condo, heading down to get his Harley.

From the parking lot, he could hear the barking and mewling. The large industrial warehouse had been converted to a good-sized animal shelter. As he walked into the brightly colored lobby, he noticed the wall behind the receptionist's desk was stenciled in neon paw prints. There was something childlike and fun about the atmosphere. He noted a pile of balls in a basket, with a sign instructing dogs and their would-be owners to 'Take one and play'.

An older woman with grey hair swept up into a bun, manned the desk. "Why hello there! Adopting?" she asked expectantly.

"Not at this time, I'm afraid. I'm here to see Dr. Williams. My friend Logan's here with her," he managed. In awe of the lobby, he couldn't remember ever seeing such an upbeat animal shelter. It was a far cry from the city pound. He knew Kalli co-owned it and wondered if the grandmotherly woman in front of him was her partner.

"Ah yes, we've been expecting you, Mr. Livingston. I'm Sadie. Dr. Kalli and Logan are just around the corner." She unlocked a door and ushered him into the corridor. A large Malamute barked a few times while jumping up to lick his hand. A half wall kept Fido inside of an enormous indoor running and play arena, complete with blue and green playground equipment. Tristan guessed that at least twenty dogs were running and playing, while a young man kept watch, occasionally throwing a ball to them.

As Tristan gave the burly pup a rub on the head, Sadie laughed. "Oh don't mind him; he's just a big baby. We'll find him a forever home one of these days. Come on now, Ace, leave Mr. Livingston be. Go on," she instructed. "Just this way." She pointed to a glass-encased conference room, which looked as if it also functioned as an office. Colorful paintings depicting grass and flowers on the bottom half of the glass, obstructed his view.

"Tris, over here," Logan called, coming out of a room to the left. Cats of all different kinds were silk screened onto the door.

"Hey."

"Mr. Logan," Sadie crooned. "I have a feeling you'll be leaving here with a kitten yet."

He shrugged, giving her a warm smile. "As soon as I get permission from my landlord."

"Okay, then. Well, I'll leave you two. Gotta get back to the front desk." Sadie shuffled down the hallway.

Tristan began to laugh. "Seriously bro? A kitty?"

"Yeah, why not? Can't a wolf get some love?"

"Sure, I'll rush right out and get you that 'Real wolves love cats' t-shirt you've always wanted," he joked.

"So?" Logan asked without stating the real question.

"What?" Tristan replied indignantly.

"Why'd you rush down here, Tris?"

"I missed you." He grinned.

"Yeah, right. You here to see her?"

"Maybe," Tristan admitted, looking over to the dogs.

"You know I respect you. You're my Alpha. We grew up together. We've hunted together. Hell, you know where this is going. Listen, about Kalli…"

"Don't, Logan," Tristan warned.

"Don't what? Tell you to go easy, because I'm going to. Damn, we're all torn up about Toby. But sending her out to me last night. That was cold, man." Logan looked over to the glass, wondering if Kalli could hear them.

"I know. But I needed to get her away from me. You don't get it, Logan. She's driving me crazy. One minute she's submitting to me on the balcony and the next thing I know, she's involved in creating this hideous drug. I was so freakin' pissed. I can't see straight when I'm around her. And now that I know she's wolf…fuck, what am I supposed to do?" Tristan rubbed his eyes with his fist. The more he talked about her, the more agitated he became.

Logan walked over to a sofa that sat next to the office and fell down onto it. He let the back of his head rest on the pillows, staring up at the ceiling.

"Let me tell you what happened last night when I, that's right *I*, took Kalli to *my* home….in *my* bed." He lowered his chin, eyeing Tristan again.

"I can't know, Logan. Don't tell me. What part of 'I can't think straight when it comes to her' don't you understand?" He held up his palms as if that would stop Logan's words from assaulting him.

"I'll tell you what happened. Nothing. Not a goddamned thing. She cried halfway home. Then I had the pleasure of watching her collect her things from your house like someone had kicked her in the stomach. Then, like the jerk I was for listening to you, I showed her into my guest room. And for the next thirty minutes, I heard her crying until she finally fell asleep."

Tristan fisted his hands and turned his back on Logan. As if he didn't feel enough like shit, Logan was forcing him to come to terms with what he'd done.

"Why are you telling me this? I'm the one who told you to take her. I knew there'd be consequences to my order," he bit out.

"This morning," Logan groaned, holding his hand to his heart as if reliving a great memory. "Aw man, do you know how beautiful she is when she wakes up? Prancing around in her underwear as if she's alone? She's totally unaware of what she does to a wolf."

Tristan grunted. Oh he knew how beautiful she was, all right.

"So when she asked me to bring her here, what was I going to do? Her eyes were all puffy, but thank the Goddess she'd stopped crying. She needed to see her animals, so how could I not oblige? It could've had something to do with those pink shorts barely covering her...well, you get the picture. Did I mention that she cooks in her underwear? She says they're pajamas, but they hug her in all the right places." Logan smiled as if he was the cat who ate the canary.

"Enough, Logan. I get the picture. You damn well know that as Alpha, there are times when I'm forced to make difficult decisions. And some decisions that aren't always popular, but that's what leadership is about. I need to think of what's best for the pack. I need to get my head on straight. Toby's dead because of her drug. Her lies," he reminded Logan.

"No, Toby's dead because some asshole out there is attacking our pack. And it's not her. Did she lie? Yes. But I've never known you to be anything but fair and compassionate with your wolves. She needs that part of you, Tris."

Tristan just shook his head. He loved Logan like a brother, but only an Alpha understood the weight of responsibility he carried. He couldn't afford the distraction. He needed her to help catch the perpetrators, nothing more, nothing less.

"Come here," Logan told him, almost instantly recognizing his insubordinate tone.

Tristan cast him a cautionary glare.

"My Alpha," Logan asked, respectfully lowering his eyes. "Tell me that this person, this abused she-wolf, this one right here is a danger. Look at her and tell me that she's a danger to your sanity, to the pack."

Tristan walked over and peered over the painted grass to view Kalli lying upon a carpet, covered in puppies. On her tummy, she was holding one up to her face, whispering endearments while blowing kisses at the furry baby. Two of the little pups were asleep, curled up with their heads on her feet. Wrestling over a rope toy, two others rolled as one in a ball.

Tristan sighed at the sight; his heart flooded with warmth. "She'd make a wonderful mother," he blurted out. As soon as the words left his lips, he cringed. *What the hell?*

Logan coughed, choking at the statement. "Shocked you noticed, let alone just said that out loud, but yes, yes she would."

Kalli could feel his presence without even looking up. She'd skipped her dose of CLI this morning, feeling as if she'd vomit at the sight of it. It was the reason that boy was dead. Being around Tristan was confusing her; thoughts of running wolf flitted around in her mind. She wanted so badly to hate him, to never speak to him after he'd sent her away. But her heart and wolf begged to be back in his arms.

"Hi," she said nonchalantly, not looking up at him as the door opened. She feared she'd start crying again.

"Hey." Goddess, she looked resplendent, puppies and all, but he held himself back.

"Do you want a puppy?"

"Um, uh, I don't think I have the time right now to take one on…" he stammered. Big Alpha male to bumbling teenager within thirty seconds, he thought to himself. This is exactly what she did to him and why he'd needed some space.

"No, I mean, do you want to hold a puppy?" She asked as if she was extending an olive branch. And in many respects she was. This time she'd give him a gift.

"Um, yeah, sure. Where do you want me?" Looking down at her firm bottom, he knew where he wanted to be.

She sat up, sliding her legs from under the warm puppy heads. Reaching over, she gently put a puppy into his big hands.

"His name is Lowell. Don't tell the others but he's my favorite," she whispered as if they could understand her.

"Little wolf?" Tristan smiled, cuddling his black and white pelt. The way she talked to them he was tempted to believe maybe they really did understand her.

She gave him a tiny shrug. "They make me feel better. I know technically they need me. But I need them. They're like children. These guys," She picked up a white one and kissed its furry head. "Their mommy got hit by a car. She didn't make it. So I've been raising them, since they were three weeks old. They're mutts. Beautiful, sweet mutts."

"Kalli, I'm sorry," he apologized softly as he nuzzled the pup. She was right; they did make him feel better, he thought. Or maybe it was the relief he felt, apologizing for his outburst.

Kalli stilled at his words. "It's okay. I was fine at Logan's." She looked away, willing herself not to cry. "I talked to that detective last night and told him everything. I plan on sticking around to help you find who did this to Toby. I won't try to leave…not that I'd be safe anywhere else."

"Thanks. I appreciate it. Tomorrow we've got a big meeting with the New York Alpha. I'll need you to be there."

"Okay," she quietly agreed. The very last thing in the world she wanted to do was be in the company of yet another Alpha. It was as if her self-imposed wolf drought had caught up with her and now she was facing a tsunami of them.

"The other thing is that we need to start working on an antidote to CLI. Regardless of whether we get the wolves who did this, the fact remains that they have some of your pills."

Kalli thought about it for a minute before rushing to speak. "I've got my research still, so I can certainly start on devising an antidote. I'll need a laptop and eventually lab equipment. I've gotta tell you, though, it could take a while to make it. Weeks at best but probably more like a month."

"Whatever it takes. I can get you the things you need. What else?"

"The thing is that there were only around thirty pills in the container that they stole. And honestly, the actual process for creating CLI is pretty complicated. So even though they'll probably break down the chemical composition fairly quickly, it'll be more difficult to duplicate the process with an end product that is the same. The point is that we've got a little bit of time, before they can make more and distribute it. But you should also know that once they figure it out, it's only a matter of time before someone decides to make it into a more functional weapon, like putting it into a bullet or dart for example. It could be honed to effectively thwart shifting if someone really tried," she reasoned.

"Good to know. Well, not really 'good to know', but that gives us all the more incentive to find these guys quickly." Tristan shuddered at the thought of how CLI could be used as a tactical weapon. Not only could wolves use it against each other, it could be used by humans and vamps against wolves as well.

"One last item. Tonight there's a charity function I need you to go to. The mayor's having a gala to raise money for the libraries. Aside from having committed to it months ago, I want whoever's responsible to see you out in public with the pack. It could help draw them out of the shadows." Tristan surveyed the flash of fear that flared in her eyes then left as quickly as it came. His little wolf had grown adept at hiding her emotions. He made a mental note that he'd need to help her with that. She wasn't doing him or herself any favors hiding her feelings.

Her stomach roiled at the thought of going out in public, but she owed him, owed the Lyceum Wolves. And she couldn't help but notice that he didn't say, 'out with him'. He specifically said, 'out with the pack'. Aware of the difference and ripe with anxiety, she reluctantly nodded.

Tristan put the pup down on the floor, picked up the rope toy and waved it in his face. Immediately, the puppy clamped down on the fibers, refusing to let go. Giving the rope a tiny shake, the puppy copied Tristan's motions. Before he knew it, the puppy was growling and shaking it hard, refusing to give up his prize.

"Look at your Lowell, Doc. He's really something," Tristan laughed. "What a tough boy you are," he sang in his best dog voice, making soft growling noises. He smiled broadly, feeling proud the puppy held on so well.

"He likes you," she acknowledged, grinning at the way Lowell ferociously challenged Tristan. There was something about watching the most lethal Alpha on the East Coast play gently with the tiny whelp.

Tristan's face fell into a soft wolfish grin, pinning Kalli with his gaze. "He's an Alpha, Kalli. Look at him holding on tight. He's claiming it, unwilling to share with another wolf. I don't let others take what's mine either."

"Is that right, huh? Takes one to know one? Perhaps that's why I love him so much," she flirted.

"Yes, he definitely isn't sharing. He knows what's his." Tristan continued to maintain eye contact, giving her a sultry smile.

Kalli's breath caught, feeling as if he was looking into her soul. Embarrassed, she lowered her head into a puppy once more. Was he insinuating that she was his? Last night, he'd been so angry, justifiably, but still, he'd sent her to stay with his beta. Maybe she'd misread his intention, but he'd surely pawned her off to his friend. And it wasn't as if Logan was chopped liver. With his thick brown hair, chiseled jawline and lean, muscled body, she was sure the girls flocked to him in droves. But while she found Logan attractive, she wasn't necessarily attracted to him.

With Tristan, however, he lit every nerve she had on end, filling her with desire just about every time she saw him. Even though he was fully clothed, dressed in denim and a black t-shirt, she struggled to resist the urge to devour him on the spot. She reasoned she could skip her meals and lick him head to toe. Shaking her head, she flushed at the thought. Her wolf must be putting these ideas into her mind. But still, she'd have to be six feet under not to want to at least kiss each one of his abs that she'd felt last night. It was as if she'd only had an appetizer, and she was still starving for the whole meal. It wasn't as if they were doing anything remotely sexual; just sitting on the floor, petting dogs. Yet the insane chemistry managed to infiltrate every single one of her carefully constructed emotional shields she'd built last night in Logan's guest room.

She realized, in that second, that there was more to what was going on between them. Not only did she want his apology and forgiveness, she wanted every part of him. The impending feelings threatened to tear her heart in shreds if he didn't return them. But the reality of the situation was that in a single act of not telling him the truth, she'd destroyed the fragile sense of trust they'd erected since they'd met. Sitting on the floor, she could feel it mending, albeit not fixed, but there was an air of openness that hadn't existed before. No more secrets. No more lies. Emotionally, she was bare. He could either make her his or walk away.

Tristan refused to release her from his gaze, watching the conflicting emotions on her face. He could tell she was struggling to hide her arousal, and he loved that even after everything they'd been through the night before, she couldn't conceal her reaction to him. But she'd lied, and well, he'd acted like a complete jerk by sending her to Logan as if she were nothing more than a female to be used by males. Something he knew would cut her to her core, given her past experiences in a pack.

He regretted the action, but was unsure how to proceed. Well fueled in anger the previous night, he'd asked Mira to accompany him to the gala. He justified it by telling himself that he needed Mira with him to field business questions. But as he sat next to Kalli in a room full of puppies, he was second guessing taking Mira. As he contemplated his predicament, his phone alarm went off, reminding him of an important meeting, one he couldn't miss.

"Kalli, I...I'm sorry, I have to go. Got a call to Japan in thirty minutes, and I need to get back to the office," he explained. "I meant what I said. I'm sorry about how I reacted last night. I'm torn up over what's happened to Toby, and it just got out of hand."

"I'm sorry for not telling you the truth sooner. If I had told you, maybe the boys wouldn't have gotten hurt," she responded in a barely audible whisper. As much as she tried to push the pain down, she found herself starting to cry again. A tear ran down her already reddened cheeks; her mouth parted as her tongue darted out to lick her upper lip.

"Chérie, look at me." Tristan cupped her face with one hand and wiped her tear with his thumb. He resisted letting his thumb slide in between her warm pink lips so she could suck his finger. Who was he kidding? He wanted her to suck more than his finger....just the thought of those plump lips, wrapping themselves around the hard length of him sent blood rushing down to his groin. He tried shaking off the dirty images running through his mind. *Don't be a selfish prick, Tris. Get it together.* He had to look away and take a deep breath before continuing. He tried to focus on his words and not the very naughty things he wanted to do to her.

"What happened is not your fault. As for you and I, we'll see, okay? I'm still kind of processing what happened, and I need to be on the top of my game in the next few days. Listen, I'll see you tonight."

Kalli swore he was going to kiss her as he ran his calloused thumb near her mouth. But instead of a kiss, he gently hugged her and stood to leave.

After he left, his words reverberated in her head: 'As for you and I, we'll see, okay?' What was that supposed to mean? They'd almost made love yesterday, and now they were at 'we'll see'. She smiled sadly, wondering if everything she'd been feeling was real or if it was all in her imagination. It sure as hell felt real, but his lack of intention made her wonder if she needed to protect her heart. Emotionally exposed, she could not have felt more vulnerable.

Although playing with puppies blanketed her with love and happiness, a hot shower really helped to relax Kalli's thoughts. It was if she let the stress wash down the drain while resolving to put on her big girl panties. She reasoned that no matter how much her hormones drove her crazy with lust, it'd be in her best interest to let her brain do the talking in the future. Allowing her heart to dictate how she handled the next few weeks in and around an Alpha would only lead to heartache. She was a well-educated, compassionate doctor, and it was about time she started acting like it. Forlorn lovesick teenager wasn't at all working for her. Either Tristan would forgive her and own up to his feelings or he wouldn't. In the meantime, it was time to buck up and get her act together. As the hot spray hit her face, she decided that it was time to snap out of it. Whether she liked it or not, she was stuck living with Logan, while trying to help catch killers.

Exiting the bathroom in nothing more than a towel, she gasped in surprise to find Logan waiting for her. Fixing his hair in the mirror, he turned and gave her a huge smile. She couldn't help but blush as she admired how gorgeous he looked in his tuxedo. While she wasn't generally modest, she felt extraordinarily underdressed, given she was naked under her tiny towel.

Logan looked her up and down. No harm done looking, he reasoned. Tristan was a damn fool for sending her away, and he might as well be the one to reap the rewards. He grew hard watching her nervously pull at her towel that barely covered her breasts. If she turned around, he was pretty sure that he'd be given another show of her firm little cheeks. Her long black wavy hair tumbled down her back in wet curls. Wide-eyed, she started laughing as he spun in a circle, showing off his fancy duds like a model.

"Nice tux, Logan. You're looking good," she commented. "But you do know as much as I love coming out of my bathroom to find a hot man waiting for me, this seems a little awkward." She smiled and went about drying her hair with a towel, wondering what Tristan would think if he came in here this very minute and found her nearly naked with his beta sitting on her bed. He'd probably go ballistic. And he'd deserve it, the still angry part of her thought.

"Hot, huh? Wait until you see my slick dance moves, girl. Fred Astaire, baby," he joked.

"Didn't you tell me that Julie was bringing me something to wear to this Godforsaken ball?" she asked, changing the subject. One could only hope that she'd forgotten and then Kalli would have a valid excuse to bail.

"Ah yes, well, there is something special that was delivered. Not by Julie, though," he affirmed with a wry grin.

She gave him an inquisitive look, wondering what it was and who had picked out the outfit. Walking over to the closet door, she saw an elegant deep red satin gown. Matching pumps sat on the floor.

"This is...it's exquisite. Really, I've never worn anything like this in my life," she exclaimed, admiring it up against her in the mirror.

"Come on now, don't you docs do these shindigs all the time?"

She rolled her eyes at him. "Uh, no way. I'm strictly a working class girl. Did you do this, Logan?"

"No ma'am. It seems you've got yourself a secret admirer. But I've been sworn to secrecy so don't bother asking," he teased with a wink. "And as much as I've enjoyed looking at your fine body in that little towel of yours, we've gotta go soon or we'll be late." He stood and walked over to the doorway.

Kalli approached him, and on her tiptoes, kissed him on the cheek.

Logan put his hand to his face as if he'd been lovingly branded. "What's that for? Not that I mind even one little bit."

"For being such a great person to me after everything that went down last night; for taking me down to the shelter today; for letting me stay here. Lots of things," she bubbled happily, guessing that Tristan had bought her the amazing dress. She returned it to the closet and went back to the dresser to brush out her hair.

"You're welcome, Kalli. You know, you're important to this pack, and to Tristan. Far more important than you even know," he said cryptically.

Kalli smiled, unsure of how to respond. Whatever he was referring to was a mystery to her.

"Not so sure about that, but I swear I'll do my best to help," she promised.

He turned to leave her, and looked over his shoulder. "Oh, and Doc. Don't forget to look in the box there on the dresser. There's something special there that will look great on you."

He wanted to tell her that Tristan had brought everything over for her, but it wasn't his place to do it. All in good time, he thought, but hoped that he'd tell her soon. It could prove to be a long, miserable evening if Tristan didn't address his feelings for her before they left. As Logan walked down the hallway, he prayed things would go smoothly.

⊰⊗ *Chapter Fifteen* ⊗⊱

The limo ride over to the Four Seasons had been nothing short of a nightmare. From the minute Tristan picked up Mira, she'd been peppering him with questions about Kalli and their relationship. In addition to the nonstop interrogation, she seemed overly affectionate, which only meant one thing: trouble.

It didn't help that he couldn't stop thinking about Kalli, since he'd left the shelter. His anger had dissipated after reflecting on her reasons why she'd been afraid to tell him. It wasn't as if he didn't know how tough things used to be in wolf packs. Forced matings and brutality used to be commonplace, but progressively, most packs had given up old practices. Both he and Marcel had consciously led their packs with authority and fairness, refusing to live barbaric existences. Burning with rage, he wished he could have prevented the abuse Kalli had suffered at the hands of wolves. It was no wonder she'd been afraid of him and Logan.

Intrigued, he'd found his attraction to her only grew deeper after talking with her at the shelter. Even though she was vulnerable, she still wanted to help him. Yes, she needed his protection. But she could have gone to the police and asked for protection. He was certain Tony would have given her sanctuary. And he returned the favor by sending her to Logan, as if they hadn't shared intimate moments. He saw the hurt in her eyes, knew she'd been crying because of him, yet aside from apologizing, things felt unresolved. He felt empty, as if he hadn't said what he needed to say. Treating the request for her attendance at the gala like a business transaction, he'd neglected to mention that he was taking Mira, something he normally wouldn't give a second thought to doing. But his connection to Kalli pulled strongly at his heart.

On the way home, he decided he needed to try to fix the mess he'd made of things. Even though cancelling with Mira wasn't an option, he'd be damned if he didn't straighten things out with Kalli during the gala. After his conference call, he'd visited with Ryan, happy to see that he was taking advantage of the female attention he'd been receiving at Julie's. Thankfully, he seemed a little better emotionally and was even asking about getting back to work. While he was there, he consulted with Julie about the best place to procure female attire for the gala. At some point during his spree, he considered that he must have gone mad, to be shopping for a woman. And perhaps he had. He wasn't usually the type to shop for himself, let alone someone else. In an effort to make amends, he sought to do something special for Kalli; to make it up to her even if his words hadn't soothed her hurt feelings. If he was truthful with himself, he'd just admit that he wanted every man in the room tonight to know she was his, that she was wearing something that he'd given her.

The cynical part of him, who had invited Mira out of anger, claimed the purchases were nothing more than business expenses. Kalli was a means to an end. A decoy. A lure. Whoever was targeting him was keeping tabs on his pack, so he'd give them something to think about. They had the pills, but they didn't have the research. He wanted them to know that he knew what they knew and was coming for them. A public show of confidence, in the wake of the death of one of his wolves, spoke of his strong constitution and power in this city. His wolves were not sheep, awaiting slaughter. They were wolves, out in the open, strong with their pack and ready to strike for the kill.

While it was true that he did want her at the gala for all those reasons, the primary reason was that he was fascinated with her. Secrets out of the way, he craved her touch, her kiss. Tonight she'd be his in every sense of the imagination.

"Tristan, do be a dear, and pour me a Grey Goose. This traffic is horrendous tonight," Mira commented, jolting him from his thoughts. They'd come to a screeching halt in the evening gridlock.

Tristan poured and then handed her the tumbler. This was going to be a helluva night, he thought. The only saving grace would be seeing Kalli in the incredible dress he'd procured.

"Thanks." She slowly sipped the warm liquor, wondering how long she'd actually have to work. "So anything I need to know about tonight? Parker and Mainer will both be there. Both have passed clearances, so I'm going to work them tonight, try to get a feel for whether or not they'll consider selling their waterfront properties." She rubbed a hand on Tristan's thigh, coming precariously close to his crotch.

Tristan gently grabbed her wrist and placed it back into her lap. "Not tonight, Mir," he warned. "And yes, I'd appreciate it if you'd chat up the mayor as well to see if there are any big deals or new players in town. He likes you and seems to have loose lips when in your company. Gotta keep an eye on the competition."

"No problem, but you owe me a dance," she flirted.

"We'll see," he hedged.

She pursed her lips, and rolled her eyes. "Seriously, Tristan? What's going on? This night should be fun. And by fun, I mean we eat, drink, dance and then leave here and dance some more, like naked in the bedroom. You, me, maybe Logan, although he's got his hands full with the human."

He glared at her.

"Oh sorry, excuse me, hybrid, whatever that means. Come on, even you have to admit that if it looks like a duck, walks like a duck, quacks like a duck…well, you get the picture," she sniffed.

"She's wolf. She just doesn't know it yet," he informed her.

"Yeah right, good luck with that."

"I don't need luck, chére. I'm Alpha, and she's all mine," he drawled.

Mira sat perfectly still, tensing every muscle in her body. "Are you fucking kidding me? Did you just say what I thought you said?"

"Watch your language, Mir. Geez," he sighed. "I'm not going to repeat what I just said, because it won't make a difference to you. You need to accept this, because eventually she will be part of Lyceum Wolves. I know you're not crazy about it when I date other women, but jealously is so not becoming."

Tristan expected that Mira would freak out when she found out he was going to bring Kalli into the pack. It wasn't as if he planned to ask Kalli right away to join, because he didn't want to scare her off. The more he considered the situation, the more he embraced the idea of keeping the lovely doctor in both his bed and his life. He wasn't sure how it would work out or if they'd last, but without a doubt, she belonged in his pack, with him. Last night, he'd been so close to making love to her on his balcony. Even though he swore he needed the truth from her, he couldn't be sure that if Logan hadn't interrupted them that he wouldn't have taken her anyway.

The electrifying connection between them was unyielding. And his wolf wanted her like he'd wanted no other. It scared Tristan, because deep down he knew the animal within would never be satisfied until he had her screaming his name, submitting to him in pleasure again and again. It conjured up all kinds of thoughts. Goddess almighty, he'd told Logan today that she'd make a good mother, and when he'd said that, he wasn't just thinking of anyone's kids. He was thinking of his own. He shook his head, laughing inwardly. Logan must have thought he'd lost his damn mind. He tried to stifle the longing, attempting to negate how deep his feelings ran.

Mira shifted in her seat, aware that he was thinking yet again of that stupid woman. Clearly he had a screw loose, she thought. "I cannot believe you'd even consider seriously letting that mongrel into our pack. After everything that's happened? Ugh. You're leading with your dick not your head," she accused.

Tristan straightened in his seat, putting distance between himself and Mira. It was true they were friends, but there was a limit to how much nonsense he'd endure, even from her.

"Mira," he growled loudly. "Knock it off. Kalli belongs with me. Do not antagonize her or me this evening. Am I clear? If you insult me again, there will be consequences." He was done discussing his love life with her. If she didn't get where he was coming from, then that was too bad, because frankly it didn't matter. As Alpha, he would do what he wanted. She needed to move on and get over it.

Mira hadn't been happy about Sydney either, but she'd survived it. But this was different; Kalli was wolf. The idea of another female wolf replacing her in his bed, let alone his heart, was driving her abhorrence. He knew it would come to a head, but tonight was not the time. She'd better curb her nasty tone, or she'd be punished. He wasn't beyond admonishing her publicly just to prove the point.

"Look, here we are. Thank the Goddess we can get out of this car," he breathed in relief.

To say Kalli had been disappointed when she found out that Tristan wasn't accompanying her to the gala would have been an understatement. The fact that he was taking Mira with him only compounded the situation, curtailing any lofty dreams she'd held about pursuing their relationship any further. If someone had taken a fire hose and sprayed her down, her hopes couldn't have gotten anymore dampened. The second Logan told her, she considered stomping back into her room, tearing off the dress and jumping into bed under the covers. But regardless of her previous lie, she was generally a woman of her word. She'd told him she'd go so she'd do it, even if she spat tacks the entire time.

As she and Logan advanced into the grand ballroom, the lull of conversation was accented by the orchestra playing Bolero. Arm in arm, they glided into the sea of attendees, joining the upper echelon of Philadelphia society. There were so many people, drinking, dancing and conversing, Kalli failed to see the purpose of their attendance. No one would even notice her.

Logan's chest puffed out slightly, honored at having such a beautiful date. When she had come into the living room earlier in the night, he'd nearly fallen onto the floor. She looked gorgeous in her form-fitting, sleeveless satin gown. The deep red fabric hugged her entire body from her breasts to her calves; a sash tied into a bow accentuated her small waist before falling into a long train. Her upswept curly raven hair gracefully displayed the lovely diamond stud earrings he'd delivered for Tristan.

Kalli had been beaming, right up until the moment he'd explained that Tristan wasn't coming with them. At the news he was going with Mira, her mood flattened. No tears marred her perfectly applied makeup, yet her tightly drawn lips and hurt eyes revealed her swirling emotions. Logan wished Tristan had just broken his date with Mira, given his extraordinary shopping spree during the afternoon. While she was showering, Tristan had slid into her room unnoticed, bringing her dress and shoes. He had given Logan the earrings, telling him to make sure she wore them, and then made him swear not to tell her. Logan had tried talking him into taking Kalli, but Tristan insisted that he and Mira had business to attend to during the gala.

After essentially calling him out as an ass, Tristan had torn out of his apartment. Logan had been on the receiving end of Mira's tantrums, so he understood why Tristan didn't want to break the date. Mira would have been fit to be tied if Tristan had dumped her at the last minute. Tristan also persevered with his main excuse for not taking Kalli, which was that he was unable to concentrate on business around her. While that may have been entirely true, Logan was finding it hard to concentrate as well. Tristan knew damn well that he needed to make things right with Kalli. A few puppy hugs were hardly enough to mend fences.

In Logan's opinion, they needed to either talk or fuck. Whichever would do just fine as long as they'd get it over with so things could progress. Logan had silently congratulated himself when he'd heard she was part wolf. His visions made complete sense now. Still, Tristan needed to learn of his mate on his own timeline. As much as it killed him, Logan refused to interfere.

Logan glanced over to Kalli as they made their way through the crowd. The opulent ballroom was overwhelming and magnificent at the same time. He could tell that Kalli felt as if she was balanced upon a ball and could come crashing down any second.

"You're okay," Logan reassured her, patting her arm.

"Thanks. I just didn't know what to expect. Do you all go to these things often?"

"Every now and then. Tristan donates a lot of money, and the parties serve a business purpose. Lots of current and prospective clients to talk to. That's probably what he's doing now."

"Yeah, right. Business, I'm sure," she commented sarcastically.

"He really is working, Kal. But I have a feeling he won't quite be himself until he sees you. Come this way."

He steered her toward the bar where he ordered two glasses of champagne.

Securely leaning against the heavy mahogany counter, Kalli turned to people watch. Her breath caught at the sight of Alexandra coming straight toward her. She grabbed Logan's arm, squeezing so tightly she'd thought she'd nearly drawn blood. *What was she doing here?* Tristan hadn't warned her. Like a missile approaching a submarine, it was too difficult to maneuver out of the line of fire. Too late, she thought, steeling her nerves.

"Ah mouse, I see you've landed the beta. Well done, I'm sure," she sneered.

Fear and hate washed over Kalli's face; a bright red flush rose to her cheeks. Alexandra's jibe was the last straw that broke the camel's back, sending Kalli spiraling into an unavoidable outburst. Having still not taken the CLI, her wolf lunged. A low growl emanated from within her, one she didn't even want to restrain. Her beast wanted out as the rage spilled forth at the vampire.

"Back. Off. Bitch," Kalli spat at her loudly enough so her voice was audible to the surrounding guests. "That's right, look around to see who's looking. You'll notice I don't give a damn who sees or hears me, given that this is the first and probably last time I'm invited to one of these things. I'm telling you right now, stay away from me or that silver carving knife over there in the roast beef will be the last thing you see before I slice your throat."

Alexandra gasped, astonished at Kalli's eruption. Logan watched with curiosity, surprised at how effectively she'd put the socially conscious Alexandra in her place. Embarrassing her at a public function was nearly a fate worse than death to Alexandra, who loved more than anything to be a 'who's who' in Philadelphia.

"Ah, I see the mouse grows her fangs. Hanging out with the wolves is doing that to you, I suppose." She rolled her eyes in disgust. "Very well, no need to get all riled. Just thought it polite to say hello, but I can see you're not ready to make nice. Ta-ta!" she sang, seething in retreat. Waving to the mayor, she turned and crossed the room as if the ugly incident had never occurred.

Tristan froze at the sound of a growl. *What the hell?* This was a mixed function, humans and supes. There was no growling at charity galas. Which one of his wolves was causing a ruckus? Quickly scanning the room, he searched for the owner of the snarl. Within seconds, he caught sight of Kalli laying into Alexandra. Whatever she said must have caused the bloodsucker to flee.

Stunned by her beauty, he could barely breathe. Goddess, the woman was spectacular. The fiery red gown clung to her in all the right places, and he noticed a small smile grow on her angelic face, presumably pleased that she had castigated Alexandra. He needed to get to her, hold her. As he rushed across the room, Mira stopped him with a hand to his arm. She gestured toward an elusive client standing to her left.

Logan laughed, seeing Kalli triumph over the demon spawn who ran the vampires. "Hey girl, I hate to point it out, but man you laid her out...and that growl. What was that?"

"Dance with me, Logan," Kalli declared, needing to move.

"Your wish is my command."

They crossed the floor, and Logan swept her into his arms. As amazing as Logan looked, she yearned for Tristan. She could feel he was close. As the music grew louder in her ears, she swayed along to the classical beats, hyper-aware of his presence. Leaning her head on Logan's shoulder, she finally spied Tristan near the buffet, surrounded by Mira and a short bald man.

His eyes caught hers, and her heart started to race. She wasn't sure whether it was his pensive expression or aggressive stance, but she could clearly sense he was agitated. Logan spun her, and she lost his eyes only momentarily, then caught them once again. His predatory gaze electrified the room, sending goose bumps over her skin. As he stalked toward them, her breathing hitched. Like a rabbit alert to the wolf, she froze save for the mindless dance steps she made while blindly following Logan. As Tristan came upon them, she forced herself to face him directly. Larger than life, Tristan was sophistication etched in dripping sexuality. His dominance was apparent to every man, woman and supernatural in the room; there'd be no denying him.

Even Logan stopped dancing to respect his Alpha. Lowering his eyes in submission, he bowed slightly. "Thank you for the dance," he whispered, releasing her.

Before she had a chance to say a word, Tristan wrapped a hand around her waist, pulling her tightly to him so they pressed together. She could feel his barely restrained erection nudging her belly. Suppressing a moan, she felt herself grow wet. She clenched her thighs hoping to hide her arousal; every supernatural within fifty feet would know of her excitement.

"Don't," Tristan ordered.

"Don't what?" she managed to ask.

"Don't try to hide it. Your delicious scent."

"But they'll know I …" Kalli's words trailed off as she lost her train of thought. God, he felt incredible.

"I want them to know. I want them all to know you're mine."

"But I thought…I mean you came with her." Her eyes darted to Mira.

"Business only, nothing more. Still, I'm very sorry I didn't bring you with me. Clearly I was an idiot to leave you alone with my beta. Every man in this room is looking at you, Kalli."

"No," she denied, shaking her head.

"Yes. And they should. Because you're magnificent. Everything about you from that alluring dress I bought you to your sexy growl. My Goddess, do you know what you do to me? Feel it," he whispered, grinding his groin against her.

"Tristan," she breathed. She was on the verge of orgasm from just dancing with the man. She couldn't imagine what would happen if they made love.

"Did you enjoy dancing with Logan?

"What? Logan?"

"Yes, Logan. Did you enjoy having your sweet body pressed to his?"

"Oh God, Tristan."

"It's all right, Kalli. Did you find it arousing? Tell me the truth."

"Another test?" she sighed.

"Truth?"

"Okay yes, but he's not…he's not you. No one I've ever met in my life is like you," she admitted.

"Ah, see how easy it is to tell the truth, ma chérie? Perhaps you'd like to explore two men at once?" he teased with a sexy smile as if he'd thoroughly enjoy it.

She blushed, not denying it.

"Someday we'll explore that little kink of yours, but tonight you are mine. In fact, I think you'll be mine for quite a long time."

"Confident, huh, wolf?"

"Would you ever expect anything less?"

He spun her around, continuing to brush against her. Tightening the grip around her waist, he ran his palm up her arm to her neck, until he reached her face. Caressing her cheek, he ran his thumb across her lower lip. "I want you so much, Kalli. I'm so sorry for everything. I shouldn't have sent you to Logan's. I was angry, but damn, I need you."

She groaned and threw her head back, publicly baring her neck to him. Submission, truth, she'd give it to him all right. But what he needed to learn was that he was hers as well, and after tonight she had no intention of letting him go.

Chapter Sixteen

The sight of her submission plunged Tristan over the edge. "We're leaving. Now," he urged, leaving no room for disagreement. Gathering her into his arms, he ushered her off the dance floor while Logan smirked at the sight and Mira glared. Within seconds, they'd reached the perimeter of the room. Tristan shoved open a door which led to a bridal lounge, and pulled Kalli inside, hastily locking the door. Tristan couldn't wait; he needed her now.

Without words, he captured her lips in an all-encompassing kiss. Kalli wrapped her arms around his neck, feverishly sweeping her tongue into his mouth, as he did hers. Starved, the passionate kiss only further ignited their arousal.

"Dress. Off now," Tristan ordered through their lips.

"Um. Yes. Zipper. Side," she agreed breathlessly.

Reaching downward, he deftly unzipped the dress until it pooled onto the floor.

"Aw chérie, you're so gorgeous." His lips quickly moved to suck and bite at her neck.

"Yes," she cried, as she threw her head back against the wall, lost in the feel of his mouth all over her skin. She panted wildly, anticipating where he'd touch her next.

"Baby, I can't wait. I need to be in you," he grunted. Goddess, she was so exquisite that he didn't know what to touch first. As his lips moved to her pink areola, he sucked hard, while massaging the smooth skin of her bottom. Moving his fingers around to the rim of her thong, he gripped it, ripping it from her body. Palming her torso, he slid his hand down her belly until his fingers brushed over her mound. Stroking up and down, he slipped his middle finger into her soft lips, finding her center of pleasure. Unrelenting, he pressed his thick digit into her hot sheath, and then followed it with two. He wanted to go slow, but lost in the moment, he pressed in and out, bringing her close to release.

"Oh my God, Tristan, please, it feels so good," she cried. "Fuck me, please."

Unable to wait any longer, he unzipped his pants, releasing his rock hard shaft. He stroked himself, while continuing to work magic with his fingers. "I can't wait, baby. You ready?"

"Yes!" she screamed in frustration as she felt him leave her warmth. He spun her around so she was facing the wall. She was so close to coming, feeling as if she'd come apart any second.

Tristan cuffed her wrists in one hand, flattened her palms against the door and spread her legs with his other hand, bending her over slightly, so he could see into her.

"Ah Kalli, you're so wet. So ready," he panted, sliding his finger over the crack of her bottom until he found her wetness. "I want to be gentle, but I need you fast. You're so..." Before he'd finished his sentence, he'd thrust himself all the way into her tight channel.

"Yes! That's it! Oh God!" Kalli screamed. She didn't care if every last person in the ballroom heard her.

"Fuck, Kalli, your pussy is so tight. So very, very tight. Are you okay, chérie?" As badly as he wanted to take her, Tristan was not a selfish lover.

Kalli could swear she felt herself stretch; the pain subsided within seconds, and she needed more. "Please, don't stop. I need...I need..." She was thrashing her head. She was so close, but she needed him to move.

Tristan began pumping in and out of her, slowly at first, building the rhythm. Soon he was pounding against her, his balls slapping against her ass. He reached around to caress her breast, but could sense she was on the edge of coming. Damn, he really wanted their first time to last longer, but the intensity more than made up for the time. With his thumb and forefinger, he pinched her nipple.

"Yes, more," she demanded. Reaching behind her, she grabbed a fistful of his hair.

Encouraged by her roughness, Tristan reached round with his other hand to touch her. Finding his prize, he brushed her clit, lightly at first, and then he increased the pressure.

Kalli felt as if she was out of her own body. She relished the feel of his cock slamming into her. Her body was on fire; his hands were everywhere. But when he increased the pressure on her sensitive nub, she splintered into delirium as an orgasmic wave washed over her. Shaking in release, Kalli shouted his name so loud she swore the people in the next building would hear her.

Tristan saw stars as her pussy tightened around him. He came hard, erupting inside her. He heard her calling his name, but it was as if he was sucked into a vortex of pleasure from which there was no escape. Pulsing into her, he resisted the urge to bite her smooth neck. Goddess, but he wanted to mark her. Make her his, not just now but forever. His wolf howled in ecstasy, begging to mate her. Tristan tried to ignore it. It couldn't be. It wasn't true. It couldn't be. Shoving the agonizing need aside, he resisted the impulse.

"Kalli, baby, are you okay?" He'd wanted to be gentle their first time but seeing her on the dance floor drove him into a wanton frenzy, craving her more than air. He hoped he hadn't scared her by their amazing yet animalistic tryst.

"God yes. That was amazing. Please take me home…so we can go again," she added, giggling, her forehead pressed against the door.

Tristan laughed a low sexy laugh. "My little wolf, you want more, huh?"

"I'm not all wolf," she reminded him. She didn't want to spoil the mood, but she was acutely aware of how others would view her hybrid status.

"You're mine. I don't care what you are," he assured, pulling out of her. He returned himself and zipped, then turned her around, anxious to see her flushed expression, the one he'd put there. "That's what's important, you know."

He lovingly cupped her face; he could see right through her anxieties. What he'd told her was true. He didn't care whether she was hybrid; he just wanted her to be true to her nature. He wanted her to feel safe, protected and loved enough to revel in her own skin.

"You're beautiful after you make love," he commented absently. His chest constricted at the thought of ever losing her.

She blushed, still engrossed in the afterglow of the moment. As her skin cooled, she was reminded that she was nude. "You're quite dashing yourself there, but this is hardly fair. You're completely dressed and me…well." She laughed and gestured to her naked body. Donning her gown, she quickly zipped it. Giving up on her now mussed updo, she pulled out the pins and sexily shook out her curls, combing her fingers through her hair.

"Wonder how fast that limo can go?" He teased. "I'm thinking that I can't wait to get you in bed so we can 'go again' as you put it".

She shot him a look, feigning shock.

"Hey, you're the one who suggested it. And this wolf aims to please," he winked.

"Well then, if you are asking, I bet it can go really, really fast," she purred, leaning in to kiss his cheek.

"Let's go home, ma chérie," Tristan suggested, hugging her to his heart. His home was now her home, and he realized that he didn't want it any other way.

After sneaking out the back entrance, Tristan held Kalli nearly the entire ride home. She'd fallen asleep in the car after their intense lovemaking, and he found it fascinating how enjoyable it was to simply watch her at rest. When the limo arrived at Livingston One, he easily cradled her in his arms, lifting her out of the car and walking into his private elevator. By the time they reached their floor, her eyes fluttered as she awoke. Smiling, she ran her hand down his cheek along his jawline.

"We're home? Oh my, now this is service," she teased with a yawn.

"I like the sound of that," Tristan replied, growing accustomed to the space in his heart she'd taken.

"What?"

"The sound of your voice calling my condo home. And don't tell Logan I said that. He'll call me soft."

"My Alpha, there is nothing soft about you," Kalli flirted, running the palm of her hand down his abs.

"You're insatiable, and I do like it." He softly kissed her warm lips, gently, in stark contrast to their kiss in the hotel.

Slowly separating from their embrace, they held each other's hands, both in awe of the emerging connection. The attraction wasn't just physical, as perhaps Tristan had hoped; it was more than that. Both Kalli and Tristan stood in the foyer, unable to articulate the visceral gravitation drawing them together. Cognizant of the overwhelming emotion brewing, Tristan broke contact and waved for Kalli to follow him down the hallway.

"Come with me," he grinned, gesturing her toward the guest room she'd previously occupied. "I've had your things moved back in while we were at the gala. Of course, I'd much rather have you in my bed from now on."

Kalli could hardly believe that he'd done this while they'd been away. The man was a force of nature.

"Confident, much? How did you know I'd want to come back?" she teased.

"Confident is my middle name, baby. And of course you'd come back. What girl can resist my southern charm?" he drawled.

"Charm? Is that what you call what happened on that dance floor, huh?" She raised an eyebrow at him.

"What happened between us…" He instantly came up behind her, running the palms of his hands up her belly to rest just under her breasts until he heard her release a small gasp. "That, my little wolf, is raw sexual energy between a man and a woman. It's unstoppable, you know. A crime to even try. And there's more where that came from. Much, much more."

Kalli felt her head fall backwards onto his shoulder. His sexy voice, laced with pure seduction, sent her reeling. But before she could completely set herself at ease, he stepped back toward the door. Damn, the man was unsettling. Yet again, he had her so excited she felt as if she was walking a high wire.

"Go ahead and freshen up. I'm gonna go get a bottle of wine. Meet you in my room." He wagged his eyebrows at her.

Kalli released a deep breath that she wasn't even aware she'd been holding. She was beginning to realize what it meant to be Alpha. It was as if he could do almost anything. He was so sure of himself and everything he did. Yet instead of being overtly overbearing, Tristan's flair for humor sparkled through the dominance. And like a cat drawn to a Christmas tree, she simply couldn't resist playing with the ornaments.

After going to the bathroom and brushing her hair, she removed her shoes with a groan.

"Sore? Why don't you let me kiss it all better?" Tristan leaned on the doorjamb.

Kalli nearly fell off the bed in surprise. He was fast and stealthy. *Sneaky wolf.*

"I think I might need to put a bell on you," she teased as she struggled to stand up without looking terribly clumsy. It was the best she could hope for; graceful was no longer an option.

"Sorry chérie, wolves don't do bells. 'Fraid you'll have to use those wolf senses that the Goddess gave you, but we'll discuss that later. Come with me. I've got something for you."

The master bedroom wasn't exactly how Kalli had imagined it would be. In contrast to his uber-masculine, sometimes bad boy image, his bedroom was warm and inviting. Blonde bamboo flooring contrasting with Tuscan tanned walls, contributed to the sensation of a wide open space, conjuring thoughts of running through a moonlit, golden wheat field. A king sized, antiqued mahogany four poster bed with white linens commanded attention; intricate carvings adorned its long pillars. Fire danced in the gas fireplace, apparently appreciative of the soft zydeco music filtering throughout the room.

"Wow. This is just...it's beautiful. Like it belongs in Homes and Gardens beautiful."

"Thanks. Luckily since it was a new building, I was able to customize everything to my liking before we moved in."

"You designed this?"

"Why yes. There's more to me than my smooth dance skills, you know." He winked.

"Hmmm...dance skills, huh? Is that what public seduction at a charity event is called these days?"

"Baby, you ain't seen nothin' yet. Come," he directed.

As they entered the master bath, Kalli let out a sigh of amazement. Another gas fireplace blazed to life with the flick of a switch. It gave light to the spectacular bathroom. Floor to ceiling windows exposed the night sky, which enhanced the subtle lighting. The oversized Jacuzzi nestled in the corner, awaiting them.

Tristan walked over and started the water. Sprinkling in soft lavender flakes, he continued preparing the space by lighting large pillar candles which surrounded the tub.

Kalli stood speechless. She'd never known a man like him in her entire life. "Alpha, you are something else," she managed, having lost all ability to articulate her astonishment.

"Well of course I am, chérie," he joked as he proceeded to pour two glasses of wine and set them on a restored trunk that served as a table. "You expect less?"

"I've just never…never…well no one has ever done this kind of thing for me," she croaked, unable to finish. Struggling to conceal the bubbling emotion surging in her throat, she wiped away a single tear.

Tristan regarded her. So strong and beautiful, yet she was incredibly fragile. The knowledge that someone had once abused her enraged him. It was no wonder that she tried so hard to swallow her feelings. He couldn't imagine that she'd never had someone treat her with kindness, the sort of kindness that was done out of a person's heart, unconditionally, without anything expected in return.

"Come over here, Kalli," he ordered in a soft voice.

She complied, still taking in her surroundings.

"You're way overdressed, do you know that?"

"As are you," she countered.

"Well, then," Giving her a closed grin, he silently indicated his intent. He reached over to her side, finding the hidden zipper he'd made himself familiar with earlier in the evening, and pulled downward. As her dress dropped to her ankles, she reached for his collar.

Stark naked, she slowly pulled at the silken fabric of his tie, taking care to unknot it, and then tossed it on the floor. She gave him a sizzling smile as she unbuttoned each tiny shirt button. His cufflinks clanked to the floor just before she removed his jacket and shirt. The man looked like a

Greek god, she thought as she placed butterfly kisses on his bared abs.

Keeping her spine perfectly straight while maintaining his eye contact, she knelt to the floor, unbuckling and unzipping. His erection sprang forth as his trousers fell to the floor. Without touching his newly exposed skin, she continued undressing him, removing his shoes and socks.

Tristan tensed in arousal, watching Kalli slink down his body, slowly stripping him. Her warm breath teased his rigid thick cock. But he was mostly fascinated by the clouds of passion that lurked within her eyes. While most people didn't dare look him directly in the eyes, she did so with reckless abandon, challenging him to come to her.

As much as he wanted her warm lips wrapped around the length of him, he first needed her to feel loved. After the rough way he'd taken her earlier, in an alcove of a ballroom, nonetheless there was nothing he desired more at the moment than to simply care for her.

"Come, Kalli," he breathed, ignoring his pulsing need. Content with her compliance, he led her to the steaming water, and shut off the spigot.

Kalli allowed him to help her into the bath. She'd been so close to swallowing him whole, while kneeling before him. The scent of his masculinity enticed her, driving her craving to lick every inch of his body. But at his words, she acquiesced, allowing him to lead her into the heavenly vessel that awaited them. He always seemed to know what was best. *Was he ever wrong?* The question spun through her head as she relaxed, submerging into the sublime paradise. It was just what she needed, and he knew it. She found herself staring at him, wondering how he knew just about everything.

He quickly followed her into the bubbles, but lounged into the opposite side. As if sensing her impending protest at the lack of contact, he tugged on her feet, as his feet rested on either side of her hips.

Kalli gasped, slipping deeper into the tub.

"Give me those pretty feet." He began to inspect her perfectly pedicured, metallic blue painted toes. "You think too much."

"What?" she muttered.

"I can see you thinking, chérie. Whatever it is, you just need to accept it." He smiled knowingly. Rubbing her insoles, he was rewarded with a grateful moan. "You ladies with those high heels. As much as I enjoyed taking you from behind with you wearing nothing but stilettos, and damn you were hot by the way, I wouldn't last five minutes in those torture chambers."

Kalli laughed. "Hmm…somehow I think you'd manage it. After the past couple of days, I'm wondering what exactly you can't do?"

"I'll be happy to teach you my tricks."

"I just bet you would. Something tells me that I'd enjoy your lessons." She brushed one foot over his thigh playfully.

"The secret is taking advantage of all life gives you," he mused.

"Work hard. Play even harder?"

"Something like that. But it's more. Take you, for instance. I've thought long and hard about why you took those pills. But it's deprived you of your nature."

She quietly listened.

"Tell me about South Carolina, Kalli."

"I told you most of it. You know how it is in a pack. You're not just raised by your parents. My mom, she'd somehow managed to live in that hellhole. My Dad was verbally abusive from as far back as I can remember, but Mom was the one who protected me. When she died...I was alone. The Alpha, Gerald, he was nothing more than a bully. And by the time I was sixteen, my body was starting to look less like a child's. So I guess that was his cue to send for me one night. Of course, I went, because who says no to the Alpha?" Kalli quieted, as if she was reliving the horrifying experience.

"Did he rape you?"

"No, thankfully. He grabbed for me, ripped my shirt off, tried to maul me...but I fought him. I managed to grab one of those old-fashioned phones he had sitting on his desk; smacked him in the head with it. Of course, that earned me a good backhand. And that's when he informed me of my 'role' in the pack. Guess he didn't want me tainting his precious bloodlines. A few days later, I took off for New York City. Hid out. Got through college. You know the rest." She absentmindedly ran her hands up and down the tops of his calves.

Tristan forced every muscle in his body to relax as he listened to her recount what had happened to her. Strung out in anger, he tried to focus on her and not his own feelings.

"You know, I've been alive for a long time, watching the way most packs have progressed. These days we welcome hybrids, outlaw forced pairings and matings, et cetera. I can't take away the pain, but I'll promise you this," Tristan said, a serious expression washing over his face. "If this Gerald is still alive, he won't be for long."

As Kalli listened, she didn't bother telling him no. She wanted Gerald dead; the wolf in her screamed for his throat.

"When did you first shift?" He changed the line of questioning while still staying on the topic he wanted to learn about the most; her past.

"Not until my sophomore year in college."

"How'd you manage that?" Most wolves had shifted by their early teen years.

Kalli bit her lip, embarrassed to tell him what she'd done to thwart it. "I starved myself."

"What?" Tristan asked incredulously.

"I know, it's awful. I ate barely enough to sustain myself. But if I'd let myself change while in the pack, you know I'd have been raped within a full moon. Whatever... it worked. Of course as soon as I left, I started eating normally again. Still, it took a couple of years for my system to recover. And then one day, I just couldn't stop her."

"And?"

"And I found a safe, isolated place for me to shift in upstate New York. I'd shift alone," she admitted, knowing he'd ask her if she wasn't forthcoming. "But when I started taking the CLI about two years ago, it was the first time in my life that I could really stop hiding. Well, I guess I was still hiding, but it was in plain sight. People could sniff me all they wanted, and for all intents and purposes, I was human. No wolf to be found."

"Well now you can stop hiding. I mean it, Kalli; I won't let anything happen to you. You can stop taking the pills," he stated flatly.

"I don't know about that, Tristan."

"You need to learn to trust me. Do we need another lesson?"

"I think your lessons could be addicting," she smiled. "Seriously, I know you're there for me. It's just that, my wolf, she scares me. Well maybe not her exactly as much as the actual shifting. I've only shifted by myself…alone. Believe me when I tell you that it has unequivocally sucked, for lack of a better term."

"Maybe you just need a good teacher."

"A strong virile Alpha, perhaps?"

"Yes, someone who'd love nothing more than to see an enchanting she-wolf in the forest. With that raven hair of yours, I can't wait to see your coloring."

"I need to think about it," she hedged.

"Better think fast, chérie. After the summit tomorrow, we're heading up the mountains for the next week or so. Full moon is coming in a few days. I reckon if you don't take any more of those pills, you might be able to shift. It may take a little more time for you to be able to shift on demand though. It's not nice to mess with Mother Nature." Tristan leaned forward, letting his hands roam up to tease her inner thighs. His fingers magically massaged her. Nearing the apex of her legs, he trailed back toward her feet, purposely teasing her need.

Kalli sank further down into the tub, actively seeking his hands. "Ah…" she sighed in frustration, trying to concentrate on what he'd been saying. "Mother Nature, huh? Is that right?"

"The Alpha is always right," he joked, leaning back again.

Unable to take a second more of his teasing, Kalli sat straight up. Her hair fell forward as her tiny hardened tips poked through the long wet curls. She leaned over, crawling toward him on her hands and knees, until she was face to face with Tristan, mere inches from his lips. Her knees straddled his as she leaned over to kiss the hollow of his neck. Seeking to break his restraint, she continued her assault, pressing her lips everywhere but on his. As she brushed a kiss over his eyelid, she felt his hands on her waist pulling her toward him. She leaned into his ear. "I need you in me...now," she whispered.

Unacquainted with being prey, Tristan distinctly got the feeling she was about to make him hers. He struggled to lie still, letting her take the lead. Yet as her slippery flesh rubbed his, he just about snapped. "Kalli," he groaned. "You're killin' me." Seeking out her brazenly exposed breasts, he captured a taut rosy peak in his mouth. Feasting on her like a starving man, he switched to the other side, alternating his affections.

Kalli reached between his legs, closing her hand around his swollen shaft. Aching with need, she could feel her own sheath contracting in anticipation of him. Fisting his sex up and down, she rubbed the tip of him through her throbbing folds.

"Fuck, yeah." Tristan pushed his hips upward as she cuffed his sex with her fingers.

Slipping the head of his shaft slowly through her lips, he pressed at her pulsating core. She stilled a moment to catch his gaze before fully impaling herself on his cock.

"Tristan!" Kalli sucked a sharp breath as the walls of her sex expanded to accommodate him. Holding onto the sides of the tub, her head fell backwards in ecstasy.

"Yes, baby!" Tristan hissed. "Ride me. Ride me, hard." Pumping up into her, he held her waist. Goddess, she was so fucking perfect. Watching her rise up and down, milking him, he thought he'd pass out.

Pressing down to meet his every thrust, Kalli writhed against him while digging her fingertips into his shoulders.

She could feel her clit rub against his pelvis, hurling her toward orgasm. As he let go of her waist, she felt his hand reach around to her bottom. She sucked a breath at the sweet sensation of his fingertips descending down the crease of her ass. His unexpected touch only served to fuel her as she increased the pace of the rhythm.

Tristan grunted as his hard muscled flesh penetrated her tight depths. As her hot core clamped down on him, he fought back his release. From the sound of her panting, he knew she was on the edge, readying to come. Brushing his forefinger against her bottom, he circled the tight flesh, envisioning taking her there someday.

"Oh God, please, yes, do it," she encouraged at the feel of him.

"Oh yeah, let me in, Kalli. Take all of me, amour." While teasing her rosebud from behind, he leaned toward her breast. Taking a wet, shimmering bud into his mouth, he gently tugged at her tight nipple with his teeth.

Overwhelming sensations seized her body, catapulting her into an orgasm like she'd never known. Water sloshed out and over the side of the tub as she convulsed in pleasure, screaming his name.

"Goddess, yeah!" Tristan roared, as the hottest, longest climax of his life ripped through him. As his seed pumped deep within her womb, he fought the urge to mark her. He knew in that moment that he'd eventually have to give in to the internal struggle to claim her as his own; his mate. It was hard for him to fathom, but his wolf demanded it.

Recovering from her release, Kalli gently lifted off him, and laid back into his arms. Her heart raced as she contemplated the scenarios of how things would play out in the long-term. Like no other man or wolf she'd experienced,

Tristan swept her up in a tornado of lust and emotion. She wished that was all she felt for the man holding onto her tightly. The more he told her she was his, the more she was starting to believe him. Scared of her own feelings which grew deeper by the hour, she found all that she could do in that moment was to hold him back. She reasoned that if things continued, she might never let him go.

~⊛· *Chapter Seventeen* ·⊛~

Making love in the morning was exceedingly satisfying, Tristan thought to himself. It had been the first time he'd spent the night at his own home with a woman, and he certainly could get used to having Kalli live with him. Watching her make breakfast, this time only in the apron, proved to be yet another perk. Determined to get started on an antidote, Kalli asked to use his laptop, and he'd set her up in his office to do her research. While she worked, Tristan chose to conduct his business outside, having to follow-up with the clients from last night's gala. Sitting on his balcony, he relaxed; catching some sun felt good. Winter would be coming soon, and the cool breeze wouldn't feel quite as delightful.

The only thing troubling him was the bittersweet need he'd felt to mark her after making love. The gnawing urge threatened to grow into a compulsion, and he wasn't sure how to contain it. He'd been so content all these years as a lone wolf. The need to mate was simply a myth as far as he was concerned. How one wolf could give up his freedom to commit to an eternal lifetime with another was beyond comprehension. Until last night, he'd only heard stories about the unnatural craving that afflicted both the man and wolf.

He prayed it wasn't happening; denial was such a pleasant place until his wolf clawed his way back into his psyche, demanding to be fed. Unlike the man, the wolf cared not of a human male's desire for freedom. He had all the freedom he ever needed within the sanctuary of the pack. The mate completed his being, needing her like a fish needed water to survive. There was no deep thought about whether or not he should claim her; rather, he accepted the mating as easily as he accepted his need to feed.

Tristan contemplated how he really felt. At one time, he'd asked Sydney to move in with him, made love to her whenever possible. But he hadn't ever considered marking her; claiming her or mating her. The thought never even entered his head, no matter how good the sex was. Yet with Kalli, not only had he thought about it, he'd actively restrained himself from biting her; marking her as his for all others to see. He feared the need was growing stronger, and was unsure of how many more times he could make love to her without doing it. Logically, there was no solution to the enigma except to acknowledge that perhaps he'd found his mate. He reasoned the best he could do was hold on tight for the ride, because he knew for certain that he wasn't getting off the train.

As his thoughts drifted to business, he couldn't curb how jacked up he was in anticipation of tonight's summit. If Jax Chandler was in any way responsible for Paul or Toby's death, he was primed and ready to kill. Revenge was not something Tristan took lightly. People had families. Death always brought consequences to both the executioner and the prisoner. Unfortunately as Alpha, he'd been forced to mete out justice more times than he'd like to count, but that was the burden and responsibility of his position. The scars on his bloodstained soul spoke of the heavy price an Alpha paid in return for the safety of his pack.

Tristan heard the sliding doors open and caught a glimpse of Logan making himself a cup of coffee. He could have sworn he heard laughing before Logan poked his nose around the glass doors.

"Hey George, how's it goin'?"

"What?"

"George Hamilton, you know. Tan man. I'd ask you to put some clothes on but that's like asking a shark to become a vegetarian," he joked, noticing Tristan was sprawled out on the lounger wearing nothing but his boxers.

"The boys have to breathe. Besides, when you've got it and whatnot," he laughed. "Goddess, isn't this weather great? I love September."

"Glad to see you're in a good mood today considering we're about to go kick some ass tonight."

"All part of the job my dear Watson. And I must say that it's about fucking time." Tristan adjusted his sunglasses. "Everyone ready to roll?"

"Yeah, Simeon and Declan are coming with us. They're good to go. Kalli, coming with?"

"Oh yeah. She's ready as she's gonna be. It is what it is. You stick close to her, okay?"

"Why I'd love to, Alpha," he said drawing it out as if he was really going to enjoy it.

"Yeah, don't get used to it, smart ass."

"So, are we going to talk about it?" Logan asked with a broad knowing smile.

"Talk about what? I may be Alpha, but I'm no mind reader." Oh, but he knew exactly what Logan was asking.

"You. Her. Dance floor. Oh and the distinct sounds of screaming that only come with hot sex. Nothin' like the sound of 'Fuck me' reverberating throughout the Four

Seasons. Classic, bro." Logan slapped Tristan on the shoulder, busting at the seams laughing.

"What about it?" Tristan replied with a coy smile.

"You're done, man. Not that I blame you. Kalli is one sweet wolf. Ah, I love when I'm right," Logan declared.

"About what?"

"Oh, nothing. Sometimes it's best to let nature take its course. But you'd know all about that, wouldn't you, Alpha?" Logan chuckled, falling back into the chair.

Tristan scowled. Damn Logan and his visions. Tristan didn't want to even know what images had been flashing through his beta's dreams. It was nothing but trouble. Business was a different story, but his love life was off limits. Deciding not to encourage Logan, he ignored his comment. An Alpha knew when to hold 'em and when to fold 'em; therefore he kept his mouth shut.

On the ride over to the summit, Kalli kept quiet as she listened to Tristan and Logan run through different scenarios. Each and every one of them had dressed in all black with sturdy boots, in case there was debris in the meeting place. Due to the high probability of both shifting and violence, the facility chosen was selected for its privacy, not comfort. They'd agreed on an abandoned building in an isolated area of Camden for the summit. Considered neutral territory, the New Jersey Alpha had granted them permission to use the facilities, given the recent death of the Lyceum wolf.

The limo pulled up to the dilapidated building, and they poured out onto the street. Simeon, a muscular wolf, who rivaled any World Wrestling champion, led the pack, alert for any sign of an ambush. Simeon nodded, signaling an all clear to Tristan and Logan. Surrounding Kalli, they proceeded toward the two story, red bricked building. Once a neighborhood firehouse, the windows had all been boarded over; graffiti was scrawled across the whitewashed plywood.

The deafening silence reminded Kalli of the desolation she'd felt during her childhood. But tonight, there was a good chance that the disconcerting reticence would be sliced with the screams of death before dawn. Kalli swore she smelled the sickly odor of wolves from her old pack, yet the five men who stood at the long wooden table were unfamiliar. As they approached the table, the strangers rose.

"Alpha." Tristan nodded in respect toward the tall attractive wolf who held court in the center of the table. Exuding power, his strong facial features accentuated his Nordic complexion; cropped blonde hair gave way to piercing pale blue eyes. When he took notice of Kalli, she instinctively bowed her head in deference, and held tight to Logan's arm.

"Alpha, I'm pleased to meet with you tonight," he replied coolly.

"Shall we sit?" Tristan suggested, preferring to take them off guard by feigning a relaxed positioning. Yet his body was coiled tight; like an asp he was ready to strike. His wolf paced, eagerly awaiting battle.

"Certainly. This is my beta, Gilles." Kalli could have sworn they were twins, but kept her thoughts to herself. The last thing she planned on doing was talking at this meeting. The only reason she'd agreed to come was to identify wolves, if presented with the opportunity.

"And you know Logan. This, here, is Dr. Williams. She's here in the capacity of witness. You should also be aware that she's mine and under my protection."

"I see," Jax commented, looking Kalli over. She swore she could feel him undressing her even though she was buttoned up tighter than the queen's girdle. Opting for a simple nod, she swallowed, continuing to clutch poor Logan's arm, hoping she wasn't cutting off his circulation.

"As much as I'm enjoying the elegant accommodations, let's get to business. A little over a week ago, two wolves set fire to my club, Eden. The same wolves are suspected in the murder of a young wolf that occurred two nights ago. Sketches of the suspects have been provided to you via Logan. I'd be remiss not to mention that circumstances and specifics that led to a lupine death are confidential at this point as there is an ongoing police investigation. While P-CAP has presumably been notified of the murder, I believe we'd agree that as wolves we prefer to abide to our own rules," Tristan paused as Jax silently acknowledged his words with a small grin.

"In addition, as you may have been notified by Marcel, another young wolf was killed in New Orleans nearly two weeks ago. New York plates were found on the stolen car. I understand that he's forwarded the sketches of the dead wolves who drove the car, but to date, no Alpha has claimed responsibility. I am formally requesting your assistance in the apprehension of the suspects in both murders. With all due respect, and this is in no way an accusation, I need confirmation from you that your pack is not involved in either of these matters."

A deeply serious expression fell across Jax's face, and he addressed Tristan. "Alpha, please accept my sincere condolences on behalf of me and my entire pack. I take no offence to your need for confirmation, and I am pleased to inform you that I have not condoned nor have I ordered an attack on either the Lyceum Wolves or Marcel's pack. However, after viewing your sketch and careful distribution of the picture, I have brought you a gift. Call it a peace offering after the misunderstanding we had regarding your sister, if you will."

Tristan stared intently at Jax. He could feel his wolf readying to shift having smelled blood. The energy in the room thrummed with tension; he was aware he'd have his prize.

"Bring it out!" Jax barked, never taking his eyes off of Tristan.

A bright red wooden door with peeling paint flew open, and a stubby, dirty man wrapped in heavy silver chains was thrust into the open space by a burly, unyielding thug holding a gun.

Kalli eyes flashed to the weapon. She guessed silver bullets came with the shiny gun; ones meant to kill wolves. *Breathe deeply. Breathe deeply.* She swore by how quickly her heart was racing that she'd need a healthy dose of oxygen by the time she got out of there…if she got out alive. But as soon as the man was shoved into the spotlight, she gasped. *Sato. South Carolina Wallace Pack.* Relief momentarily swept through her until she realized that number one, the other wolf wasn't in attendance, and two, punishment would be served.

Easily identifying the man as one of the wolves from the sketches, Tristan turned to Kalli. "Do you know this man, Dr. Williams?" he asked formally.

"Yes, Alpha," she croaked, shrinking into Logan. It was as if she was a young girl again, cowering. She felt Sato's eyes bore into her and looked away. "I...ugh..I think his name is Sato. I'm not one hundred percent on the last name. But without a doubt, this man was at the fire, and he's part of the South Carolina Wallace Pack."

"You fucking bitch!" he screeched at her. Even chained, he was formidable. Baiting Kalli, he continued to yell. "You're nothing but a traitorous hybrid whore! Gerald's still waitin' for you, missy. Oh yeah, you owe him. He'll have ya on your back in no time spreading those filthy legs and..."

Before he had a chance to finish, Tristan slammed him into silence against a wall, crushing his larynx with the brunt of his forearm.

Kalli fought for air, attempting to quell both her burgeoning anger and fear. She glanced across the table and caught a glimpse of Jax smiling as if he was enjoying watching Tristan's attack. As if sensing that Kalli was about to lose it, Logan pulled her close to his side, putting a protective arm around her, and placed his finger to his lips, signaling her to remain silent.

"You killed my wolf; my son," Tristan roared, unrelentingly maintaining his hold.

An evil smirk broke across the man's face. "Not so tough now, Alpha, are ya? That kid was your weakness. We gutted him good."

A loud crack resounded throughout the room as Tristan smashed the wolf's head against the wall, leaving a dent in the sheet rock.

"Where's the other wolf?" Tristan spat at him.

"Like I'd tell ya. But don't worry, he's still out there. In fact, he'll probably find you first....he torched your club good after we got thrown out. And your bitch, Gerald is looking for her. You can kill me but this won't be the end for any of you," he sneered, spitting saliva into the air with each spoken word.

Tristan's steely eyes settled on the killer. In a cold, low voice, he deliberately and slowly delivered the death sentence, each word laced with intent. "Tonight you're goin' to die just like Toby. And like him, you will run for your life. As confusion and despair threaten to overtake your senses, dread will engulf your entire being. You will beg the Goddess for your despicable worthless life as I watch the life drain from your eyes. You've got a thirty second lead, but know this; within the next five minutes, your life will end."

Tristan released him, ripping the chains off of the man as easily as if he was pulling apart string cheese. The acrid odor of burning flesh from the silver burning Tristan's hands hung in the air. Like a caged animal, the man took off running, clothes flying in the process as he prepared to shift.

Kalli held her breath, trying not to hyperventilate at the sight. Witnessing Tristan's furor first hand jolted through her like electricity. She'd never seen an Alpha so fierce and primal; a purely spectacular male. Hating Sato and everything he represented, she felt no sympathy for the killer. Her only regret was that she wouldn't be able to witness his death.

Tristan ripped off his leather jacket, t-shirt and jeans within seconds. As soon as the air hit his naked skin, he instantly shifted into his beast. Turning his head just once to glance at Kalli, he howled and ran out into the darkness.

Stealthily, the black wolf weaved in and out of the shadows, scenting his prey. He crouched low to the ground, hearing a whine in the distance. Sprinting at full speed, he took off toward the enemy, who was attempting to hide in a nearby shed. Images of Toby flashed through his mind, surging the rage; the need for revenge. The thirst for blood danced on his tongue.

As he rounded the corner, the grey matted wolf darted into a deserted house, and Tristan closed in pursuit. Inwardly, he laughed, knowing the wolf had essentially trapped himself with his own irons. Hunching down, he quietly padded into the blackened entranceway. He could smell the blood of the wolf in the room; he must have cut himself in the street.

A rat squeaked in the corner, momentarily distracting Tristan. He growled menacingly toward the rodent, and it scurried off. Still smelling Sato's scent, he launched himself up the stairs, which led into a parlor of sorts. The waiting enemy snarled, beckoning Tristan to attack quickly, increasing the chance he'd make a mistake. But Tristan wouldn't make this quick. Sato had shown Toby no mercy, chasing him down, eviscerating him slowly. So he'd planned do the same to Sato, inflicting the exact pure terror Toby must have felt. Circling Sato, Tristan bared his teeth, approaching and then receding and back again. He snapped at him, tearing off a chunk of Sato's fur; blood sprayed the floor. *Is that how you made Toby feel? The pain of the bullets tearing through his skin. The scent of his own blood filling his nostrils as he tried to shift.*

Sato whined in pain, but refused to retreat. The large grey wolf advanced with great speed, jumping at Tristan's head. Teeth sliced through his ear as blood and fur flew into the air. Refusing to yelp, Tristan let the pain ignite his rage. He quickly flipped himself around, until his teeth were firmly rooted in Sato's pelt. The harder the other wolf tried to shake him off the harder Tristan held on, not killing him…yet. Sato twisted and turned until he finally fell to his back, baring his belly submissively. As Tristan went to release his hold, Sato gnashed his teeth in one last attempt to maul the Alpha. Anticipating his strike, Tristan struck, sinking his teeth into the soft tissue under the chin. Blood flooded his mouth as he shredded the wiry fur and flesh. Slowly he tore it apart, bit by bit, until his prey stopped moving. Releasing the wolf, Tristan circled around the body, until it transformed into the remains of a shell that used to be Sato. Throat torn out, the sanguine cord of the spine laid on the dusty floor, providing evidence of the kill.

Tristan howled in mourning for the wolf spirit; there was always a consequence for taking a life. As Alpha, the heavy scar on his soul settled. Responsibilities and vengeance to the pack ran deep. In his actions and thoughts, he felt he'd brought Toby a step closer to peace. Others would pay as well, but for tonight, he'd avenged for his pack.

Tristan strode into the warehouse, naked and bloody, fresh from the kill. Kalli screamed his name, struggling to break free of Logan's hold. Stifling her cries, the silence seemed to mirror Tristan's tenebrous disposition. Although he'd been gone for less than fifteen minutes, his somber expression spoke of war. Deftly pulling on his t-shirt and jeans, he slipped on his shoes and approached the table.

"I am in gratitude for your gift, Alpha. Clearly, this is just the beginning. One battle. You should be advised that after today's news, we'll be going after the Wallace Pack.

Please contact me directly should you receive any more information on the other wolf," Tristan stated emotionlessly. His normally warm amber eyes appeared darker, tinged in sadness.

"You are very welcome," Jax remarked. Standing up from the table, he extended his hand. As Tristan shook it, Jax caught sight of his wariness. "Alpha, it had to be done. If there's one thing I know, it is the weight we both share. Good luck to you going after the others."

Tristan nodded in understanding. Taking Kalli from Logan, he hugged her tightly. "Let's go. Our business is finished here."

Before leaving, Tristan turned to Simeon. "Body's in the third house on the left. After we get home, grab a couple of the boys and ship it to South Carolina."

"Got it boss." Simeon knew the drill without Tristan saying any more. It was a message to the Wallace Pack wolves, and he'd be happy to help him deliver it.

-❦ *Chapter Eighteen* ❦-

The macabre vibe continued well after they'd left the warehouse. Rather than a slew of consolatory comments, a muted contemplation blanketed the car. On the way over the bridge to Philadelphia, Tristan received a call from Tony informing him that the body of Lindsay, Kalli's assistant, had been found in the UVH parking lot earlier in the evening. She'd been found stuffed under her car, throat slit. The cowardly act had been caught on tape, and one of the sketches matched the suspect; the second wolf, Morris.

Tony said they believed that both wolves had visited the hospital in search of Kalli, while she'd been held by Alexandra. During that visit, an exchange of information had taken place between Lindsay and the suspects. An intensive computer search showed evidence that Lindsay had been responsible for hacking into several computers at the hospital, including Kalli's. A large lump sum of money had been recently deposited in Lindsay's account, suggesting she'd sold Kalli out, and possibly others. Tony said it was too early to tell at this point. They weren't exactly sure of the motive for her killing, but reasoned that perhaps the wolves wanted to tie up loose ends after Toby's murder.

The news of Lindsay's slaying and betrayal angered Kalli. But she held the emotion in tightly, refusing to shed a tear or waste her thoughts on the foolish girl who'd helped kill Toby. The incident only served as a further incentive to help Tristan track down the other wolf. Seeing Tristan's display of power earlier left no doubt he'd be caught.

When they finally reached Livingston One, they were greeted by both Julie and Mira, who both offered assistance. Logan quietly confided what happened at the summit with both women, while Tristan and Kalli retreated to his condo. Normally jovial and confident, Tristan seemed distant and uncharacteristically reserved. Like Tristan, Kalli knew that things were far from over, especially since they suspected that the CLI was in Gerald's hands.

"I've gotta take a shower," he muttered, walking toward the master bedroom. "You wanna join me?"

"Sure, um, I've just got to stop by my room a sec, okay?"

"Okay, meet you in there."

She nodded, wishing she could take his hurt away. He needed comfort tonight, and she swore she'd do everything in her power to help him. The killing appeared to come at a great cost to him, or perhaps he was mourning Toby. Observing Tristan in the element of battle had been both exhilarating and exhausting. She couldn't even imagine what it had done to him, but she'd go to him, care for him, and make him whole again. But Kalli knew there was a critical singular task she had to complete before she could give herself to him fully; one which would allow her to start her life anew.

Going into her bathroom, she stared at herself in the mirror. Taking a deep breath, she peeled off the black clothing she'd donned for the summit. But even once her clothes were gone, the morose film of violence still clung to her skin. She needed to shake off this evening's events as much as anyone, but she couldn't stop thinking about Tristan, the man and the wolf. Reveling in his animalistic display of dominance, she could no longer deny her true self.

Stark naked, she wrapped her fingers around the tan bottle on the countertop, which contained the CLI. Remorse for Toby's death still remained, but pride for surviving all those years without detection surged through her veins. There was no use in regretting what her childhood could or should have been. There was only now. And without a doubt, Tristan and Lyceum Wolves commanded her future. In her mind's eye her alter ego awakened, enthusiastically prancing in anticipation. Unscrewing the white top, she took one last look at the pills before flushing all of them down the toilet.

Instead of going to his room, Tristan had decided to turn around and head toward the kitchen. He'd torn off his clothes, removed his shoes, and threw them into a black plastic bag. Texting housekeeping, they arrived within seconds to take it to the incinerator for disposal. The scent of the dead wasn't something one could wash out of clothing. Snatching a bottle of cognac and a couple of glasses, he retired to his private sanctuary.

Tristan let the hot spray sting his skin as his consciousness drifted to Kalli. Mulling it over all day, he'd struggled to comprehend the urge to claim her. Yet deep down, he knew exactly why. Although Logan's earlier cryptic comments had irritated the hell out of him, he realized at some point later in the afternoon that his beta knew for certain what he'd been renouncing. But his stubborn attitude could no longer deny fate. Never truly understanding what it was like for other mated wolves, the calling of his mate was a song he craved like no other.

Accepting and acting on this newfound realization were two entirely different things. Kalli hadn't even accepted her own wolf, so he wasn't about to slam her with this new information any time soon. Reflecting on the summit, he prayed he hadn't frightened the hell out of her. But like he'd told her, there was no hiding one's true nature. And his was lethal.

He placed his forehead against the cool tile as the calming scent of Kalli wafted into the room. Out of his peripheral vision, he could see her white robe drop to the floor, giving way to her silky olive skin. Through the beveled glass blocks, he watched the black curls spill down her back as she removed the band and pins, which had bound her hair.

In the reflection of the mirror, Kalli's breath caught as she noticed his sexy silhouette; like a powerful animal, he stretched his arms upward, leaning against the shower wall. Slipping around the enclosure in search of Tristan, she admired the sight of his bronzed dripping wet skin. The muscled planes of his back gave way to the solid curve of his buttocks and long powerful legs. Jets of water sprayed from each wall, and by the time she reached him, warm drops poured down her lithe but curvy body.

Within inches of his body, she placed her hands on his shoulders tracing her fingers upward until she reached hold of his rock-hard biceps. Giving them a gentle caress, her hands trailed down the hard muscles of his back. She heard him hiss; his head lolled backward in contentment. Her hands explored his trim waist until her arms were wrapped all the way around him. Pressing forward to embrace him, her swollen bosom crushed against the expanse of his back and her legs straddled his. Spreading her fingers, she touched his wonderfully broad chest down to the rippled abs beneath his warm bare skin.

"You okay?" she asked lovingly, closing her eyes while the cheek of her face pressed softly against his back.

"Chérie, there is no place I'd rather be right now," he mumbled. "Goddess, you feel so good. So perfect." He moved to turn around to face her, but she stilled his movement.

"Shhhh...My Alpha, let me take care of you tonight," she whispered, reaching for the soap. "Relax, baby."

Lathering the bubbly cleanser into her small hands, she sluiced slippery liquid over his clavicles, massaging his neck until he released a small moan. Her hands continued their assault, rubbing the globes of his bottom and down his crease. Brushing his thighs, she gently turned him until he faced her.

He stood silently watching her, enjoying the feel of her smooth palms on his skin. She rinsed her hands to fill them with cleanly scented shampoo. Reaching up into his hair, her pebbled pink tips grazed his chest. He sighed in aching need at the feel of them, but allowed her to thoroughly wash his blood-matted hair. Squeezing out the excess lather, she gently tilted his head back into the spray.

Again, she resumed washing him with suds. Moving from under his arms to his biceps, she carefully attended to him all the way down to his fingers. Kalli's breath caught at the sight of his tanned, sculptured chest. He opened his eyes to catch her gaze as she cleaned him all the way down to his belly. Keeping eye contact, she let her fingers deliberately trace the muscularly cut v that led to his groin. Whisking her palms downward, she spread his legs, stroking the juncture of his thighs. A ragged gasp escaped his lips as she cupped his velvety sac; his head fell backwards to rest on the tile, delighting in the sensation. Wrapping her other hand around his straining erection, she pumped him up and down, smoothing her thumb over the plump head.

Tristan had never in his life been so open and vulnerable to a woman, letting her roam free on his body. From the first touch of her fingers to his shoulders to the graze of her nails on his chest, he tensed in excitement, letting her work her magic. She'd asked him to relax, but the agonizing arousal coursed through his body like he'd touched a live wire. It took every bit of self-restraint to not rush to make love to her. Rather, he willingly submitted to the sweet pain of her titillating stimulation, anticipating her next touch. As if she was performing a purification ritual, he felt the dark cloud in his soul lift.

As he peered into the depths of her eyes, the intense affection he felt for Kalli teased his lips. He wanted to tell her how much she meant to him. More than lust, he was falling fast without a parachute. He bit his lip in resistance, thwarting the words that threatened to expose his heart. A jolt ran through his body as her tiny hands massaged his hot swollen flesh.

"Kalli," he cried out in pleasure before she released him. Lovingly, she turned his body once more, rinsing him clean. He gave into her direction, again his eyes meeting hers.

As if performing a sensual rumba, she refused to release him from her trance. Smiling, she gracefully knelt before him, combing her fingernails down the front of his thighs. Tristan sucked a blissful breath. The sight of his beautifully bared female on her knees, parting her lips, sent blood pulsating into his already hard cock. Incredibly stunning, her drenched hair clung to her skin. Puckered nipples brushed across his thighs, as she leaned forward. Darting her tongue outward, she licked the underside of his engorged shaft. He could have sworn he'd died and gone to heaven as her warm lips encased him.

Kalli relished his taste as she sucked him deeply. Releasing his sex from her mouth, she fisted his swollen staff while she laved his testicles, rolling them over her tongue. Once again she took his rigid flesh into her mouth, slowly swallowing all of him. Digging her fingers into the cheeks of his ass, she pulled him toward her until he began to pump himself in and out of her lips. She moaned, as the excitement of tasting him incited her own passion; her core ached with need, begging to be touched.

As the intoxication of her actions spread throughout his body, Tristan struggled to speak. "Mon amour…please." He grasped her hair. "I can't stop. I'm going to come."

His words only inflamed her arousal, taking him faster and deeper. Refusing to let go, she grasped his bottom, encouraging him to thrust harder, edging him closer to his impeding orgasm.

No longer able to resist as her lips tightened around his throbbing hardness, he screamed her name, gasping for breath, "Kalli!"

His cry of deliverance resounded as he abandoned himself to his erotic release. Groaning as she took all of him, he poured himself into her, her unrelenting lips and tongue mercilessly milking him dry. He reached for her, pulling her up into his embrace, the warm water of the shower caressing their intermingled bodies.

Kalli's chest felt tight, so swollen with emotion, she couldn't look at him without revealing her feelings. Resisting the temptation to fall in love with him was going to be difficult, she thought. Everything about him from the way he playfully conversed to his resplendent black wolf captivated her. Her Alpha, the magnificent man within her arms, was hers.

⤜⚙ *Chapter Nineteen* ⚙⤛

"Anastas," Kalli confided.

"Hmm," Tristan replied, lazily drawing circles on the inside of her palm while they lay entwined in his bed. After turning off the shower, Kalli had insisted on drying every square inch of him with a warmed, fluffy towel. Within minutes, they both fell comfortably into Tristan's large inviting bed.

"Anastas. Kalli Anastas. That's my real name."

"Anastas," he repeated, the word rolling off his smooth tongue in a Greek accent. "It suits you. Thank you for trusting me with it. See, my lessons are working."

"Yes, professor, indeed they are, although I'm afraid I may require many more lengthy, hands-on demonstrations." She brought his hand up to her lips for a brief kiss.

Tristan chuckled.

"And I have something else to share with you," Kalli continued.

"Do share."

She quieted, pushing up onto her forearms and tummy so she could look at him directly. "The pills. They're gone."

"Gone?"

"Gone as in I flushed them gone. Gone as in I'm returning to my nature as a wise Alpha encouraged me to do." She grinned, remembering their previous discussion.

Tristan pulled her up into his arms and kissed her slowly and gently. "Mon amour, I was hoping…but you had to make the decision on your own. And now there's nothing stopping us."

"Stopping us from what?" She eyed him inquisitively.

"It's just that I'm looking forward to sharing that part of myself with you. I want to run and hunt and…" He let his words trail off on purpose, unsure of how much of his feelings he should disclose.

"And?" She left the question hanging, yet it went unanswered.

He simply smiled at her, somewhat stalling, somewhat just lost in her altogether.

"Mr. Livingston," she challenged. "Trust goes both ways. Do you need me to teach you a lesson?"

"I'm sure you would, chérie. The scary part is that I might like it."

"Come on Tristan. Spill it," she whined, in an attempt to rush the conversation, dying to know what he wanted to do with her.

"First let me ask you something." He stilled in preparation for her response. "Tonight at the meeting. What were your impressions? Truth."

"At first, I was terrified. It was suffocating in there. My whole life I've lived in fear of wolves. And then, there I am at a summit of all things, with two seriously lethal Alpha males." She rolled her eyes.

"Lethal?"

"Damn straight lethal. And then seeing Sato, I was torn between cowering and attempting to kill him myself. The thing is that I know that there is this part of me, a very big part, that abhors violence, but I wanted Sato dead. Not only did I want him dead, I was exhilarated by your power, your strength. I wanted to watch while you took him down." She let out a deep breath. "Oh God. It sounds awful, doesn't it?"

"No. Vengeance is bittersweet. No doubt he had it coming after what he'd done to you, even if it was indirectly. And he'd killed Toby. The man lacked remorse. He'd do it again," Tristan concluded thoughtfully.

"So, now that you know all my secrets, what gives? What else do you want to do with me? Besides having your wicked way with me?" She laughed.

He cupped her cheeks in his hands, letting his thumb brush her lips. "Kalli, I…I've been alone for such a long time. But now. Meeting you. My wolf. Fuck, I'm incredibly inarticulate tonight," he huffed in frustration.

Kalli giggled and cuddled closer, lying her back down on his chest again. Maybe it would be easier for him if he didn't look at her while saying whatever it was he needed to tell her?

"Okay, here it is. I've never in my adult life lived with a woman. Came close with Sydney, but she wasn't my mate. And I never felt this urge…this urge to claim her…Mira neither. I've never felt that craving…that need to mark someone. To claim them."

"What are you saying?"

"I can't resist any longer…this need. I don't know how to explain it. At first I blamed it on my wolf. It is, but it isn't. You and I…there's something serious between us. I mean the sex is amazing but it's not just that. I've got to have you…have you as in 'you are mine'. And not like 'mine' meaning part of the pack either. It's more. So much more than that." He blew out a deep breath, fearing he was fucking up the entire conversation.

"It's okay, Tristan. I know. I feel strongly about you too." *I'm falling in love with you.* "I wish I could play coy and pretend I don't feel it, but I just can't. I want this…what's happening between us. And my wolf, well, she's been at me since the minute you put me in your lap in your car," she admitted softly.

"I want to claim you, Kalli. Mark you. Do you understand what I'm saying?" Done with hedging the issue, he put all his cards on the table. If he didn't tell her now, he'd end up doing it the next time they made love. The call was beyond his control.

Kalli's stomach danced with butterflies. She'd never been claimed before but she knew that it would be a sign to the pack that she was his potential mate. Her wolf rolled in submission, baring her neck, awaiting his mark. "Do it. I want to be yours. I know it's taken me a while to trust, but you've shown me how important it is to be myself. But the next moon…I'll need your help."

Tristan's pride swelled at her words. He breathed a sigh of relief; she'd felt it too. Not ready to mention he truly believed she was his mate, he celebrated the fact that she wanted this.

"Baby, you've got no idea how much I'm going to help you. Your first shift with the pack; I promise you that it will be a magical experience," he declared. "You'll carry my mark. But you must know that there is no other for me from here on out." He moved his hand downward, now circling her very pretty, very hard, pink tips.

"Alpha, are you giving up your naughty ways?" she teased.

"No way, chérie. I'm only providing full disclosure. All kinky practices are now officially reserved for you." He pinched her nipple, enjoying hearing her squeak in pleasure. Declaring his intention to mark her ignited her excitement. Her delicious scent filled the room. His little wolf was terribly aroused. Goddess, he loved that she was so responsive. Truth be told, he loved everything about her.

"Ah," she moaned at his touch. "Do tell me all about these kinky practices. Hmm....I don't think I can wait." She found herself involuntarily grinding her hips against his leg.

He shifted, reaching over to slide open a bedroom drawer, retrieving a small black bag. A dark smile broke across his face, aware that he was about to push her limits.

"A mystery?" she queried, nervously biting her lip. *He'd been planning this? What was in the damn bag?*

"What? I know how to shop for more than dresses and earrings. In fact, I think this little store may become one of our favorite spots," he boasted, anticipating playing with her. She'd nearly fallen apart at his dark intrusion the last time they'd made love. He opened the bag, gesturing for her to look inside it.

Kalli gasped as she pulled out the small plug. Her eyes widened at him in disbelief.

"I...I don't know, Tristan," she stammered, trying to conceal her excitement.

"No hiding your real feelings, chérie. I know the truth. The way you flew apart last time I touched you with my fingers, I thought a little toy was in order. As much as I'd love to take you there, and I would," he crooned in a low sexy voice, melting away her concerns, "that's not happening tonight. But I know you'll love this little toy, here. Don't you trust me? Perhaps you need another lesson?" he breathed, sliding his palm down her belly.

"Ah, yes," Kalli moaned in anticipation, his fingers teasing below her belly button.

"The very thought of me taking you there excites you, doesn't it? Your lovely flushed skin and rapid breathing gives you away," He slid his hand down into her slick heat, pressing a finger up into her core. "Ah, yes. You're soaking wet."

"Tristan, yes."

"I've gotta taste you, baby." Tristan flipped Kalli onto her back, settling his face between her legs. His warm breath skated across her mound while he continued gliding his finger in and out of her hot sheath. With his other hand, he ran two fingers down her nether lips, gently separating her to expose her treasured pearl.

"Mon amour, your pussy is so fucking beautiful. So smooth. Now relax, let me taste you," he ordered right before he delved into her aching sex. With a broad sweep of his flat tongue, he brushed over her clit, and she cried out in ecstasy.

"Oh my God." She reached to grab onto the sheets, balling them up in her fists. As his satiny tongue rubbed her sensitive bud, she nearly flew off the bed. She began panting wildly as he relentlessly laved her.

He darted his tongue through her folds, relishing her honeyed cream. Adding another thick finger, he pumped into her while increasing the pressure on her swollen nub. Over and over he flicked, storming her senses.

Kalli thrashed her head back and forth as her orgasm danced within reach. Panting gave way to incoherent screaming as she begged for release. "Tristan, please, I can't...I need...yes."

Her pleading was music to his ears. As her walls began to quiver, he sucked on her clitoris, pressing his tongue against it at the same time.

A slamming release shook Kalli to her very core. "Tristan!" she mouthed, over and over, feeling as if she'd left her body. Thrusting her hips up into his mouth, she sought to milk the shuddering climax which ripped from her head to her toes. By the time he'd released her, she was breathing so hard it was as if she'd run a marathon. Her face flamed as she descended back into reality, cognizant of how she'd lost it.

Giving her no time to think, Tristan roughly flipped her over on her stomach. He adjusted her positioning so that her arms and head comfortably rested on the pillow. Pulling her hips upward, he spread her legs so he fit nicely at her entrance.

Frustrated at the emptiness, she mewled in protest.

"Easy, baby," he cajoled. "I could feast on you all day, but it's time for your toy."

Kalli nodded into the pillow in agreement, eager for him to enter her. She was on fire with need. His finger ran through her slippery folds yet again, and she released a gasp in relief. As Kalli wriggled toward him, seeking his touch, she felt a cool liquid run down her bottom.

"Relax now, Kalli. Push back," he instructed as he slowly pressed the small plug into her back hole.

"Ahhh...Tristan. It's...it's...I can't," she hissed, while pushing backward.

"You're doing it chérie. That's it. Almost there."

The small burn she'd felt, was quickly replaced with a fullness she'd never experienced. Foreign yet erotic, she loved the feel of it inside her. She moved back to him, enjoying the strange stimulation that roused her hunger for him.

"It's all the way in, baby. Just get used to it for a minute." He pushed the rubber stub in further, twisting it back and forth. The way she was writhing on it, he reckoned she'd come if he kept at it. "There you go. Just feel. Breathe."

"Yes, Tristan. I need you in me now."

His erect manhood throbbed in excitement. Sliding a hand under her belly and holding the plug in place, he edged the head of his erection at her most tender flesh. Inch by glorious inch, he eased himself into her until he was fully seated.

Kalli sucked a breath as he entered her. There were no words to describe the incredibly overwhelming sensation of being entirely filled. As he began to move, she found herself pushing back onto him in cadence. Quickening gasps accompanied by ripples of pleasure flowed deep within her womb, taking her to the edge. As he played with the plug, pulling it out and then pressing it back in, at the same time he thrusted.

She shuddered, no longer able to hold back the tidal wave threatening to crash over her. "Tristan! Fuck me! Harder! Yes! I'm coming. Please," she yelled into the pillow, convulsing into orgasm.

As her tight core fisted his cock, sweat broke across his brow. The feel of the plug through the thin barrier, stroked his manhood, as she pulsed around him. As she began to scream, he sank himself into her again and again, harder and harder. The sound of his flesh meeting hers echoed in the room. Breathing hard, his body seized in the frenzy of the simultaneous explosion. With an unfettered cry of fulfillment, he reached up under her belly with both hands until her back was pressed to his chest. With a final thrust, he roared. Canines extended, he bit down hard onto her shoulder, forever marking her as his.

Kalli reared up to accept his bite, still lost in the crescendo of her climax. As his teeth met her golden skin, she cried out in delight as the power of her Alpha entered her body. As much as she was his in that moment, he was hers in return.

⊸◈ *Chapter Twenty* ◈⊷

The ride up to the mountains took a little over two hours. Tristan had explained that the burial wouldn't take place until dusk. This time of year the sun set around seven thirty, so they'd have plenty of time to get settled in before the ritual began. Logan had already left for the mountains, as had most of the city wolves. After finishing several business calls, Tristan and Kalli set off around noon in a large SUV that towed a small Harley trailer. The warm September weather was a great time to ride, and Tristan was looking forward to taking Kalli out on his bike.

Since it was early in the month, some of the leaves were beginning to change color, preparing the trees for their winter slumber. By late September, the foliage would be at its peak. From Mountain Maples to Sweetgums, the leaves frolicked in the warm autumn wind. The scenic drive helped to soothe Kalli's racing thoughts. She absentmindedly fingered the spot where Tristan had marked her. While the skin was not broken or scarred, the sweet tingle of his bite remained. Growing up, she'd been told that each pack had its own distinctive markings. Once claimed, the mark would either grow more prominent as the couple forged their way toward mating or conversely, it would fade if the pair separated.

When she'd looked at her shoulder in the mirror that morning, it looked like a tiny rose-colored tattoo in the shape of an infinity symbol, as if two loops were intertwined. She supposed it suited her, reminding her of how she and Tristan fit perfectly together. As soon as he'd bitten her skin, her wolf had awakened. She struggled helplessly to emerge, begging to claim him in return. But since she hadn't turned in so long, it was impossible. She needed to shift again in order to mark him.

She wondered nervously what it would be like to shift into her wolf with Tristan at her side. In the past, it had been an exceedingly lonely experience. But the more time she spent with Tristan, the more she wanted to share everything with him: her body, her mind and her wolf.

"Hey, we're here," Tristan commented, jarring her from her contemplations.

Large pine trees towered over and around an imposing grid-ironed fence, which looked like it could easily impale someone if they tried to climb over it. Tristan pulled the car up to a security panel. Punching in a code, the doors opened, allowing them access to the unmarked compound.

"See there." He pointed to a large A-framed building. "That's the clubhouse. Tennis courts and the pool are behind it. There's a small general store in there that we run. Carries sundries, a small selection of groceries...stuff like that. We kind of run the place like a resort, but some of the people stay year round."

They continued down and around a curvy road, which led into what could best be described as a development of cabins interspersed between the enormous trees.

"These, here, are mostly owned by families. We've got a condo building too, where a lot of the single wolves stay.

My place is up here near the top of the mountain. Logan usually stays with me most of the time, even though he's got a condo. It's got plenty of rooms, and I like the company," he explained.

As they passed a flat clearing, Kalli was surprised to see several horses in a rolling field; a barn sat in the distance. "You keep horses?"

"Yeah. Janie's in charge of the stables. She gives lessons to the pups, and some of us pay her to care for our horses."

Making a right turn into a winding driveway, a two-story home sat enclosed in forest. "And this is home," he declared.

"It's beautiful, Tristan, really." Admiring the tan-colored log cabin, Kalli wondered what it would be like to grow up here. A stark contrast to the sleek skyscraper, it was warm and inviting.

"You like?" he asked proudly. It was his escape from the city, and he hoped his urban woman would enjoy the country. He treasured his time in the mountains, and this truly was his sanctuary. It was important to him that she loved it as much as he did.

"What's not to like? Hey, do we have time to go for a hike?" she asked excitedly.

Tristan laughed. Warmth settled in his chest. As his mate, she fit him like a glove. The more time he spent with her, the stronger their bond grew. He loved being with her, talking to her, making love to her. He shook his head silently as it hit him. The mark; it was only the beginning. As much as he wanted to deny the feelings deep within his heart, he was falling in love with her. And it all felt natural, like it was meant to be.

He never thought he'd live to see the day when he considered mating a female. But now, happily, his world had been turned upside down by a raven-haired half-wolf who enjoyed cooking in her underwear. He laughed.

"What?" Kalli smiled as if she read his thoughts.

"Nothing. Just thinking about how I like to see you cook in your underwear."

Kalli began laughing with him. "Well, I guess it is a good thing we found each other, considering your penchant for nudity, Alpha. I can see why you like this isolated house," she teased.

"Wait until you see the hot tub. I've got plans for you," he promised, getting out of the car without waiting for a response. His cock jerked just thinking about her hot little body sitting on top of him while the hot bubbles massaged their skin.

A high vaulted ceiling with a floor to ceiling stone fireplace greeted them as they entered his home. The home's airy feeling was counterbalanced by the glow of the gas-lit fire. A U-shaped, sienna leather sectional sofa facing the hearth sat on oak planked floors. The general décor was clean and classic with exposed woods offset by earthy brown tones. A modern white kitchen, complete with black speckled granite countertops merged seamlessly with the great room.

Considering Kalli had spent her entire adult life living inside matchbook-sized apartments, the spacious house felt extraordinarily cozy and relaxing. Conjuring up thoughts ranging from roasting marshmallows, to making love on the floor in front of the fire, to chasing toddlers, Kalli wrapped her arms around herself. She inwardly questioned her own feelings. It was not like as a girl or even as a young woman she'd ever dreamed of getting married or having a family. But everything about Tristan was changing how she saw the world, how she felt about everything. He was like a missing piece in the puzzle that was her life.

As she explored, Tristan set down the bags and got to work preparing something special. "I've got a surprise for you," he announced from the kitchen.

She looked over to see him mulling about in his kitchen. *Was he preparing a meal?*

"Does the surprise include food? Because if it does, I'm in."

"Did you bring jeans?" he asked. "As much as I love easy access, you really need pants for this surprise. Also, boots or sneakers would be good."

"You're bad! Easy access, huh? Somehow that does not surprise me. You are something else, wolf," she chuckled.

"Hey, I am *the* wolf, to you."

"That you are," she assured him. "Well, I do love a good surprise. But I love food even more." *I really just love you.* The words ran through her head, and she smiled at the thought. God, she was in deep with no means of escape. At this point there was no fighting the tide. Crossing the great room, she reached over the counter, snatched up a piece of cheese and stuffed it in her mouth before she could say anything else that would divulge her true feelings.

"No guessing. And no more food either, until we get to our secret destination," he said mysteriously.

"Meanie," she jested, wondering what was in store for her next. A myriad of emotions stirred. She was already nervous about meeting his pack. How would people react to a hybrid that hadn't shifted in two years? A hybrid who'd created the drug that prevented Toby from shifting? Would they blame her for his death? And then there was the mark, his claim on her body and soul. How would they feel about their Alpha, who'd marked her as his female? Her mind raced trying to figure out what he possibly could have cooked up as a surprise. In the recesses of her mind, she considered the enlightening, very sensual lessons Tristan had given her. *Trust.* She took a deep breath as she attempted to put her education to good use.

"This! Is! Awesome!" Kalli squealed while trying not to frighten the horse or fall off it, both of which seemed like possibilities. "I love it! Really. I can't believe this was my surprise. Thank you so much!"

"Easy, chérie. Snowflake is very relaxed, but you gotta watch where you're going," Tristan warned. He'd made her cover her eyes on the way over to the stables. When she saw the dressed horses, she jumped up and down like a kid at Christmas. Such a basic way to get in touch with nature - a ride through the woods. But for Kalli, he could tell it had been a first. He wished he could create many firsts for her as they built their life together. Struggling not to move too quickly, he'd sworn to himself that he'd patiently let her adjust to being a wolf again, and then tell her that she was his mate.

At this rate, Tristan honestly couldn't understand how she didn't know. Though they'd only known each other for days, his wolf could recognize the soul for whom he'd been waiting for over one hundred years. It was the human part of Tristan who'd resisted. First he'd fought through the cloudy confusion, unsure of how he could possibly want to mark a female. But now his primary concern was ensuring that her shift was pleasurable, and ultimately, that she was accepted by the pack. Acceptance was something she'd have to earn herself. But she was exceedingly strong, despite her hybrid status. If given the chance, he was quite certain she'd attain both their respect and trust.

As they approached the lake on horseback, Tristan eyed one of his favorite spots to rest. Whether in human or wolf form, he loved lying in the soft grass, listening to the sounds of nature, relaxing by the water.

"Whoa. Pull back on your reins, Kal. We'll stop here," he instructed. Dismounting his horse, he gave it an appreciative pet. Pulling off the bridle, he slid on a halter, which he'd kept in his backpack, and then tied the leather lead around a low tree branch. As wolf, he was considerate of the horse's comfort, since he planned a leisurely late lunch that might take several hours. Kalli followed his example and also dismounted. He repeated the procedure with her horse, ensuring that both the mare and stallion were secure and content.

"This is the best surprise anyone has ever given me, you know. Okay, maybe it is the only time anyone has ever done something like this for me. It's just so...I don't know. It's special. Amazing. The horses. The mountains. The lake. And you," she marveled. It was Tristan who'd changed her perceptions about pack life and what it meant to be Alpha.

Tristan came up behind Kalli, wrapping his arms around her waist. He kissed her ear and for a long while just held her, while they both stared out toward the water.

"Tristan," she whispered.

"Yeah, baby.

"No one's ever done anything like this for me," she croaked, trying not to cry. "Don't say it's no big deal, because it is."

"I want to do this for you. Even if there wasn't this thing...this connection between us. I just want to see you be happy, not locked up in a human's body, denying your wolf her due."

"As usual, you are right," she joked lightly.

"See, I knew you'd start seeing things my way." He smiled broadly. "Come on, let's eat lunch, then we'll talk. I'd say 'I'm so hungry I could eat a horse', but I don't want to offend our rides."

Tristan proceeded to spread a thin blanket onto the soft knoll while Kalli set out the food and drinks. After enjoying a leisurely picnic in the sun, they laid back on the warm fabric, taking in the sun.

"You're too far away," Tristan complained. "I need you next to me."

Kalli complied by rolling from her back onto her stomach, resting her head on his chest. She lazily draped her jean-clad thigh across his legs.

"Much better, mon amour."

"Hmm...yes," she replied.

"We need to talk about tonight. Toby's funeral. It's probably going to last several hours. To be honest, I haven't attended too many wolf burials. You know that whole immortal thing. But it happens from time to time."

"What's going to happen?" Kalli inquired, rubbing her hand on his chest.

"The first part is not all that different than some human rituals. We gather around the gravesite; talk about our experiences with that person, what made them special. It takes a while because there are many of us. Then we run, and mourn. We celebrate Toby's life, comfort each other."

"I can't run," she commented.

"I know, baby. That's why I wanted to talk."

"I'll go to the human part and skip the other. I mean, I can't shift, and to be honest, I'm a little worried about how the pack will react to me being there at all."

"They'll be fine. You're mine. Trust me." He pinned her with his eyes.

"Okay," she sighed, knowing he was probably right but that that wouldn't stop her from worrying.

"We won't be gone long, though. I'll be home right after the run." Tristan squeezed her tight, wishing she could run with him. "But then tomorrow night...we will run together. It's the full moon."

"Yes it is." She breathed in a deep breath and blew it out.

"That's the other reason we need to talk. You've never shifted with other wolves. It...it can be overwhelming...Things can happen."

"Things? What things?" Kalli sat straight up in worry, looking down into Tristan's warm amber eyes. She tried not to panic but 'things' did not sound good.

"Come back here and relax," he ordered, pulling her back into his arms. "It's not bad. It's just that sometimes when we shift in a pack, all your senses are enhanced. And at the same time, you're in touch with others."

"Yeah." That didn't sound so bad, she thought.

"You know that we are very sexual, chérie. Not that we can't control our urges, because we can. But the temptation is there; wolves can partake or refuse. It's up to each and every wolf how far they want to go. And of course, no means no, even to wolves. Most wolves have great restraint and control. But often on a full moon, they, for lack of a better word, 'indulge' in their impulses."

Kalli tensed in his arms. "Are you saying what I think you're saying?

"Okay, here's the thing. Tomorrow, your hormones, your libido is going to react strongly to the pull of the pack. Before you run, after you run...you're going to want...well, you know, a release."

"Sex?"

"Well, yes, but it can be overwhelming. But, I'll be there for you. In fact, I think that tomorrow, when you change, maybe just you and I should run together. I don't want you getting lost or hurt."

"Or getting screwed?" she blurted out, on the verge of freaking out.

"No, chérie. It won't happen as wolf. But after..."

"What, Tristan? What's going to happen after?" She heard her voice rising as her anxiety worsened.

"After, we're going to go home. You and me. And I'm going to fuck you senseless, baby," he teased. "But remember the other night at the gala?"

"What about it?" she snapped, knowing where this was leading.

"Logan's my beta. I trust him with my life. And as much as it will kill me, I trust him with you, with us...together. After this first shift with the pack, you'll be able to control it. But this first time, I want it to be special for you, Kalli."

"I know. But Tristan, what exactly are you saying? It's not that I'm not open to experiencing different things with you. I won't lie, Logan's nice and he's good-looking, but he's so not....he's not...you. You're the one I want to claim."

Tristan leaned forward, capturing her lips in a soft kiss. "I know, baby. I just want us to be good...for the change to be the most incredible thing you've ever experienced. Logan cares for you. You'll be safe with us. We'll take care of you, I promise."

"Are you sure about this, Tristan? You do know that you're freaking me out. I don't want to turn into some kind of a sex crazed maniac tomorrow night," she insisted.

Tristan laughed. "It's not like that at all, Kal. In fact, I'm doing a pretty shitty job of explaining this whole thing. All I can tell you is that it will be beautiful; your shift, our lovemaking, everything."

"This is so crazy. It's not like I haven't shifted, but it's just been me, though. How pathetic is it that I don't even know something so basic, like what color I am or how to hunt with another wolf?"

"It'll come naturally. All of it. Our bond, Kalli, that's what's new...for both of us. Can you feel it?" he whispered.

"Yes." She skimmed two fingers over her mark. "I've never felt so strongly for anyone else in my entire life, Tristan."

"I feel the same way. My mark," Tristan slid his fingers under hers, tracing the symbol, "I want everyone to see it so they know you're mine. You've changed everything for me."

"Not nearly as much as you've changed things for me. I've been scared for so long, I've forgotten who I was or how to trust. And you're changing that, and it's unbelievable to feel again. But I can't imagine what I've done for you."

"Let's put it this way, I've been alone a long, long time. And I've never once in all those years wanted to be with one female...one woman." God, he wanted to tell her how she was his mate and how much he loved her. But she hadn't even shifted yet. He didn't want to scare her.

"When you say all those years, what do you mean? How old are you?"

Tristan laughed. "Old enough to know I'm robbin' the cradle when it comes to you, my little wolf."

"But you look like you're maybe thirty in human years. And even that is pushing it. Fess up," Kalli pressed with a smile.

"Born in 1862. You do the math." He grinned.

"So that puts you around one hundred and fifty?" She quickly calculated.

"That's what I get for falling for such a smart woman. Pretty quick on the math facts, huh?"

"Did you know that as a half breed I carry the benefit of immortality too? Ironically, both my parents are dead, anyway."

"Ah, but your mum was human. And your dad, well, he fought and lost. Even vampires can die. It's just the way of..."

"Nature?" Kalli finished his sentence, laughing.

"See? My lessons are rubbing off on you, young grasshopper," Tristan teased. "I've got lots of wonderful things I can't wait to teach you."

"I think it's time I teach you a lesson or two, oh great one," she jested, moving her hand over his leg, skating across the juncture of his thighs. "Although being the student definitely has its perks."

Tristan tensed as her hand skimmed over him. The evidence of his growing arousal pressed against the zipper of his jeans. Pulling her closer, he kissed the top of her head.

"Baby, whatever role you want is fine with me. You up for a little 'how to' in the great outdoors kind of lesson?"

Kalli cried his name in delight as he flipped her over onto her back. Straddling her, he ran his hand up under her tank top, caressing her breast.

"Yes please," she moaned, ready to take anything and everything he was willing to give her. Her heart was lost to him.

~❀ *Chapter Twenty-One* ❀~

After making love at the lake, Tristan and Kalli rode back to the barn, turned over their horses and hurried back home to get ready for Toby's memorial. Unsure what to wear, Kalli settled on rolled-up jean capris and a black tank top. By six-thirty, it had cooled only slightly after a ninety degree day, and Tristan had warned her that they'd be sitting for a while and to dress comfortably. Sliding on a pair of sandals, she bounded down the stairs to find Tristan and Logan lounging on the sofas but engaged in a serious conversation. Assuming it was about Toby, she quietly sidled up to Tristan.

"Hey there, we were just talking about how we're going to run things tonight. Fortunately, we don't need to have many funerals 'round here."

"Hi Kalli," Logan greeted, looking handsome in jeans and a white t-shirt, his bare feet crossed and rested on the coffee table.

"Hey Logan," she replied, looking to Tristan for guidance. For some reason, she'd become slightly worried about how people would react to Tristan's mark, his claim on her.

"He knows, Kalli. It's okay. We talked about everything," Tristan assured her, giving her thigh a quick squeeze.

Like how I'm going to turn into a sex craved maniac tomorrow night, she thought to herself.

As if Tristan could read her thoughts, he continued with a sexy grin. "He knows about us, and yes, we've talked about tomorrow night."

Logan interrupted, wanting to put Kalli at ease. "It's okay. I understand why you created CLI and hid your wolf. Self-preservation is pretty damn important when you're alone. But now you have us." He looked to Tristan and then back at Kalli. "And we won't let anything happen to you. Not tonight, tomorrow or any other day."

"Thanks," she acknowledged, willing herself to remain composed. "It's…it's not easy growing up in a pack like I did…alone. I just want you to know that I really appreciate you and Tristan looking out for me."

Tristan wrapped an arm around her, pulling her to him. "Soon, the whole pack will be there for you. You'll never be alone again."

Kalli gave him a small smile, giving in to her need to snuggle him, to touch him.

"I can't imagine what it was like for you all those years…shifting alone. It's just not right. You're going to love running with the pack. Tristan said he's running with you tomorrow night. I'll lead the pack then meet up with you guys later." He caught Tristan's eyes and smiled. "I won't lie, Kalli. I'm honored to be a part of your shift and helping you with your…um…needs. You know…should a *need* arise."

"Oh my God. This is so embarrassing," she gasped, putting her hands over her eyes. Her cheeks flamed. "Is there nothing you guys don't discuss?"

Tristan's eyes fixed on him with a glare. "What don't you understand about 'be cool'? As for tomorrow, don't get used to it, wolf. She's mine."

Logan laughed, enjoying riling up his friend. "Yeah, yeah, yeah. As if I was ever not clear on that. Come on...I am the great seer."

"Do share your visions...seems like you've been holdin' back on me, bro," Tristan accused.

"I can't share all my secrets. It's fate, anyway. I mean, look at your mark, it's beautiful."

"That it is. She's mine, and I want the whole pack to know it."

"Thank you, both. I couldn't be happier to wear it. And soon, I will be leaving my own mark on you, my Alpha," she purred openly. She didn't care if Logan was there to hear her. The way she felt, she'd shout it from the mountains. Claiming him would be one of the first things she did once her wolf reemerged.

Tristan gave her a quick hug. "Hey, I'll be right back. I just want to check on something before we go, okay?" He ran up the stairs, leaving Kalli and Logan alone.

"So are you staying here tonight?" Kalli asked Logan. "Tristan said that you usually stay here with him, and I want you to know that just because I'm here I don't ever want that to change. You guys have your thing, and I don't want to intrude or make things weird with me being here."

"Weird, no. Better, oh yeah. I'm really looking forward to watching you make breakfast," he grinned wolfishly, referring to her cooking attire or lack thereof.

Kalli laughed. "Hmm...I guess there really is no denying my wolf. She gets hot when she cooks."

A knock at the door interrupted them. Kalli got up to answer it. As she went to turn the handle, the hair on the back of her neck pricked.

Surprised to see Kalli in Tristan's home, Mira stood frozen in the entranceway. "What are you doing here?" she sniffed. "May I come in?"

"By all means." Regardless of her instinct to say no, Kalli ushered her into the foyer. A rush of anger flooded her body, and she struggled not to lose it. *Who the hell did this she-wolf think she was?*

"Where's Tristan?" Mira barked.

"Mira, come sit," Logan insisted, sensing things could get dicey.

"Why is she here, Logan? This is pack business. I want to talk to Tristan."

Logan stood. "Come on, Mir. Let's have a drink before we go. Don't do this."

Mira turned to Kalli, readying to lay into her, when she noticed Tristan's mark. Furious, she stalked up to her, gesturing to her neck. "Tell me this isn't what I think it is? Tell me now!"

While Kalli was more than accustomed to dealing with irate humans in the ER, Mira's mere presence in Tristan's home infuriated her. It wasn't just Mira's anger toward her. No, this woman threatened her bond with Tristan, and she had no tolerance for the intrusion. Her wolf, recognizing the aggressive alpha female, sought her submission; nothing less would suffice.

When Kalli didn't respond right away, Mira attempted to walk upstairs in search of Tristan. Instantly, Kalli growled and blocked her access to the staircase. With her hands clasping the railings, she refused to let Mira walk another step.

"Let's get something straight, Mira. Tristan will come back down here when he's damn well ready and yes, this is exactly what you think it is." She pulled her strap aside so Mira could get an unobstructed view of Tristan's mark, then she leaned toward Mira, staring her down.

"Tristan has claimed me. And after tomorrow night, he will be claimed as mine. So you have two choices: you can either be respectful in this house or you can get the hell out. I realize you've been friends with Tristan for a long time, but I'm warning you that I won't tolerate this nonsense. I don't want to hear one more word out of those finely painted lips of yours until you make your decision. And if you're thinking of challenging me, bring it."

Silence fell over the house as Kalli stood firmly planted, waiting for a response. Logan bit his lips in a tight smile and looked up to Tristan, who'd come to rescue Kalli after hearing Mira's rant. Tristan grinned back proudly at Logan, raising a knowing eyebrow at his beta. They'd briefly discussed this possibility earlier. While it was natural that Mira would feel threatened, both Tristan and Logan agreed that Kalli wouldn't allow another female to intrude on her relationship, especially now that she'd stopped taking those pills. Her wolf, who he suspected was also very much an Alpha, would seek to protect her mate. Not wanting to interfere, both men waited on the females to resolve their conflict.

Mira, sensing Tristan, lowered her eyes in submission. There was no arguing his mark; he'd selected Kalli as a potential mate. Even though she knew she wasn't Tristan's mate, she was devastated that he would claim a half breed. Worse, it meant she'd be cast aside in favor of his mate.

"I will be respectful in this house," Mira bit out. She turned on her heels and stomped toward the door.

Logan went to stop her. "Mir, wait."

"I'll meet you at the funeral," she spat, not looking back at him. Slamming the door, she set off toward the field.

Tristan descended the steps, and smiled at Kalli. "Okay?"

"Yeah, sorry. I'm not putting up with that 'I'm the alpha female' shit from her. I know she's your friend, but…"

"Hey, I'm proud of you. And I agree she was being disrespectful. I care about Mira, but you're my…." *Mate.* "You're mine. She needs to learn her place. Besides, I love how you want to claim me. I am so looking forward to it, too." He wrapped his hands around her waist and kissed her gently on her lips.

"I'm yours," she whispered in response.

❦ Chapter Twenty-Two ❧

Tristan had assigned Willow to lead the memorial service. In traditional preparation, an unmarked grave had been dug in a field on the property. Toby, wrapped in plain linen cloth, had been carried to the site by Tristan, who with the help of others, had lowered the dead wolf to his final resting place. The open gravesite was canopied by a clear starry sky. Settling around it, several pack members laid towels and blankets on the dewy grass.

Kalli quietly sat, watching the proceedings. While she'd attended several human funerals, she hadn't experienced one within a pack. Silent in her thoughts, she glanced over at Mira who was casting her an icy stare. She ignored her. It wasn't the place for arguments. No, it was a time for mourning and reflection. And Kalli, more than anyone, could appreciate loss.

Tristan stood solemnly before his pack and released a breath in preparation for the eulogy. "Lyceum Wolves, tonight we celebrate our young Toby's life. Whether studying hard or working hard, Toby always had a kind word for everyone and did his best to support our pack. From chasing the pups and teaching them how to hunt, to chasing the ladies, Toby lived life to the fullest. He'd shown many Alpha attributes, and perhaps would have led his own pack one day. Our brother's great spirit now shines within

Lupus above, sparkling down on us. Tonight we share our experiences and our love with him and each other."

Many of the pack members smiled recalling his actions, and openly wept in sadness, realizing he was really gone. It was one thing to find out someone had died; it was another to see the empty shell of their body lying in the dirt. The finality of his violent passing could not be denied. Noticing that Kalli sat alone, Logan got up and sat next to her, protectively wrapping an arm around her shoulder.

"But before we begin the reminiscence, I want to take a few minutes to make sure every one of you knows that danger remains. The boy lying in this grave serves as a cold reminder that the immortal are susceptible to the call of death. Pack must remain strong in the throes of battle, as the survival of our species is a never ending war. Enemies shall never cease to exist, my friends. In only a few more days, we will once again go on the offensive to eradicate those who seek to harm us. Until they are contained, we must remain diligent at home in our efforts to protect the pack and our territory," he declared.

Tristan was planning an attack on the Wallace pack, but kept his strategy under wraps, given the circumstances. It was clear to him that Sato could not have been working alone. Perhaps at one time Sato had feigned lone wolf status in order to travel freely within territories. But Tristan's investigation of Gerald indicated that even though their pack was not large, they'd been committing atrocities for well over a century. Tristan could not accept another attack on Lyceum Wolves or Kalli. They needed to be dealt with, swiftly and without mercy.

Bringing his thoughts back to Toby, he gazed upon the grief-stricken faces and continued. "As many of you know,

Toby's untimely death was met with vengeance last night. The blood of a wolf responsible for his death was shed in retribution. But the fight is not over. There's another wolf who shares culpability in this heinous act; one who will soon meet the same fate," he growled.

"But tonight, we honor Toby. Then we'll mourn in remembrance, as only wolves do. I'll begin." Tristan gently knelt, looking down into the grave. "Toby. Son. I'm going to miss you so much. Teaching you how to ride a motorcycle was a memory I'll always cherish. Even though you scratched my Harley up good your first try, you made me proud." He laughed softly at the memory. "The look on your face when I got you your own bike for your birthday last year…it was like I was the one who got the gift. Little brother, you were more than an adopted pup to me. As I run tonight, I know that you'll always be there in spirit with us. Be at peace, Toby." Tristan gave a small smile up toward the constellations, as a lone tear ran down his cheek.

Kalli began to quietly cry as she listened to Tristan talk to the boy he loved. She wished she could go back in time and find another way to hide instead of creating CLI. If he hadn't taken it, he might still be alive. Perhaps her mere presence in the Lyceum Wolves territory had brought war by the Wallace Pack. Even after all these years, she should have known they'd never simply let her go. While she may have been lower than an omega, they viewed her as their property. Sato's vile words toward her had confirmed that their hate was alive and well.

One by one, the wolves shared their goodbyes, sharing memories of Toby. The experience reminded her of a Quaker funeral she'd once attended for one of her colleague's parents who'd passed. Beautiful stories were met with both laughter and tears. Sitting with Logan and Tristan, listening to the crickets sing their music, she felt oddly at ease within the pack. By the time everyone who wanted to speak was finished, it was nearly midnight.

Tristan whispered in Kalli's ear, as the last speaker finished. "Chérie, we're gonna run now. I'll meet you at home in a few hours." He kissed her on the cheek, stood and walked over to pick up a shovel.

"And now my wolves, we'll return Toby's body to our great Earth. We're pack in life and in death." Tristan shoved the cold metal into the massive pile of dirt. With a heave, the red and brown particles scattered over the linen-shrouded form below. Several joined in to help, digging and pitching, until the burial site was sealed. Young pups placed wild flowers and seeds onto the loose terra, in an effort to bring forth a new circle of life onto the otherwise barren covering.

Wolves didn't leave headstones, for with scent, they'd always know where their loved one was buried. And in their hearts, they believed that lost souls returned to the Goddess of nature from whence they came. Their land was life. When they played or rode through this field, they'd be reminded of Toby and of his great spirit within their pack.

In preparation for their run, pack members began to strip. Feeling like an interloper, Kalli flicked on her flashlight and began to walk back toward the cabin. Out of curiosity, she briefly stopped and turned back, to catch a glimpse of her Alpha shedding his clothes, right before he turned into his spectacular black wolf. His lean, tanned body glowed under the stars giving way to shiny raven fur. Fascinated, Kalli quietly sat down on a rock, voyeuristically watching the remarkable sight. From afar, she admired her

Alpha, and her heart tightened as she yearned to be with him.

Falling in love with a man like Tristan was easy. His physical beauty paled in comparison to his charismatic personality and cunning intellect. It took her breath away how he approached every single thing in his life with passion and vigor, from business to making love. She'd never witnessed such compassion and dominance in one man. Tonight, observing him command his wolves both as human and beast, exhilarated her.

In that reflective moment, Kalli realized she'd fallen in love with him. There was no mistaking the ache in her heart. As her mark tingled upon her shoulder, she was reminded that she was his. Her wolf begged to claim him in return. *Mate.* The word ran through her mind as if it was as natural as swimming on a warm summer day. Kalli released a small gasp as Tristan ran back and forth, playfully corralling the pups who sought to frolic on the outskirts. She indulged in her own fantasy, imagining him playing with their own children. He'd make a wonderful father. Raking her hand through her hair with a sigh, she once again wished she could run with him, to ease his pain. Speaking her thoughts aloud, she whispered, "I love you, Tristan. Run well tonight."

As if he'd heard her, the black wolf stopped to gaze upon her. His penetrating glare told her that he'd known she'd been watching all along. Giving him a small smile, she waved from the distance and slowly began her track back to the house.

Tristan heard the words, a mere whisper upon her lips. His heart beat wildly at her confession. His mate loved him. He wished to go to her, to tell her that he loved her as well, and make love to her all night long until she screamed his name over and over. But it would have to wait a few hours; his responsibility to the pack came first. He released a celebratory howl, and the pack snapped to attention, readying to follow his orders. Respecting his command, Lyceum Wolves raced into the night.

It had been nearly two days since she'd taken CLI, and her proximity to the pack had left her skin itching to shift. But only the draw of the full moon could initiate her change after suppressing her wolf for so long. Her wolf was clawing to escape, to run with her Alpha. By the time Kalli got back to the cabin, she felt on fire with the need to shift. Like in the past, she could feel the change coming. But instead of resisting the transformation, her body and mind craved it. Even though she was still terrified, Kalli knew that, with Tristan, she'd be safe. And like her wolf, she planned to mark him the first chance she got.

Being with the other wolves pulled at her emotions in ways she'd never thought possible or expected. Seeing their naked skin melting into fur drove her into a muted exhilaration. She rubbed her limbs, which tingled in anticipation. Everything seemed amplified; sound, touch, smell. Safely within the wooden walls of Tristan's home, the cries of the night were still audible to her hypersensitive hearing. All senses on alert, she took a hot shower, hoping it'd subdue the overwhelming sensations racking her body.

Even though the warm water had helped to take the edge off, she felt like she was clinging to a precipice, rocks slipping under her feet. Wrapping her bare skin in Tristan's thin cotton robe, she made a cup of calming chamomile tea.

But finding the chocolate truffles in his pantry was like finding gold in a mine. When it came to chocolate, the answer was always 'yes' as far as Kalli was concerned. As she bit into the tasty delicacy, a small gasp of pleasure escaped her lips. *Oh yes. Next to sex, it was the best thing on the planet.* Grabbing her warm mug and a book off one of Tristan's bookshelves, she trudged upstairs on a mission to lose herself within its pages.

After thirty minutes of reading on an overstuffed chair, she gave in to her exhaustion and opted for the mattress. Within seconds of lying down in Tristan's bed, she found she could no longer keep her eyes open. The smell of him on his pillow calmed every nerve in her body. Like an animal, Kalli rubbed her face into it, wishing his strong arms were wrapped around her. Shedding her robe, she slipped into the soft cool linens and embraced sleep, awaiting his return.

"Hmm, Tristan," Kalli purred, breathing in the masculine scent of her Alpha. Kissing his skin, eyes still closed, she brushed her tongue over his nipple, teasing it with her teeth until it hardened. Feeling his arms pull her closer, she slid her hand down his chest. Finding the growing evidence of his arousal, she wrapped her soft fingers around him.

"Kalli," he groaned. Tristan had thought of nothing else but Kalli for the past three hours. *She loved him.* After running, he quickly showered and slid next to the warmth of her body. He could tell she wasn't quite awake but not asleep either. The touch of her hand sent blood rushing to his cock. Dominance still fresh in his system, he cuffed her wrist, demanding he take the lead.

She protested with a small moan, but was rewarded with a long, drugging kiss, bolting passion throughout her blood. In a fluid motion, he turned her onto her back, nudging her legs apart with his knees until he was comfortably settled on top of her. Supporting his weight with his elbows alongside of her head, his fingers pushed through her hair, fisting large spools of black curls as he continued kissing her deeply and thoroughly.

Kalli breathlessly kissed Tristan back, intoxicated by his essence. She welcomed the pressure of his body restraining her against the bed, allowing him to command their lovemaking. Wanting to be utterly possessed by him, she opened her heart and mind, submitting to their pleasure. The womanly heart of her ached to be taken. Moist and desperate for his touch, she acquiesced to the agonizing anticipation.

Releasing her lips, Tristan lowered his head to suckle a bared rosy tip. Gently, he swirled his tongue around the quivering areola until the throbbing peak stood stiff. Switching to the opposite breast, he continued his arousing assault.

"You are so perfect," he murmured as he licked and sucked her sensitive skin.

"Tristan," she whispered in response, altogether lost in his touch. She pushed her hips upward until she felt the tip of his straining sex.

"Kalli. Open your eyes," Tristan urged.

With heavy-lidded eyes, she peered up into the universe of his soul.

Tristan gazed into her eyes as he trailed his thumb along the seam of her lips. "I love you too. You're mine as I'm yours. You're my mate," he professed as he slid the hard length of him into her slick heat.

Her mouth opened in a soft cry as he buried himself in one swift motion. He gently cupped her cheek, pushing his thumb into her mouth. She wrapped her lips around his finger, allowing him to pull her cheek against the cool pillow, baring her neck to him. She moaned in response to the thrilling sensation of being purely dominated by her loving Alpha. Her mouth, the stretching walls of her tight depths, her swollen breasts and the rest of her soft curving flesh was his to take however he wanted. She offered it up to him on a platter, reveling in the ecstasy streaming through her consciousness.

At her passionate submission, Tristan nearly came. It was if he could sense the exact moment Kalli gifted him with her boundless trust. She gave herself freely, and he sought to take everything she offered.

"Feel me, Kalli," he instructed as he began to move within her. "Feel us."

He began thrusting his thick hardness in and out of her core, teasing every last moan from her body. Kissing her taut neck, he gently bit down on his mark, reminding her of his claim. She dug her fingernails into his back, feeling as if she'd explode any second. Her entire being, ignited in arousal, ached for release.

"That's it baby, feel me inside of you," he encouraged as she set free a cry of pleasure. "We are made for each other."

Tristan ground his pelvis against her clit, and she writhed upward, savoring every second of their joining.

Propelling her to the edge of rapture, he plunged into her again.

"Please," she beseeched him. "I need to come. It's so good...so close...please."

Ravishing her mercilessly, he continued to work her into a frenzied state of euphoria. He fought for his own breath as she panted, releasing cries with each deep thrust she received. As his powerful fullness built up her orgasm, she moaned as the clenching spasms racked her body. She screamed his name, embracing the uncontrollable quivering waves of climax, grinding herself into him as he slammed against her.

"Fuck, yes, Kalli, I can feel you around me. So tight. I'm coming," Tristan yelled, as her warm sheath pulsed around him. Abandoning himself to his orgasm, he bit her again, stifling his masculine groans of satisfaction while exploding deep within her core.

"I love you," she whispered, slowly recovering from the erotic release.

Tristan gently slid out of her, yet never let go. As he fell on to his back, he brought her with him so that she rested on his chest. With one hand intertwined with hers on his belly, he caressed her hair with the other.

"Mon amour, what you do to me." His heart bloomed with emotion. Loving her would consume him forever, and he couldn't imagine living his life any other way.

⊰⊱ Chapter Twenty-Three ⊰⊱

From the minute Kalli woke, her senses were uncontrollably sensitive. While making love throughout the night had brought tears of joy, she now felt unsettled, overwrought with a thousand sensations bombarding her body and mind. She knew immediately that the rudimentary signs of her impending transformation had officially commenced. But this was different. Symptoms exaggerated exponentially; she assumed the influence of the pack drove the intensification of the effects. Every nerve and sense stood alert. The smell of the wildflowers. The sound of the birds. It was all too much. And then there was her hunger.

Tearing through the refrigerator, she cooked a huge feast of eggs, bacon, pancakes, sausage and toast. Ravenous, she ate five eggs, several pieces of bacon and two pancakes. While Tristan normally loved watching his little she-wolf make breakfast, he sought to comfort her. But there was nothing much he could do to ease the evidence of her affliction. Her first shift around pack would be difficult, he was certain. But once she got over the hump, she'd learn control over the way the pack heightened one's already animalistic ways.

Tristan stood behind her while she sat drinking tea, hands shaking as the amber liquid washed over the lips of the cup. Rubbing her shoulders, he worked the knots; she moaned in relief.

"Chérie, how about we take a run? It'll help release some of the tension."

"I'm sorry, Tristan. I don't know what's happening to me. Everything was so special last night..." her words trailed off, as she remembered the intensity of the evening.

"It's okay. Come up here." Tristan took her by the hands, pulling her upward and hugged her. "Tonight will be even more special than last night. I can't wait to see your beautiful wolf. I promise that it's going to be incredible. You'll learn how to trust in the reckless abandon of being wolf. The smell of the trees and animals. The taste of the hunt. We're going to run and then come back, take a hot tub...celebrate. As for the sexual release, it will be what it is...and with you it's always incredible."

"But what if I get lost? Go crazy? And Logan...I could seriously die of embarrassment that I could attack him as if I'm in heat," she huffed.

"Remember who's Alpha, chérie. No matter what happens later, you are mine. Trust me when I tell you that your wolf will not forget, nor will Logan's. I'll control what happens, I promise. Come on, now. Go get your shoes on. We're going for a walk. I want to show you around in the daylight, before tonight. It's beautiful here."

"Tristan," she said quietly, looking up into his golden eyes. "I know we didn't talk about things last night. About mating...I want you to know that I meant what I said. I love you. I want to claim you tonight...after the shift."

"Aw baby, you will. And believe me, I can't wait." He gave her a broad smile. "And after this mess is cleaned up with the Wallace Pack, we'll announce our mating to all of

Lyceum Wolves, and hold a formal ritual...just you and me."

"I don't know how...I mean, I haven't been around wolves long enough to know how it works. I can just feel it within me. I want you...to be with you. God, this is so crazy."

"No it's not. But in a way, I know how you feel. Before you, the whole need to mate never made a lick of sense. But now, it's perfectly clear."

She smiled, knowing that everything always came back to nature for Tristan. Kalli wished she could be so confident, knowing what to do and say. But every minute she spent with Tristan, she grew more and more aware of the mating bond. More than a human's love, it bound their wolves eternally. Organic and instinctive, their mating would bond them irrevocably throughout time.

Tristan had taken Kalli for a long and winding walk through the woods, stopping to teach her about the plants and even point out the natural habitats of small game and reptiles. As a veterinarian, she found it fascinating. She was amazed at how much he knew about the environment and conservation. By the time they reached a small spring, she was unusually relaxed. He showed her how they'd fostered the spring. The cool clean water ran from the pipe in the rock into his stainless steel canteen as he filled it. As she drank the nectar, she eyed him thoughtfully, wondering exactly what he couldn't do. Whether it was riding a Harley or identifying a copperhead snake, he did it all with a cool air of confidence and a smile.

By the time they got back, Tristan directed her to eat lunch and take a nap, one that, regretfully, he insisted did not include sex. Instead, he'd stripped her bare, massaging every last muscle until she'd fallen asleep at his hands. He knew that her body was storing energy for the shift. Eating. Drinking. Exercising. And finally sleeping. It was everything she needed to make a smooth transition to lupine.

After a long nap, Tristan woke Kalli. Red streaks painted the dusky sky as the sun fell below the horizon. Wearing only cotton bathrobes, both Kalli and Tristan stood on the last step of the large cedar deck which wrapped around the back of the cabin. The harmonious sounds of the cicadas and crickets blanketed tranquility over Kalli's mind.

In the distance, she heard the yips of wolves, already singing in celebration of the full moon. Tendrils of her Alpha's power danced along her skin as she disrobed. Fully bared to the twilight, she closed her eyes and took a cleansing breath in preparation for her shift. Her wolf rejoiced in appreciation, no longer confined to the deep recesses of her soul. No, tonight the wolf would command her very being and in truth, Kalli delighted at the prospect. The gravitational force of the pack's quintessence reminded her of how this change represented a threshold to a new life. No longer a lone wolf, she'd claim her mate and belong to pack.

Turning to Tristan, she lifted her eyes to meet his. He smiled down at her, enjoying the sheer bliss she'd been experiencing at finally coming to acceptance of her nature. Tonight, he'd watch out for her, making sure she learned the land and was comfortable with him before introducing her to the pack. He expected that certain females such as Mira might try to challenge her. And while he was fully confident of her Alpha tendencies, tonight there'd be no fighting. Tonight was about helping Kalli while she rediscovered her wolf and learned to control the exhilarating, but sometimes distracting, assault to both one's senses and libido when in the presence of other wolves.

"I'm ready, Tristan," she breathed. "My wolf is here and can't wait to run."

"Okay chérie. Remember what we talked about. The tendency to want to go with the others will be strong, so pay attention to me. We'll introduce you to the pack another night. Logan's with them and he'll let them know you're around, but they've been instructed to leave you be." He tossed his robe onto the wooden planks, and took Kalli's hand in his.

His eyes narrowed into a serious expression. "That being said, expect their influence to be significant. This means you might feel unusually aggressive if one of them nears, especially given your need to claim me. You also will be extraordinarily hungry, so we'll hunt. Given that you've only hunted alone, I'll teach you how to hunt as a pair. Then eventually, we'll hunt with the pack, as a team. It's much better that way...power in numbers and all. Plus, we work collectively to teach the pups how to catch prey."

"Anything else I should know?" She smiled, listening to him reiterate what he'd already told her on their walk. She loved the way he cared so much about taking care of his pack, her, and making sure that she was prepared for what would happen. Given her terrifying past experiences, she had high expectations based solely on the facts that Tristan had told her. She laughed to herself, realizing how much she'd grown to trust him. A week ago, she'd considered her life that of a human, revolted by the life of a wolf. It was amazing how her Alpha had changed her thinking, her life.

Tristan wrapped a finger around one of her long curls and gave it a little tug, in an attempt to get her to focus. He could see the wheels spinning, and needed her to remain on task, so she'd be safe and calm within the forest. With a closed smile, he reminded her about the other topic she really wanted to avoid discussing. "The last thing I want to remind you of is one of my favorite topics, sex. I know we talked about this, but your libido will be on fire. Any full moon revs us all up, but this being your first around pack is going to make you one little randy girl," he teased, winking at her.

She rolled her eyes. "Please, let's just not talk about it."

"Don't be embarrassed. It's just our way…to want to be close to those that we love. And in your case, you'll learn to control it, but don't worry about it tonight. We'll just see how it goes after we shift back. I've got a nice set up for us afterwards to help you relax. No matter what happens tonight, I'll be there to protect you…always. Never forget that, Kalli." His voice took on a serious tone. "Ready now?"

Kalli gave a self-assured smile. Thanks to Tristan, she honestly was ready. "Hell yes. Let's do this thing. See if you can catch me, wolf!"

Untwining her hand from Tristan's, she broke free into a full sprint, seamlessly shifting into her wolf.

Tristan gasped in awe at the beautiful sight of her. Splendid white fur touched with grey down her back and legs, she darted across the green grass. She circled round him, running quickly, purely engrossed in her release. As Tristan stood erect, still in human form, she ringed once more, slowing as she came to face him. Falling at his bare feet, she playfully bowed her head toward the ground, looking upward at him with her tail wagging, hindquarters raised high in the air.

Reaching forward, Tristan ran his palm over her small head, in approval, rubbing her ears. "Chérie, you're stunning. Just beautiful, baby," he crooned.

She barked in response, and began chasing the wind in large circles as if to encourage him to shift. Taking off like a missile toward him, she swiftly missed him and ran toward the woods. Coming to a halt, she looked eagerly over her shoulder, waiting for him to change.

He laughed at her exuberance. After all the angst regarding her change, she was the one running circles around him. Or so she thought. Fluently, Tristan metamorphosed into his handsome, magisterial wolf. Stalking toward her, he sought her submission. Expecting pursuit, Kalli took flight toward the woods. Spotting his prey, Tristan flew past her, corralling her to the ground. Gleefully, she rolled to her back, baring her neck in defeat. He licked her muzzle, assuring her of his affections. With a nip, she reminded him that it was time to hunt; her wolf hungered for a kill. Free to run the land, she sought exploration and sport. Tristan nudged her belly, encouraging her to roll to her feet. Following her Alpha, they bounded into the night.

Rounding a clearing, Kalli spotted a rabbit in the field. Tristan sensed her distraction, waiting to see how she'd handle hunting with him near. Wagging her tail, ears up, she instinctively focused on her prey. Tristan watched intently, prepared to rush the rabbit from the other side should she miss. Quietly approaching the rabbit, she struck out in a sprint, snapping its neck, resulting in an instant kill. Sharing her spoils, they ate the small snack then ran to the spring for a drink.

While lapping up the water, Kalli froze; she sensed the pack was approaching. Ears down, the hair on her back bristled as the first wolf came into sight. A smaller white she-wolf followed a silky grey male. Kalli, unused to being in pack, immediate recognized them as Mira and Logan. Subordinates trailed, staying cautiously behind the pair. Tristan stepped forward to block their access. *What the hell were they doing?* He'd told Logan that he didn't want them near Kalli. Growling, he warned them to come no closer. Yet Mira ignored him, and continued to pad toward him. While she lowered herself in submission, she advanced nonetheless. In a sign of dominance, Tristan sent her a hard stare.

Upon seeing Mira close in upon Tristan, Kalli's posture straightened. Threatened, she lifted her tail and edged around Tristan. Emitting a low growl, she locked her eyes on Mira in an angry menacing act of intimidation. When she refused to submit, Kalli maintained her confident stance, and bared her canines. Ready to attack, in the moment she resisted the aggression that begged to escape. Not only did she want a subtle signal of submission, she wanted Mira on her back.

Within seconds, Mira looked away and whined, yielding to Kalli's threats.

Logan, watching the interaction play out, knew that Tristan would be pissed as hell that he'd let the pack come near Kalli. But they'd been running for over an hour and happened to be near the spring. He'd hoped that Tristan would have moved Kalli in time. He could sense the confusion and surprise of the subordinates as Kalli, who hadn't been formally introduced as pack, not only stood marked as Tristan's but had just forced Mira to publicly submit.

Tristan nearly had a heart attack when his little wolf challenged Mira. After witnessing Kalli dressing down Mira in his home the previous day, it was just a matter of time before she confronted her without reserve in front of the pack. Even though he knew it had to be done, he was hoping to delay any confrontation until Kalli had had a chance to be comfortable within her wolf. He also wanted time to announce his intention to mate Kalli so that when Mira submitted it would be a less bitter pill for her to swallow. While Mira was currently the Alpha female, she was not his mate. The pack subordinates would expect his mate to be the strongest, most intelligent female, and after her little display of dominance, she was.

As the pack ran off, Kalli howled in jubilation. There was no way that, after everything she'd been through, she'd allow another female near her male. Mira, without a doubt, was formidable. She reckoned that it would not be her last challenge. Yet confidence raced through her veins. Forcing Mira to physically submit would be a pleasure that her wolf would someday see to fruition, of that she was certain.

Tristan howled along with Kalli, proud of her courage and assertiveness. His woman matched his own authoritative constitution. And while he trusted in fate and nature, he couldn't help but be amazed at how she fit him precisely in every way. Nuzzling his muzzle along her side, she returned his action in kind. The sheer adrenaline of the night brought forth a surge of emotions they both longed to explore. Nudging her forward, he willed her to follow; it was time to celebrate their first successful run together, one of many in their eternal lifetime.

⊷❀ *Chapter Twenty-Four* ❀⊶

❝**T**hat was phenomenal!" Kalli exclaimed, letting the hot spray clean her skin. An oversized nozzle delivered the warm water into the open-aired shower which sat next to the outdoor Jacuzzi. Overwrought with both desire and exhilaration, she squealed in delight as Tristan delivered a spank to her bottom. "Hey, what's that for?"

"I couldn't resist with you wagging your tail at me like that all night. A man can only take so much. Seeing your wolf has given me some very naughty ideas...ones that I'm sure you'll like," he promised in a sexy low voice. Slipping out of the shower, he grabbed a clean beach towel off a hook and slung it around his waist, beads of water dripping off his lithe body. "I'm goin' inside to get a few things. Go 'head and get in the hot tub, and I'll be right out."

Kalli sighed in anticipation, washing the last of the dirt off her skin. As usual, he'd been right about everything. She'd been ravenous when she'd attacked her prey, and then, with her aggression toward Mira, protecting her Alpha had been foremost in her wolf's mind. And now desire for him raged like a wildfire. She had no idea what he was getting or planning but he'd damn well better hurry up.

Easing into the hot tub, she hissed as bubbling water caressed her in all the right spots. "Oh. My. God. This feels so good," she declared, sinking in all the way up to her neck. Closing her eyes, she laid her head against the soft padding along the rim. A door opening caused her to lift her lids. Gloriously naked and erect, Tristan exited the house with a tray full of goodies. Food? Champagne? Something else that she couldn't quite identify?

At this point the only sustenance she required was Tristan, as he was, and in her. She lazily smiled, watching him pour three glasses, presumably a third for Logan, who hadn't yet arrived. She wondered if he was okay, given her fight with Mira. She knew the three of them had all been childhood friends, and she wished things could be different, but now that she had Tristan, she wasn't letting some she-wolf try to push her away. There was a new sheriff in town, and she wasn't going to tolerate Mira's nasty interference.

Tristan lowered himself into the tub slowly, reaching for Kalli. The sexual tension between them crackled the air. She needed him, and so much more. And as promised, he was there for her.

"Come here, mon amour," he purred into her shoulder, licking over his mark, sending a bolt of desire to her already pulsing core.

"Tristan, I am so....I can't wait to have you in me, please," she begged. Every nerve screamed for his touch.

"Yes, baby, I know. I know what you need." He pulled her on top of him, so she sat straddling his legs. Reaching down between her legs, he brushed his thumb over her clit. He planned to take her hard and fast the first time.

She screamed at the brief caress of her nub. "Oh God, yes!"

"That better? How 'bout this?" Guiding his engorged head to her entrance, he pulled her downward, impaling her on his rock hard cock. So deep inside her, he filled her completely. "Ah yes, Kalli."

"Yes, that's it. Fuck me!" she screamed loudly into the night.

Knowing how to take the edge off, Tristan passionately captured her lips, sweeping his tongue into her mouth. Wrapping her long hair around his fist, he kissed her, engrossed in her ambrosial essence.

Kalli returned his bruising kiss, sucking and biting. As the animalistic excitation overtook her being, she took all he gave and demanded even more. "Oh yes! Harder! Yes! Tristan! So close!"

"That's it. Yeah, take me all in. Feel how hard you make me." Seeking to give her the release she needed, he slid his hand in between her legs. Circling and pressing against her ripe nub, he felt her convulse around him. "Let it go."

As he applied pressure to her sensitive pearl, she flew apart, screaming his name, grinding herself hard against his pelvis. In the heat of her climax, she extended her canines and bit deep into Tristan's shoulder, effectively claiming him forever. A part of her wished it could have been a gentle process, but her wild territorial wolf insisted she claim him on her terms, deliberately carnal. There could be no mistaking her intentions.

Tristan nearly split in half as she marked him. The pleasure of her bite racked through him and he struggled not to come. "Yes, Kalli. I'm yours," he grunted through the sweet pain.

Kalli laved over her bite, resting her head upon his shoulder, while he remained stiff inside her. Feeling unchained, she could feel the ache start to build once again.

Tristan sucked her neck, kissing behind her ear. "Goddess, I love you, woman. You feel so good around me."

"I love you too," she moaned as she relaxed against him.

"Rest a minute, chérie; we're just getting started." He looked up to find Logan smiling at him from across the hot tub; he'd been watching them make love. Like Kalli and Tristan had done, he was taking a shower.

Kalli caught a glimpse of Logan as he tilted his head back and closed his eyes to rinse the bubbles off his taut skin. Like a sculpted statue in a fountain, water sluiced off his corded muscles. The sight of him rubbing his hands over his hard masculine form caused her sheath to clench even tighter around Tristan.

Intellectually, she knew that whatever sexual feelings she had toward Logan were only driven by the extraordinary experience of learning to shift with the pack. Tristan had warned her that this would happen. She wasn't in love with Logan, in any sense of the imagination, but the overwhelming sexual attraction of the night pulled at her. A pang of guilt stabbed her, aware that her libido was out of control. Mortified at her hidden desires, she buried her face into Tristan's shoulder, looking away. God help her, she wanted to make love to them both tonight.

Tristan felt Kalli vise around him, her eyes darting to Logan. Sensing her interest, he was torn between finishing what they'd started and wanting to wait for Logan to join them. Loving his beta and his mate, he sought to exhaust her heightened sex drive in unison, certain that it would prove to be both a wondrous and provocative adventure. His most visceral animal instincts encouraged the sexual interaction;

he loved them both unconditionally and as Alpha, whatever happened, both Kalli and Logan would be under his command.

He smiled down at her, appreciating that she was truly a babe in the woods when it came to living as wolf. It was no longer about secretly shifting once a month to get it over with…no, she was learning how to saturate her mind with the experience, learn the power of the pack and accept the happiness that came with being wolf. Their mating would be both a life affirming and life changing experience, one that would eventually affect every member of Lyceum Wolves. Nothing would ever be the same, and he didn't want it any other way. And while for most of his life, he'd never imagined or wanted a mate, he knew for certain that now he had Kalli in his life, he'd never be able to live without her.

Tristan slid out of her, but still kept her pulled against him in an embrace. "It's okay, Kalli, I want this too," he whispered into her ear. "Remember that nothing will happen that you don't want to happen."

"I am out of control," she confessed, refusing to look at him.

"No you're not. You're just in touch with the pack and your shift. It's all good. Nature, baby, remember? Next time you run with the pack, you'll still feel a little bit like this, but you'll have better control. I promise I'll take care of you. Tonight, just enjoy how you feel, how we make you feel."

"As opposed to feeling like I could crawl out of my own skin just to get off," she joked, finally looking him in the eyes. "God, I really am a wolf in heat."

"Hmm, not yet, but someday. And I won't lie, I am looking forward to that, chérie," he purred. The thought of her pregnant with his children tugged at his heart. She'd make a wonderful mother.

"Don't even tell me what will happen when I go into heat. All I know is that I can't keep my hands to myself as it is. I can't believe the dirty thoughts running through my head," she laughed. "Are you sure this is normal?"

"Perfectly. Now does someone need another lesson in trust?" he asked with a chuckle, aware of all the naughty things he planned to do to her lovely little body in just a few short minutes.

"I suppose I do," she teased back, kissing his cheek softly. "You were planning on teaching me, Alpha?"

"Hey people," Logan interrupted with a smile. "Looks like I'm missing all the fun."

"Hey yourself," Kalli replied as she drank in the view of his glistening body.

"Come on in, bro," Tristan called over to him; a look of mutual understanding passed between them. They'd discussed in detail how the shift would affect Kalli and others in the pack. As leaders, they were ultra-aware of the implications of adding another pack member and the side effects of Kalli's shift. While it was unusual to be a lone wolf as Kalli had been, it wasn't unheard of, so they knew what to expect.

Logan languidly slid into the hot water, groaning in pleasure. "Oh man, that feels good."

"Yes it does. You know what feels even better?" Tristan raised an eyebrow at him. "Hold her for me, will you? I want to rub her feet. My girl ran hard tonight."

Kalli's heart pounded, hearing Tristan offer her up to Logan like a piece of roast beef. *What the hell was he doing? Trust, trust, trust.* Oh God, she knew she should trust

Tristan after everything they'd been through, but he wasn't making it easy.

Tristan pulled her toward him once again and gently kissed her. "You're okay, chérie. Now give me your feet." Easily maneuvering Kalli's small frame, he set her so that her back was against Logan's chest. "That's it. Just relax and let us take care of you."

Logan didn't attempt to touch Kalli; he simply let her rest against him as if she was sitting in a chair. They both kind of just relaxed into the hot steam.

But once Tristan went to work on the insoles of her feet, Kalli gave a satisfying moan. "Oh my, that feels amazing. Please, do not ever stop." Letting her head loll back onto Logan's chest, she closed her eyes.

Tristan smiled at Logan, who was waiting for instructions. "Logan, why don't you massage our little wolf? She did so well tonight, don't you think?"

Logan returned the smile, given permission to touch her. "Yes she did. And I must say that I enjoyed watching her go all alpha, standing her ground."

"What a bitch," Kalli snapped. "I know you guys are friends, but I'm not backing down."

"Nor should you," Tristan agreed. "But that shouldn't have happened tonight, because I asked Logan to keep the pack away. You are a ferocious girl, you know that. But really, Mira damn well knows that she shouldn't have approached me out there, especially since I claimed you. I'm sure her submission did not sit well with her, but Mir's ego will survive."

"Yeah, I'm really sorry about that, man, but I thought you guys were on your way out of the spring. But damn, if watching your woman growl didn't turn me on," he chuckled. "Dominance is hot." He wiggled his eyebrows, and they all laughed.

Logan gently took his hands to Kalli's shoulders, moving slowly down her arms. When he finally reached her fingers, he moved to her hips, adjusting her so the firm ridge of him nestled in her bottom. Sliding his palms up her belly, he finally arrived where he wanted. Collecting her tantalizing breasts in both hands, he gently squeezed them.

Kalli's pulse raced in arousal. Her eyes flew open to Tristan, who watched her intently.

"Breathe, Kalli," he reminded her. "Goddess, you are so radiant tonight. Seeing you in Logan's hands...it really turns me on, baby."

At his words, arousal took flight within her once again. The predatory look in Tristan's eyes made her pussy tighten. She wanted him in her again. Having Logan touch her while he watched, only served to ramp up her desire even more.

"She's so soft," Logan commented to Tristan as he placed a kiss to her ear. The evidence of his growing arousal pressed up against her backside and Kalli squirmed in excitement.

Running his palms from the tips of her toes to the inside of her thighs, Tristan brushed over her mound then pulled away again, edging her up with desire. Hearing her breath catch as he nearly touched the heart of her sent a surge of blood to his groin. "Logan, sit up on the edge. I need to taste her...that's it," he encouraged.

Using his muscular thighs, Logan pushed up so that he and Kalli sat along the wide border of the hot tub. Bared to the night, Kalli sucked a breath as the cool air hit her skin; her exposed ripe peaks hardened.

Like a lion stalking his prey, Tristan's eyes locked on hers, advancing until he pushed both Kalli's and Logan's knees wide open, his face mere inches from the apex of her thighs.

"Hmm…such a pretty pussy, look, Logan. She's so wet for us, aren't you Kalli?" Tracing his forefinger through her slick folds he stroked up and down, avoiding her swollen center.

In the past, Kalli would have been offended at such dirty talk, but Tristan's words sent her into overdrive. No longer a scared and timid human wannabe, she sought to experience all and everything Tristan offered. Logan's hands continued to massage her, now paying special attention to her nipples, rolling them between his forefingers and thumbs. Kalli pushed her hips upward seeking his mouth, unable to wait. She strained as Tristan's breath brushed over her lips.

"Tristan, please, don't tease me," she begged.

As much as Tristan wanted to draw out her pleasure, he knew that tonight of all nights, she desperately craved release. Her body would be on fire with arousal and he planned to drench her in his love. Darting his tongue forward, he licked open her seam and pushed two firm fingers up into her at the same time.

"Yes!" Kalli screamed.

"You taste so sweet," he mumbled into her wetness. Circling her with his tongue, he dragged a flat broad stroke against her golden flesh. He lapped at her honeyed cream, gently taking her into his lips. Turning his fingers upward, he petted along the long strip of nerves that ran deep inside her.

"There, oh yes, there," she confirmed. Writhing, she raked both hands through his hair, clasping him to her. As he wrapped his lips around her clit and sucked, her orgasm slammed into her hard. She fought for air, shaking in Logan's arms as Tristan continued to pull on her little peak, draining every last wave from her.

"Tristan," she gasped, unable to string together a coherent thought. The things this man did to her sent her over the edge and then some. Just as she was starting to recoup, he spun her around so she was on her hands and knees on the step of the tub.

"Kalli, take Logan, while I take you." She heard Tristan say. Opening her eyes, her gaze flew to Logan's. Nestled between his legs, Logan's hard shaft begged to be touched. He reached down to stroke himself, but she stopped him.

"Logan, come to me," she commanded. God help her, she wanted him too. He'd given her nothing but assurance since she'd met the man. And here he was before her, gorgeous and hot with need.

Obeying his Alpha's mate, he leaned forward, his hardness so close to her warm mouth. In the heat of the moment, no longer embarrassed, Kalli craved him. Tristan wanted this as much as she did, so when he pressed at her core, she parted her lips and dragged her tongue over Logan's straining sex. He tasted of maleness, spicy and delicious. She took him all the way into her mouth. She mewled softly, and Logan threw back his head, willing himself to let her suckle him at her own pace.

The sight of his woman pleasuring Logan sent a hedonistic pulse to Tristan's already throbbing hardness. Slowly, he pushed into Kalli's tightness, stretching the walls of her body. "Aw, Kalli," he groaned. "So amazing."

She moaned in excitement, reveling in the feel of Tristan inside her while she sucked Logan harder and harder, bringing him pleasure.

Tristan surged into the warmth between her legs. "Ah yeah. Feel how good we all are together." Settling his hands on her bottom, he slowly rocked in and out, all the while watching Kalli attend to Logan. The quickening energy flowed between all three of them, building the sexual tension to a new high.

Massaging her smooth cheeks, Tristan ran his finger along the crease of Kalli's ass and brushed over her rosebud. She moaned in response, wriggling back toward his touch. Remembering how she'd so enjoyed the anal play the other night and the way she came apart with the toy, he'd been dying to expand their repertoire.

"Mon amour, I want to take you here tonight," he breathed, pressing a finger into her puckered flesh while continuing his sensual rhythm. "It will be so good." He swore he'd make it the most amazing, pleasurable experience she'd ever known.

Her senses flooded, her pulse quickened at the thought. Momentarily releasing Logan from her mouth, she hesitated to admit what she secretly wanted. "I...I don't know," she breathed.

"Trust," he reminded her with a soft smack to her ass. The sting sent a jolt to her already aching pussy, elevating her desire. She swore she could feel the wetness flow in response to his demand.

"Ah yes. Yes, do it," she responded with urgency. Part of her wondered what was wrong with her that she liked the feel of him slapping her bottom. But then again, everything he did felt so good. Her body thrummed in excitement, awaiting his next move.

"I think she likes being spanked," Logan remarked as she took him once again into her mouth. "Oh yeah, definitely. Kalli, that feels so good."

Kalli hissed as a cool liquid ran down her backside, realizing what Tristan was doing to her. As his generously lubricated finger probed her, she pushed back into him. "Tristan, yes. Please."

He added another finger and a small burning sensation hit her. "I...I can't...."

"Breathe, baby. Just give your body a minute. We've got to slow down."

Relaxing into his touch, the burn gave way to fullness as he pushed in and out, his fingers now scissoring her, preparing her for him. An erotic pleasure that she'd never known coursed through her body, every part of her full with the men she trusted.

Logan removed himself from her mouth, resting her forehead on his legs, so she could relax as Tristan entered her. Lying back onto the wide rim, perpendicular to them, he looked up to their faces. The position also freed him so that he could stroke his rigid sex and have one hand to touch Kalli.

"Okay, chérie, I'm going to go slowly. I'm right here. Now push back a little as I push into you," he instructed. Kalli gasped into Logan's thigh as Tristan pushed the first inch of his rock hard cock into her tight ring.

The slight pain soon gave way to a blissful wholeness. She took ragged breaths as he slowly entered her, anticipating his entire sinewy length. "Oh my God, Tristan.

Please, don't stop," she screamed at the feel of his dark intrusion.

"You feel so good, Kal. So tight. You okay?" he asked, his hand gripped to her hips.

"Yes, please…make love to me," she cried, nodding her head. Filled with a hunger she'd never known, she couldn't take any more. So out of control, yet so filled with ecstasy, she needed all of him, every last bit he was willing to give.

Carefully, he moved in and out of her, taking care to make sure she was enjoying every stroke. Sliding his hands around her belly, he pulled her upward until they were both up on their knees. His chest against her back, he held her breasts, pinching her nipples into firm nubs.

She released a groan, overwhelmed with the feel of his hands on her, the fullness. "Tristan, I love you," she moaned.

"Love you too, baby. Feel us."

Logan was about to burst at the sight of them together, so beautiful. Tristan eyed him, willing him to remain in contact. With his free hand, Logan pushed a long, thick finger into the slick wetness of her arousal, thumbing her clitoris.

"Oh my God, I…I…" She ecstatically shuddered at yet another touch to her body. Tristan pushed in and out of her rosebud as Logan pressed inside her core. Sinfully delighted, she hurtled toward her orgasm. Screaming Tristan's name over and over again, a frenzy of convulsing waves rippled throughout her whole body. Tristan held her tightly, as she thrashed back and forth, crying out in reckless fervor.

As she spasmed, Tristan groaned low and hard, stiffening in release. "Ah, I'm coming!" He held tight to her body as the fiery culmination of their explosions continued to rack their bodies. Logan grunted, a hard climax rocking him, his seed jetting upon his rock hard abs.

For a long minute, the trio rested in their respective positions, unable to move. Slowly, Tristan pulled himself from Kalli, scooping her up into his arms. Taking her over to the shower, he turned on the warm spray, carefully washing her body as she laid her face against his chest.

The night could not have been more perfect, Kalli thought as she clung to Tristan. As if she'd been born again, she'd breached the curtain of apprehension and fear that had plagued her life. She was wolf and woman, inside and out. Her Alpha. Her pack. Grateful for her awakening, she whispered, 'I love you', before finally submitting to the gratifying exhaustion that took over her body and mind.

❧ Chapter Twenty-Five ❧

The birds serenaded them from the tree branches as the streaks of sun burst through the skylights. Kalli could have sworn she'd died and gone to heaven after the magical night she'd spent running with Tristan, and then making love to him under the stars. Not even Logan's participation felt awkward in retrospect. It all was as Tristan had said it would be; natural and loving.

She felt like the luckiest woman in the world. After the years of abuse and hiding, she could finally embrace her wolf and everything she was. True, she was still a well-respected veterinarian, who would continue her work at the university and shelter. But it was as if a huge piece of her being had been discovered: lover, mate and pack member. For the first time in her entire life, she felt complete.

"Hey, what are you thinking about?" Tristan asked sleepily.

"How do you do that?"

"What?"

"Know what I'm thinking?" she laughed.

Tristan kissed the top of her head. "It's not that I know exactly what you're thinking. I can't really explain it except to say that I bond with every single pack member. I feel them and they, to some extent feel me. I can push forth feelings, power, for lack of a better word. It can cause excitement or calming; things like that. Intimidation, if challenged. It's hard to explain; it's just part of me."

"And with me? What do you feel?" She trailed her fingers along the contours of his chest.

"Ah, with you I feel every emotion tenfold, as if it's magnified somehow. I sense how you are feeling, what you're thinking. It's all part of me claiming you and you claiming me. Our bodies and minds work in preparation for our mating, so that we get used to working as one, leading as one. As my mate, you'll have status within the pack. But the dominance you demonstrated over Mira yesterday, as wolf, well. Let's just say, tongues will be wagging instead of tails this morning."

"And how does the pack feel today?"

"They feel good about the stability of me taking on a mate, something they've wanted for a long time but never thought they'd get. And frankly neither did I. But now that I have you, I'm not letting go."

"About that…our mating. I don't know…I mean I never had a female to explain it to me. I've met mated wolves but never really understood how…the details."

He smiled, remembering her naivety. "Not that complicated really. I mean technically we're halfway there, having claimed each other and all." He traced her mark with his forefinger. "We just have to declare our commitment to each other while making love and then exchange, you know, bites. But a little harder this time, so that we have a blood exchange. Of course, afterward, we'll formally announce our mating in front of the pack. We can hold a more traditional reception if you want. It'll be beautiful, like you. And from then on, we'll be mated, be able to have children. So, how do you feel about that?"

"It sounds wonderful," she responded, mentally paused on the thought of children.

"How do you feel about children?"

"Honestly? I never gave it a thought before I met you. But watching you the other day at the funeral, playing with the pups… I really would love to have your children someday. You'd make a great Dad."

"And you'd make a great mother. Seeing you with your puppies…makes me want to have a whole litter," he halfheartedly joked, hoping not to scare her too much.

Tristan's heart had constricted on hearing her words. She wanted *his* children. He'd never thought he'd mate, let alone have kids until he saw her that day in the shelter, caring for all the animals. He laughed to himself, taking note of the one-eighty he'd made over the past week. He had always subscribed to the idea that one should not mess with Mother Nature. And boy was she ever teaching him a lesson.

Changing the subject, he inquired how she felt about last night. "So how do you feel today? About your run? About our mad lovemaking session in the hot tub?" He laughed.

"You get right to it, don't you?" she giggled. "I feel amazing. A bit sore in all the right places, but I am just feeling so whole. So complete. Shifting with you last night, was the single most phenomenal thing that has ever happened to me. Well, aside from what we did afterward. That was pretty awesome too."

She quieted in a serious manner, cupping his face and gazing directly into his piercing amber eyes. Unprecedented emotions rose in her chest; tears threatened to fall. "I just…I want you to know how grateful I am to you. And no, don't even say it's nothing. Everything you've done for me, I've never had this before...you've made me...you've made me whole. I can't even say 'whole again' because I've never felt like I belonged or even felt comfortable in my own skin. Then all those years, being terrified. Because of you, I'm safe, true to my nature and most importantly, loved."

Tristan leaned in, kissing her tears, and just held her. He loved her so much. He knew she didn't want his pity. She just wanted to say thank you, and he welcomed her appreciation with love.

The sound of the phone ringing broke the moment, and he reached over to pick it up. "Tristan," he answered.

Holding the phone to his hand, he addressed Kalli. "Janie wants to know if you can look at one of our mares. She's sick. Doc Evans checked her a few days ago but Janie would feel better if you came by to check on her again today...since you're here and all."

Kalli nodded, smiling in agreement. Secretly, she was thrilled that someone from the pack would think to ask her for help. Even though she and Tristan would only be up the mountains on weekends, she'd be happy to help care for the horses in the future.

"She can make it. I'll drop her off in about a half hour on my way to the clubhouse. Later." Hanging up the phone, Tristan stretched slowly, wrapping his hands back around her. "Well baby, as much as I'd love to stay in bed all day, you've got a date with a horse and I've got an early meeting. We're running through the plan for when we go to South Carolina tomorrow."

Nearly jumping out of the bed, Kalli sat straight up and shot him a questioning look. "South Carolina? When are we going? Did they find him?"

Tristan returned her look with a serious expression. "You, my lovely little wolf, are not going anywhere. And yes, we've found Gerald. I expect the wolf who killed Toby will be with him, or he'll know his location. Logan's got all the intel, and we're flying in tomorrow night on the jet."

As much as Kalli wanted to see Tristan rip Gerald's throat out, she still held a healthy fear of the man who'd wanted to hurt her. All things considered, she should be happy that Tristan didn't want to take her with him. But her protective streak couldn't let him go alone.

"Tristan, here's the thing, I know that place. I know how to get around in the woods, where they hide, the wolves. I can help," she suggested, trying to convince him to let her go.

"Not an option, baby." Swinging his legs off the bed, he strode across the room. There was no way in hell he was putting her in danger.

"Please. Just think about it. Gerald, he's ruthless. He doesn't play by the rules."

Tristan turned before going into the bathroom. His eyes narrowed into the predatory scowl she'd seen at the Summit. "There won't be anyone left when this is done, Kalli. I'll spare the women and pups, but subordinates who support him will die. I've got this. As for you, you're staying here. End of discussion."

Kalli's stomach lurched as she thought about Tristan, Logan and the others going after the Wallace pack. Merciless, they'd go for the kill every time. While she was confident that Tristan could best Gerald one to one, they played dirty, often employing human weapons that could injure wolves, weakening their prey. Maybe Tristan thought her going wasn't an option, but losing him wasn't an option either. Quietly, she resolved to try and talk him into taking her after she checked the horses.

"Stop worrying," Tristan ordered as he pulled the car in front of the barn. "Seriously, you've got to let it go and trust that I will handle this. I've got news for you; it's not my first time to the rodeo. I won't be able to do my job if you're there with me. It's literally impossible to concentrate when I'm within five feet of you." He gave her a small smile. "Now go take care of my baby...my big four-legged baby, that is."

"Baby, huh?"

"Jellybean's the one who's sick. She's a sweet girl, picked her out myself. And yes, she's my baby. So go give her a look, would you? Janie can give you a ride back if you want."

"Nah, I think a walk back to the house would do me good. I'll take the path you showed me yesterday. Should only take me about ten minutes, right?"

"Yep, the cabin's open. I should be done in a few hours, okay?"

Kalli leaned over, giving him a brief kiss on the lips. As she contemplated kissing him more deeply, she ran her tongue across the seam of his lips. He reluctantly resisted, softly laughing.

"If you keep this up, I swear I'll have you up in that hay loft within five seconds. I don't think Janie would appreciate us going like rabbits in her stables."

She smiled against his lips. "Later. You owe me," she teased seductively.

With a peck to his cheek, she opened the car door, shut it and walked into the barn. Janie, a pixie-sized woman with red cropped hair, waved her over. Looking around, Kalli considered maybe taking a ride, but regretfully, she hadn't thought about it when dressing in a pair of shorts. She admired the neatly kept facilities. The stable already housed around twelve horses, and it appeared as if it could easily hold twelve more.

"Janie?" Kalli asked, extending her hand.

"Kalli?" They shook hands and she quickly ushered Kalli toward Jellybean's stall. She was a beautiful palomino American Quarter Horse, standing fourteen hands high with a small refined head and strong muscular body.

Slowly approaching her, Kalli flattened her palm, letting the horse sniff her before gently stroking her neck. "That's a girl. Now what seems to be wrong? You a sick baby?" she crooned.

Janie shot her a broad smile. "You really are Tristan's mate, aren't you?"

Kalli nodded, smiling in kind. "Yes, I am. Or, I should say that I will be. Why?"

"They're his babies too, you know. I'm glad to have you in the pack. He needs a good woman," she offered. "And I couldn't be happier now that we've got ourselves a pack veterinarian."

"I'd love to help with them when we're here, but I'm more of a generalist. Not a lot of expertise with these big babies, I'm afraid. But I'd be happy to check her vitals. What did Dr. Evans say?"

"He said she was doing better. She had been diagnosed with influenza. She seems all right, but I get worried, ya know. She's been on stall rest, isolated. I figured since you were here, you could give her a looksee."

"I'd love to. Got a stethoscope handy?" Kalli happily opened the stall and began her exam.

After checking all of Jellybean's vitals, she was happy to report that the big girl was making a speedy recovery. Janie and Kalli talked horses for over an hour before she decided to get home. Promising to return later in the day for a ride, she took off toward the path.

Enjoying the warm afternoon, Kalli took her time on the trails, thrilled that she actually remembered her way through the forest after their run. Approaching the spring, she sat on a rock, trying to decide the best way to convince Tristan to take her with him to South Carolina. She was sure she could help him, even if she agreed to stay in the car. Perhaps if she remotely assisted via a wire, she could feed them information about location.

Deep in thought, she heard a branch snap. Her lupine senses, having returned to normal, didn't detect any kind of animal or wolf. She sniffed into the air again, wondering if perhaps she was mistaken. The altogether familiar scent of a human wafted into her nostrils. She knew that sometimes humans came onto the compound to bring in supplies to the clubhouse or help with the horses, but was also certain that none should be in the forest.

Like a deer on alert, she stilled, scanning the trees. Seeing nothing, she decided to shift. At the very least, she'd get home more quickly. At worst, she'd outrun any human predator. Crouching down into a defensive stance, she readied to shift, calling her wolf to the surface. But as she went to lift her shirt in an effort to strip, a dark covering fell over her. Struggling to remove it, she hissed in pain. Laced in silver, she'd been effectively blinded and trapped. Strong arms wrapped around her as she fought to escape. The silver restrained her from shifting, weakening her entire body. Screaming for help and writhing, she jerked as a sharp needle pierced her thigh. *Tranquilizer.* Mouthing Tristan's name in silence, she hit the forest floor, enveloped in darkness

They'd spent hours reviewing intel, including maps and names, in preparation for their attack. Logan, in charge of weapons, had worked with Declan to load the plane and procure the necessary bulletproof equipment. While Tristan normally didn't do weapons, he was aware that Gerald liked guns. And he planned on taking him out by any means possible.

'*Do you know where Kalli is?*' buzzed across his cell phone screen as he finished up with the wolves. The text from Janie didn't automatically send him into a panic, until he realized it was nearly five o'clock in the afternoon and he'd been gone for four hours.

Tapping Janie's mobile number, he waited. "Where is she?" he barked when Janie picked up the line.

"I don't know, Tris. We were supposed to go for a ride hours ago. I tried calling the house, but no answer. I was hoping she was with you."

"Lock up the barn, Janie. Lock all the doors until Simeon comes for you."

"What's wrong?"

"Just do it. Don't let anyone in. Grab the shotgun in the office and wait for Simeon now."

Ending the call, he yelled over to the group. "Logan! Kalli's missing. Simeon, over to the barn, now! Take Declan. Go wolf when you get there, start running the property. Something's wrong. I feel it. Logan, car! Let's get over to the cabin now. Call Mira; tell her we're on lockdown. All wolves need to be inside and ready to shift."

Running out of the building, Tristan and Logan jumped into his car and sped up to the cabin. By the time they got there, Tristan was furious. They tore through the cabin, but he could tell by the scents that she hadn't been home since the morning. She was gone.

Tristan began pacing like a caged tiger, working through where she could be, who'd taken her. "Goddammit, Logan. How'd they breach our property? There's no way in hell any foreign pack could make one step on our land without someone scenting them. The only way anyone could have gotten in is as human. What deliveries did we have today?"

"There was a scheduled food delivery early this morning, but if anything had been wrong, the food service manager would have called us. But you're right; a human has to have done this. The wolves would know if another wolf breached our property. And if someone did go after her, why wouldn't Kalli shift? She should be able to shift on demand by now…after last night," Logan reasoned.

"A human. A fucking human. Or…" He stilled as the horrifying possibility ran through his mind. "A wolf pretending to be a human. The CLI. No one would have scented them. They could have taken her over the fence just about anywhere. We've gotta run the perimeter. Fuck!" He pounded his fist into the wall in frustration.

"And if they silvered her, maybe drugged her, they could stop her shift," Logan added.

Tristan felt as if someone had reached into his chest and pulled out his heart by its bloody roots. They'd come into Lyceum Wolves and taken her. His blood pumped in rage. Stripping off his clothes, he instantly transformed, sprinting off across the yard and into the field. Logan followed in pursuit. By the time they reached the furthest boundary, they'd almost given up hope, but soon Tristan screeched to a dead stop and shifted back to human. Running over to the fence, he peeled off a small scrap of red flannel. Holding it to his nose, he breathed deeply, memorizing every last molecule of its odor.

"Wolf. Not ours," he barked out, raking his fingers through his hair. Handing it off to Logan, he peered over the fence that led into a thin patch of woods next to a small road. No car. No trash. No clues. It didn't matter, because he knew where they'd taken her. And he knew for certain who exactly took her. When he found Gerald, he swore he'd rip his throat out vein by vein. If he weren't a dead man before, he'd just signed his own death warrant.

"Back to the clubhouse. I want every wolf there. I want to make sure no one else is missing and if anyone saw anything," Tristan ordered.

Silently, Logan nodded. His Alpha was about to go on a tear, and he prayed they'd find Kalli. Cursing his damn visions, he couldn't believe he hadn't seen this coming.

Pack members filled the large all-purpose room in the clubhouse. A hum of nervous conversation echoed off the cedar walls. After a quick change of clothes in the locker room, an agitated Tristan entered the open area, parting the sea of people. Instantly it became so quiet you could hear a pin drop. Everyone sat, cautiously watching their Alpha.

Looking to Logan, who'd dressed quickly as well, Tristan assessed the situation. "All wolves accounted for?"

"Yeah, everyone's here except for Simeon. I sent him to the airstrip to make sure the jet was ready tonight, and to change flight plans. We're set to go."

"Listen up everyone," Tristan began in a deadly serious tone. "We've suffered a security breach this afternoon. We believe that at least two persons, possibly wolves taking CLI, came onto Lyceum Wolves' property via the north gate. Somewhere between the barn and my cabin, they abducted Kalli."

The crowd released a small roar of murmurs at the news.

"Settle down," he ordered. "Now I know that most of you noticed her on last night's run…at the spring. I was planning on a formal introduction to the pack later this week, but now it seems there's no other way for me to do this. So for those who haven't been listening to gossip, she's mine; I've claimed her."

A few gasps could be heard. Tristan nodded in response. While most wolves knew he'd claimed Kalli, it seemed as if a few hadn't heard the news. Most of the pack was still happily surprised that he'd found someone after leading Lyceum Wolves for over fifty years as a single wolf.

"And she's my mate," he added, as the room fell silent once again. They all registered the seriousness of the situation. An Alpha's mate kidnapped. Tristan and the pack would suffer enormously if anything happened to her. He would simply not recover from such a loss. While he would assuredly go on without her, he'd probably have to step down as Alpha due to the excruciating grief. There'd be infighting and challenges for his position, despite Logan's status.

"Like I said, I planned to formally introduce her to you after we took down the Wallace pack. We were going to complete our mating afterward. But now…" His words temporarily trailed off as the thought of Kalli dead raced through his mind. It killed him, but he refused to show weakness in front of his pack. As always, they needed him to be a rock, and he never disappointed them. "Tonight we go in to take out Wallace. But before that happens, I want to know who was on the property today. Ellie said the clubhouse was locked up tight. No humans were there after the morning food delivery. Janie told me Doc Evans was out of town; that's why she called on Kalli to check the horses. Somebody here must have seen something, scented something. If you've got anything to say, now's the time. I want the truth," he demanded.

A barely audible cough came from the back of the room as Julie stood. "Alpha." She lowered her eyes. "Coming back from town in my car, I passed the stables. I noticed the mares were in the south field. The boys were in the northern field. I saw two men near them, but I just assumed they were Doc Evan's workers. The interns, you know. They come with him sometimes. I didn't stop. I should have stopped. I…I'm so sorry." A tear escaped at the realization she could have seen the intruders.

"Were they going toward the barn or the field?"

"Toward the fields, into the woods."

"Julie, this is really important." Tristan fixed her with his stare. "What else do you remember? What were they doing?"

"Just walking. They had on backpacks, but again, sometimes Doc has a pack too. I had the windows down, and smelled the humans. Nothing appeared strange...so I kept driving," she muttered.

"Did you see or scent anyone else besides Janie, Kalli or the horses? Humans? Wolves? Animals?"

Recognition flashed across her face. Her eyes darted across the room and then to the floor.

Tristan rushed to her, taking her by the arms. "Look at me, Julie," he insisted forcefully. "Who else was at the barn?"

Julie raised her gaze to his, then her eyes settled on Mira, who'd been sitting up toward the front of the room. Inspecting her perfectly manicured nails, she pretended to ignore Julie.

"Are you sure?" Tristan spat out; his voice rose.

"Yes, as wolf. I didn't see her, but I scented her at the barn. I'm certain," Julie confessed, shaking her head.

The atmosphere in the room crackled with a surge of fear as if they were waiting for a volcano to erupt.

Tristan closed his eyes, taking a deep breath as he contemplated the scenarios of Mira's involvement. It couldn't be possible. She'd been mad about Kalli from the very beginning, jealous even. The public submission at the springs had only served to stoke her anger. But they'd been friends for so long. She knew he'd claimed her. It would crush him, but by Goddess, he needed to know if she was involved in the abduction.

"Mira!" Tristan yelled as the others cowered slightly. Every wolf could sense the powerful waves of anger emanating off of their Alpha.

Mira's head snapped to attention upon hearing her name. With a confident stance, she stood up and faced him, placing a hand to her hip. Inwardly she shook in fright, but she couldn't let them know. She'd done the right thing in sending her away. Kalli was a half breed whore who'd pollute the pack. She didn't belong in Lyceum Wolves. He'd thank her eventually.

"Yes," Mira responded flatly.

"Mira, you've been my friend for a very long time, but I'm only going to ask you this question once. I expect truth. Do you understand?" Tristan growled.

Lowering her gaze slightly but still maintaining eye contact, she nodded. "Yes, Tristan. As always."

Logan started to approach the pair, but Tristan held up a hand, halting him. He shot him a warning look and then narrowed his eyes on Mira once again.

"Were you involved in Kalli's abduction?" Tristan asked in a low menacing voice.

"I...I was just out running. I didn't do anything," she protested.

Sensing deception, Tristan did something he normally didn't do. Opening himself, he let his mind touch Mira's. He wanted her to feel a mere sliver of the sheer wrath that pulsed throughout his being.

As it hit her, Mira gasped in pain. "Tristan, don't," she pleaded.

Logan ran forward. As beta, Tristan's emotions ran through him as if he were experiencing them himself. Tristan held up his palm again, stopping him from moving, all the while never taking his eyes off Mira.

"Stand down, Logan. Do not challenge me," he ordered. "Mira, what did you do?"

Looking to the floor, she shook her head back and forth in denial, yet she felt compelled to tell him. He'd know. There was no way to lie to him. Surely he'd understand that she'd done this for the pack. Steeling her nerves, she looked directly into his eyes. "No, I did not take her personally. But yes, I called them to take her. She's not pack."

As the words hit him, the slicing agony of betrayal cut at his heart.

On your knees!" he commanded, enraged by what she'd done to him. When she refused to listen, his power discharged, spilling over, forcing her to the floor. Standing back, he held his fisted hands at his sides. "Why Mira? We've been friends for over a century. How could you do this to me? To the pack?"

Mira stumbled to the ground, submitting. Tristan's surge of anger held her at the carpet.

"I did this for the pack! She doesn't belong here," she cried in defiance. "I am Lyceum Wolves. Daughter of Alpha. I know how things should be. You wouldn't listen. Something had to be done. She has her own pack! And now she's there! You'll never get her back!"

"Correction, Mira. You were the daughter of Alpha. You were Lyceum Wolves. I can't believe you'd let others come onto our territory...take my mate. But you betrayed me. The pack. You put everyone at risk. I can't understand this." Tristan shook his head, still unable to believe that his best friend had done this to him. Petty jealously was one thing; questioning his leadership was a direct challenge. None of it could go unpunished.

"Mira, if you were a male, I'd kill you on the spot for treason. But in deference to our friendship, I hereby strip you of your lineage."

Mira screamed as she realized what he was about to do to her. "No Tristan! You can't!"

"Silence!" he bellowed, delivering another wave of his power, muting her defiance. "Not only have you engaged in treason by inviting dangerous enemies onto our land, you've challenged your Alpha. In a physical challenge, it'd be unlikely you'd survive. Therefore, I must consider a suitable alternative. You will start a new life in another pack. I will notify other possible Alphas this evening. In the meantime, you will be confined to your cabin and are not allowed to leave this compound. Tomorrow, I'll inform you of your new location."

Mira beat the floor with her fists, "No, no, no…this is my pack. You can't do this!"

"That's where you're wrong, Mir. It's already done. Do not challenge me further, or I'll take drastic action. Now get up off your knees and get out of my sight. Declan, assign guards to Mira. She's no longer Lyceum Wolves. As such, she's not allowed to leave her cabin or interact with the others."

"Yes sir," Declan nodded.

"Logan, find out who Mira spoke to from the Wallace pack. See what she knows and then meet me over at the jet. I'd do it, but I swear I might kill her. Honestly, my wolf is demanding no less than her death, but she's been with us forever. Goddess help me, I've got to show her mercy."

A frozen glare glossed over Mira's face as Declan led her out of the room. Pack members looked away, incredulous that she'd deliberately bring strangers into their sanctuary. It was a miracle no one else had been taken or killed. Tristan, aware of how his anger had affected them, concentrated on sending an air of repose into the otherwise distressed crowd.

"My wolves," he addressed them calmly. "Keep diligent watch until I return. Willow's in charge while I'm gone. I'm asking that you stay indoors, no running until we're sure the situation in South Carolina's been contained. Understood?"

With a nod toward Willow, Tristan pounded out to his car. He'd expected that Mira would have been hurt by him taking a mate, but never had he anticipated such treachery. She'd put the entire pack at risk out of some misguided sense of loyalty. Unforgiveable, yet he couldn't bring himself to mete out the deserved retribution; death. Hoping she'd find peace in a new pack, he fired up the car and let his thoughts drift back to Kalli.

Instinctively, he assumed Gerald would keep her alive, perhaps torture her, rather than kill her. Reports indicated that there were only two females left in the pack after he'd killed them off, one by one. No pups had been listed, although Tristan suspected that they could have somehow gone undetected in the flyover. Eleven remaining males kept court at all times of day.

Now that Kalli could shift, she'd have a fighting chance of staying alive. She was strong and intelligent. If an opportunity for escape presented itself, he was confident she'd take it. Rubbing a hand over his face in frustration, he considered how they would have transported her. Drug or silver would be the easiest way to ensure she couldn't shift. Surely they would have flown Kalli out of Pennsylvania, realizing he'd tear the state apart looking for her? Glancing over to the clock, he saw it read seven o'clock. If they managed to leave within the hour, they'd arrive by ten. Every muscle in his body tensed. Blood boiling, he was ready to embrace the retributive justice that would come at his hands tonight.

⊸❧ *Chapter Twenty-Six* ❧⊷

K alli vomited onto the floor, unable to control the nausea. Unsure of what drug they used, she thought it had to be some kind of an animal tranquilizer. Wiping the spittle from her lips, she cracked her eyes open, trying to assess her surroundings. The irrefutable smell of human urine and feces permeated the small cemented room in which they'd placed her. Her wrist burned as the silver handcuff, attached to an old metal cot, cut into her skin. The threadbare mattress chafed at her legs, but at least they hadn't entirely restrained her. She struggled to sit up, but managed with a sigh, as she leaned against the cold concrete.

Although it was dark, her eyes quickly adjusted to the light. Taking in the barren accommodations, she noticed a small square window in the wall half way toward the ceiling. More of a hole really, it left no room to escape. The one foot by one foot portal was missing its glass, allowing a cool mountain breeze to seep into the room. Sniffing into the air, a stir of painful memories told her exactly where she was. *Wallace pack.* Heart of the Blue Ridge Mountains; spectacular waterfalls, scenic vistas, wild flowers. Yet the only thing this place held for Kalli was a lifetime of abuse and torture.

Heart racing, she struggled to remain calm as the door to the room flew open. And although the ray of bright light blinded her, she'd never forget the horrific scent of Gerald or the smell of whiskey on his breath. Telling herself she was stronger this time, she fortified her mind, readying for his attack.

"Look who the cat dragged in. Our little hybrid slut thought she'd hide from us. We always find what's ours," he cackled as he approached her, shining a spotlight into her face. "Old Morris lucked out, didn't he? Thought he'd find something up in the big city. We was lookin' for some bitches to bring back here. We're low, ya see. But we knew there'd be plenty of girls we could take. Big city won't miss 'em. Little did he know he'd find you."

"I'm not who you think I am," she protested.

"Oh, yeah, I know who ya are. Fancy degrees, I hear ya made a drug to hide your wolf," he laughed. "Worked real well too. Dumb ole Lyceums didn't know we was even there. Well, now that we got ya, you're gonna make more of those pills. We can sell 'em on the streets. Got big plans for ya, you know?"

Overwhelmed by the odor, Kalli cringed in his presence. As if she were in a swamp at night with gators, she could see the red flecks of light reflecting off his cold black eyes. She wanted so badly to shift, but as long as she was silvered, she couldn't. If somehow she could get the cuff off, she could summon her wolf. In her mind, she'd made the decision to die fighting. Dying seemed a preferable option compared to a lifetime in Wallace. No matter what happened to her, she wouldn't let him manufacture the CLI. He'd never be able to do it without her.

"I don't belong to you anymore," she spat at him. "My mate. He'll come for me."

He ran a finger down her neck. Linking a claw into the rim of her t-shirt, he tore it open, revealing Tristan's mark. "Claimed, I see. But mated, not yet. I can tell a mated bitch, and you're not one. Close but no cigar."

Refusing to give quarter, Kalli defiantly sat with her bra exposed, refusing to let him see how terrified she was.

"My mate will come for you. You'll be dead by morning."

"Maybe you'll be the one who'll be dead after I let a few of my men go at ya. Not many bitches around here. Now here you are, fallin' into our laps."

He ran his hand down her chest, but when he attempted to paw her breast, Kalli struck him between the eyes with the palm of her hand, ramming his nose.

"Fucking bitch," he screamed as blood spurted from his nostrils. In response, he struck Kalli across the face with the back of his hand. Her head smashed into the cinderblock with a resounding crack.

She saw stars as the pain radiated throughout her face and then through the back of her head. Feigning unconsciousness, she kept her eyes closed. It wasn't hard to fake given the injury to her head. She sighed in relief as she heard the door slam as he left, leaving a string of curse words in his wake.

Racking her brain for a way to escape, she needed to get out of the cuff. She was no Houdini, but she'd watched plenty of television shows where people unlocked their own handcuffs. *What did they use? A credit card? No, that was for doors. Come on Kalli, think. A paperclip? A pin?* Where the hell would she get a pin? Her hair, still in a ponytail, only had a rubber band in it. She still had on her shoes but they only held laces. Then it occurred to her that she was wearing a wired bra. She wasn't crazy about the idea of stripping inside of her hellhole prison but if she could get the cuff off, she'd open the door, shift and wouldn't need her clothes.

After managing to unhook her bra, she bit at the fabric with her teeth until a small hole emerged. Threading the wire out, she bent it back and forth until it broke into two pieces. She proceeded to shim the lock by inserting the small wire between the notches and the ratchet. Within a minute, the lock clicked open. Smiling to herself, she had her own plan for Gerald, and it involved him and a dirt bed.

Challenging the Alpha while silvered may not have been the brightest idea she'd had, but damn if she'd deny her mate. Tristan was coming for her. Released from the poison shackle, she could feel it in her blood. Her wolf called to the surface, and she swore she could sense him on the land, in the air. She was certain, in that moment, that Gerald would, indeed, end up a cadaverous, lifeless piece of flesh by sunrise.

Locked and loaded, Lyceum Wolves hit the ground. In a smooth landing, the plane taxied onto the private airstrip nestled on a small strip of land within the mountains. As soon as they came to a grinding halt, Tristan, Logan, Declan, Gavin and Shayne poured out of the plane into two waiting SUVs. Tristan could feel her as soon as they hit the rocky soil. The smell of blood hung in the air, and he swore he'd have vengeance.

The Wallace compound was set against a mountain face, with a myriad of trails leading into the dense brush. They'd parked about a mile outside of the perimeter. Nearly midnight, the waning moon lit the forest floor as they stealthily navigated the terrain. As they neared the housing complex, Tristan signaled to Simeon to take the highest point. Simeon, a former Navy SEAL, was a precision shooter. Aware that the Wallace wolves had a proclivity toward weapons, Tristan had instructed Simeon to pick off any wolf brandishing a gun. But not Gerald. No, Gerald was Tristan's only.

Holding a hand up, Tristan pointed to the right, around the large dilapidated structure. Scenting Kalli, he could tell she was close, within a hundred yards at the very most. Logan, also catching her scent, had been assigned to take Kalli to safety. As beta, he was the only wolf Tristan trusted to ensure her rescue. No words were needed to convey his meaning as they exchanged glances. Furtively, Logan took off with Gavin around the building, as loud music whipped a cadence into the night.

Tristan's primary mission was to annihilate Gerald. The man was a menace who needed taming. In a deliberate manner, with his usual confidence, Tristan strode up to the front door. Armed with silver bullets, Declan and Shayne flanked him. Like a homing missile, Tristan kicked in the door and strode into the melee. The sounds of bullets breaking the windows resounded, while Tristan shrewdly assessed the wolves around him, searching for Gerald. Shayne and Declan started fighting as soon as they entered. Shifting into wolf, the fur literally started to fly. Five wolves fell to the ground in a pool of blood as Simeon carried out his orders.

Tristan's eyes locked onto the stocky wolf crouched in the corner, growling as each of his wolves hit the ground. Intrepidly approaching the wolf, his feet never stopped moving. Images of Toby lying dead in the ground ran through his mind followed by his mate, abused and nearly broken, at the hands of the monster before him. Tristan didn't want to kill Gerald quickly; he planned on making him suffer the way he'd done to the others.

"What you want wolf? Can't you see here that we're just enjoying a drink?" The words had barely left Gerald's mouth before Tristan had him by the throat.

"Gerald? Alpha of Wallace pack?" Tristan asked with a snarl.

"Yeah, what's it to ya? This is my land, here. Ya need to get off."

"Where are the women and pups?"

"I got a bitch downstairs if ya want her, but we don't got any others right now. We've been pickin' them off up north," Gerald freely admitted, not recognizing Tristan as Alpha of Lyceum Wolves.

"Declan! Downstairs, now! Make sure Logan's got Kalli out of here," Tristan shouted.

Furiously shaking Gerald by the scruff of his shirt, he jammed him up against the wall. A tiny red dot appeared above Gerald's brow as Simeon's laser locked on the broad prominence of his forehead.

"Stand down, Si," Tristan instructed, holding two fingers into the air. A bullet to the brain was too good for Gerald; too easy. After all the pain and suffering he'd inflicted on men, women and children over the years, he'd go down old school. Tristan, not one to be accused of going outside of pack protocol, sought to have him submit as wolf, and die as wolf. There was no other way that would make amends for the bloody atrocities the man had caused to so many.

With a grunt, Tristan threw him clear across the room where he slammed into a pile of aluminum chairs. Aside from the sound of scraping metal, Gerald's heavy panting was the only audible sound. Dead Wallace wolves, well departed from life, provided a macabre background to Gerald's impending demise. Tristan smiled coldly as he noted that Morris, the wolf who had helped to kill Toby, lay among the dead, a silver bullet to his head. Simeon had picked him off; still dressed, the wolf gripped a small handgun. Giving the lifeless body a nudge with his boot, a small bottle of pills spilled out of his front shirt pocket. *CLI.* Never taking his eyes off Gerald, Tristan effortlessly scooped up the bottle and tossed it over to Shayne, who'd shifted back to human.

Disgusted by Toby's needless death and Kalli's abduction, Tristan stalked toward Gerald, who was eyeing a Glock that had fallen into the debris. Kicking the grey metal out of reach, Tristan stood towering above the seething brawny wolf. With an ominous delivery, Tristan informed him of his death sentence as if he were a judge in a courtroom. His menacing stare bored into the malevolent creature who'd taken his mate.

"Gerald, wolf of Wallace. Consider yourself informed of my challenge to your pack. From this minute forward, any females or pups you've hidden will be placed under my protection. I command you to shift. In front of my wolves, we will do this challenge," Tristan demanded, with a cool demeanor. It had to be done this way. The respect of his own wolves was as important as eradicating Gerald. Wolf versus wolf, it was how he was raised, and how he would die.

Tearing off his shirt and pants, Tristan transformed to wolf within seconds. Gerald's husky brown wolf charged at him, jaws snapping, but Tristan sidestepped the attack, snarling in response. Standing proud, the black Alpha wolf circled around the brown, eyes locked on his. With his ears forward and tail lifted, Tristan bared his fangs. His wolf demanded the death of the one who'd dared to challenge him for his mate. Eyes wild, threatening and locked onto Gerald, Tristan's wolf kept low to the ground, readying for attack. Taking flight, he rushed Gerald, and in a submissive move Gerald took off out of the building. With his prey on the move, Tristan gave chase; a rush of adrenaline flooded his system, anticipating the kill.

Gerald only made it a few hundred yards before Tristan pawed him downward, dragging him to the leaf-covered ground. Engaged in a ritualistic combat as old as time, Tristan pinned the brown wolf with his forepaws, exposing his vital areas. Unwilling to submit, Gerald continued to fight, biting a small gash into the black wolf's back leg. With an arched neck and bared fangs, Tristan seized Gerald's vulnerable soft throat, tearing out a huge chunk of fur and flesh. The smell of fresh blood spattered the woods. Furious and violent, Tristan tore apart the brown wolf's neck until the head dangled by a single vertebra.

Tristan. Kalli felt him the instant he landed on the mountain ridge. His unique scent, carried to her on the wind, provided a renewed energy. She hoisted herself to her feet, but wavered. Overwhelmed with dizziness, she fell back to the dirty cot. She thought she should shift, but her head pounded in protest. Reaching her hand into her hair, she felt the large knot of swelling on her skull. *I need to shift.* But then a rustling outside her window called her to the night. Feeling as if she'd faint, she grunted, pushing onto her knees until her fingertips felt the rim of the small window.

"Tristan!" she screamed over and over, praying someone would hear her.

Her breath hitched as a hand found hers. Unable to see, she desperately grabbed onto it.

"Kalli!" Logan yelled into the small dark cavity. He could barely make out Kalli's face through the mask of blood; tendrils of black curls adhered to her skin. As he peered in further, he swore. Tristan was going to kill Gerald a thousand times over for attacking his mate.

"Logan. Please," Kalli coughed. Between vomiting and screaming, her throat was raw. "Door's locked. There's no way out. I need to shift. My head."

Logan looked to Gavin. "Kalli, this here's Gavin. He's ours."

Gavin knelt down next to Logan, and allowed Logan to put his hand into Kalli's.

"Take his hand. It's okay. He's gonna stay with you. I'll come round to get you. I'll be right there. You're going to be okay."

"Tristan? Where is he? Please, nothing can happen to him," she cried.

"Trust me, Kal, Gerald's the one who's got to worry. Tris will be fine. Just hold tight. I'm coming." He heard her give a small sob at his words. She might have been strong, but he could tell she was on the verge of breaking.

Without a doubt, Tristan was going to go ballistic when he saw Kalli's face. His Alpha, a well-oiled killing machine, didn't need yet another reason to rip into Gerald. Fearing the sight of her could distract him in his quest, Logan took off in a full sprint. Once he found the back entrance, Logan heard growling followed by an eerie silence emanating from another room. Staying focused, he made his way to a staircase that was tucked into an alcove in the kitchen. Making his way down the steps, he found himself in a complicated series of tunnels.

Taking a minute to sniff the dank musty air, he caught her scent. In the dark recesses, he heard crying, voices of children and women. Exploring the cavernous passages, Logan swore, realizing this was some kind of underground prison. He'd need to work on freeing these wolves, but Kalli's injuries warranted his immediate attention. Finally arriving where he believed she was being held, he pulled on a rusty doorknob. *Locked.* A noise alerted him that someone was close behind. Relieved, he found Declan's wolf padding toward him.

"Hey Dec. I need you to shift. Help me break open this door."

Declan shifted back and prepared to help Logan. Heaving their shoulders into the heavy wood, it splintered open. Logan rushed into the room, finding Kalli stretched upward still holding tight to Gavin. Gently uncurling her fingers from Gavin's, he took her into his arms. She was shaking, presumably from shock. Logan wrapped his shirt around her. He needed her to shift so she could heal.

"Come on Kalli, girl. You're okay," he cajoled, more trying to convince himself than her. He felt the significant goose egg on the back of her head. Blood still trickled out of the gash on her face; her eye was swollen shut. Tristan was going to freak the hell out knowing they'd done this to her.

"You need to shift, baby," he insisted.

Kalli shook her head, shivering in his arms. "I know...I just need a minute. I'm tired. My head..."

"You've got to shift, Kalli." Feeling as if he was losing her, he made a split decision to take her to Tristan.

Caught up in the kill, Tristan froze at the scent of Kalli's blood. He quickly turned his head and caught sight of his beta, carrying a broken and bloodied Kalli in his arms. Trudging into the forest, Logan fell to his knees.

"Tristan, please. She needs to shift. I'm guessing she's got a concussion, but I don't know how bad it is. She's in and out. Please," he pleaded softly, aware that Tristan was still very much wild; his feral beast on edge. Seeing his mate hurt would only inflame his animalistic fervor, but Logan knew that she needed her Alpha. He was the only one who could reach her, force her wolf to resurface.

Releasing a growl, Tristan eyed Logan, holding his injured mate. The animal in him, already agitated, possessively snarled at Logan. *His mate. Blood.* He stalked toward him, baring his fangs.

Logan lowered his eyes and gently laid Kalli onto the cool earth. "Tristan," he whispered. "Your mate. Gerald, he hurt her. She needs you to tell her to shift. I think she knows she's gotta shift but she's too weak. But she'll listen to you, her Alpha."

Logan slowly backed away from Kalli's body, careful not to look at Tristan directly. The other wolves lowered their heads and flattened their ears, closing their eyes to slits, demonstrating submission. Satisfied that no challenges would come and all wolves were reverent, Tristan crept over to Kalli and licked her face. His wolf whined loudly as it continued to nuzzle her.

As consciousness of Kalli's predicament took hold, Tristan shifted to his human form. Pulling her gently into his arms, against his naked skin, he brushed the hair from her face.

"Mon amour." He stifled a cry. What had they done to his mate? "I need you baby, come on now. I need you to shift for me."

Kalli's eyes fluttered open. "Tristan," she whispered. *Her Alpha.* He was near.

"Chérie, listen to me now, you've got a bad head injury there. I'm going to help you, okay? Close your eyes, that's it," he coaxed in a gentle tone as she obeyed. Willing himself to remain calm was extraordinarily difficult, but he needed his aura to remain placid. Taking a deep cleansing breath, he concentrated on sending her his power; tendrils of love flowed from his mind to hers.

"Remember our trust, Kalli. Picture your wolf. She's right there on the surface. Now shift," he commanded.

Kalli felt a wave of emotion rush through her psyche. The sound of Tristan's voice spoke to her inner wolf. Listening to the command of her Alpha, she emerged. Cuddling into his arms, she ran her muzzle along his chest, licking, tasting.

Tristan blew out a breath, thanking the Goddess she'd listened. His little wolf was perfectly nestled in his arms. Safe. He caught a glimpse of Logan, who'd watched in awe. Nodding in thanks to his beta, Tristan returned his attention to Kalli.

"You're beautiful, baby. Look at you." He kissed her head, rubbing her pelt until her head fell back in pleasure.

"Logan, we've got to get out of here," he told him, not letting Kalli move away from him.

Logan shuffled up to his feet. "Tris, there's women and pups below. Maybe seven or eight souls from what I could scent. I don't know for sure, but we've gotta get them."

Wiping his face with the back of his hand, Tristan groaned. "Christ, I knew he couldn't have done away with all the pack. Take Dec and the others with you. Get em' out. We're taking them home. When we get back, we'll figure it all out." Tristan looked around, spotting Simeon in a tree.

"Simeon, get the plane ready. Any chance we can get a charter set up for the others?"

"Yeah, sure boss. I'm on it," he replied, climbing down.

"Right, thanks." Tristan acknowledged. He looked back to Logan and extended his hand upward to his beta. "Logan, I can't thank you enough for getting her out. I'm going to take Kalli back now. I'll meet you back at the cabin."

Logan took his Alpha's hand, with great respect. What they'd done hadn't been easy, but it had had to be done. No longer under threat, they'd return to their territory.

As Logan turned to retrieve the imprisoned pack subordinates, Tristan transformed back into his black wolf. Waiting patiently for Kalli to get her bearings, he contemplated loose ends. What still remained a mystery was who had staged the attack on Marcel's wolves. Neither Gerald nor Jax had claimed responsibility. Yet, clearly the wolves who'd attacked his sister belonged to an Alpha, he was sure. Lone wolves rarely engaged in territorial war tactics. He reasoned that Marcel still had cause to remain cautious.

Kalli approached, jarring his mind back to his first priority. Watching her pad toward him, his heart swelled. *His mate.* As soon as they returned, they'd make it official. Soon he'd rule Lyceum Wolves, no longer alone.

☙ *Chapter Twenty-Seven* ☙

It'd been exactly twenty-four hours since they'd left South Carolina, and for the first time in her life, she felt free. Like an eagle soaring in the sky, she rejoiced in the majestic landscape that was her new life. Fully healed from her shift, they'd agreed that tonight they'd officially mate.

With no reservations, she'd laid perfectly bare on his bed, waiting for Tristan to come to her. As he opened the bathroom door, he gave her a sultry smile, his own nude body attuned to her need. Never one to be dominated, Tristan promptly flipped her onto her stomach, straddling her legs.

Not quite sitting on her bottom, he supported his weight with his well-toned legs. As he leaned forward to massage her back, his hard arousal bulged against her skin. She wriggled against the bed in anticipation, thoroughly enjoying the feel of his velvety hardness against her own skin.

"Yes," Kalli mewled as Tristan ran his magical fingers down the base of her spine.

"Did I tell you today how beautiful you are?"

"Hmm…maybe only five times," she smiled.

"Ah, then I'll have to tell you again and again until you forget the exact number." He kissed her shoulder lightly. "But first, tonight, we're going to mate. And rumor has it that we'll be in for quite the ride once I taste your sweet blood."

"Is that right?" she murmured into her pillow, enthralled by his touch.

"So I've been told. But the only way to know for sure is for us to," he paused to kiss slowly up and down her back, giving her the chills, "experiment. Put things to task as they say. You ready, my little wolf?"

"More than you'll ever know." Stretching her neck to view him, her eyes caught his. "My Alpha, take me."

Tristan reached his arms around her small body. Capturing a warm breast with one hand, he dipped his other down into her wet heat, circling her center of nerves. Continuing to lick and kiss her back, he smiled as Kalli moaned in delight.

Grinding against his hand, Kalli felt the rush of desire. Her orgasm edged her psyche, the painful ache in her core, needing relief. As his erection pressed against the crease of her bottom, she shuddered in arousal. "Tristan, oh, God."

"That's it, baby. So close aren't you?"

"Yes!" she screamed as he inserted a finger into her hot sheath. Unrelenting, he applied pressure to her clit, pushing her over into climax. She shook against the bed, his hard hot body pressed to hers, his chest to her back.

Before she had a chance to recover, he rolled her to her side and gently kneed open her legs, slowly intertwining their limbs. Nestled together, he took hold of his swollen manhood and slid the hard shaft up and down her glistening folds, coating himself in her juices.

Cupping the cheek of her face, he let his gaze fall upon her eyes, as if seeing deep into her soul. Locked on each other with intent, he slowly rocked up into her warm tight channel. Kalli's breath caught as he entered her, but they never lost eye contact. Reaching for him, she wrapped a hand around his neck, threading the fingers of her other hand in his hand.

Face to face, chest to chest, they made love. One singular moment in time, they wordlessly connected, the emotional intensity vised around their hearts like a steel band. Thrusting in unison, slowly and deliberately, their desire mounted. Breathless, their pulses raced in hunger for each other. Tristan began to lose control as they reached a pinnacle of pleasure.

"Kalli," he panted. "I love you with all that I am. You are mine. My soul. My mate."

"Tristan. You're my everything. My mate."

Before she had a chance to say anything else, Tristan kissed her. A passionate, loving kiss representing their eternal love and connection pushed them into simultaneous orgasm. Spilling himself deep within her, Tristan extended his canines. Piercing into his mark, her honeyed blood solidified the mating bond.

Kalli shuddered around him, clamping down on him, her release finding its way through every cell in her body. As she bit into Tristan, his powerful essence assuaged her heart and soul. Everything that was Alpha and man, merged into her psyche. Like a solar flare, flames of love ignited, dancing into their universe.

Coming down from the climax, they held tightly to each other. Both Kalli and Tristan relaxed into the sweet embrace, not willing to relinquish the intimacy that had passed between them. A bond forged in love and trust that neither had ever dreamed could exist. A new world of leading Lyceum Wolves awaited them.

❧ *Epilogue* ❧

A s the private plane landed in New Orleans, Logan's mind raced. It had been a long time since he'd been home, and he was looking forward to helping Marcel figure out who may have killed Paul. He glanced over to the women and children he'd rescued, who were huddled closely in their seats. He and Tristan had made the decision to relocate the remaining Wallace pack wolves to his old pack instead of keeping them in Philadelphia.

Three women and four children, all dirty and battered, were going to get a new lease on life. After talking with them, he gleaned they'd been kept down in Gerald's makeshift prison for well over a year. Apparently, the former Wallace pack Alpha didn't want to have to even see their faces, let alone hear from them. So he'd condemned them to living in the subterranean hell.

Logan was disgusted that anyone would treat another soul in such an inhumane manner. Sure, he'd grown up hearing the rumors of violence within the old packs, but never in all his years had he witnessed such a horrific sight. It was no wonder Kalli had been so afraid of wolves and created the CLI in order to remain hidden. As he reflected on the women's fate, he reasoned that they too could begin new lives for themselves. But like Kalli, they'd probably be emotionally traumatized by the violence. Even with a new home and pack, life wouldn't be easy for them, regardless of everyone's good intentions.

Julie had accompanied him on his long flight. He observed how she'd taken the initiative and was helping them exit the jet. Goddess, he hoped a good dose of her healing would go a long way to help them assimilate. He waved over to Katrina, Tristan's sister, who'd come to the airport to help. She was taking them to Marcel's bayou compound. She gave him a sad smile and a nod as she helped the women and their pups get settled into a large limo that was waiting on the tarmac. While reluctant to let them go, he was assured they were in good hands. Waving goodbye, he entered into a separate limo that waited for his arrival.

Instead of going toward the country, Logan headed toward the city. Marcel was held up in his Garden District mansion, working on business, and Logan sought to debrief him as to what had occurred in South Carolina. Most importantly, he needed to make it clear that there was still someone out there, who he feared planned another attack on the wolves. Neither Jax Chandler, the Wallace pack nor any other packs had claimed responsibility for Paul's death. And his visions told him there was more death to come....another dead wolf. So when Tristan suggested that he accompany the South Carolina wolves to their new Louisiana home, he eagerly agreed to go. He felt that if he could talk to Marcel in person, he could get a better handle on what was happening, clarify his dreams and help catch the killer.

Strip malls, churches and infamous above-ground cemeteries flashed by his line of vision on the short drive into the city. As they entered the Warehouse District, he was reminded of memories from long ago. During the late eighteen hundreds, Marcel, Tristan, Mira and he would take weekend trips to the French Quarter, attending masked Carnival balls, socializing into the wee hours of the morning. Then later, at the turn of the century, they'd witnessed the beginnings of Jazz played in the Storyville cabarets. And to this day, he never tired of walking the streets, appreciating the historic architecture. No matter how long he'd lived in Philadelphia, New Orleans was home.

As he reflected on happier times with Mira, the thought of her betrayal cut deep. When Tristan had sent her off to live with his eldest brother, Blake, in his Wyoming pack, he'd wholeheartedly agreed with the decision. Even though he loved her, he'd never be able to trust her again after she'd put the entire pack in danger. She was lucky Tristan hadn't killed her. Perhaps in time, wounds would heal, he thought, but not anytime soon.

As he opened the car door, he took a deep breath, reminded of his intentions. Cicadas sung in the night as he drew in the warm southern air. He loved everything about New Orleans, from pralines to eating creole shrimp to sitting in his boat in the swamp, listening to music while watching the gators sun themselves. There wasn't much he didn't like about the Big Easy. He sighed, wishing this trip was for pleasure, but alas, it wasn't.

The sound of a low growl emanating from the house first alerted him that something wasn't right. He quickly ran up the steps and burst through the large front door. As he darted into a large moonlit parlor, he heard the sound of gunfire as Marcel fell to the floor. A burly, masked man dressed in black stuffed the gun into his pants and ran toward the back door.

"Go," Marcel gurgled, holding the side of his neck as bright red blood spurted onto the cream-colored Italian marbled floor.

Logan fell to his knees and ripped off his shirt, holding it against the gaping wound. "You've gotta shift, Marcel," he pleaded.

"Let me go. Don't let him get away with this. Go get him," Marcel ordered. A sobbing woman raced to his side, bringing a towel to help stop the bleeding.

"Call 911," Logan yelled before sprinting after the man, determined to follow Marcel's wishes. He pursued the attacker, wondering where Marcel's beta was. *Where was everyone? Who was the young woman?* Unable to reason through what was happening, he focused on his task. Within seconds, Logan caught up with the perpetrator as he was trying to escape from the rear exit. Unsuccessfully but furiously, he yanked at the lock that prevented him from leaving. Logan scented that he was wolf and reached forward to subdue him.

"What the hell?" Logan yelled as the man spun around and punched him across the mouth. Logan staggered, but managed to wrestle him to the ground, grabbing onto his waist. They both hit the ground with a thud, struggling for control. The man extended his claws, scratching at Logan's face as he attempted to shift while still clothed. But Logan managed to hook a strong arm around the assassin's neck, squeezing until a loud snap resounded throughout the room. The dead wolf collapsed immediately upon Logan. Without hesitation, he cursed, removing the hood. *Calvin. Marcel's beta.* He'd challenged Marcel?

Logan threw Calvin's body aside and ran back to Marcel's side; sirens wailed in the distance. Logan stilled as he came upon the sight of him sprawled on the floor. Oh Goddess no. He fell to his knees, grasping his old friend, pulling him up into his lap.

"Marcel, please man. You've gotta shift," he begged.

"Too late...it's silver," Marcel whispered. "Not gonna make it."

"Goddammit, Marcel. We need you. You can't leave me. Tristan. Katrina. Hell, your whole pack. Your family. We need you. Now come on and shift," he demanded.

Marcel coughed up blood and shook his head.

"Where the hell is 911?" Logan screamed, glancing over to the unidentified sobbing woman crumpled in the corner.

"Calvin. It was Calvin," Marcel grunted.

"Yes. He's dead. I killed him." Logan couldn't think. He'd killed Marcel's beta. Calvin was the second strongest wolf in the pack. And Marcel, the Alpha, was dying in his arms. This couldn't be happening.

"Logan, you're Alpha now."

"No...listen Marcel, you're going to make it. I'm not..."

"Yes, you are. Tristan will understand. This is how this works. You know it. You're my brother too...you've got to do this. You have no choice."

Logan was crying, shaking his head, pulling Marcel's head to his breast. *Goddess no. Please Goddess no.*

"Say it," Marcel choked out, commanding him.

"No, I can't. Please don't leave, Marcel."

"Say it!"

Resigned, Logan took a deep breath. He could hear Marcel's heartbeat flutter. Tristan was right about nature and fucking goddamn fate. No one could fight her. Logan held his friend silently, listening as his pulse slowed. He swore revenge for his friend…for his pack. As the life faded from Marcel's eyes, Logan held his gaze and assured his friend.

"I am Alpha."

About the Author

Kym Grosso is the author of the erotic paranormal romance series, The Immortals of New Orleans. The series currently includes *Kade's Dark Embrace* (Immortals of New Orleans, Book 1), *Luca's Magic Embrace* (Immortals of New Orleans, Book 2) and *Tristan's Lyceum Wolves* (Immortals of New Orleans, Book 3).

In addition to romance, Kym has written and published several articles about autism, and is passionate about autism advocacy. She writes autism articles on PsychologyToday.com and AutismInRealLife.com. She also is a contributing essay author in *Chicken Soup for the Soul: Raising Kids on the Spectrum.*

Kym lives with her husband, two children, dog, cat and guinea pig. Her hobbies include autism advocacy, reading, tennis, zumba, traveling and spending time with her husband and children. New Orleans, with its rich culture, history and unique cuisine, is one of her favorite places to visit. Also, she loves traveling just about anywhere that has a beach or snow-covered mountains. On any given night, when not writing her own books, Kym can be found reading her Kindle, which is filled with hundreds of romances.

♥ ♥ ♥

Social Media/Links:

• Website:
www.KymGrosso.com

• Email:
Kym.Grosso@AutismInRealLife.com

• Facebook:
www.facebook.com/KymGrossoBooks

• Twitter:
@KymGrosso

• Goodreads:
www.goodreads.com/author/show/5785692.Kym_Grosso

Printed in Great Britain
by Amazon